She knew she was in danger of losing herself in his eyes, in his voice, in his arms. She couldn't say another word. With one look, he completely stole her breath away. This man had been everything to her—friend, enemy, husband...lover. *What would he be now?*

D0424054

ONE TRUE LOVE

You never take a risk. You always play it safe.
His words echoed through her head. It was the most honest thing he'd ever said to her. And she knew he was right. But she was about to take the biggest risk of her life.

Lisa's heart sped up. She put a hand to stop him from coming closer, but touching his bare chest only made it worse. Instead of pushing him away, her fingers curled in the dark strands of hair on his chest.

"God, I've missed you doing that," he said huskily, his gaze dropping to her mouth. "And I've missed doing this."

He covered her mouth with his, pushing, prodding, persuading until she could do nothing more but open her mouth and kiss him back the way he wanted her to.

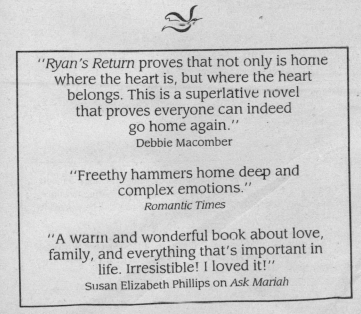

Other Avon Books by
Barbara Freethy

ASK MARIAH
DANIEL'S GIFT
RYAN'S RETURN

BARBARA FREETHY

One True Love

AVON BOOKS  NEW YORK

This is a work of fiction. Names, characters, places, and incidents either are the product of the author's imagination or are used fictitiously. Any resemblance to actual events, locales, organizations, or persons, living or dead, is entirely coincidental and beyond the intent of either the author or the publisher.

AVON BOOKS, INC.
1350 Avenue of the Americas
New York, New York 10019

Copyright © 1998 by Barbara Freethy
Excerpt from *Forever After* copyright © 1998 by Adeline Catherine Anderson
Excerpt from *Sealed With a Kiss* copyright © 1998 by Pamela Morsi
Excerpt from *The Night Remembers* copyright © 1997 by Kathleen Eagle
Excerpt from *Stranger In My Arms* copyright © 1998 by Lisa Kleypas
Excerpt from *One True Love* copyright © 1998 by Barbara Freethy
Excerpt from *That Scandalous Evening* copyright © 1998 by Christina Dodd
Inside cover author photo by Dave Dornlas
Published by arrangement with the author
Visit our website at **http://www.AvonBooks.com**
Library of Congress Catalog Card Number: 97-94933
ISBN: 0-380-79480-2

First Avon Books Printing: August 1998
First Avon Books Special Printing: March 1998

AVON TRADEMARK REG. U.S. PAT. OFF. AND IN OTHER COUNTRIES, MARCA REGISTRADA, HECHO EN U.S.A.

Printed in the U.S.A.

WCD 10 9 8 7 6 5 4 3 2 1

To Terry,
Always and Forever

Chapter 1

Wind chimes blew in the warm breeze, a robin sang out for its mate to finish the nest before the babies came, and Nick's guitar played a soothing melody of sleep and love. The porch swing creaked as Lisa stroked her baby's head, letting the fine strands of black silk curl around her fingers. She pressed the baby closer to her heart. She'd never felt so happy, so complete. Then Nick hit a false chord, a shrieking note that clashed with the springtime harmony. The robins squawked and fluttered and flew away, leaving their nest dark and empty . . .

Lisa Alvarez jolted awake, her heart racing, her breathing ragged. "It was a dream," she told herself. "Just a dream." The pounding on her office door brought her back to reality.

"Elisabeth?" her secretary called.

"Come in," Lisa said somewhat weakly, still disoriented by the vivid dream.

Her secretary, Marian Griggs, walked into the office with a brightly wrapped box in her hand. "I know you told me not to disturb you, but this just came for you. I thought it might be a wedding present, and well, you know how I am about presents." Marian set the box down on the desk in front of Lisa and sent her a curious look. "Are you all right?"

Lisa pushed a sweaty strand of hair behind her ear. "I'm fine. I just put my head down for a minute. I was so tired after working all night, I guess I fell asleep."

1

"Open the gift," Marian encouraged.

"There's no card." Lisa's hand shook slightly as she slipped the ribbon off the box and removed the lid. She carefully pulled away the white tissue paper to reveal a charm bracelet that held only one small charm, a pair of gold baby shoes. "Oh, no," she whispered as she touched the shoes with her fingertip. "Oh, no." The metal burned her fingers, and she slammed the lid down on the box and took a deep breath.

"What's wrong?" Marian asked with concern.

"Please, go. Just go."

Marian looked like she wanted to argue, but then she nodded. "Okay. I'm going." She walked out of the room, shutting the door quietly behind her.

Lisa took several calming breaths. Why was it all coming back now, when she finally had her life together? After a long moment of indecision, she opened the box once again. This time, she reached for the small envelope lying beneath the bracelet. She slipped it out and opened it.

"Eight years, Lisa. You can push the rest of us away. You can marry this safe, older man, but I will not let you forget her—Robin Nicole Maddux. This bracelet was blessed. If you hold on to it, you will feel the magic. Believe in it now and come home, before it's too late."

Eight years, and her mother, Silvia Alvarez, still hoped for a miracle. When would Silvia learn that there was no magic in the world—only foolish dreams?

Lisa looked at the bracelet once again. It had been blessed by her great-aunt Carmela, who drank tequila for "medicinal purposes" and fashioned jewelry out of gold nuggets she believed were from an ancient Aztec city.

Her mother might believe Carmela was a descendant from the mystical Aztecs and therefore had special powers, but as far as Lisa was concerned, Carmela was nothing more than an old con artist. That's why Lisa had left the bracelet behind all those years ago—as she had left everything else behind.

Lisa set the box on the edge of the desk and walked over to the window, resting her palms on the windowsill. Below, the streets of downtown Los Angeles bustled with activity, but here in her third-floor office, she was protected from the heat and the smog, the mix of languages, the car horns, the curses, the smells of burritos and quesadillas being sold in tiny taquerias tucked in between the glass and chrome skyscrapers.

She had left Solana Beach, a suburb of San Diego, to come to the sprawling city of Los Angeles, to lose herself in the crowds. It was easy to do that here. Her Mexican/Irish heritage raised few eyebrows in this city of immigrants. She heard three or four languages every time she stepped on the elevator. No one questioned why her hair was so black, her eyes so blue. No one asked, because no one cared. That was the trade-off.

For almost eight years she'd lived in L.A., working her way up from a receptionist in a public relations firm to a senior account executive at one of the most prestigious advertising agencies in Los Angeles. She had changed jobs every few years and apartments almost as frequently, never letting herself get too close or too settled—until now.

In less than a month, she would marry her boss, fifty-two-year-old Raymond Curtis, a man twenty-one years her senior. The age gap didn't bother her. Raymond was the first man she'd felt comfortable with in a long time. She couldn't keep running for the rest of her life. It was time to settle down.

Her mother thought she had chosen Raymond because she wanted a father figure, but Lisa had stopped looking for a father years before. Patrick O'Donegan had taken off two days after Lisa's birth, knowing his family couldn't accept a child who wasn't pure Irish.

In truth, Lisa didn't feel Irish or Mexican. She felt alone. Her mother said she'd been born with an insecure chip on her shoulder. Maybe so. After all, her father had taken one look at her and run screaming for the hills. Was it any wonder she always anticipated rejection?

As Lisa turned, her gaze was caught by the sudden fluttering of a bird outside the window. The bird had a bright orange chest and a gray coat. An American robin. Lisa s lowed hard as the bird settled on top of the streetlight just a few feet from her office window. She couldn't imagine how the bird had come to be here, amidst the concrete, the buildings and the smog. She closed her eyes against a wave of memories. But in her mind she could see another robin, a tall tree, a budding nest and Nick holding their baby . . . no, she wouldn't remember. She couldn't.

A knock came at her door, and Lisa opened her eyes. The robin had disappeared. Perhaps she had simply imagined its appearance. With a sense of relief, she turned away from the window as her fiancé entered the office.

"I'm back," Raymond Curtis said, offering her a broad smile.

Raymond was an attractive man with thin brown hair, graying sideburns, and a narrow face. Of average height, he had a lean, wiry look that came from hours of exercising. A noted clotheshorse, he had a closet full of suits and ties for every occasion. Today, he wore his trademark charcoal gray Armani suit, which he fondly referred to as his "pitch" suit. Judging by the smile on his face, his latest pitch had gone well.

"How did it go?" Lisa asked.

"Exceptionally well." He kissed her on the cheek, then set a box of cereal down on her desk. "I hope you like graham cracker cereal with marshmallows."

"Can't say I've tried it."

"It's new, and the Nature Brand people want to launch the cereal with print, radio and television ads. This is going to be great, Elisabeth." His eyes lit up at the prospect of landing a big new client. "I need an initial proposal, campaign strategy complete with various slogans and artwork four weeks from today. We're competing with one other firm, and we're talking million-dollar account."

Lisa stared at him in amazement as he rattled off a hectic schedule of meetings and appointments with the Nature Brand people. "Raymond, have you forgotten? We're getting married in four weeks."

"I know." The light in his eyes dimmed slightly. "The timing isn't the best."

"That's an understatement."

"This account is too good to pass up." He smiled persuasively. "The wedding details are pretty much set. All we have to do is send out the invitations."

Lisa's eyes drifted over to the box of invitations sitting on her credenza. The engraved ivory cards still needed to be addressed, sealed and stamped. She tucked a strand of her hair behind one ear.

"I wouldn't say that's all we have to do, Raymond. I still have the final fitting of my gown, presents to buy for the bridesmaids you insisted we have, last-minute decisions about flowers, and—"

"Let Mrs. Carstairs handle it."

"I'm still not comfortable with a wedding consultant planning my wedding."

Raymond laughed. "That's her job. Look, I know I'm asking a lot, but this account is just what we've been waiting for, especially since losing Bailey Brothers to Beverly Wickham earlier this year. This one will put us back on top."

"Is Beverly competing for Nature Brand, too?"

Raymond tugged at the knot in his tie. "Unfortunately, yes. There's one other thing. The honeymoon."

Lisa stared at him with dismay. "You're not planning on cancelling the honeymoon?"

"No, of course not."

"Good, for a minute there . . ."

"Just cut it short a day or two. If we get this account, Monty Friedman, Nature Brand's CEO, has asked that we meet the week after our presentation to work out a detailed game plan. I can put him off until Wednesday or Thursday, of course."

"Of course," Lisa echoed with a sigh.

"Once we have the campaign up and running, we'll take two weeks off and go wherever your heart desires. What do you say?"

What could she say? She couldn't deny Raymond the

portunity to land a big account. The agency was more than just a job to him. It was his life—hers, too. "All right," she said.

"I knew I could count on you. So, what have you been up to today?" Raymond glanced at her desk, immediately zeroing in on the package. "Hey, what's this? Did we get a wedding present already?" He reached for the box before she could stop him.

"No. It's not a wedding present. It's—"

"A bracelet." His gaze turned puzzled as he looked into her eyes. "Baby shoes?"

Lisa swallowed hard as she stared at the gold charm bracelet swinging from his fingers. In her mind, she saw another man's hand, heard another man's voice.

"I wonder what other charms she'll get over the years, a baseball bat, a mitt, a basketball," Nick said with a laugh, *his curly brown hair still mussed from his daughter's restless fingers, his light green eyes twinkling with pleasure.*

"She's a girl," Lisa replied.

"She can still be an athlete."

"Like her dad." Lisa felt Nick's strong arm slide around her waist.

"Or a writer, like you. In fact, she can be anything she wants to be. As long as she's happy."

"Oh, Nick, you make it easy to believe in the impossible."

"I don't believe in the impossible. I believe in you—in us."

Lisa closed her eyes. Damn that bracelet. She didn't want to remember.

"Elisabeth, what's wrong?"

She took a deep breath and opened her eyes. "Nothing is wrong. The bracelet is a gift from my mother. Something old for luck."

Raymond didn't look satisfied with her answer. "You did tell her we're not planning on having children, didn't you?" he asked, worry running through his usually placid brown eyes.

"Yes, but my mother doesn't hear anything she doesn't

want to hear. My father was gone for ten years before she admitted he might not be coming back. The woman is the queen of denial.''

''Elisabeth, I raised a son, and I don't want to do it again. Frankly, I was never good at being a father. Just ask Ray Junior, if you don't believe me. He's twenty-five now, and I still don't know what to say to him.''

Twenty-five! His son was twenty-five, only six years younger than herself. When she'd been in the first grade, Raymond had been having a child. Lisa took another deep breath. The age difference didn't matter. They had the same goals now. That's what was important.

''I don't want children,'' she said. ''I don't need to be— a mother.''

He looked deep into her eyes. ''Are you sure?''

''Absolutely, positively sure.'' She refused to let any doubts creep into her voice.

He glanced down at the bracelet in his hand, fingering the tiny gold baby shoes. Finally, he set it back in the box and checked his watch. ''What time are you meeting Mrs. Carstairs?''

''Five-thirty at the bridal salon,'' she replied with a sigh.

Raymond sent her a curious look. ''What's wrong?''

''Nothing.'' She hesitated. ''Don't you think it would be better to have a small, intimate wedding?''

''How small would you suggest?''

''You and me and two witnesses,'' she said hopefully.

''Don't be silly. I have family, friends, business associates. I want to show you off. Every time I see you I thank God no one snatched you up before now.''

Lisa's heart stopped. She had to tell him. She'd been trying to for days, but the right moment had never arrived.

''Raymond—''

She stopped as the intercom buzzed, feeling both relieved and annoyed by the interruption. She reached over and picked up the phone. ''Yes?''

''Maggie Scott on line one, Elisabeth,'' the receptionist said.

Lisa hesitated. Maggie Scott—another voice from her past. Why were they all coming back now—when she finally had her life under control? "Tell her I'll be with her in a minute."

"Problems?" Raymond asked.

"It's an old friend of mine, Maggie Scott. We grew up together in Solana Beach. We used to be best friends."

"Used to be?"

"She got married, had kids. I moved away." Lisa waved her hand in the air. "I guess we drifted apart."

"That happens."

Lisa nodded, knowing they hadn't just drifted apart. She'd turned her back on Maggie, the same way she'd turned her back on her mother and . . .

"Stop by my office when you're done," Raymond said, turning toward the door. "We'll discuss our plans for the weekend. Monty Friedman has invited us to a party tomorrow afternoon. Everyone will be there. It will be a good opportunity for you to meet the key players."

"Okay," Lisa replied, her mind more on Maggie than the upcoming party. She was suddenly filled with a sense of foreboding. The past was catching up to the present, and she wasn't ready yet.

Maggie Scott pulled the phone cord around the corner of the desk in the upstairs hall, searching for a quiet place to talk. She could hear her thirteen-year-old daughter, Roxanne, practicing cheerleading routines in the living room with three other giggling, adolescent girls. Her eight-year-old son, Dylan, was playing Sega Genesis on the television in the family room, yelling "Victory!" every time he knocked out a warrior. Her five-year-old daughter, Mary Bea, was having a tantrum in her bedroom. Even with the door closed, Maggie could hear Mary Bea crying, her sobs intermixed with defiant shouts of "I don't like you, and I wish I had another mommy!"

For a guilty moment, Maggie wished the same thing. Not that she didn't love her kids; they were just driving her stark, raving mad. She had them twenty-four hours a day, seven days a week, without relief.

Of course, that's the way she'd wanted it. After her husband, Keith, had died last year, Maggie had proudly told her loving family she could handle things on her own. She could be a single mother. She could manage her house and her children.

For ten months, she'd held it together. She'd smiled and laughed through her heartache. She'd learned how to fix the toilet, change an electrical fuse, and mow the lawn. She'd even bought a jockstrap for her son. Through it all, she'd pretended that Keith was coming home any minute, that he'd be proud of her accomplishments, and she'd finally have some help. But Keith wasn't coming home.

Maggie's stomach churned at the reminder. Her breath caught in her throat, and she felt claustrophobic, scared, anxious. The attacks of panic had begun two weeks earlier when a card had arrived in the mail addressed to Keith. The letter was signed Serena Hollingsworth. Maggie had never heard Keith mention a woman by that name, but the letter had suggested a personal relationship.

Serena had asked why Keith hadn't contacted her as promised. She said she'd been travelling but had checked her messages faithfully, hoping to hear from him.

The first thought that came into Maggie's mind was that her husband had had an affair. Then it occurred to her that Keith had been dead for almost a year and this woman knew nothing about it. How close could they have been?

Maggie had thrown the card away, then dug it out of the wastebasket and stuck it in her "to do" pile, which never seemed to get done. She'd decided to simply notify the woman of Keith's death, only she hadn't gotten around to it. She hadn't wanted to confront the fact that Keith had had a friendship with a woman she knew nothing about. For the first time, she wondered what else she'd known nothing about. The memory of her loving husband, the foundation of her solid marriage, seemed suddenly unstable.

The thought once again sent adrenaline pulsing thr

her veins. In the past two weeks, she'd suffered several anxious moments when she felt her heart racing over something illogical, silly almost. She'd become afraid of so many things. She'd drive down the street and imagine how easily a car could swerve and hit her head-on. She'd get on an elevator and picture herself plunging to the basement in the express ride from hell.

Yesterday she had let Dylan take a bus trip to the zoo and had worried all day that the bus would get in an accident, that Dylan would get lost, or the zoo would suddenly become the target of a terrorist attack.

Maggie was losing control. She felt as if her fingers were clinging to the edge of a cliff that was crumbling beneath her hand. The kids were suffering, too, and she couldn't help them. She yelled at them unnecessarily, making her fears their fears. By bedtime, all four of them were usually in tears. She wasn't being fair to them, and she had to do something soon before she destroyed what was left of her family.

"Mom, can we have a snack?" Roxy yelled up the stairs.

"I'm on the phone," Maggie replied, walking around in circles, searching for a quiet place to sit. Her room was a mess, with a pile of laundry on the bed, waiting to be sorted. The desk in the hall alcove was covered with bills she had yet to pay. Just looking at all those envelopes made her anxiety level rise yet again.

Maggie jumped to one side of the hall as Dylan and their golden retriever, Sally, ran up the stairs.

"Sally found a dead bird in the backyard," Dylan said with excitement. The dog barked in delight. "Do you want to see it? It's in the kitchen."

"No. I'm on the phone." Maggie sighed as Mary Bea marched out of her room with her backpack in one hand and her cherished blanket in the other. Her face was streaked with tears, her blond curls a mass of tangles. "Where do you think you're going, young lady?"

"I'm running away unless you say you're sorry for yelling at me."

"I'm on the phone," Maggie replied for the third time.

"And if anyone is going to run away from home, it will be me."

"Mom, we're starving," Roxy complained from the bottom of the stairs.

"I'm on the phone," Maggie yelled back. "Can't anyone see I'm on the phone? Do you think this receiver is an earring?"

Dylan and Mary Bea looked at her in bewilderment, then Mary Bea started to cry. "You're yelling again," she accused.

Maggie opened the door to the hall closet and walked inside, shutting herself in among the coats, the umbrellas and the tennis rackets that hadn't been used in years. She sat down on the upturned end of a suitcase she'd meant to store in the basement, but like so many things in her life, it had gone undone.

"Mom, why are you in the closet?" Dylan asked.

"Are you playing hide-and-seek?" Mary Bea asked hopefully. "Can I play, too?"

"She doesn't want to play with you," Dylan said.

"Yes, she does."

"No, she doesn't."

"Go away," Maggie yelled. "I'm on the phone."

"Maggie?" Lisa's voice came over the receiver like an answer to a prayer.

"Lisa. Thank God, you're there." Maggie took a deep breath. Eight years ago what she needed to say would have come easily. Now there were barriers between them, years when they hadn't seen much of each other, layers of grief and disillusionment that weighed heavily on their friendship, but Maggie had nowhere else to turn. "I need you." She closed her eyes, waiting for Lisa's response.

Lisa stared blindly at her desktop, not seeing the work spread out before her, hearing only the anguish in Maggie's voice. *I need you.* Three short words that demanded so much, coming from a woman who had always asked for so little. They had been best friends forever. Maggie Maddux Scott with her golden hair, her big booming laugh and wide gen-

erous smile had befriended Lisa on her first day at a new
middle school. She didn't care that Lisa was different, that
she was too shy, too skinny, too nervous, too everything.

Maggie's friendship had come like the sun after a long
winter's storm. She'd introduced Lisa to the joy of laughter,
to the secrets of best friends. With two older brothers, Maggie was dying for a sister, and Lisa fit the bill. They'd been
inseparable for years, until . . . Lisa's gaze drifted to the
opened box on the desk, to the bracelet that gleamed against
the tissue paper.

"Did you hear me?" Maggie asked.

Lisa started. "Yes, of course. What's wrong? Is one of
the kids—"

"No. It's me." Maggie's voice sounded edgy. "I'm losing
it, Lisa. The walls are closing in on me. I can't breathe."

"Are you in the closet again?" Lisa demanded.

"Yes, I'm in the closet. It's the only place where I won't
be interrupted, where I can have two minutes to myself. It's
not the closet that's making me crazy. It's everything else. I
can't do this anymore. I can't fight with Roxy every morning
about her clothes. I can't drive Dylan all over town so he
can play these damn sports, and I can't take Mary Bea into
Wal-Mart ever again, because my five-year-old stole two
peanut butter cups and a giant-sized Hershey bar and I didn't
even notice until I got home and found chocolate smeared
across her chin."

"Slow down," Lisa said. "I don't think Wal-Mart will
toss you into jail over a couple of candy bars."

"I'm supposed to be okay, you know. It's been almost a
year. I should be getting over this by now."

"Honey, he was your husband. And you've been in love
with him forever. You married him right out of high school.
You might never get over him."

"I know, but I'm so angry, Lisa. He had to die and leave
me with all this. It was Keith's idea to buy this big, stupid
house, you know. I never wanted this elephant of a mortgage,
and it was his idea to have three kids; I would have stopped
at two. It was his idea to go into the lab that night . . ."

Maggie's voice faltered. "If he hadn't gone to his office, he wouldn't have been there when the lab exploded," Maggie sobbed, as her emotions spilled out. "I told him to wait until the next morning . . ."

Maggie's sobs tore at Lisa's heart. "Please don't cry."

"He wouldn't listen," Maggie said with a sniff. "He never listened to me."

Every word Maggie uttered reminded Lisa of her own guilt, her own anger. And it was so pointless. "Maggie, you have to stop torturing yourself."

"Why? I'm torturing everyone else."

"You're not."

"I am. I need you, Lisa. I'm desperate."

"Me? What about—your brothers?" God, she was pathetic. She couldn't even say his name out loud.

"I can't reach Nick. He might be away for the weekend, Joe moved up to Monterey last year, remember? And his wife is expecting a baby any day now. My parents are finally taking their second honeymoon. I can't ask them to come home."

"What do you want me to do?"

"Watch my kids for the weekend. I know I shouldn't ask. You're getting married in a month, and you must be busy, but I could use a friend right now." Her voice tightened. "And—and you owe me, Lisa. There, I said it. I've felt it for a long time, and now I've said it. You didn't even come for Keith's funeral. I still can't believe you didn't come."

Lisa's stomach turned over at the anger and bitterness in Maggie's voice. Maggie was right. Lisa had been a lousy friend. "I came down the week after," she protested.

"So you wouldn't have to see Nick and my parents and my kids. Your feelings came before mine."

"You're right. I was scared." *And selfish.* Lisa twisted the phone cord between her fingers. She'd felt guilty for weeks. She still did. "I should have been there for you. If you don't want to be my friend, I won't blame you."

"You're not getting out of it that easily. I need you now, Lisa. You have to come. You just have to."

"I'll be down as soon as I can, a couple of hours." Lisa mentally ran through the list of what she was supposed to accomplish that weekend. Raymond wouldn't be happy. Neither would Mrs. Carstairs, but Maggie was right. Lisa owed her this. Heck, she owed her a lot more than this.

"Really?" Maggie's voice filled with hope. "I know you hate it here, all the memories and Nick . . ."

"I can handle the memories; it's your children I'm concerned about. Are you sure you want to leave them with me?"

"I wouldn't trust anyone else," Maggie said softly.

Lisa's gaze dropped to the charm bracelet once again. Someone else had trusted her, and she had let her down. "Are you sure?"

"It's the only thing I am sure about. Lisa?"

"What?"

"Hurry."

Lisa hung up the phone, worried more than ever by the note of panic in Maggie's voice. Maggie had always been the cool one, sensible, reasonable, dependable—nothing like her older brother, Nick. Lisa's heart raced at the thought of him. But just because she was going back to San Diego didn't mean she had to see Nick. She'd managed to avoid him for almost eight years. Surely, she could make it through one more weekend.

~ *Chapter 2*

Nick Maddux was surrounded by pregnant women. Every time he turned around, he bumped into some-one's stomach. Muttering yet another apology, he backed into the corner of his ten-by-twelve-foot booth at the San Diego Baby and Parenting Fair and took a deep breath. He was hot, tired and proud.

His handcrafted baby furniture was the hit of the show. He had taken three orders for cradles, another two for cribs, and one for a matching crib, dresser and rocking chair. A couple of the items he had in stock, but the rest he would have to make. In some cases, it would be a challenge to have his furniture arrive before the stork, but Nick thrived on chal-lenges, and Robin Wood Designs was finally on its way to becoming the profitable business he had envisioned.

Nick couldn't believe how far he'd come, how much he'd changed.

Eight years ago, he'd been twenty-five years old, working toward getting his contractor's license, and trying to provide for a wife and a child on the way. He'd kept at it long after they'd gone, hammering out his anger and frustration on helpless nails and boards.

Every evening he'd drink himself to sleep, and every morning he'd wake up more sad than he could ever have imagined. Two years had gone by before he ran out of work, out of booze and out of money. Finally, stone cold sober, he'd realized his life was a mess.

15

That's when he'd met Walter Mackey, a master craftsman well into his seventies but still taking joy out of carving wood. Walter made rocking chairs in his garage and sold them at craft fairs. Nick had bought one of those chairs for his mother's birthday. She'd fallen in love with the beautifully crafted design, the smooth feel of the wood. She'd told Nick he'd given her something that would last forever.

It was then Nick realized he could make something that would last forever. His life didn't have to be a series of arrivals and departures.

Walter had taught him everything he knew, and Nick had done the rest himself. For five years, he'd worked two jobs, construction during the day and woodworking at night. He'd helped Walter with his business and begun to dream of having his own.

Last year, he'd purchased a retail space on Pacific Beach Drive in San Diego. His designs, with his signature robin in the corner, had caught on, and now he was reaching out for more customers, more opportunities to put his piece of forever into someone else's life.

Nick had decided to focus on baby furniture because something for one's child always brought out the checkbook faster than something for oneself. Besides that mercenary reason, Nick had become obsessed with building furniture for babies that would nurture them, keep them safe, protect them.

He knew where the obsession came from, just not how to stop it. Maybe he didn't need to stop it. Maybe Robin would be proud of all that he'd accomplished in her name.

Robin. The thought of her made him smile even as his heart broke yet again. He wondered when he'd ever stop feeling the familiar ripping pain that ran through his body every time he said her name, thought of her sweet face, remembered.

He looked around his booth at the two pregnant women checking out his furniture. One had come with her mother, the other with her adoring husband. As he watched, Nick saw the husband rest his palm on his wife's stomach and whisper something into her ear. She smiled. The man kissed her on the brow tenderly, lovingly.

Nick felt himself drawn into the past. In his mind he saw Lisa with her round stomach, her glowing smile, her blue eyes lit up for the world to see. She'd been so happy then, so proud of herself. In the few months since their marriage, Lisa had blossomed into a woman loved and secure. He'd taken pride in knowing it was because of him. He'd brought that smile to her face. And in making her feel special, he'd made himself feel special. He was no longer the invisible middle child, not the oldest or the brightest or the youngest or the cutest—just the one in the middle.

He'd felt the anonymity of that place every day of his life. His father had focused all of his energies on Nick's older brother, Joe. Joe was the smart one, the one who could calculate algebraic equations in his head, the one who would go on to a brilliant career in finance, just like his father. And Maggie was the darling, the joy of their family, the silly little girl whose imagination took more flights than their father's frequent business trips across the country.

Nick loved all of them, but he'd never felt loved for himself—until Lisa. She'd looked past the cocky insecure arrogance and seen who he really was and loved him anyway. When she'd become pregnant, they both thought they'd won the lottery.

He closed his eyes for a moment as the pain threatened to overwhelm him, and he saw her again.

"I can't believe I'm having a baby." Lisa took his hand *and placed it on her abdomen. "Feel that? She's kicking me."*

Nick's gut tightened at the fluttering kick against his fingers. It was the most incredible feeling. He couldn't begin to express the depth of his love for this unborn child, but he could show Lisa. In the middle of the store, he kissed her on the lips, uncaring of the salespeople or the other customers. "I love you," he whispered against her mouth.

She looked into his eyes. "I love you, too. More than any-

thing. I'm so happy it scares me. What if something goes wrong?"

"Nothing will go wrong."

"Oh, Nick, things always go wrong around me. Remember our first date—we hit a parked car."

He smiled. "That wasn't your fault. I'm the one who wasn't paying attention."

"I'm the one who distracted you," she said with a worried look in her eyes.

"Okay, it was your fault."

"Nick!"

"I'm teasing. Don't be afraid of being happy. It's not fatal, you know. This is just the beginning for us."

It had been the beginning of the end.

Nick blinked his eyes open as the woman in his booth asked him a question, intruding on his memories. "Excuse me?"

"How much is the cradle?" she asked with a curious smile.

"One hundred and thirty dollars."

She nodded. "It's expensive, but it's also gorgeous. Are you the craftsman?"

"Yes."

"You do beautiful work."

"Thank you." Nick ran his calloused fingers along the side of the cradle, sending it into a gentle rocking motion.

"It's so quiet. We've looked at a lot of cradles, but yours seem—special. I can almost see my baby lying there, rocking."

"Me, too," he muttered, but it wasn't her baby he was seeing, it was his—Robin with the tiny curls of black hair and the bright blue eyes, so like her mother's. Nick shook the thought out of his head.

"We'll take two," the woman said.

He raised an eyebrow.

"We're having twins," she explained with a laugh, patting her rather large abdomen.

"Congratulations."

"Good luck would be more appropriate."

Nick smiled as he took down her name, address and phone number and set up a delivery date. When she and her husband left, the booth was empty, save for two lanky teenagers. So much for sentimental moments. It was time to get on with the business of breaking down the booth.

"Hey, boss. It's almost five. Can we start packing up?" Ernie Mackey asked.

"I'm starving," David Schmitz added.

Nick smiled at the teenagers, whose pants were three sizes too big and whose shirts trailed down to their knees. Ernie was Walter's grandson and had absolutely no interest in making furniture, only in making money. He was a high school senior who needed wheels and cash for the prom, so he'd agreed to work for Nick after school and on the weekends. David was Ernie's best friend.

"You guys have already eaten your way through the food court," Nick replied. "I think you can make it another half hour."

"Aw, man," Ernie complained. "You're a slave driver."

"You want to work for a slave driver, try working for your grandfather."

"You're right. He's worse, but at least he doesn't do baby shows," Ernie said with disgust. "I've never seen so many screaming, ugly babies or pregnant women in my entire life."

"Yeah," David agreed. He leaned over and dropped his voice a notch. "I didn't know so many people in San Diego were having this much sex. And some of them are really old."

Nick laughed. "Like forty, right? Now you know what's in store for you if you have unprotected sex."

"No way. I'm not having kids, not until I'm at least thirty," David said. "I want to have fun, man."

"Just remember that every time you have fun, and I do mean every time," Nick said pointedly.

"You sound like my father," Ernie complained.

He did sound like a father, but he wasn't one—not anymore. "Why don't you guys take down the crib? I think we're just about done." Nick slipped the orders he had taken into a manila envelope.

"How did you do, Nick?" Suzanne Brooks asked from the booth adjoining his.

"Okay," he said.

A slender woman with a sleek cap of red hair that framed her face and emphasized her brown eyes, Suzanne owned an expensive baby clothing store in La Jolla, and they had become a source of referrals for one another. They had gone out a few times. Nick enjoyed her company but was wary of her eager interest in him. Suzanne seemed to be pushing for a deeper, more personal relationship, and he wasn't ready for it. Although as soon as the thought came to mind, he felt like a fool. Just when the hell was he going to be ready? It had been almost eight years, well past time to move on with his life.

"Do you want to get a drink after work, maybe some dinner?" she asked, straightening her emerald green suit jacket. "I didn't have a chance to get lunch."

"Sure."

"Really?"

"You sound surprised," he said with a grin.

"No, I'm pleased. Shall we go to the Glass House? It's supposed to be very good."

Nick frowned. "I'm more steak and potatoes than pheasant under glass, Suzanne. I'm not sure I could find a suit if I needed one to be buried in."

"Well, wherever you want to go then."

"Ruby's Chili House."

"Oh, okay. That sounds interesting."

She looked a bit disheartened by his choice, which didn't totally surprise him. Suzanne was a lovely woman, but her tastes were more sophisticated than his.

"I'm not very good with spicy food," she added. "Is the chili hot?"

"Hotter than hell," he said cheerfully. Lisa had loved Ruby's chili. He could still see the sweat beading along her forehead with every bite, the fire in her blue eyes, the rosiness of her cheeks. She'd been as passionate about food as . . . God, where had that thought come from? "Never mind," he said to Suzanne. "Let's go somewhere else. You pick. Just don't make it black tie, okay? I'm a working guy."

"You're a successful business owner, a great-looking man. Most of the women stop by your booth just to look at you."

"Yeah, right."

"It's true. I don't think they can fathom how such a big, brawny guy can make such beautiful furniture. I wish you could see yourself as others see you."

Nick smiled somewhat awkwardly as he dug his hands into the pockets of his worn blue jeans. If Suzanne could really see him for what he was, she'd run as far away from him as possible. Sure, he'd seen desire in a few women's eyes over the past couple of years. But he still remembered that one scathing look of complete and utter rejection.

"Nick?"

He shook himself, not understanding why the memories had begun again. It probably had something to do with Silvia, Lisa's mother. Two days earlier, Silvia had asked him for the key to the storage locker where they'd put Lisa's things all those years ago. She'd said she wanted to get something out, something important.

Nick hadn't asked what. He hadn't been to the storage locker in years. He probably should have cleaned it out or at least sent Lisa the bill, but for some reason, he'd just kept paying it.

"Nick?" Suzanne repeated. "Shall I come by your place and pick you up?"

"Don't like riding in my pickup truck, huh?" He knew the battered blue Toyota wasn't much to look at, but it was handy for moving furniture. "I can bring the jeep. I know it's not much better, but at least it has a solid coat of paint."

"That's fine."

"Why don't I pick you up at seven-thirty?" he suggested. She hesitated. "Is there something you're hiding in that house of yours? You've never invited me in. I'm beginning to think you have a wife stashed away inside.''

"No wife," he said bluntly. ''If you'd rather I didn't come by, we can forget the whole thing.''

"No, no.'' She put a hand on his arm. ''I'm sorry, Nick. I didn't mean to pry. You can pick me up. You can even stay for breakfast if you want.''

He saw the seductive invitation in her eyes and knew she'd make good on her promise, but what about the morning? What about breakfast, lunch and dinner? He had a feeling Suzanne Brooks didn't sleep with a man for the hell of it, and that was the only reason he'd slept with anyone in the past eight years.

Walter kept telling him it was time to move on, to settle down, to get on with the rest of his life. Perhaps the old man was right. He could get used to breakfast at Suzanne's. He could forget that her skin wasn't dark, her eyes weren't blue, her hair wasn't the color of the night.

Or maybe he'd spend the rest of his life haunted by a memory, by a woman he would probably never see again—at least if she had anything to say about it.

Raymond Curtis took the elevator downstairs. Instead of descending to the underground parking, he impulsively stepped off at the lobby level. He didn't feel like going home yet. His Spanish-style house in the San Fernando Valley with its cool red tiles and slick hardwood floors would be neat and clean and waiting for him. The evening paper would be on the dining room table, and his housekeeper would have something warming in the oven, but Elisabeth wouldn't be there.

No, Elisabeth was on her way to San Diego to rescue some childhood friend from a panic attack. Raymond frowned, still angry at Elisabeth's abrupt and sudden departure. He didn't like unpredictability. He didn't appreciate people doing what they weren't supposed to do.

That was one of the reasons he'd stayed single for fifteen years after his first marriage ended in divorce. Margery had never done what she was supposed to do. She'd been impetuous, impulsive and impossible. *She'd been young.*

The little warning voice returned to his head. Elisabeth was young, too. The difference was him. He was older now. He could handle a young wife. He wouldn't make the same mistakes he had made before.

As Raymond walked through the lobby and into the crowded Irish bar serving up happy hour, he thought about the strange present Elisabeth's mother had sent them, a charm bracelet with baby shoes, of all things. What an odd gift. He didn't like it. It made him feel uneasy. Elisabeth had been upset by the present, too. Did she want children? Was she simply pretending she didn't, ready to trap him into fatherhood once they were married?

He hated to think she could be that devious. He'd certainly never seen that side of her. She was always open and honest in her dealings with coworkers and clients. No, he was simply imagining problems. Pre-wedding jitters, he told himself, as he stepped up to the bar and ordered a gin and tonic.

He'd asked Elisabeth to marry him the same day he'd discovered a new bald spot on the back of his head. He'd never admit that the two events were related, but deep down in his heart, he knew they were. He was getting older. He didn't want to end up alone.

Not that he didn't love Elisabeth. Who wouldn't love her? She was gorgeous, with her dark hair and striking blue eyes. She had great breasts, beautiful legs, a sharp mind. And she didn't talk much. She didn't question him about the past. She didn't analyze their lovemaking. She didn't ask him for anything.

His uneasiness increased. *She didn't ask him for anything. She didn't need him.* Raymond took another sip of his drink to calm his unreasonable fears. Elisabeth looked up to him, he knew that. She respected his business decisions. She'd told him she cared a great deal for him.

Cared. It was a word he'd used a lot. Now, he hated it coming back at him, because he knew it didn't mean the same thing as love. But if she didn't love him, why the hell was she marrying him? For money, security? He hoped not. He wanted her to love him, to lust for him, to adore him.

So why was he planning the whole goddamned wedding, while she took off to San Diego?

Raymond picked up his drink and slammed it down his throat. He had half a mind to go after Elisabeth, to track down this friend of hers and make it clear that he was the most important person in Elisabeth's life.

"Alone on a Friday night? You're slipping, Raymond." Beverly Wickham slid onto the bar stool next to him and ordered a Manhattan.

"Beverly," Raymond said in cool, even tones. Beverly had worked as an account executive for him six years earlier. When he didn't promote her fast enough, she'd left him to start her own agency and had become one of his toughest competitors.

A tall, statuesque blond in her late forties, Beverly wore a teal-blue Armani suit, matching high heels and sheer stockings. Although her face didn't have the natural glowing beauty of a younger woman, it was perfectly made up. She knew how to make the most of her assets, he'd say that for her.

"Raymond," Beverly said, her hazel-colored eyes lighting with mischief. "I hear we'll be going head to head on the Nature Brand account. I do love a good fight."

"It won't be a fight. It will be a knockout."

"I seriously doubt that. Who's writing the copy—Elisabeth?"

"Of course."

"Of course," she echoed mockingly. "Where is she tonight? Picking out pink bridesmaid's dresses?"

"She's visiting a friend."

Beverly arched an eyebrow. "You don't sound happy about it."

"I couldn't care less. We don't live in each other's pockets." He looked down the bar, hoping to catch the bartender's eye. He needed another drink.

"Not yet anyway," Beverly said. "When is the big day?"

"April twenty-seventh."

"That's four weeks from—"

"Tomorrow."

"Oh, my." She shook her finger at him. "Time is running out for you, Raymond."

"I'm getting married; I'm not dying."

"Then why the long face, the empty glass?"

"I'm tired and I was thirsty."

"Let me buy you a drink."

Raymond hesitated. Beverly loved to push his buttons, and she seemed to know exactly how to do it. In many ways they were alike—both ambitious, tough, and in love with the world of advertising.

"Another gin and tonic for my friend," Beverly said as the bartender came over. "That is what you were drinking, isn't it?"

He looked into her perceptive eyes and smiled. "Good memory."

"You're actually paying me a compliment? I'm impressed."

"You'll get over it." When the bartender set down the drinks, Raymond handed him a ten dollar bill. "I'll take care of these."

"You don't want to be indebted to me, even for the price of a drink?" Beverly asked, putting her wallet away.

"I don't let women pay for my drinks."

She shifted in her chair, sending him a thoughtful look. "One of the last few gentlemen in L.A. So, how do you plan to get married and dream up an advertising campaign for Nature Brand at the same time?"

"The wedding is all done. Elisabeth and I have plenty of time to concentrate on Nature Brand, not to mention the fact that I have several other talented people at the agency upon whom I can call for help."

"True. But one might think a man's thoughts would be more focused on his lovely bride than on cereal."

"That's the beauty of marrying a coworker. We're both willing to make sacrifices for the company."

"Sounds like the perfect marriage."

"It will be."

Silence fell between them.

"Do you want to have dinner?" Beverly asked.

Raymond took a sip of his drink. "I don't think so."

"Because we're competitors, or because you don't like me?"

He shrugged, not sure how to answer such a pointed question. "I haven't given it much thought."

"I have." She ran her finger around the edge of her glass. "I'm forty-nine years old and all the men my age are dating younger women, some of them much younger. I don't understand it. I mean Elisabeth is what—twenty-seven?"

"Thirty-one," he said through tight lips. "I don't want to discuss this with you."

"She's only six years older than your son, Raymond. When you were in Vietnam, she was in preschool. Does she even know about Woodstock? What on earth do you have to talk about? Or is talking not one of your priorities?"

Raymond felt the color rise in his cheeks. "Elisabeth and I have a great deal in common."

"Okay, maybe you do. Maybe she's the love of your life, but just out of curiosity, have you ever dated a woman of your own generation?"

"I married one."

"That was years ago, when you were both young. I'm talking about recently, the past fifteen years since your divorce."

Raymond finished his drink and slid the glass across the counter. "I have to go."

"Why do older women scare older men?" Beverly persisted, putting a hand on his arm as he attempted to stand up. "I'd really like to know, because I don't want to spend the rest of my life alone, but I also don't want to spend it with some young twenty-year-old to whom JFK is as unfamiliar as George Washington."

Raymond peeled her fingers from his suit sleeve. "You'd be lucky to find a twenty-year-old, Beverly. It's not your age.

It's you. You talk too much. You push too much.''

Beverly's hand dropped to her side. She didn't look insulted, just thoughtful. "Maybe you're right. I just want to meet a man who understands me, who knows my mind, who can relate to where I'm coming from. All the men I want seem to be taken by younger gals. I just don't get it. I'm a lot better at sex now than when I was twenty, believe me. I'm in better shape, too. Some day, somebody is going to have the thrill of his life.''

Raymond swallowed hard, his gaze drawn to her ample breasts, the curve of her hips. Simple physical reaction, he told himself. He certainly had no interest in Beverly. She'd eat him alive. "I have to go.''

"Don't worry. I wasn't going to make a pass at you.''

"I wasn't worried.'' Although he couldn't help wondering why she wouldn't make a pass at him.

"After all, you're in love with Elisabeth, right?''

"Right.'' And he'd better get the hell out of this bar before he forgot that. "I'll see you around.''

"Raymond? If I was thirty . . .'' Her eyes met his. "Any chance?'' She shook her head before he could answer. "Never mind. I don't really want to know. Sometimes, it's better just to live with the fantasy.''

As Raymond left the bar, he realized Beverly had just pushed another button. She wasn't the one living the fantasy, he was—a fifty-two-year-old man and a thirty-one-year-old woman. He could have been Elisabeth's father. A wave of doubts washed over him, almost drowning him in insecurity and fear.

He knew why he wanted Elisabeth; he just didn't know why she wanted him. And he was afraid to ask.

Chapter 3

Normally Lisa could make the trip from Los Angeles to San Diego in about two hours, but on a late Friday afternoon in early April, it took almost three. It was seven by the time she reached the strip of highway that ran alongside the sandy beaches and blue rocking waves of the Pacific Ocean. As she turned off the freeway, the sun dipped past the horizon, making a glorious, fiery descent, reminding her of all the sunsets she'd watched from the beaches of this southern California city.

She rolled down her window and helplessly inhaled the ocean breeze, the distant scent of jasmine. It smelled like home. She'd grown up here amidst the palm trees, the boats and the beaches, graduating from middle school, high school and finally San Diego State University.

At one time, she'd thought she'd live here forever, near the sand and the sea and the people she loved. But San Diego had changed over the years, and so had she. It was no longer a sleepy beach town but a busy metropolis, expanding in the south from immigrants pouring out of Mexico and in the north from weary, disillusioned city people escaping L.A.

Everywhere she looked she saw new buildings, unfamiliar signs. San Diego was a stranger, and so was she.

She'd been foolish to fear coming down this road. It was not the same road she'd left. Just because she'd come back did not mean she'd come home.

Maggie's street didn't bring back memories either. The

house Maggie lived in now was a recent purchase, bought a few years earlier when Keith had taken a job as a chemist at Bellarmine Labs. The job had brought Keith a hefty increase in salary, and he'd wanted a house to show for it, so he and Maggie and the kids had moved out of their small apartment into this new subdivision of modern two-story houses.

Lisa had only visited once, shortly after Keith's funeral, almost a year ago.

Lisa stopped her car in front of Maggie's house. As she stepped on to the sidewalk, she smiled to herself at the homey touches. Maggie's windows boasted planter boxes filled with irises and daisies. A porch swing blew in the breeze. As she made her way to the front door, Lisa noticed the welcome mat on the ground, the brass knocker with the name "Scott" engraved on it.

Home and family. That's all Maggie had ever wanted. She'd been the anchor in their group, the one who wanted to nest, to savor simple pleasures. For awhile Lisa had wanted the same things, until her life had gone in a different direction. She smoothed down the skirt of her navy blue business suit, suddenly worried that she and Maggie would no longer have anything in common.

Maggie threw open the door before Lisa could ring the bell. "Thank God, you're here," she said, pulling Lisa into a warm hug. "I thought you'd changed your mind."

"The traffic was bad. Everyone wanted to get out of town, I guess."

"I know that feeling. Come on in." Maggie led the way into the house. "I have to apologize—the house is a mess."

The sight of clothes, toys, dishes and general signs of chaos in the living room, dining room and kitchen startled Lisa. Maggie's disclaimer was not the usual polite apology of a hostess caught unawares. The house truly was a mess, which disturbed Lisa even more. Maggie had always been neat. A place for everything and everything in its place.

Lisa followed Maggie up the stairs and into her bedroom. Maggie shoved the pile of laundry from the bed to the floor and sat down. She looked Lisa straight in the eye. "I think I'm losing my mind."

Lisa tried to smile reassuringly, but Maggie's pale face, her tangled blond hair, her old jeans and sweatshirt didn't indicate a healthy state of mind. "Okay, what's wrong?"

Maggie took a deep breath. "Two weeks ago Keith got a letter from a woman named Serena Hollingsworth. She wondered why Keith hadn't been in touch."

Lisa stared at her in bewilderment. "I don't understand . . ."

"I never heard of this woman, Lisa."

"You don't think Keith was seeing someone on the side?"

"No, of course not," Maggie said immediately, then her voice faltered. "At least, I don't think so. I don't know. All of a sudden, I don't know."

Lisa sat down on the other side of the bed, trying to think of what to say. She didn't know what she'd been expecting, but it certainly wasn't this. "Keith adored you and the kids. He wouldn't have cheated on you. He was too honorable."

Maggie stared at her for a long moment. "He increased his life insurance two months before he died, Lisa. He never told me he was doing that."

"He was providing for you."

"Maybe. There's something else. The day before he died, Keith made a huge cash withdrawal from our savings account, eight thousand dollars. We were saving it to buy a new car. I have no idea what he did with the money." Maggie's gaze drifted over to the picture of Keith she still kept on her dresser. "I thought I knew everything about him. Maybe I didn't know anything."

Lisa plucked at the bedspread with her fingers. She didn't like what she was hearing, a strange woman, insurance money, cash withdrawals. None of it sounded like Keith. He'd been an intellectual, a family man, not a womanizer. "You're probably worrying about nothing," she said finally. "Maybe Keith took the money out to put a down payment on a car to surprise you. He loved to surprise you."

Maggie didn't smile or look comforted. She flopped onto

her back, staring at the ceiling. "I wondered about the money before, but I put it out of my mind. When I got that letter from Serena Hollingsworth, it all came back, and I panicked. I couldn't breathe. I couldn't sleep. I kept wondering about her, about him, the money, the life insurance, the fire. There was nothing left but ashes and some teeth that could have . . ."

"That could have what?"

"Belonged to anyone," she said flatly.

"They checked Keith's dental records."

"Right. He had a filling in his third molar. So what? You don't think anyone else has a filling in their third molar?"

"They found bits and pieces of his clothes, his briefcase. The security guard said he'd seen Keith go inside just minutes before the explosion."

Maggie sat up and slid off the bed. She began to pace restlessly around the room. "I know. Keith is dead, and I'm just imagining things." Her eyes met Lisa's. "I think I might be having a nervous breakdown."

"Maybe you should see a doctor."

"Maybe. I can't let the kids down, Lisa. I have to be here for them, but right now, I just want to get away. I got in my car yesterday to drop the kids off at school, and I almost didn't come back. The urge to leave was incredibly strong. I can't believe I'm saying that. I'm a mother. What kind of a mother wants to leave her children?"

Lisa stood up, put her arms around Maggie and hugged her tight. "A mother who is at the end of her rope."

Maggie stepped back with a sigh. "I love them. You know I do, but—"

"But you've been on your own for the past year."

"Yes." Maggie's mouth trembled. "I hate failing."

"You're not failing. You're just being human. You want to get away, Maggie? Just go. I'm here. I'll watch the kids. Check into a hotel for the next two nights, pamper yourself. You deserve it."

Maggie's eyes lit up. "Really? I wanted to ask you, but I wasn't sure. Although I have to admit I already packed my bag.'' She paused. ''You would really do this for me, Lisa?''

''What are friends for?'' Lisa paused as she looked into Maggie's eyes. ''I should have been here for you. I should have taken care of you the way you took care of me. I was incredibly selfish. And I am so sorry. I know it's not enough to say that. I wouldn't blame you if you hated me.''

''I don't hate you,'' Maggie said softly. ''I know why you've stayed away. You're afraid to love people. You always have been.''

''Afraid—don't be silly.''

''I'm not being silly. We may not have seen each other much the past eight years, but I still know you better than anyone else. I remember all those nights we slept out in my parents' backyard. I'd look up at the stars and dream up a wonderful story about my future husband and children and house in the suburbs. You wouldn't let yourself dream, not even then.''

''I did dream once. Look where it got me.''

''You could have tried again.''

Lisa shook her head. ''I'll never try again, not like that, not with so much of me on the line.''

''You're getting married in a few weeks. Does your fiancé have any idea how much you're holding back?''

Maggie's words hit too close to the mark. ''I thought we were talking about you.''

''I'm worried about you, too, Lisa.''

''I'm fine. Now, do you need some money for a hotel?'' Lisa asked.

''I've got a credit card. I'm just not sure if I should leave the kids.''

''Because of me?'' Lisa asked. ''I'd understand if . . .''

''No, God no. How could you even think that?'' Maggie paused, taking Lisa's hands in hers. ''You still blame yourself, don't you, even after all these years? Why can't you let it go?''

''Because it's always there.''

Maggie sighed. ''Yes, I guess it is.''

''Speaking of letting something go—you're not thinking

of chasing down this Serena Hollingsworth, are you?''

"No, of course not," Maggie said quickly. ·

"Honey, there's no point."

"I know that. I do," she added.

Before Lisa could say anything else, the doorbell interrupted their conversation.

"Who could that be?" Maggie muttered.

Lisa's stomach twisted into a knot. *Please, God, don't let it be Nick.* Slowly, she followed Maggie downstairs.

Maggie opened the front door and gasped. "What on earth?"

Lisa peered over Maggie's shoulder. On the porch stood a short, stocky older man with a square face and the blackest, bushiest eyebrows she'd ever seen. His right hand was clasped around the neck of Maggie's thirteen-year-old daughter, Roxanne, and his left hand was around the neck of a pimply-faced adolescent boy.

"I was checking the perimeter of the property, Mrs. Scott, as I do every evening, and I caught these two trespassers at 1900 hours in the back alley," the man said, stating his report as if he were in the military. "I'm sorry to report there was mouth-to-mouth contact."

"Mouth-to-mouth?" Maggie repeated in a daze, looking at her daughter's guilty face. "You're supposed to be in your room, not in the back alley."

"I was giving Marc the homework assignment," Roxanne muttered.

"Since when are you studying mouth-to-mouth resuscitation?"

"Mom, you're embarrassing me." Roxy slid a sideward glance at the boy, who was staring at the shoelaces on his high-top tennis shoes.

"I can't begin to tell you what you're doing to me," Maggie declared. "Thank you, Mr. Bickmore. I'll handle this now."

"As you wish, Mrs. Scott." Mr. Bickmore saluted her, turned on one sharp heel and walked down the path to the sidewalk.

"You can go home now, Marc," Maggie said, drawing Roxanne into the house.

Marc ran off as if he'd been released from a cannon.

Once the front door closed, mother and daughter stared at each other in bewilderment, neither one understanding the other.

Finally, Maggie threw up her hands. "I'm leaving," she said.

Roxanne's mouth dropped open. "You're going away?"

"Yes, for the weekend. Aunt Lisa will stay with you."

Aunt Lisa. Lisa shivered at the words. She hadn't thought of herself as Aunt Lisa in a very long time.

Roxanne sent Lisa a skeptical look that reinforced her doubts about her ability to care for three children, especially one intent on kissing boys in the back alley.

"Why can't Uncle Nick stay with us?" Roxy asked her mother.

Nick. Lisa couldn't stop the automatic, stomach-twisting knot that came with the mention of his name.

"Because I don't know where Uncle Nick is. I left him two messages, and he didn't call me back." Maggie took a few steps toward the kitchen and cupped her mouth. "Dylan, Mary Bea. Come here."

Dylan ran in from the kitchen, Mary Bea wandered down the hall, holding her blanket in one hand, her other thumb planted firmly in her mouth.

"I'm going away for a couple of days," Maggie said. "Your aunt Lisa will watch you."

"Where are you going?" Dylan asked.

"I'm not sure. I'll call you tomorrow and tell you where I am." She turned to Maggie. "You met Mr. Bickmore. Harry is his first name. He's a retired marine sergeant and guards this neighborhood as if it were Fort Knox. No one comes on to this property without Harry knowing about it. In fact, he almost shot the·gardener once."

"That's comforting."

"I've written everything down on a piece of paper." Maggie looked around. "Where did I put that paper? Oh, I know

I left it upstairs on my dresser. I wrote down the name of the kids' pediatrician, our insurance plan, my permission in case you need to take them to the doctor. I'm not sure where I'll be, but I'll call and leave you a number. Let's see what else?" Maggie ran a hand through her hair. "I also wrote down the kids' schedule. It's on the refrigerator. Oh, this is so complicated. How can I go?"

"Just go. We'll be fine."

"Why are you leaving, Mommy?" Mary Bea asked, her eyes welling with tears.

"Because Mommy needs time to relax, so she can stop yelling so much." Maggie squatted down and drew her two younger children into her arms. They hugged for a long minute. Then Maggie opened one arm and motioned for Roxy to join them. After an awkward, reluctant moment, Roxy shuffled forward and hugged her mother.

This time when Maggie drew away there were tears in her eyes. "I love you guys, very, very much. But I have to get away—just for a little while."

"Are you coming back?" Mary Bea asked.

Maggie drew in a sharp gasp of breath. "Of course I'm coming back."

"Daddy didn't."

"She's not going to die, stupid," Roxy said sharply.

"I'm not stupid."

"Yes, you are."

Maggie sent Lisa a helpless, desperate look. "I—I can't do this. It's too selfish, irresponsible. The kids need me."

"They need you healthy and happy and strong." Lisa picked up the overnight bag Maggie had set by the front door. "We'll see you on Sunday."

"Will you be okay?" Maggie asked.

"We'll be fine. Don't worry about a thing."

Maggie kissed each one of her children, then fled.

For one long minute the house was filled with disbelieving silence. The children looked from one to the other, confused, unsure of what had happened.

Lisa couldn't blame them. She might be Aunt Lisa, but in

truth she was a stranger. She hadn't spent any time with these kids. She was Roxanne's godmother, but aside from sending her a Communion gift and cards on birthdays and Christmas, she barely knew the girl. And Mary Bea had been a baby when she'd last seen her. As for Dylan, Lisa remembered when he'd been born, just a month before Robin.

Robin would have been his age now, his size. Lisa's breath caught at the thought. How could she bear to be around Dylan, Roxy and Mary Bea, to see their joy, to feel their love, when it would only remind her of Robin? She wanted to call Maggie back, but she was long gone, and Lisa was alone.

"What are we going to do now?" Dylan asked.

Three pairs of eyes turned to her.

"I was going to ask you the same question." She tried to sound cheerful and confident. "I'm sure we can have a great time together."

"Maybe we should call Uncle Nick," Roxy said.

Lisa put a hand on her arm. "Don't be silly. We'll be fine. There's no need to call your uncle—Nick."

Mary Bea looked at Lisa and began to sob, her cries growing louder with each passing second. Her little face turned red as she screamed. "I want my mommy."

Lisa put her arms around the little girl, trying to draw her close, but Mary Bea would have none of that. "I want Uncle Nick," she said this time.

"It will be okay. I'll play a game with you. We'll tell stories. We'll watch television."

"Uncle Nick, Uncle Nick," Mary Bea yelled.

"Honey, calm down," Lisa tried again.

Mary Bea screamed louder.

"You better call Uncle Nick," Dylan said. "She might never stop screaming."

Lisa's anxiety level rose with each cry. Mary Bea's face turned blotchy, and she began to cough in between her cries as if she couldn't catch her breath. Lisa felt suddenly terrified. What if something happened to Mary Bea? What if she couldn't get Mary Bea to stop crying? What if she fainted? What if she stopped breathing?

Lisa drew in a long breath of air, as memories of the past hit her in the face. Robin in her crib, screaming, her tiny face turning a blotchy red as she pounded her little fists against the sheets. Then hours later, Robin, so still, so lifeless, her skin so cold. Oh, God! How could she do this?

"Aunt Lisa," Roxanne said.

Her voice sounded far away. Lisa could barely focus on Roxy's face. She kept thinking of Robin. The baby had cried so much at first. In the middle of the night, after two and sometimes three trips to the nursery, Lisa had begged and prayed and pleaded for one long night of sleep. Finally, the silence had come, the horrible, deafening silence.

Roxanne ran to the phone and dialed a number. Lisa couldn't raise a voice to stop her.

"Uncle Nick," Roxanne said. "Mom went away and Mary Bea won't stop crying, and I think . . ." She paused, staring at Lisa in uncertainty. "I think Aunt Lisa needs you."

No, don't say that, Lisa begged silently. The last thing she wanted was for Nick to think she needed him, but it was too late. Roxanne hung up the phone.

"He wasn't there," Roxy said. "I'm sure he'll come over when he gets the message." She turned to Mary Bea. "It's okay. Uncle Nick will be here soon. Everything will be all right. You'll see."

Lisa turned away, feeling as panicked as Maggie. She couldn't handle the memories or the kids, and she certainly couldn't handle Nick. She wanted to run away, but this time there was nowhere to go.

Aunt Lisa needs you. The words ran around in his head as Nick played the message one more time. He couldn't believe his ears. Why would Lisa need him? Why would she even be in San Diego? He rewound the tape to the messages left earlier that day. Maggie's voice came first.

"I'm burning out, Nick," she said in a rush. "The kids are driving me crazy. They fight all the time." She paused to tell one of the kids in the background to be quiet. "I can't

even talk on the phone without being interrupted. Some days,
I feel like I can't go on—''

The desperation in her voice touched a deep, resonant
chord within Nick. He remembered that feeling of not being
able to get up, to get dressed, to go on. He also remembered
Maggie standing behind him, supporting him.

Guilt swept through him. He should have been there for
Maggie this past year, but he'd been so busy launching his
business that he'd let it consume his life. When he'd asked
Maggie if she was all right, if she needed anything, she'd
always said no. Why hadn't he seen she was just covering
up, pretending?

Because he hadn't wanted to see. No one had. After the
funeral, after those first few weeks of grief, they'd all gone
on with their lives, believing that Maggie had cried all her
tears. He should have known better. It wasn't until later that
the real grief came, that the inescapable truth of being alone
hit home.

Maggie's voice came back as the machine played the next
message. ''I need to get away, Nick, at least for the day.
Could you watch the kids? I hate to ask, but Mom and Dad
are gone. I won't even think of calling them and ruining their
trip. I'm not that bad.'' She tried to laugh, but it sounded
forced. ''I just need a good night's sleep. Anyway, call me
when you get in.''

The next message was from Roxanne. Apparently unable
to reach him, Maggie had called Lisa. That didn't surprise
him. What shocked the hell out of him was that Lisa had
actually come.

He couldn't stop the sudden surge of energy that ran
through his veins, the anticipation, the fear. For a long time
he'd wanted Lisa to come back. But as the weeks turned into
months, then years, he'd let anger and disillusionment build
a huge, impenetrable wall around his heart. Now that it was
complete, the last thing he wanted was to tear it down.

Aunt Lisa needs you. Roxy's words rang through his head.
He tried to drum up the anger. So what if Lisa needed him.

Hadn't he needed her? Hadn't she turned her back on him? Why the hell should he help her?

The phone rang. He started, giving it a wary glance. What if it was Lisa? What would he say? The phone rang again and again. The machine picked up and after a moment, he heard a woman's voice. It wasn't Lisa; it was Suzanne.

"Nick? Are you there? I made reservations for eight o'clock at the Bella Vista in La Jolla. I hope that's okay."

Nick reached for the phone. "Suzanne. I'm here."

"Oh. I made—"

"I can't go," he said abruptly.

"You can't go? Why not?"

Nick took a deep breath. "My sister isn't feeling well. When I got home there was a bunch of messages from her. I need to go over there."

There was a long silence on the other end of the phone. "I didn't even know you had a sister."

"Maggie is three years younger."

"Do you have brothers, too?"

"One older brother. I'm in the middle."

"You never mentioned them to me. I thought you were all alone here in San Diego."

Nick sighed at the unhappiness in her voice, feeling both defensive and angry at the same time. He'd deliberately kept Suzanne away from the family for reasons he couldn't even bring himself to define. "My brother doesn't live here, just Maggie and my parents. If you want to meet them, you can meet them."

"Really? Why don't I go with you, then?"

"No," he said flatly. "Maggie's upset." *And Lisa will be there.* "Look, I'm sorry, but I have to go. I'll call you, okay?"

"All right. Good night."

Nick hung up the phone, debating whether or not he should call Maggie or just go over to her house. He reached for his keys on the side table, catching his reflection in the mirror. He couldn't help adjusting the collar of his white chambray shirt, running a hand through his curly brown hair.

He hadn't seen Lisa in five years, not since Mary Bea's birth. He'd accidentally run into her in the hospital corridor outside of the nursery. It had been the worst possible place for them to meet, the memories of their love and their pain coming together in a rush of emotion. He'd seen the tears in her eyes as she'd turned away.

He'd called after her, but she'd kept going. Lisa always kept going. Leaving was her specialty. Every time she left, she took another piece of his heart. Not this time. This time, he would make sure he left first.

Chapter 4

"Would you like assistance with your luggage, Mrs. Scott?" the reservations clerk asked with a cheerful smile.

Maggie glanced down at her one worn overnight bag and didn't think it merited a bellboy's tip. "No thanks, I can manage."

The clerk handed her an envelope with her key enclosed. "Have a nice evening."

A nice evening. Maggie glanced around the lobby of the San Diego Court Hotel and smiled. Marble floors, gleaming chandeliers, lush green ferns, cozy table lamps and comfortable armchairs for reading or conversing decorated the lobby. It was a grown-up room for grown-ups, not a child in sight. Thank goodness!

Maggie walked toward the elevators, feeling like a stranger in a strange land. Most of the people in the lobby were dressed for business. The men wore suits, the women wore dresses and heels. Some people had nametags on, boasting the name of their convention group. The hotel obviously catered more to business than to tourism, or else the noisy children and their tired parents were tucked away in some distant wing.

Maggie hadn't stayed in a hotel since Keith had surprised her on their wedding anniversary three years earlier. He'd taken her to the Biltmore in Los Angeles so they could have

41

some time alone together, the first night they'd spent away from the kids since Mary Bea's birth.

It had been wonderful, incredible. Keith had ordered champagne and chocolates, surprising her with the unexpectedly romantic gesture, which had been completely out of character but very welcome. They'd planned on dining in the restaurant but never made it past the king-size bed in the bedroom. Instead they'd ordered room service at midnight and fed each other like young lovers instead of two people who'd been married for ten years.

Maggie's smile faded as she blinked back a sudden tear. She was not going to cry. She was not going to waste the evening in a deluge of tears. Thrusting her chin in the air, she walked over to the bank of elevators and pushed the up button.

A man in a navy blue business suit stood off to one side, impatiently tapping his foot against the marble floor. He was a handsome man, and Maggie breathed in his musky male scent with a sense of hunger, a wash of longing for what she no longer had.

The man sent her a curious look. "Are you all right, ma'am?"

Ma'am? Maggie suddenly felt as old and haggard as she obviously looked. "I'm fine," she said sharply.

He shrugged, obviously dismissing her from his mind. His expression lit up, however, when an attractive blond in a tight black dress, so short it should have been illegal, walked by the elevators, her high, high heels clicking against the floor.

The woman paused and offered the man a dazzling smile. "Aren't you Jonathan Harman?" she asked.

"As a matter of fact, I am." He stood a bit taller under her scrutiny.

"I heard you speak earlier on the role of venture capitalists in today's changing economy. You have incredible insight."

"Thank you."

Maggie frowned. The way the man was beaming, you would have thought she'd said he had an incredible . . .

The elevator bell rang, and the doors slowly opened. Maggie walked inside. The man and the woman stared at each other but didn't move.

"Anyone going up?" Maggie asked, holding the door open with her hand.

"You're not turning in, I hope?" the woman said to the man with a pouty twist of her mouth.

"I could be persuaded not to."

"Then let me persuade you. Have a drink with me?" She tossed her hair back over one shoulder.

Maggie cleared her throat. The man turned to her. "You have a nice evening, ma'am." He put a hand on the other woman's back, and they walked away.

Maggie had a feeling he'd be having a much nicer evening than she would. Ma'am. She made a face as the elevator doors closed. The word made her sound old, like someone's mother. Which, of course, was exactly what she was. She couldn't help looking down at her jeans and her sweatshirt. Her hair was a mess; she hadn't brushed it in hours, and whatever lipstick she'd put on that morning had surely vanished. No wonder he'd called her ma'am.

The doors opened, and Maggie walked slowly down the hall. Her room was on the sixth floor, just around the corner from the elevators. After struggling with her card key, Maggie opened the door. The room was clean, elegant and quiet—oh, so quiet.

As the door shut behind her, she dropped her bag on the floor and walked to the window. She had a view of downtown San Diego. It was a view she'd seen before. She turned and saw the bed, the king-size bed, the one she'd be sleeping in alone.

What was she doing here?

Maggie sat on the bed and stared at the phone. She could call Lisa and see if the kids were all right.

At the thought of her children, the anxiety returned. A myriad of terrifying possibilities raced through Maggie's mind. What if Mary Bea started crying and Lisa panicked? What if Lisa couldn't calm Mary Bea down?

Or what if Roxy got angry and ran off with that pimply faced, hormone-crazy boy? Lisa wouldn't know how to find her. And what if Dylan logged on to the internet and invited some crazy person to visit him?

Why on earth had she left them? All kinds of terrible things could be happening.

"Get a grip," Maggie told herself out loud. She took several deep breaths, forcing herself to relax. She hadn't been gone two hours. If she called, the kids would probably talk her into coming home, and deep down she knew that home was not where she needed to be right now.

Maggie reached for her oversize purse, hoping to find some gum or a leftover peppermint. After pulling out a hairbrush, a box of crayons, three of Mary Bea's barrettes, a parking ticket, a troll doll, three plastic spiders and twenty-seven Safeway receipts, Maggie gave up on finding anything edible.

Unfortunately, the only thing left in her purse was a white envelope—the letter from Serena Hollingsworth. She didn't know what had possessed her to bring it with her. It wasn't as if she was going to see the woman. She didn't need to know why Keith had promised to contact Serena. It had nothing to do with her. Besides, she trusted her husband.

Maggie needed a distraction, so she picked up the television remote control and turned on the set. She flipped through twenty-seven channels with a sudden rush of delight. Instead of cartoons or reruns on Nickelodeon, she could actually choose an adult movie. Maybe this wasn't such a bad idea after all.

Kicking her feet up on the bed, she leaned back against the pillows and let some of the tension ease out of her body. She'd made the right decision to get away. She needed some time alone, to breathe, to let go of all the stress. The kids would be fine with Lisa and maybe, just maybe, getting to know the children would remind Lisa of everything and everyone she'd walked away from.

*   *   *

The children hated her. As Lisa looked around the kitchen table, she could see it in each of their faces. They didn't want her. They wanted their mother. And so did she. Lisa knew nothing about being a mother. Her brief stint had only proved how incapable she was of taking care of one child, much less three. She didn't belong here in this noisy, chaotic house. She belonged in her cool, clean, organized office where she knew how to do everything, where there were no surprises, no uncertainties.

"Mom always makes us eat a vegetable with dinner," Roxy announced, picking up a potato chip and deliberately placing it in her mouth. The resulting crunch was as loud as any verbal accusation.

"Would you like me to make you some corn? I think I saw some in the freezer," Lisa suggested, watching the ketchup drip out of Dylan's hot dog bun. Her first dinner was high on fat, low on nutrients, but Maggie's refrigerator had been empty. At least the children were eating something, and Mary Bea's sobs had dwindled down to an occasional sniffle.

"I hate corn." Dylan wrinkled his nose at the thought.

Lisa watched in fascination as his freckles danced along his cheeks at the motion. He was all boy, big front teeth that didn't quite fit his face, blond hair that stuck up in cowlicks at the back of his head, and the dirtiest hands she'd ever seen. She sighed, recognizing yet another mistake. She should have made the children wash their hands before dinner.

"You hate everything," Roxy said with an air of superiority.

"And you like everything, including that dweeb, Marc." Dylan made a smooching sound with his lips.

Roxy threw a potato chip at him. Mary Bea sat up, looking more interested in their fight than anything Lisa had tried to bring up.

"That's enough," Lisa said sharply, trying to assert some sort of control. Three pairs of eyes fixed on her face, and she panicked. She'd faced down heads of companies, boards of directors, but here, in front of these three children, she felt like a complete idiot. And they knew. She knew they knew. In two minutes, they'd seen right through her efficient facade and recognized the bumbling, uncertain woman she'd once been—maybe always would be—at least when it came to family.

"When is Uncle Nick coming?" Mary Bea demanded.

"I don't know," Lisa replied. It wasn't the right answer. Mary Bea's lip turned down and trembled. "Soon. He'll be here soon," Lisa added hastily. "Look, we can do this. We can have fun and get to know each other while your mom is gone. What do you normally do after dinner?"

"We watch TV and play video games all night," Dylan said.

"And talk on the phone to our friends," Roxy added.

"Mommy doesn't let you play video games all night," Mary Bea said.

Dylan glared at her. "What do you know?"

"Well, she doesn't. She always makes you stop when you start yelling at the TV."

"How about homework?" Lisa asked. "Who has homework?"

"It's Friday night," Roxy said with disgust.

Lisa sighed. "Okay, no homework. Why don't I clear the table and we'll watch some television together, maybe play a board game?"

"I'm too old for games," Roxy said.

"Then you don't have to play."

Roxy frowned. "How come you divorced Uncle Nick?"

The question came out of the blue, stunning her with its utter simplicity.

"I—I—" The words wouldn't come. Maybe because she'd never even answered the question for herself, much less for anyone else. "We just didn't get along," Lisa said finally. *They'd gotten along great in the beginning.* "We didn't love each other enough." *They'd loved each other passionately in the beginning.* "We found we each needed more space." *They'd slept wrapped in each other's arms in the beginning.*

"Why didn't you just get a bigger house?" Dylan asked with simple logic.

Lisa couldn't help but smile. "We didn't think of that."

"I want to take a bath," Mary Bea announced. "I want to see if my new Barbie can swim underwater."

Lisa latched on to the idea with thankful enthusiasm. "That sounds great." She stood up and began clearing the table. "Could you start the bathwater, Roxy?"

"All right." As Roxy and Mary Bea left the room, Dylan pushed back his chair. "Can we have popcorn?"

"Popcorn? Aren't you full?"

"No, I'm starving."

"After two hot dogs and a bag of chips?"

"Mommy says I'm growing."

"Do you have popcorn?"

"Yes, and I know how to make it. I learned how at Billy's house."

"You did? Well—" The doorbell interrupted her statement. Lisa's heart raced at the sound, with anticipation, exhilaration and stark fear. The bell rang again sharply, decisively, impatiently. Nick, it had to be Nick. Oh, God, what was she going to do?

Dylan stared at her. "Aren't you going to answer the door?"

"Sure. Of course. I'll do it right now." Lisa walked slowly to the front door. She didn't ask who it was or even peer through the peephole. She just opened the door and looked into the eyes of the man she had once loved more than anyone on earth.

"Lisa."

"Nick."

She couldn't say another word. With one look, Nick completely stole her breath away. Waves of shock ran through her, followed by feelings of fear, excitement, joy, sadness. This man had been everything to her—friend, lover, husband . . . enemy. She'd once known every inch of his hard body, every freckle, every muscle, every line. But now—now he was a stranger.

Though still fit and trim, Nick had lost the boyish leanness of his youth, but there was strength in his stance, in his build, in his face. The years had brought shadows to his once brilliant green eyes, lines around the corner of a mouth that at one time had known only how to smile.

Nick crossed his arms in front of his broad chest, and Lisa's gaze was drawn down the length of him, remembering with painful clarity how it had felt to put her arms around his waist, to taste his mouth, to run her hands through his hair.

Goosebumps ran down her arms unbidden and unrestrained. Looking at him now, Lisa found that Nick still made her heart race. He still made her palms sweat. Dammit. She didn't want him to affect her. She didn't want to feel anything, not anger or hatred or love or passion—least of all passion. They were nothing to each other anymore, nothing.

Nick read every emotion that passed through her clear blue eyes, but when he got to desire he looked away. He'd always been able to tell exactly what Lisa was thinking. Now, he didn't want to know. He didn't want to believe that she felt anything for him. To believe would be to risk the peace that had been a long time in coming.

As his gaze roamed across her face, he felt every muscle in his body tighten. She was everything he remembered and more. Her black silky hair still caught every bit of light that lit up a room. Even in the moonlight, her hair came alive just like her blue, blue eyes. He'd felt as if he'd been living in the shadows until she'd come into his life, with her gentle grace, her soft lips, her stubborn chin and a body he couldn't stop touching. At twenty, she had been his fantasy. At twenty-five she had been his nightmare.

"What the hell is going on?" Nick demanded, retreating into anger. He knew how to fight with Lisa. He couldn't remember how to like her, how to love her.

Lisa stiffened. "Excuse me?"

"I get a frantic call from my niece saying her mother has taken off and you're in trouble."

She put her hands on her hips. The light of battle entered her eyes. "I'm not in trouble, and Maggie has just gone away for the weekend."

"Then why did Roxy call me?"

"Mary Bea was a little upset, but she's fine now. We're all fine. You can go home." She started to close the door, but Nick stuck his foot out.

"Not so fast. I think I'll come in and talk to the kids if you don't mind."

"And if I do?"

"Tough."

"Nick—"

He brushed past her. "Roxy, Dylan, Mary Bea?" he shouted.

The kids came running from every direction—Dylan from the kitchen, Roxy and Mary Bea down the stairs. They threw themselves into their uncle's outstretched arms, their eyes beaming with happiness.

Lisa couldn't help but feel a bit jealous at the sight. They loved him. They wanted him—not her. Of course, why would they want her? They didn't even know her. It was her fault that she was practically a stranger, but that didn't make it easier to take.

"Are you going to stay with us, Uncle Nick?" Dylan asked. "We could play Sega. I got a cool new game."

"Uh, well, it looks like you already have someone to watch you," Nick said, not even glancing in Lisa's direction. "Where did your mom go?"

"She got mad and left," Roxy said. "We don't know when she's coming back."

"She's coming back Sunday," Lisa interrupted.

"I don't think she is coming back," Mary Bea said, her face turning sad once again. "She said we were driving her crazy."

"Don't cry, please don't cry," Lisa begged.

"I can't help it," Mary Bea said with a hiccup. "I want my mommy." Her words ended with a wail.

"Everything's fine, huh?" Nick ran his hand through Mary Bea's tangled blond curls. "It's okay, pumpkin. Uncle Nick is here." He cocked his head to one side. "What's that sound?"

Lisa was so distracted by the gentle way he soothed Mary Bea that she couldn't hear anything but the pounding of her own heart.

"It sounds like someone is taking a shower," Dylan said.

Roxy clapped a hand to her mouth. "The tub."

Lisa beat Roxy up the stairs, only to find water splashing over the top of the tub, covering the bathroom floor and soaking into the hall carpet. In her rush to turn off the faucet, she slid, landing on her buttocks and slamming her big toe into the tub, which sent a rush of pain up her leg. The water soaked through her skirt in seconds. By the time she had righted herself and reached for the faucet, she was sopping wet.

When she turned around, she stared into four sets of amazed eyes. She felt embarrassed, like she'd just walked naked into the middle of an intersection. "It's all right," she mumbled. "I'll clean it up. It will be okay."

A loud, shrill, beeping noise suddenly rang through the house.

"Oh, my God, that's the smoke alarm," Lisa said.

"The popcorn," Dylan cried.

This time Nick led the rush down the stairs and into the kitchen, where kernels of corn were turning black in a sizzling frying pan. Nick turned off the burner and pushed the pan away from the heat.

"You've got everything under control, huh?" Nick asked again.

"I thought he was putting a bag in the microwave," Lisa explained, her damp skirt clinging to her legs with a coolness that sent a shiver down her spine. She hated the way Nick looked at her, like she was a failure, like she couldn't do anything right, although she shouldn't have been surprised by the accusation in his eyes. He'd looked exactly the same way eight years ago. "This is your fault," she said in defense. "If you hadn't arrived, Roxy would have turned off the water in the tub, and I would have stopped Dylan from trying to fry the popcorn."

Nick's eyes blazed. "It's always my fault, isn't it, Lisa?"

She took an instinctive step backward, knowing he wasn't talking about the popcorn or the tub and that she'd just opened a door she had no intention of going through. "I didn't—I can't—don't do this, Nick."

"It's always about you."

It was never about me. It was always about her. Robin. Our baby. The protest screamed silently through her head, but the words wouldn't come out. She hadn't said Robin's name out loud since the day they'd buried her. She couldn't say it now. Instead she took a deep breath and cleared her throat. "Go home, Nick."

He hesitated, then turned toward the door, but Mary Bea's plaintive sob cut through the silence in the room. She launched herself against him, throwing her chubby little arms around his thigh so he couldn't move.

"Stay, Uncle Nick."

Nick hesitated, obviously torn between the children he loved and the ex-wife he hated. "Maybe I should stay."

Lisa's mouth dropped open. "You can't stay. I'm here."

"The kids want me. Why don't you leave? Head back to L.A. Take off the way you always do."

It was tempting. Boy, was it tempting. Then she remembered Maggie, her best friend's panicked face, and Lisa knew she couldn't break her promise. "I told Maggie I'd watch the kids."

"I'm sure she wouldn't be surprised if you left."

His words hurt the way they were meant to. Lisa squared her shoulders. "I'm staying, Nick. I promised Maggie I'd take care of her kids, and that's what I will do."

"We all know how much your promises are worth. Zero. Or am I being too generous?"

"I never knew you had such a mean streak."

"Who do you think put it there?"

She hobbled over to the stove. "I'm going to clean up the mess."

"If only you could." He met her eyes in one long, telling look before he led the children out of the room.

Chapter 5

*L*isa managed to avoid Nick for the next hour. While he and Dylan played Sega, she cleaned up the kitchen, got Mary Bea into the bath and even convinced Roxy to help sort through the pile of laundry on Maggie's bed. By ten o'clock Lisa was exhausted. The long day, the frantic drive down to San Diego, and the turmoil of seeing Nick again after so many years had taken every last ounce of her energy. It was all she could do to finish Mary Bea's bedtime story and climb out of the small twin bed before she fell asleep with her niece.

Niece. Lisa took one last look at Mary Bea, smiling wistfully at the sight of her blond curls falling lazily across her rosy cheeks, her little hand tucked up under her chin. Lisa had once dreamed of a life like this, a house full of children, a loving husband. But dreams didn't come true. She'd known that for eight years. With an abrupt flick of the switch, she drowned the room in darkness and stepped into the hallway, running smack into Nick.

"Is she asleep?"

Nick's low, husky voice startled her. He was so close that she could feel his breath against her cheek, see the shadow of beard along his jawline. She tried to move away, but Nick took up so much space. He always had. His presence swamped her both emotionally and physically.

"Lisa?" he murmured, a questioning note in his voice.

"Could you move, please?"

Nick didn't budge. He simply looked at her with those sharp, piercing green eyes that saw everything. "My God, it's still there. After all these years, after everything we did and everything we said, it's still there."

"Don't be ridiculous." Her muscles tightened, and she tried not to look at him, but he was so damn close.

"You never could lie worth a damn."

"Let me go, Nick."

"I'm not holding you, Lisa."

But he was, with his eyes, with his voice, with his memories. They'd stood together like this before at the door to Robin's room. They'd watched their baby sleep. They'd held each other and smiled with pride and joy before they'd gone back to their bedroom to make love. She took in a deep breath and let it out. "You're not making this easy."

"Why should I?"

Lisa took another deep breath and silently counted to ten.

"You didn't answer my question," Nick said with a baiting smile.

"Where are you planning to sleep?" Lisa asked instead.

A light burned through his eyes.

"I'm taking Maggie's room," she added hastily. "I guess that leaves you with the couch."

"What if I want her room?"

"You're out of luck. In fact, you really don't have to stay."

"I promised the kids I would. I don't break my promises."

"Fine. Stay. Are Dylan and Roxy asleep?" she asked, as they walked down the hall together.

"Dylan's asleep. Roxy's reading."

"I'll get my bag out of my car then."

Nick dogged her steps down the stairs. "Why don't you go home, Lisa? I'll take care of the kids."

"I made a promise, too. I intend to keep it."

Lisa opened the front door and walked onto the porch. She paused, suddenly realizing how long it had been since she had smelled the ocean and lived in a neighborhood where crickets sang through the night.

"I can't believe you came back," Nick said after a moment. He leaned against the porch railing, crossing his arms in front of him. "The last time I saw you was the night Mary Bea was born. You ran off so fast, I didn't get a chance to say hello."

Lisa looked into his curious eyes and shrugged. "I don't think hello was what you were planning to say."

He tipped his head. "You might be right about that."

"I love Maggie, Nick. That's why I'm here. You know how much I care about her."

"I know you did love her. But you loved a lot of people—eight years ago." He paused. "It's almost her birthday, you know. A week from Sunday—Robin would have been eight years old."

"Don't."

"You can't even say her name, can you?"

Lisa didn't want to say Robin's name. She didn't want to think about her baby. She didn't want to remember. It hurt too damn much. "She's gone, Nick. Saying her name won't bring her back."

"Maybe it would bring you back."

She looked at him, confused by his cryptic answer. "I'm here."

"I don't mean here in San Diego. I mean here—in your heart." He suddenly reached out, and his palm covered the curve of her breast. An irrepressible tingle ran down her spine, a shock wave of warmth and love and sex.

"Don't," she whispered.

His hand curved around her breast. "You died that night, Lisa, as surely as she did. At least the Lisa I remember, the Lisa I married, the Lisa I loved."

His words cut her to the quick. She pushed his hand away from her body. "Died? I wasn't the one who disappeared for almost twelve hours while people were calling and crying and calling again," she said passionately. "I wasn't the one who came to the funeral home smelling like a brewery."

His face tightened. "Stop it, Lisa."

"Why should I?"

His eyes blazed with anger and pain. "Because you made your point. I wasn't there for you. I wasn't there for Robin. Everything is my fault. We've had this argument before. You've never understood what I went through."

"And you've never understood what I went through. That's why we didn't work, Nick. Maybe we were never meant to work. That's why it happened. It was an end to what never should have begun." Silence fell between them, broken only by the sound of their breathing, angry and rushed. "It's pointless to rehash the past," Lisa said finally. "It's done."

"You've never given our past a second thought, have you? Not since the day you left." Nick pulled her hand into the light of the porch. Her engagement ring sparkled between them like a traitor caught in a spotlight. "My God! Are you married?"

"No. No. I'm just engaged." She didn't know why she rushed to explain that she was only engaged. After all, she would be married soon.

Nick shook his head in confusion. "I can't believe Maggie never said anything. You're getting married."

"It's been a long time, Nick. It's not like I rushed out and grabbed the next guy who came along."

He looked at her with more pain than anger, and she felt her insides melt. "Do you remember the robins, Lisa? We sat on the porch and watched them that first spring. The male called to the female with his song and she came. They built a nest together and had baby robins."

Yes, she remembered the robins. She remembered Nick sitting on the porch, playing his guitar as the male robin sang his song, and just like the female robin, she had been drawn to the music, to the male—to Nick.

"So who is this guy you're marrying?" Nick asked more harshly than he should have for a man who hadn't seen her in a very long time.

She shrugged. "Does it matter?"

Nick didn't answer. Finally, she moved toward the edge of the porch. "I'm going to get my bag. I'll only be here til

Sunday, Nick. Do you think we can just pretend to get along for two more days? I don't want the kids to feel uncomfortable.''

"Sure, why not? We'll call a truce." He walked over to her and stuck out his hand. "Shake?"

She knew it was a mistake the second she slid her hand into his. His palm was warm, his fingers strong and tender as they curled around hers. It wasn't a handshake. It was a meeting of two electrical wires that together created a dangerous spark.

"That was cheating," she whispered, meeting the smile in Nick's eyes.

"It's still there. I knew it was still there. And so did you."

She pulled her hand away from his and practically ran down the walkway to her car, eager to get some distance between them.

"That's why you never came back, isn't it?" Nick's voice carried across the lawn. "You were afraid of me."

Lisa shook her head, but couldn't chance the words. She wasn't afraid of him. She was afraid of herself.

There was no reason to be afraid, Maggie told herself late Saturday morning as she stood outside the entrance to Serena Hollingsworth's town house in Beverly Hills. Just because she'd never met the woman and had no business showing up at her door unannounced, there was no reason to be nervous. The woman had written to Keith. If she'd wanted to remain anonymous, she wouldn't have sent a letter to his home.

Unless Serena didn't know Keith was married. After all, she didn't know he was dead. Maybe she also didn't know he was married with children, three beautiful children. Maggie took a deep breath as she looked around.

The town house sat on the edge of a luxurious condominium complex. It had taken Maggie fifteen minutes just to locate number 1207 in building number three. She had had to walk down several lush, green pathways to find Serena's town house, which was tucked away in a bower of bushes and flowers.

The entrance was private. It was the perfect spot for two people to meet, two people who didn't want anyone else to see them. A perfect spot to have an affair—except for the fact that it was two hours from San Diego. If Keith had wanted to have an affair, why hadn't he had one closer to home?

The whole thing was ridiculous. Keith could not have had a woman on the side. Maggie would have known. She would have noticed something—lipstick, a strange receipt for flowers, something. Surely, he wouldn't have been able to act perfectly natural? Wouldn't the guilt have driven him crazy? Not that Keith was a particularly guilty sort of person.

She was the one with the guilt, the one who hated to even change seats at the baseball game for fear of getting caught. And she usually did, because she wore guilt like a scarlet letter. Keith believed some rules were made to be bent. But changing a seat at a baseball game could not be compared with having an affair. The rules of marriage were unbreakable, at least in her mind.

As Maggie stared at Serena's door, she remembered the trips Keith had taken in the months before he'd died, trips to another lab in Santa Monica, and a couple even further up the coast in San Francisco. She'd never called him while he was away. He'd always insisted on phoning her, because he didn't know where he'd be at any given time. Whereas he always knew where she would be—right there in his house, taking care of his children.

Maggie's imagination took over. She couldn't stop the suspicious thoughts from running through her head, the doubts, the uncertainty. Had she married an imposter? She remembered seeing a movie where a man had kept three wives in three different cities and none of them knew about each other, until the man had gotten hurt and all three had ended up at the hospital together.

But that wasn't Keith. Until this last job, he'd barely travelled at all. He'd been content to come home every night to her and the children.

At least she thought he'd been content.

Maybe not. Maybe he'd yearned for a different life from the one they'd had.

The doubts ran around and around in her head until she felt dizzy. She had to do something to stop them. She'd driven two hours to meet Serena Hollingsworth. Wasn't it about time she knocked on the door?

Maggie strode forward before she could rethink her decision to act. She rang the bell and waited. There was no reply, no rustling sounds of someone hurrying to get the door, just silence. Serena wasn't home.

Maggie felt the wind go out of her sails, the resolve go out of her head, the strength go out of her shoulders. She felt so weak she had to sit down on the step, the white envelope still clutched between her fingers. She'd driven all this way for nothing. Nothing!

Not that she even knew what she would say to Serena, something about the letter, something about Keith's death, something . . .

A man came jogging down the path dressed in tight black bicycle shorts and a peach-colored tank top. He looked to be in his early thirties and was in great shape with lean runner's legs, a broad chest, sexy moustache and hair almost long enough to be pulled back in a ponytail.

Maggie couldn't help but smooth down the skirt of the floral sundress she'd exchanged for the jeans she usually wore. Her hair was actually brushed, and she'd even worn lipstick. Not that it mattered. He wouldn't give her a second look.

She was wrong. The man smiled at Maggie and slowed his pace as he approached Serena's town house. "If you're waiting for Serena, you're going to have a long wait."

"I am?" Maggie asked as he jogged in a small circle in front of her. "Is she away?"

"Saturday is her spa day. Are you a friend of hers?"

Maggie hesitated. She didn't make a habit of lying. But then, she didn't make a habit out of chasing down women who wrote to her husband, either. "Yes," she said finally. "I live out of town. I thought I'd surprise her, but I guess I should have called first.'' She got to her feet, feeling as if her nose had grown two inches with that lie.

''I'm sure you could find her at the spa.''

''Which spa is that?''

''The Olympia Spa on the corner of Sycamore and Doran. You can't miss it. There are Greek statues of gods and goddesses along the driveway. It's pretentious as hell, and you have to sell your soul to get in, but it's a happening place. Serena swears there's nothing better than a day at the spa— not even sex.'' His eyes narrowed speculatively. ''You don't look like the spa type, though.''

Of course she didn't look like someone who went to a spa. The closest she got to exercise was the twenty-year-old stationary bicycle in her garage. ''I—uh—I've been busy lately. Gotten a little out of shape.''

''This is L.A. Can't afford to be out of shape in this town.''

''I'm not staying long.''

''That's what I thought, too,'' he said with a smile so sexy it almost took her breath away. ''I came out from Omaha ten years ago for a one-week vacation. I've been here ever since.''

''Really?'' Goodness, she could watch this man talk forever. He had an incredible mouth.

''L.A. gets into your blood,'' he added. ''It's hot and smoggy but if you want to work in film, this is the place to be. It's where all the beautiful people are.''

Maggie uttered a short laugh. ''I don't work in film, and I'm hardly beautiful, so I don't think I have to worry.''

He didn't say anything for a moment, just studied her with light brown eyes that gleamed with hints of gold. There was intelligence in his eyes. Good Lord, the man was gorgeous and intelligent. He was right. L.A. was where all the beautiful people were, and it was time she went home.

''You're real,'' he said finally. ''You're barely wearing makeup, and I'd bet your hair is actually blond. Unbelievable.''

Maggie swallowed uncomfortably under his close perusal.

"I better go."

"I'm sorry, I didn't mean to stare. I'm Serena's neighbor. My name is Jeremy. Jeremy Hunt." He extended his hand, and Maggie reluctantly took it. "I'm a writer, and I guess I tend to analyze people a little more than I should."

"It's all right," she said, as she extricated her hand from his. "My hair is blond." Why on earth had she told him that?

He smiled again. "If you stay in L.A., maybe we'll see each other around."

My God, the man was actually looking at her like a woman, a real, live woman, not someone's mother, not someone's wife, but a sexual woman. Maggie was tempted to turn around and see if there was someone standing behind her. She hadn't had a man flirt with her in years. She didn't have a clue how to respond.

"I'm—I'm not staying," she said.

"Too bad. It's tough to find real in this town. Figures you'd be leaving. Just my bad luck."

"I'm sure there are lots of real people in Los Angeles. Maybe you're not looking in the right place."

"Maybe not. Are you sure you're a friend of Serena's?"

"Of course. Why wouldn't I be?" She couldn't look him in the eye. He'd see right through her.

"You seem different."

"Don't you have any friends that are different from yourself?"

"Touché."

"Well, thanks for telling me where Serena is. I better go find her."

He tipped his head. "Have a nice day."

"You too." She took a few steps down the path, then heard him call after her.

"Hey, you never told me your name."

She paused and glanced over her shoulder. "I know."

"I'm a writer," he warned with another one of his dazzling smiles. "I'll just make one up for you."

"I've always been partial to Crystal. It sounds expensive, delicate, strong, and pretty."

"Then I'll call you Crystal, because it fits."

Maggie smiled to herself. It didn't fit. She wasn't a Crystal; she was a Margaret. But as she walked away with the most seductive swagger she'd ever managed, she couldn't help wondering if he liked what he saw. Then the traitorous thought scared her and she hurried down the path to her car. What was she doing? She was a married woman. She couldn't be thinking about another man.

It wasn't until she slipped her key into her car door that she realized she wasn't married anymore. She wasn't a wife. She was a widow. And she had two choices. She could go back to San Diego and forget all about Serena Hollingsworth or she could go to the spa and find some answers. There was really only one choice.

He should have gone home, Nick decided as he watched Lisa brush out Mary Bea's blond curls in preparation for an upcoming birthday party. Lisa knelt on the living room floor behind Mary Bea, her hands swift yet gentle as she unsnarled each tangle without drawing one word of complaint from Mary Bea.

Mary Bea had been quiet all morning, more subdued than Nick was used to seeing her, but maybe she was exhausted from all the crying the night before. Whatever the reason, it was obvious she'd begun to accept Lisa as a baby-sitter, which meant he really didn't need to stay.

It wasn't like he didn't have anything to do. He had orders stacking up from the baby fair, not to mention the ones he'd taken in his store the past week. And while his two store clerks could work the front desk and sell the furniture they had in stock, he was the only one who could actually make the pieces to be sold. Which meant he should be working instead of standing in the doorway of Maggie's living room watching his ex-wife brush his niece's hair.

But there was something in Lisa's sure strokes, in the picture they made together that captivated him. Today, she looked like the woman he remembered. Gone was the starchy white shirt, the sterile business suit, all the armor of her current life as a businesswoman. Today, dressed in soft, worn blue jeans and a light blue sleeveless knit top, she looked like a woman, feminine, alluring, motherly.

He could almost imagine this was their home, their daughter, their life. If only . . . no, that was a path he wouldn't go down. Lisa was leaving tomorrow, going back to L.A., to her life, to her future husband. His stomach twisted in a jealous knot. He couldn't stand to think of someone else holding her, kissing her, touching her. What the hell was wrong with him? It had been eight years, and he still thought of her as belonging to him.

Lisa looked up and caught him staring. "Nick," she said, her voice somewhat flustered. "You should have said something. I didn't realize you were standing there."

"I didn't want to interrupt such an important task."

"Aunt Lisa says I look beautiful," Mary Bea said with a smile. "Do you think I'm beautiful?"

"The prettiest girl in town."

"Prettier than Aunt Lisa?" Mary Bea quizzed, determined to spell out exactly where she ranked in the list.

"You're definitely the prettiest five-year-old girl."

Mary Bea tilted her head to one side as she considered his answer. "That's okay, I guess."

"Isn't she ready yet?" Dylan ran into the living room with his baseball bat in one hand and his mitt in the other. "I'm going to be late for practice."

"You have to drop me off at the movies first," Roxy said, following close behind her brother. "I don't want to look for my friends in the dark."

"Then I'll be even later," Dylan moaned. "Girls are such a pain."

"You're right about that," Nick said, commiserating with his young nephew.

Lisa stood up. "Why don't we take two cars? I'll drop off Roxy and Mary Bea, and you can take Dylan to baseball practice."

It was a good plan. Then they wouldn't have to sit in the same car together. In fact, they might be able to get through most of the day without seeing each other.

"Fine," he said. "Let's go."

"I'll just get my purse." As Lisa reached for her purse on the coffee table, the dog came bounding into the room, knocking her off balance. The purse fell from her hand, landing open on the carpet, the contents spilling out.

Nick squatted down to help her gather her wallet and lipstick and keys—and the small white box that had somehow found its way into her purse.

"What's this?" Nick asked.

She tried to grab the box, but he lifted the lid before she could stop him. His jaw dropped at the sight of the charm bracelet. The pulse in the base of his neck beat frantically as the blood drained out of his face.

"Oh, God," he muttered as he ran the gold chain between his fingers. "Where did you—?"

"My mother."

"Silvia. That's what she wanted. The magic bracelet. I should have guessed."

"You have a magic bracelet?" Dylan asked. "That's cool. What does it do?"

"It doesn't do anything, and it's not magic," Lisa said. "I can't believe you kept it all these years." She looked into his eyes, searching for an explanation.

"It was in storage."

"Storage?" she echoed. "What storage?"

He set the bracelet back in the box and handed it to her. Then he got to his feet. "We'd better get a move on. Why don't you kids get in the car?"

"Nick?" she asked, as the kids left the room.

"What?"

"I thought you gave our stuff away."

He shrugged as he dug his hands into his pockets. "I didn't."

She pushed the box and other items into her purse and stood up. "Why not?"

"Does it matter? You told me to put all the pieces of our life into a garbage bag and throw it in the dump. Why do you care if I still have some of our things?"

"What else do you have?"

"Do you really want to know? Because I can show you. I can take you to our house, Lisa." He saw the blood drain from her face. "What's the matter? Afraid of ghosts?"

"We have to go. The kids are waiting."

"Of course you have to leave. Just once I'd like you to stay and fight to the bitter end."

"I know how to fight, Nick. I fought until the horrible, horrible end. Remember? But I've moved on with my life. I'm not stuck in the past like you." She turned on her heel and walked through the door and down the drive to her car, where Mary Bea and Roxy were waiting.

Nick watched her slide into the front seat and turn the key in the ignition. Instead of the motor catching life, nothing happened. Lisa tried again. Another click.

"Come on, Uncle Nick, we're going to be late," Dylan called out from the front seat of Nick's jeep.

"Hang on a second." He walked over to Lisa's car, watching as she struggled valiantly to get it to start.

"I don't understand. I just had the car tuned up," she muttered. "It's supposed to be in perfect condition."

"Might have a dead battery."

"Do you want to jump me?"

He couldn't help but smile. "You bet."

"The car I mean," she said crossly.

"Of course. I don't have a jump. Come on, we'll take the kids in my car and figure out what to do with yours later."

"It has to start." She tried again, with no luck.

"Maybe you should use the magic bracelet," Mary Bea suggested.

"If it were magic, my car would start," Lisa said.

"Guess you'll have to ride with me," Nick said, suddenly realizing how much he wanted her to come with him. He wanted a chance to show her what she'd turned her back on. Maybe it was ego, but dammit, he couldn't stand the way she looked at him, as if he was stuck in some sort of a time warp. "After we drop off the kids, we can go by the house," he said as she stepped out of her car.

"I have no intention of going to your house."

He grinned. "Too bad. I'm the one who's driving."

Chapter 6

"Thanks for giving me a ride," Beverly said as she slipped into the front seat of Raymond's silver Lexus. She set her purse on the floor and crossed her long, slender legs, then flashed him a brilliant smile. "You're a peach."

He wasn't a peach. He was an idiot. Not only was he giving his competition a ride to a party hosted by the account they both wanted but the competition was Beverly, of all people. Beverly, who sent his blood pressure skyrocketing thirty points every time she opened her mouth. Beverly, who wore a sophisticated, sexy scent reminiscent of Chanel that completely swamped his senses. He had always found perfume on a beautiful woman to be erotic, sexual. But this woman was Beverly, not Elisabeth, and he had no business thinking such thoughts. He turned the key in the ignition and pulled sharply away from the curb.

"I love a man who likes to go fast," Beverly said with a small laugh.

Raymond suddenly had the sinking feeling that she could see right into his head, into his thoughts. "I thought women liked men who went slow."

"Depends on what they're doing."

"Dammit, Beverly. It's one o'clock in the afternoon."

"I'm sorry. I didn't know there was a starting time on flirting."

"I'm not flirting with you. I'm giving you a ride."

"Have it your way." She sent him a curious look. "What do you think Monty Friedman will say when he sees us together?"

Raymond inwardly groaned. The CEO of Nature Brand would probably be amused, but then he'd deliberately pitted them against each other. Monty wanted to hire not just the best company but the toughest, the most willing to do whatever it took, the one still standing at the end of the fight, however dirty that fight might get.

"Monty's sister and I went to high school together," Beverly said idly. "Catholic school. She was a prig though, very straight. Wouldn't have dreamed of wearing sexy lingerie under her regulation plaid uniform."

Great, Beverly had an inside edge. He would have to watch her like a hawk. "I suppose you wore a garter belt?"

"It was red, very sexy. I thought I was so cool." She sighed. "Don't you wonder where all the time has gone? Every year, the days, the hours, the minutes—all seem shorter. Sometimes I wish I didn't have to sleep. I feel like I'm missing something by wasting those hours in oblivion."

Raymond knew exactly how she felt. His life had become a race against time, against his graying hair, his receding hairline, the rubbery muscles that never seemed to achieve the leanness of his youth no matter how many sit-ups he did.

"I envy Elisabeth," Beverly continued. "She's young, beautiful, thin, and, I hate to admit it, she's even nice. When she lets her guard down, that is. I saw her at the Children's Hospital Halloween Fair last fall. She was really in her element there, handing out balloons, painting faces."

"I don't remember her talking about that," Raymond said, reminded once again that Elisabeth didn't always share her life with him. Not that he wanted to be with her every second, but it still bothered him that she'd never mentioned her friend in San Diego. And that bracelet her mother had sent, there was something odd about it. He'd bet his last dollar it wasn't a wedding present at all. He'd met Silvia Alvarez once and only then because she'd dropped in at the office unexpectedly. She clearly hadn't liked him at all.

He doubted he'd see her again until the wedding. She and Elisabeth didn't seem to get along. In fact, sometimes he forgot Elisabeth even had a family; she so rarely mentioned anyone. Maybe he should have asked more questions. In truth, he didn't really care to know them. He'd had enough of in-laws the first time around.

"I'm surprised you didn't come to the fair," Beverly continued. "Elisabeth designed the flyers and the posters for the event. They were excellent."

"I'm sure they were. She does first-rate work."

"That she does."

Silence fell between them as Raymond stopped the car at a stoplight. Two teenagers walked slowly across the street. Their hair was sprayed various shades of red and green. The boy's pants were dragging down to his knees, and the girl wore all black clothing, save for a pair of bright red boots. They were smoking cigarettes and looking as if they thought they were the coolest pair in the world.

Raymond glanced over at Beverly. She looked at him and smiled. They both started to laugh.

"Did we ever look that bad?" she asked.

"I wore enough grease in my hair to fry bacon," Raymond confessed. "And I smoked. Drove like a maniac. I don't know why, except that it was 1962. I was rebelling—against what I have no idea," Raymond replied as the light changed.

"I wore those low-riding hip huggers with the big bell bottoms, and I parted my hair down the middle and wore it straight so that it covered my eyes."

"Were your parents okay with it?"

"Are you kidding? I went to Catholic school, remember? I gave my father gray hair. He was very straight, very religious. He even made me go to Mass every Sunday. When I got old enough to go by myself, I would hide my regular clothes in the bushes in the alley behind our house. As soon as I kissed my parents good-bye, I changed and went to Bob's Big Boy to hang out. I always wanted to be one of those waitresses at the drive-in. Ours wore roller skates."

He laughed, remembering. "It was a lifetime ago, wasn't it?"

"They were the good old days, I guess."

"Not all so good," he said with a sigh.

"You went to Vietnam, didn't you?"

"I was drafted."

"How long were you there?"

"Seven months," he said in a clipped voice. "It was worse than any hell I could have imagined. I got lucky. I broke my leg in three places during an exercise, and they shipped me back to the States."

Beverly's voice filled with compassion. "You call that lucky?"

"Compared to the alternative, yes."

"My brother still wakes up with nightmares from his tour."

"Me, too." Raymond could have cut out his tongue for uttering those damning words. He didn't know why he'd told her that. He'd never told anyone. Fortunately the nightmares came infrequently enough now that he didn't anticipate sharing them with Elisabeth. At least he hoped he wouldn't have to. He was too old to have nightmares, to need comfort. He was a man, goddammit.

"How come we never talked like this before—when I worked for you?" Beverly asked.

"You were too busy trying to climb my ladder."

"And you kept pushing Jimmy and Larry and every other young male hotshot ahead of me on that ladder."

"Are you claiming sexual discrimination?"

"I could have."

"I don't have a problem with women reaching the top. Elisabeth has never had any complaints."

"It must have been me then."

"You push too hard, Beverly."

"It's the only way I know how to get what I want. It's certainly never just come to me," she said with a trace of bitterness. "I wasn't always like this, you know. Once, I made the mistake of believing . . ." Her voice drifted away as she turned to look out the window.

"What were you going to say?" he prodded.

"Nothing you'd be interested in."

But he was suddenly very interested in why her eyes were so bright, why she looked vulnerable instead of assured.

"Patience is a virtue," he said, returning to their original topic.

"Patience be damned. You didn't have to wait to get ahead. I've read about some of your past exploits in *Advertising Age*, how you bailed out on your first employer, stealing half the accounts."

"I didn't steal them. They came on their own, and Madison went bankrupt."

"Whose fault was that?"

His gut tightened. "You know I could drop you off on this street corner and have Monty all to myself this afternoon."

Beverly shook her head. "No can do, Raymond. I told Monty you were giving me a ride, just in case you found a cliff to throw me over along the way."

"What did he say?"

"He said if we weren't both so stubborn and pigheaded, we'd probably make a good team."

"Yeah, what does he know?" Raymond growled as he turned off the street and into the long driveway that led up to Monty's Bel Air home. "You and I could never work together, not in a million years."

"I agree with you."

"You do?" He stopped the car behind a gold Mercedes. "That's a first."

"But I think we could do other things really well together, if you didn't have such a youth complex. If you weren't looking to find young Raymond in young Elisabeth."

His jaw dropped at her bluntness. "Jesus, Beverly, do you ever think before you open your mouth?"

She shrugged. "It wastes too much time." She picked up

her purse and opened the door. "Aren't you coming?" she asked when he made no move to get out.

"In a minute."

"Don't want to be seen with me? Afraid I'll ruin your playboy image?"

"Beverly?"

"What?"

"Find another ride home."

"Sure, why not. Maybe I can find a young, hard body, with a washboard stomach and bulging pecs. After all, if you can do it, why can't I?"

He shook his head in bemusement. "I'd wish you good luck, but I don't think you're the one who will need it."

"Raymond, as far as the account goes . . ." She paused, then grinned. "May the best woman win."

Raymond couldn't stop the smile that spread across his face. She was a piece of work, but he was determined to win her—make that beat her.

Maggie listened to the phone ring, two, three, four times, then the machine picked up. Darn, they weren't there. Then she remembered Mary Bea's birthday party, Dylan's practice, Roxy's movie date. Lisa was no doubt busy chauffeuring them around town. Maggie felt another surge of guilt at leaving the kids alone with a woman they barely knew. Lisa hadn't been around kids in ages. She was probably ready to tear her hair out. Maggie smiled at that thought.

As the tape beeped, she left her message. "Hi, it's Mom. I just wanted to see how you were doing. I hope you're not giving Lisa a hard time. Anyway, I'll call you later. I love you all. Bye."

As she stepped out of the phone booth, she debated whether she shouldn't just go home. The traffic along Sycamore Boulevard whizzed by, and the cars were all nice—Mercedeses, Lexuses, BMWs, even a Porsche. She looked at her serviceable Ford Taurus station wagon and sighed. You could take the woman out of the suburb, but it was tough to take the suburb out of the woman.

When she returned to her car, she checked the map on the seat beside her and realized Doran was just a few blocks away. She was so close to the spa, she might as well check it out.

A few minutes later, she saw the sparkling white nude statues that Jeremy had described, and she knew she was in the right place. She turned into the driveway and pulled her car into a vacant spot in the lot. Once again the cars spoke of wealth, as did the elegant lines of the spa, which looked more like a stately mansion than a place to get sweaty and hit tennis balls.

After fighting back another urge to flea, Maggie stepped out of the car and marched up to the front door of the spa. She still felt out of place, but she was determined not to show it. Meeting Serena Hollingsworth was worth a little discomfort. She needed answers, and there was only one woman who could provide them.

The lobby of the spa was air-conditioned to a lovely state of cool. There were impressionistic paintings on the wall, glass tables and puffy white sofas resting on thick, luxurious white carpet. At one end of the room was a large half-moon reception desk.

As Maggie approached the desk, a very muscular young man stood up. He was dressed in a short-sleeve white polo shirt and matching white pants. "May I help you?" he asked.

Hans, as indicated by his name tag, glanced quickly down Maggie's body, obviously assessing her financial status as well as her physical attributes.

"I—I—" Now that she was here, Maggie wasn't quite sure how to proceed.

"Don't be shy," he said with a knowing smile. "We all have to start somewhere."

"Excuse me?"

"You've probably gotten busy with work and social events, let a few pounds slip on during the holidays, neglected your daily facial routine and morning jog, and now you're feeling like it's time to get rid of that old, dead skin and get ready for bikini season? Am I right?"

"Exactly right," Maggie said, knowing full well she'd never put on a bikini in this lifetime.

"I'm always right," he said with a proud smile. "We have several different plans, and I'm sure we can find one that will suit you."

"Actually, I'm only in town for a few days. I'm not sure how long I'll be staying."

"No problem. We have a one-day special that lets you try out all of our facilities. In fact, we'll assign you a personal trainer to take you through our weight room and assist you with the cardiorespiratory machines."

"The what?"

"Stairmaster and Treadmill."

"Oh, of course."

"After your workout, you can take a sauna, Jacuzzi, swim in the pool, and end the day with a rubdown, massage, facial and manicure/pedicure session. In fact, I could probably get you into the salon if you'd also like a trim."

Maggie patted down her hair self-consciously. "You think I need a trim?"

"To go with the new you, absolutely."

"The new me." She liked the sound of that. "You can really make me over in one day?"

"We can get you off to a good start. I guarantee you'll feel like a new woman by the time you leave here today. In fact, you may not ever want to leave."

Maggie considered his statement. She needed to look for Serena, and she was bound to find her somewhere in the spa, according to Jeremy. Why not treat herself at the same time? "How much for the one-day makeover special?"

"Two hundred and fifty dollars."

Two hundred and fifty dollars? That was a week's groceries and a pair of tennis shoes for Dylan. How could she possibly spend so much on herself? She had three children growing out of their clothes and their shoes and their bikes. But it had been a long time since she'd spent anything on herself. And if it would make her feel like a new person, how could she say no? If it helped her retrieve her sanity, it would be money well spent.

"All right," she said impulsively. "I'll do it. I don't have any exercise clothes, though. I was just coming to look."

"We can fix you up with a leotard, T-shirt and aerobic shoes for a hundred dollars."

What the heck. She might as well go for it. After this weekend, she wouldn't spend anything on herself for the rest of the year.

"Just fill out this form, and we'll get started." Hans motioned to another man who'd just come through the pair of double doors leading into the exercise area. "Rocco, I have a customer for you."

Maggie swallowed hard as her gaze travelled up the long, stocky, powerful body of the man named Rocco. He was six foot five at least, built like a redwood tree, and rippling with muscles. Good Lord, Jeremy Hunt was right. L.A. was filled to the brim with beautiful people.

"Name?" Rocco asked.

She thought for a minute and decided to go with something new—to match the soon-to-be-new Maggie. "Crystal," she said. "My name is Crystal Scott."

"How fast can you run, Crystal?"

She could get through all twelve aisles at the supermarket in less than eight minutes. Seven if she skipped the cosmetics aisle, which she usually did. "Um, I'm not sure."

"How far do you usually run?"

She mentally estimated the distance between the couch and the refrigerator times fifty trips a day. "It depends."

"On how much time you have?"

Or how hungry, bored or depressed I am. "Exactly," she replied.

He looked her up and down. "All right. I guess we'll have to find out what you can do." Rocco snapped his fingers, and a young woman who couldn't have weighed more than eighty pounds soaking wet sprinted out of the inner office. "Lara will show you where to change. I'll meet you in ten minutes. Don't be late. We have a lot of work to do." He turned to leave, then paused. "Make sure you fill out the section on health restrictions and sign the release form."

"Release form?" she echoed faintly.

"In case you pass out or have a heart attack or something, you won't hold us responsible."

No, she wouldn't hold them responsible. They weren't crazy. She was. Out of her mind to even be considering a workout session with the Incredible Hulk.

Rocco disappeared through the double doors, but before they closed, Maggie heard him call out to someone.

"Serena, baby," he said. "Work it now. Work it hard."

Serena. Maggie stretched her neck to catch a glimpse of Serena, but the doors slid shut, and she was left with Lara, Hans and a clipboard full of release forms. But Serena Hollingsworth was inside those double doors, and Maggie couldn't give up now. She was too close to finding out exactly what she needed to know.

"Nick, I don't want to know what you've done with the house. I don't want to see it." Lisa crossed her arms in front of her as Nick pulled the car away from the baseball diamond and headed toward the beach. They'd dropped off Mary Bea at her birthday party and Roxy at the movies, and for the next two hours they would be completely on their own. Lisa wanted to return to Maggie's house, but she knew that wasn't Nick's intent. She couldn't stand the thought of seeing their house again. In fact, she felt almost panicked at the thought. Why the hell hadn't Nick moved in all these years?

"Did you see Dylan make that catch?" Nick asked as he maneuvered his way through the afternoon traffic. "The kid is incredibly athletic."

"He does seem very good at baseball. Must be the Mad dux in him. I don't remember Keith being a great athlete." Lisa paused. "I'm serious, Nick, I don't want to go to the house."

"It's not *the* house. It's *our* house."

"We're divorced. I signed the house over to you years ago."

"Semantics."

Lisa sighed. "Okay, bottom line—what's it going to take to get you to drive me back to Maggie's house?"

"A miracle." He flashed her a cocky grin. "Think you're due?"

"As a matter of fact, yes." Lisa sat stoically in her seat as the scenery grew more familiar. She remembered the Frosty Freeze where she and Nick had shared an ice cream. She remembered the library, the bookstore, the car wash, the deli, all the little stores and malls she'd frequented. She remembered the wide four-lane boulevards, the glorious palm trees, the blue-blue sky, the color of which Nick always said he saw in her eyes.

She looked at each street sign, each storefront with a bittersweet sense of longing. These streets were not the streets of just her marriage, but of her childhood as well, her youth. She remembered "cruising" the boulevard. She remembered going to the pizza parlor after the football game, eight people piled in a Volkswagen bug. She smiled at the memory, almost surprised that she still had good memories, after all the bad that had come later.

Nick turned off the main boulevard and drove through a middle-class suburban area, where the houses were older, the lawns a bit faded, a neighborhood where children's bikes and skateboards were parked precariously on the sidewalks and lawns, where people still watered their grass on a Saturday afternoon and washed their cars with good old-fashioned elbow grease.

Finally, Nick pulled into the driveway of a small frame house with a big front porch and a large oak tree that made the house seem smaller than Lisa remembered. Otherwise, it looked exactly the way she'd left it. The porch swing still hung from two rusty chains that creaked with the breeze. She couldn't count the times she'd sat in the swing, sometimes to escape the southern California heat, sometimes to listen to Nick play the Spanish guitar, sometimes to watch the birds build their nests in the sturdy branches of the trees.

They had rented the house at first. When one of the elderly

owners had died, the remaining spouse had offered it to them for a steal. They'd felt like the luckiest couple on the face of the earth. They were married. They had a home. They were expecting a baby. They thought their life together would be happily ever after.

"What do you think?" Nick asked, as he shut off the engine. The tightness in his voice told her any answer would probably be the wrong answer. He was itching for a fight. She could see it in the tension of his shoulders, hear it in the coldness of his voice.

She looked away from his penetrating eyes and focused on the house. "It could use a new coat of paint."

"The salt from the ocean tears the paint right off. I put a new coat on a few years ago, but it didn't last."

Great, they were talking about paint. They'd once made love in every room of the house, and now they were talking about chipped paint. She waited for him to say something more, but now that they had arrived, he seemed strangely reluctant to even get out of the car.

"Why are you doing this, Nick?"

For a moment she didn't think he would answer her, then his words came stiff and unyielding. "You never looked back, Lisa, not once. I watched you from the window. You just got in your car and left."

"How would you know? You were drunk the day I left."

"I was drunk, deliberately drunk, because the tequila was the only thing that took the edge off, that kept your knife from plunging all the way through to my heart." His voice faltered for a moment, then gained strength. "I'm not proud of the way I behaved, yelling at the doctors and at you. I just hurt so damn much. And you wouldn't talk to me. You wouldn't look at me."

And she couldn't look at him now. She couldn't bear to see the pain in his eyes, the accusation.

"You're doing it again." He pulled her chin around with his hand, his gaze revealing more anger than hurt. "Tuning me out. I hate when you do that. I remember that night, about a week after the funeral. You practically jumped out of your skin when I accidentally touched your breast, as if the feel of me was so repulsive you couldn't stand it.''

Lisa clapped her hands over her ears. "Stop it!"

"Why? It's the truth. I came to you naked, wanting, needing, and you walked away.''

Lisa heard the bitterness, the anguish, the accusation in his words, in his voice. She couldn't deny what he was saying, but whereas he had drunk to escape, she had closed off every emotion so she wouldn't feel anything. "I couldn't make love to you,'' she whispered. "I know you wanted a release from all the tension, but I couldn't give it to you.''

"A release?'' he asked in amazement. "That's what you thought I wanted? My God, we'd just lost our daughter. You were so distant, so cold. I didn't want a release. I wanted you. I wanted to feel your heartbeat beneath mine. I wanted to be with you, so I wouldn't feel so damn alone.''

Lisa sucked in a breath of air, suddenly feeling as if she were suffocating. Nick had always been passionate and personal, unafraid to talk about the most intimate details of their life. At one time, she'd thought it good that he was so willing to tell her how he was feeling, but after— after it happened— she had hated his desire for conversation. She hadn't wanted to talk about any of it. She had felt like a failure, and talking about it only made her feel worse. Nick had kept pushing, and she'd kept withdrawing, until they were both angry. Finally, they'd given up.

Nick threw open the door, letting a blast of fresh air into the car. "We're here. We might as well go in.''

"So you can prove to me—what?''

"I don't know. I just think you should see the house.''

"When she—when it happened,'' Lisa amended, "everyone wanted me to forget, even you. My mother told me to think only of the good times and to go on with my life. She said I'd have other babies.'' Lisa's mouth trembled, and she fought back a wave of emotion. "She said someday I would understand why it had happened.'' She shook her head in bewilderment. "I've never understood.''

"You did forget.''

"No!" she yelled. "I didn't forget. How can you forget when a part of you dies?" She stared down at her hands, subconsciously twisting the engagement ring around her finger. "But I did move on, Nick. I wish you had done the same thing."

"If you've truly put everything that happened in the past behind you, why are you afraid to go into the house?"

She couldn't answer his logic, so she gave up. "Fine. I'll go into the house. I'll look in every room. But I won't relive that night with you. I won't talk about what happened or why. Not now. Not ever."

Lisa stepped out of the car just as a bird swooped across the yard and lit on one of the lower branches of the tree. Her heart stopped. The first robin of spring.

Chapter 7

"*I*t's too early," Lisa whispered, turning to see the same stunned expression on Nick's face.

He looked into her eyes. "They haven't been back since Robin died."

"No."

"Yes. That spring they built their nest, but something happened, and they never came back. Don't you remember?"

She shook her head. "I don't remember."

"I guess you put them out of your mind like everything else, but I couldn't. It seemed so symbolic, that goddamn empty nest. I used to sit out there in the late night and the early morning, staring at that nest, wondering why they were gone—wondering why Robin was gone."

Lisa watched as the robin flew from branch to branch, as if it weren't quite sure where it wanted to be.

"Are you trying to tell me that what happened had something to do with the birds' abandoning their nest?"

"Maybe. Your mother thought it meant something."

"Well, she would. If the robins left that spring, it's because they found a better place to go. It didn't have anything to do with what happened."

"Then how come the robin has come back now—with you?" he challenged.

"It's not with me." But was it? Lisa remembered the robin in L.A., the one she'd seen outside her office building. No, it couldn't be the same bird. Los Angeles was a hundred and fifty miles away. She strode briskly toward the house. "I thought you wanted me to see the place. I'm here, so let's go."

"Fine." Nick followed her up the steps and unlocked the front door. He motioned her inside. "After you, milady."

His voice faltered.

"Oh, Nick." Her eyes filled with moisture as she remembered.

"This is our palace, milady," Nick said with a grin as he carried her up the stairs, her wedding gown trailing over his arm and down to the floor of the porch. "I'm the king and you are my very beautiful queen." He lowered his head and kissed her warmly on the mouth.

Lisa sighed with pure pleasure. She had just married an incredible man and was about to be carried over the threshold into her very own home. She didn't think she could be any happier. "If this is a dream, I don't want to wake up."

He looked into her eyes with a seriousness she hadn't expected. "It's not a dream. It's reality. It's us. I've wanted you forever, since Maggie brought you home in the seventh grade."

"You sure waited long enough to ask me out. Like six years." She punched him on the arm. "A little slow, weren't you?"

"I was afraid of you, afraid of the way you made me feel, like I was out of control, like I was starving for something I couldn't have."

"You made me feel the same way." She traced his face with her fingers, loving the feel of his strong jaw, his smoothly shaven face. It was the first time she'd felt the silkiness of his skin. Usually he wore a five o'clock shadow by three o'clock in the afternoon. "Did I tell you that I love you, Nick Maddux?"

"Yes, but keep saying it." He paused. "I love you, Lisa Maddux."

"I like the sound of that." And she did, not just because it was Nick's name, her married name, but because it wiped away the traces of her past, her mixed heritage, all the un-

certainty, the anticipation of rejection that had filled her every waking moment. She knew who she was now. And she liked who she was.

Nick struggled to open the door without dropping her. Finally, he got it open. "This is it." He carried her over the threshold and gently set her down on her feet.

She looked around and gasped in amazement. There were flowers everywhere, bouquets on every available table, filling the room with the scent of roses, gardenias and jasmine. "You did this?"

He laughed and shook his head. "Are you kidding? This has your mother written all over it."

Lisa frowned, knowing her mother was a hopeless romantic, a believer in everything magical and mystical. "Do you mind?" she asked somewhat anxiously.

Nick shook his head. "How could I mind? Don't you get it, Lisa? I love you no matter who your father is, no matter what your mother does, and no matter what you do. I'm never going to leave you. So you better get used to having me around for the next fifty years. You and I—we're bound for life."

"Lisa?" Nick's voice brought her back to painful reality.

The room was no longer filled with flowers. In fact, the sofa was new, and so was the armchair. The coffee table was covered with sports magazines. There were no rose petals. There was no love left in the room. At least she didn't think so, until she turned and stumbled into Nick's arms.

His hands clasped her shoulders to steady her. "Careful."

"I didn't realize you were standing so close to me."

"I was going to tell you to watch the edge of the carpet. It's easy to catch your foot in it. I've been meaning to do something about it."

She heard his words, but they weren't registering. She couldn't concentrate on the carpet when her face was just inches away from his, when she could feel his warm breath blow across her cheek, when she could see the old scar that ran across the edge of his chin.

"Lisa?" he asked, his eyes gazing into hers.

She didn't understand the question. "Nick?"

He touched the side of her face with the back of his hand, a tender caress that drew goose bumps along her arms. She silently willed him to move away, at the same time praying that he wouldn't. His gaze dropped to her mouth. She licked her lips in helpless anticipation.

Slowly, he lowered his head, giving her enough time to plan an escape from a high-security prison, when all she really needed to do was take one step backward. But she couldn't move.

When his mouth finally touched hers, she felt like a volcano had just erupted. The heat of his mouth set her heart on fire. His tongue slid along her lips, teasing her until she opened her mouth and he slipped inside in a kiss so deep, so personal, so intimate she forgot for a minute that they weren't married anymore, that she had no business kissing him.

By the time she remembered, Nick was already pulling away, removing her arms from his neck, and setting her aside, as if she were unwanted, as if she had instigated the kiss instead of him.

"Go ahead, look around," Nick said briskly. "I have to make a phone call." He disappeared into the kitchen, slamming the door behind him.

Lisa sat down in the armchair, stunned by Nick's actions and her own passionate response. She told herself it was the house, the memories that had made her kiss him back. She certainly didn't feel anything for him—not any more, not after everything that had happened.

A wave of painful guilt followed her rationalization. She was engaged to marry Raymond. She had no business kissing her ex-husband, no right to feel so—so completely overwhelmed by a man she didn't love anymore.

Damn Nick anyway!

When her pulse had steadied and she'd caught her breath, Lisa stood up. She knew she couldn't leave this house until she'd walked down the hall, looked in the bedrooms. Maybe it would be better to do it on her own, without Nick hovering beside her.

The first door she came to was their old bedroom. The door was ajar, and she pushed it all the way open. The room was the way she remembered—yet different. As usual, Nick hadn't made the bed, and his clothes were tossed over the exercise bicycle instead of hung neatly in the closet. The painting over the bed was new, as was the dresser and the night tables. The furniture appeared handcrafted, and she took a step closer to look at it.

Running her hand over the smooth wood of the dresser, she wondered where Nick had bought it. The detailed ornamentation on each corner of the dresser was incredible.

"Like it?" Nick asked.

She turned to see him standing in the doorway, an inscrutable expression on his face. He looked more distant than she'd ever seen him. Yet only minutes ago, they'd been in each other's arms. She looked back at the dresser, preferring the safety of a conversation about furniture than one about themselves.

"It's beautiful," she said. "Where did you get it?"

"I made it."

"You did?" she asked in surprise.

"Yeah." He smiled somewhat cynically. "Didn't think I had it in me, huh?"

"I didn't think about it." She glanced at the dresser one last time, then moved away. "You got rid of the bed, I see."

"The day you left." His eyes darkened with bitterness. "It seemed appropriate."

Discussing their bed was the last thing Lisa wanted to do, so she moved purposefully toward the door, edging past Nick, who didn't make it any easier for her to get by. Once in the hall, she squared her shoulders and headed toward the second bedroom. She didn't know what to expect—a crib, baby toys, the mural they'd painted together. She wasn't sure she could bear to see any of it.

The door was closed, but the cool knob turned easily in her hand. She felt like she was opening a door to the past, a door she should have kept closed. But now that she was here, now that she was so close, she couldn't do anything but move forward.

The door swung open, and she let it go, barely noticing when it hit the back wall.

The room was empty, absolutely and completely empty, not one piece of furniture, nothing on the walls, not even a carpet on the floor. It was stark, cold and dark. There was nothing left to remind her of their baby.

It suddenly hurt again, the pain as fresh as it was the night she'd discovered . . . Lisa couldn't finish the thought. Her stomach twisted into a knot. She felt dizzy, nauseated, and completely overwhelmed. Turning quickly, she ran out of the room and down the hall to the bathroom. She slammed the door and promptly threw up.

"Lisa?" Nick pounded on the door. "Are you all right?"

She sat back on her heels and wiped her face with a towel. No, she wasn't all right. Why had she ever come back here?

"Lisa, if you don't answer me, I'm coming in."

She couldn't let him see her like this. She couldn't let him know. "I'm fine. I'll be out in a minute." She stood up and let cool water pour over her face, then dried her skin with a rough terry-cloth towel until her cheeks stung. Finally, she opened the door.

He looked at her with worried eyes, obviously concerned but still wary. "Are you all right?"

"I'm fine."

"You're still lying to me? After all these years, you can't admit that you hurt, that you ache inside, that you miss the love we had, the child we made."

"Stop!" She put up her hand in protest. "I don't hurt anymore. I've moved on. I've put the past in the past where it belongs. I don't want to go back. I don't want to cry. I don't want to feel any of it ever again. Don't you understand?"

"I understand why you're afraid of the pain. I don't understand why you can't share it with me. I was your husband, your lover, your best friend." His voice caught and grew rough. "And you were all those things to me. I thought I could tell you anything until you shut down, until you closed me out. Why the hell do you think I started drinking? I couldn't stand how cold you were around me. You blamed me for everything. For wanting you to come to bed, for desiring you that night, for taking you away from our daughter."

"No."

"It's true!"

Lisa closed her eyes against the sudden rush of memories. *The emergency room was full that night with victims of a multiple car accident. She could still remember sitting on the hard chair, staring at a man with blood running down his face and feeling—nothing.*

"Lisa, it will be all right. She'll be okay." Nick touched her hand.

She felt as if she'd been stung by a bee, and she yanked her hand away from him. It was his fault. All his fault. "You—you did this."

Nick jerked back as if she had hit him in the face. "Lisa, please. Don't say that."

"You made me come to bed. Don't keep checking on her, you said. Let her sleep. Let her cry. She needs to learn how to go to sleep on her own," Lisa sobbed. "Well, now she knows how to go to sleep on her own. In fact, she knows how to die—"

"Don't say that. She's not dead."

"Yes, she is. While we were making love our baby was dying. Oh, God, I can't stand it." The pain ripped through her body until she felt as if she were bleeding in a thousand different places. She hugged her arms around her chest, feeling impossibly cold.

"Lisa." Nick reached for her, but she moved away.

"Don't touch me. Don't ever touch me again."

Her eyes flew open, and Lisa looked into Nick's face, suddenly aware of the truth. "You're right. I did blame you."

"I'm surprised you're willing to admit it."

She shrugged, feeling helpless to change what had gone before. "We were young, Nick, so impossibly young, so unable to handle what happened." Lisa let out a sigh. "What am I doing? I told you I wouldn't relive that night with you." She turned on her heel and walked down the hall to the living room. Nick followed her.

"Don't you think it's time we talked about what happened? We never have."

She paused, her hand on the front door knob. "We talked about it with the doctors."

"No, you talked about it with the doctors, and I talked about it with them, but we weren't together when we did it, and we never once spoke of it to each other, except to assign blame. Maybe we should talk now."

Lisa immediately shook her head. Walking down that street would be like entering an alley filled with street thugs. She'd never make it out alive. She turned her head to look at Nick. "Let it alone, please. If you want an apology, I'll give you one."

His jaw dropped open. "You will?"

"Yes, I am sorry for what I said to you that night. You couldn't have known what would happen."

"You're apologizing?"

"Don't make me say it again."

"I think I deserve to hear it again."

She gave him a reluctant smile. "Eight years has given me perspective, okay? I know now that I took everything out on you. I didn't know how to deal with my emotions, my anger. I wanted to break something, to hit someone, and you were the closest one."

"And you figured that out just now?"

"No, I figured it out about five years ago. I realized it the night Mary Bea was born, when I saw you standing in front of the nursery window. You looked at her with so much love in your eyes, and it reminded me of the way you used to look at—at our baby. You wouldn't have done anything to hurt our child." Her eyes watered, but she blinked the tears away.

"Why didn't you tell me that night?"

"You looked angry, Nick. I figured you hated me and nothing would change that, certainly not an overdue apology."

She wanted him to say that he didn't hate her, that he could never hate her, but he remained silent. She walked out to the porch. He shut the door behind them.

Lisa glanced at the oak tree, not sure she was pleased or disturbed to see that the robin had once again taken flight. "He's gone," she murmured.

"He probably realized he had the wrong house, the wrong tree, the wrong yard."

"Probably," Lisa agreed, deciding that the robins were another topic better left alone.

"So what happens now?" Nick asked.

"Now?" She thought for a moment. "Now, we pick up Maggie's kids and deal with the rest of the day and tomorrow."

"That's it?"

"That's it. I'm going back to L.A. as soon as Maggie gets home."

"To get married."

"Among other things. I have a job, an apartment, friends."

He crossed his arms as he leaned against one of the pillars of the porch. "Yeah, me too."

"That's good. Are you still doing construction?"

Nick hesitated. "Of a sort. You wouldn't be interested."

Lisa felt as if he'd shut a door between them, and it felt strange because it was the first time he'd closed the door. She'd always been the one to draw the line of privacy, of what was personal, of what could be shared. Nick had always been an open book—until now. He had changed. The thought made her feel sad.

Nick had always been an optimist, expecting the best, living his life in the clouds of idealism and hope. When the bad news had struck, she'd been prepared, because she always expected the worst. Nick had fallen much further and much harder. If she'd wanted to, she might have been able to catch him, or at least to break his fall. Instead she'd let him crash and burn, wanting company in her misery, wanting to punish him, because he was the one who'd convinced her to believe in happily ever after. As Lisa turned toward the car, she vowed she would never make that mistake again.

"Is it really possible to lose weight by hanging upside down?" Maggie asked, jogging to keep up with Rocco as he moved briskly through what he referred to as the Cardiovascular Club. Gauging the amount of sweat pouring off the bodies of the men and women using the machines, Maggie wasn't sure it was a club she wanted to join.

A stunning woman walked past her in a bright purple bra and bicycle shorts, and Maggie realized the club results were impressive. For a moment, she wondered if the woman was Serena, but a man called out "Lucy" and the woman waved. Maggie felt enormous relief that the gorgeous blond was not Serena.

"Every machine works on a specific part of your body," Rocco said. "That particular one improves circulation. We have machines to trim and tighten your calves, thighs, abs, quads, biceps, breasts. You name it, we can do it."

"How about my big toe? It sort of curves to the left. Can you do anything about that?"

Rocco didn't find her question the least bit amusing. "We're going to start you on the treadmill. Warm up with a slow walk for two minutes, a faster walk for five minutes, then jog for ten minutes and cool down for three." He checked his watch, inserted the key into the treadmill and turned it on.

Maggie looked down at the fast-moving belt and wondered what he considered a slow walk.

"Let's go," he said impatiently.

"How do I get on it?"

"You straddle the belt, like so," he demonstrated, "then hop on."

Maggie eyed him doubtfully but figured he knew what he

was talking about. She jumped on, feeling the belt take off
without her. It took her a full minute to realize she was in
fact only walking. She felt better. She could do this. Five
minutes later, she realized it would not be that easy.

Rocco kept turning up the speed until she wasn't jogging—she was running the fifty yard dash with the other
Olympic hopefuls, only the finish line kept moving farther
away. With her breath coming in deep, clutching gasps,
Rocco finally slowed down the machine until she could walk.

"Let's see," Rocco said, checking the stats on the machine. "If you'd continued at that speed, you would have
done a mile in twelve minutes. Is that your usual pace?"

Twelve minutes? Hardly world record time, she realized.
"I think I run faster outside."

Rocco sent her a skeptical look. "Now that you're warmed
up, let's try the StairMaster."

Stairmaster? She was ready for the Jacuzzi. Before Maggie
could protest, Rocco had moved over to the stepping machine.

"This is a great workout for the entire body. Hop on, I'll
show you how it works." He punched several buttons on a
computer monitor at the top of the machine. "This will mea-
sure your speed, level of stairs, your heart rate and how many
calories you're burning per hour."

"Great," Maggie said faintly, realizing he wanted her to
get on. Before she did, she had to ask one important question.
"Rocco, do you know Serena Hollingsworth?"

He smiled, a big toothy grin. "Sure, everyone knows Serena."

Lisa didn't like the sound of that.

"Is she here? I'd like to see her."

"She's around. Why? Are you a friend?" He laughed.
"Or the other woman?"

"What do you mean by that?" Maggie asked sharply.

"Nothing. Nothing. It's just that the last woman who
asked for Serena wanted to blacken both of her eyes."

"Why?"

Rocco shrugged. "Don't know. Don't care. I mind my own business. It's healthier."

"Well, I'm not interested in beating up Serena. I just want to talk to her. We have a mutual friend. If you see her, could you point her out to me?"

"Sure. Hop on."

Maggie sighed and got on the StairMaster. Within ten minutes her leg muscles were burning, but Rocco continued to check her vital signs, telling her she was okay and to "work it, baby, work it." She would have told him not to call her baby, but at the moment oxygen was too precious to waste.

Finally, Rocco signalled that she could slow down and get off. While he was making notes on his clipboard, she leaned against the StairMaster pole and prayed that she could make it through the day without having a heart attack or throwing up all over Rocco's very expensive tennis shoes.

"Crystal? Crystal?"

Maggie heard the man calling out to Crystal but didn't realize he was speaking to her until his hand came down on her shoulder.

Her head bounced up at his touch, and she was shocked to find herself looking into the amused eyes of Jeremy Hunt. "Crystal?"

"Oh, hi," she said. "I didn't hear you."

"Because that's not your name." He grinned.

She licked her lips. "Of course, it is."

"Ms. Scott, are you ready to continue?" Rocco asked. "I don't want you to cool down."

"God forbid," she replied, turning back to Jeremy. "I'm doing the one-day makeover special."

"Have you caught up with Serena?" Jeremy asked. "I just saw her in the weight room. I told her you were looking for her. She didn't seem to remember you from the description I gave her."

"It's been awhile since we've seen each other."

"Really?"

He knew she was lying; she didn't know how he'd figured

it out, except that she was a terrible liar. "I better keep moving," she said. "I don't want to cool down, right Rocky? I mean Rocco," she said as the brute next to her scowled.

"Stallone's a wimp. Don't make that mistake again."

"I won't," she hurriedly promised.

"Good. Let's move on to the weights."

Maggie saw Jeremy studying her with the same interest, the same intensity she'd noted before. A tingle ran down her spine, as his regard once again made her feel feminine. It probably had something to do with the colorful leotard she had on. She hadn't worn anything so sexy or revealing in a long time, and although she had more curves than most of the women in the spa, she didn't look as bad as she'd expected to look. All the anxiety and stress of the past few weeks had actually helped her take off a few pounds.

Maggie cleared her throat, realizing she and Jeremy were still staring at each other. "Well, good-bye."

"I have a feeling we'll see each other again."

"You do?" she asked, feeling flattered and nervous. She could handle a few one-liners of flirtatious chitchat, but anything more and she'd be way out of her depth.

"I do." He grabbed her hand as she turned to follow Rocco into the next room. His fingers twisted around her small half-carat diamond ring, the one Keith had bought for her when they were young and poor and madly in love. "Is this still good?"

"You mean is it past its expiration date?" Maggie quipped, trying not to take his question too seriously.

"In a manner of speaking."

"Why do you want to know?"

"I don't ask married women to have coffee with me after their workout."

"Are you going to ask me?"

"That depends? Does the ring still fit?"

Maggie hesitated. She had a feeling she would regret her answer.

~~ *Chapter 8*

Raymond knew he would regret bringing Beverly to the party. He just hadn't expected to feel so stupid quite so soon. Since walking through the front doors of the large, elegant mansion in Beverly Hills, Raymond had felt like he was following Beverly's bread crumbs. In every room he encountered people who had just been charmed by Beverly. He couldn't believe he'd been stupid enough to let her walk into the party first. What had he been thinking?

Shaking his head in disgust, Raymond grabbed a glass of champagne from a passing waiter in the sunroom and walked out onto the redwood deck, where he found the main thrust of the party in the gardens and pool area. A live band played mariachi music, Monty's favorite. Raymond made a mental note to ask Elisabeth how they could tie Monty's love of mariachi music into the campaign.

Funny, he rarely thought of Elisabeth's Mexican heritage. She never mentioned it. In fact, she often seemed uncomfortable with the whole thing. He didn't know why. He supposed he could ask.

His thoughts changed direction as he paused by the fountain to watch the interplay between Beverly and Monty Friedman. Monty was a short, somewhat balding man in his midfifties. He had risen from nothing to run a very big company, but despite his obvious trappings of success there was still a bit of street toughness about Monty. At the moment, though, he was smiling broadly, charmed or at least intrigued by Beverly's conversation.

Raymond frowned. If only he'd brought Elisabeth. She would have stolen Monty right out from under Beverly. Youth and looks always beat out age and experience. He'd learned that lesson years ago when he'd managed to snatch the vice presidency from the hands of a man thirty years his senior.

The president of his company had told him that fresh blood and burning ambition had gotten Raymond the job. At the time, Raymond had felt nothing for the man he'd beaten, the one who'd spent twenty years of his life plodding his way slowly up the ladder only to have it snatched out from under him by a young hotshot.

Raymond wouldn't let some kid take anything from him, now that the positions were reversed. No, he could still compete with the best of them. He had the same drive, the same hunger, the same thirst as any young stud. In fact, he was damn thirsty. Raymond moved over to the bar and ordered a gin and tonic.

As he reached into his pocket for his wallet and pulled out a ten dollar bill, Raymond suddenly realized his hands looked old, weathered, wrinkled. There were even a few sun spots. The thought, the fear that he was getting old made his hand tremble, and the bill dropped to the ground.

"I'll get that for you, sir," the waiter said with impressive eagerness, hustling out from behind the bar before Raymond could bend over. "There you go, sir," he said, obviously hoping for a big tip.

Raymond scowled at the man's young face, his flat stomach, his long, gangly limbs, the compassion in his eyes. Damn that kid for treating him like a sick old man who couldn't even bend over. He was in peak condition, and if Elisabeth had been on his arm, the kid would have been looking at him with admiration, not treating him like someone's father.

The waiter handed Raymond his drink. Raymond took his change, then dropped two quarters into the glass on the counter and wandered back to the edge of the terrace. He paused by one of the many buffet tables that were being set up and helped himself to fresh shrimp and cocktail sauce. Then he headed for Monty. Beverly had had him on her own long enough.

"Raymond, hello. I was wondering where you were," Monty said.

"I'd shake your hand, but . . ."

"No, no. Enjoy yourself. By the way, Beverly tells me you're getting married in a few weeks," Monty said. "Congratulations."

Raymond smiled, feeling as if he'd been sucker-punched. Not that his wedding was a secret. In fact, he'd planned on inviting Monty, but he had a feeling Beverly had presented the upcoming nuptials in a light that wouldn't be advantageous to him. In fact, a quick glance in her direction revealed a pair of sparkling eyes. Beverly looked quite pleased with herself.

"I hope you won't be too busy to put together your proposal. I know how weddings are," Monty said.

"It's all taken care of," Raymond explained. "We have a wonderful consultant who is handling all of the details. Elisabeth and I just have to show up."

"Where is Elisabeth? I thought you were bringing her with you today. She is your top copywriter, isn't she?"

"Yes, Elisabeth is a senior account executive and my best copywriter. Fresh, original, unique—"

"Young," Beverly interjected with a pleasant smile.

"Which is an advantage," Raymond continued. "She's much closer to the age of our target audience than Beverly or myself." He turned to Monty. "That's one of the benefits of my firm, Monty. We have depth and breadth of experience, the right person for every job."

"It's too bad Elisabeth couldn't come today," Beverly said. "She's visiting a friend, right?"

"A sick friend," Raymond said, noting the speculative look in Monty's eyes. He knew Monty considered his business to be valuable enough to put all other committments aside. "It was an emergency."

"It's nice of Elisabeth to be so caring to a sick friend," Beverly said. "I've probably lost a lot of my friends because I always put business first." She took a sip of her champagne and offered Raymond a triumphant smile.

Damn, she was good, turning every positive into a negative. Maybe he should have promoted her all those years ago, then she wouldn't be here today stabbing him in the back.

"I'm sure Monty appreciates loyalty," Raymond said.

The other man nodded. "Of course." He smiled broadly. "As long as it's loyalty to me. Now, if you'll excuse me, I think I'll get some food. By the way, we're serving prime rib, and while the meat is exceptionally tender, the knives are especially sharp." His eyes twinkled. "Fair warning to both of you."

"You're making a fool of yourself," Raymond said as Monty left him alone with Beverly.

"I don't think so," Beverly said. "By the way, I won't need a ride home after all. Monty and I are going to have a quiet drink after the party is over."

"The hell you are. I brought you to this party, and I'll take you home."

"You're not invited, Raymond."

"And you are? I don't think so. What are you planning to do, hang out until everyone leaves, then tell Monty your ride left without you?"

Beverly smiled and put a hand through his arm. "Not a bad plan, is it?"

"I've got a better one." He tipped his plate so that his shrimp cocktail sauce dripped down the front of her cream-colored linen suit.

Beverly gasped in horror. "Raymond, how could you?"

He stared at the stain in bemusement, not quite certain what had possessed him to act in such a desperate manner. But now that he'd done it, he might as well use it to his advantage. "Damn, I'm sorry. Listen, I'll take you home right now so you can change. We can slip out the back. No one will have to see you.''

She frowned at him. ''That was a dirty trick.''

''You're the one who said no ground rules.''

''I thought you'd learned some finesse in your old age,'' she said, dabbing at the sauce with her napkin, which only made her look like she was bleeding all over her suit. ''This is awful.''

Raymond smiled, realizing he felt younger at this very moment than he had in a long time. ''It looks pretty bad all right. I'll buy you a new dress.''

''You're damn right you will, and it will cost you a pretty penny. Count on it.''

''Come on, let's go.'' Raymond took her hand, but she shook it free, so she could wave her finger in his face.

''I'll tell you one thing, Raymond, darling, you may have won this battle, but the war is not over yet. Not by a long shot.''

Raymond felt a rush of excitement at her words. He hadn't felt so energized in a long time. ''I like a good fight. Just don't expect to end up on top.''

She smiled at his choice of words, and her finger suddenly drifted down the side of his face in a caress. ''I always end up on top, Raymond. And trust me, when it happens to you, you'll love every second of it.''

''Don't you love that burn? Is it the most incredible feeling you've ever had in your life?'' Rocco asked Maggie, his square face glowing with almost orgasmic pleasure, as he pushed the pin into the next weight level and ordered her to do ten more repetitions.

''I'm not sure I can stand this much pleasure,'' Maggie said, feeling her calf muscles catch fire. ''If I get any hotter, you may have to call the fire department.''

''You can do it. Focus. Concentrate. Mind over body. You have to want it. Want it. Want it,'' he chanted.

Maggie finished the last repetition and laid back on the bench. ''I'm done.''

"Hardly. We haven't even begun to do your arms yet," Rocco said, extending her a hand.

Reluctantly, she took it and sat up, gazing around the weight room as she did so. There were four men and three other women working out. "Is one of those women Serena, by any chance?"

Rocco glanced around the room, then shook his head. "Nope. She's probably in the mud room or the sauna."

"Why don't I do the mud now and skip the arms?" Maggie suggested. "I really want to catch Serena before she leaves."

"We've got to do the machines in order, Ms. Scott, otherwise you'll be lopsided."

Maggie had news for him. She was already lopsided. She'd had three children, for God's sake.

Rocco didn't wait for an argument. He simply led her over to the next set of machines and prepared to torture her for another hour.

Maggie occasionally caught glimpses of Jeremy Hunt as he went through his own workout. She had to admit the man had an incredible body. Long, muscular legs, a flat stomach, a broad chest and a nice tan. Besides his great physique, his hair was incredibly thick and wavy, his eyes a nice, nice shade of brown. And he had a sexy smile, the kind of smile she'd often longed to see on her husband's face. But then Keith had not been the stuff of which romantic heroes are made.

Keith hadn't been fat, but he hadn't put much store by exercise unless it involved throwing a ball of some sort. He usually burned instead of tanned, and his hair had thinned considerably the last few years, leaving a rather large bald spot on the back of his head.

She smiled fondly at the memory. Keith hadn't been a Greek god, but he hadn't been ugly either. And she'd loved him for far more than his physical appearance. He had been a good, honest and kind man, and she'd always admired his superb intelligence. Plus, he had a bit of an adventurous streak. He'd always loved reading mystery novels and solving puzzles. He'd even taken her to one of those "murder" dinners where the guests had to solve the mystery of who was the killer among them. She remembered his zeal in tracking down clues, his imagination that led them down a hallway no one else had suspected was there.

Of course, she'd matched him in the imagination part. It was the logical reasoning where he had shined. He didn't just imagine things, he planned them out with the precision of an algebraic equation.

Maggie wished he was here now so he could solve this puzzle. Only there wouldn't be a puzzle if he was still here. With a sigh, she turned her attention to Rocco.

"Looks like we're done here, Ms. Scott," he said. "It's time for your sauna."

"You mean I get to sit in a hot room and sweat." She laughed. "I never thought the day would come when that would sound appealing."

"Lara will take over from here." Rocco motioned to the young woman Maggie had met in the reception area. "She'll show you the rest of our facilities and lead you on to the Jacuzzi and mud room, and whatever else you'd like to experience."

"Thanks. I appreciate it."

His head swung around. "Oh, there goes Serena now."

Maggie tried to see where he was pointing, but Lara stepped in front of her and all she caught was a glimpse of a hot pink T-shirt.

"Are you ready to try the sauna, Ms. Scott?" Lara asked.

"No, I want to find Serena."

"Serena Hollingsworth?" Lara checked her watch. "Serena is on her way to start a tennis match. I doubt she'll have time to talk right now. It's a club tournament, and she's serious about her tennis."

Maggie sighed. "Okay, I'll take the sauna and get dressed. Maybe Serena will be done by then."

"They usually play for about an hour and a half, then they have drinks." Lara led her into the women's locker room. "I didn't realize you were a friend of Serena's," she said as she opened the door. "Although Serena sends us lots of her friends. Of course, they're usually male," she said with a small laugh.

Maggie's suspicious antenna immediately went up. "Male?"

"That's right. Serena says she meets a lot of men in her business."

"What business would that be?"

Lara shrugged. "I'm not sure. It's not a good idea to ask questions of people who have a lot of money—especially gorgeous single women, if you know what I mean. Judging by her jewelry, I'd say whatever Serena does is very lucrative."

Maggie's imagination took those few words and shot ahead. Good heavens! Was Lara implying that Serena was a hooker, a call girl, a professional? No. There were dozens of other ways gorgeous young women could make money in L.A. She was reading into an innocent comment. At least she hoped she was.

An hour and a half later, Maggie ran out of the locker room and straight into the arms of Jeremy Hunt. Her stomach clenched, a shiver ran down her spine, and all the man had done was stop her from falling. Lord, she was pathetic.

"Steady," he said, releasing her.

Maggie felt ridiculously disappointed when he let her go, but she tried not to show it. "Sorry, I didn't see you. I guess I should look where I'm going."

"You *look* great," he said, studying her freshly scrubbed face, her shampooed hair, the slight blush she'd applied to her cheekbones.

"Really?" She self-consciously patted down her hair. She hadn't gotten it cut, but Lara had styled it away from her face in soft curls, and after being worked out, sweated, pummelled, soaked, dried, and finally made up, she felt like a new person.

"How about that coffee?" Jeremy asked.

Maggie hesitated, torn by the look of male admiration in

his eyes and the desire to catch up with Serena. "Actually, I was hoping to find Serena. I think she's playing a tennis match."

"Right. I saw her a few minutes ago. She won easily, so she was pretty happy. She goes on to play a celebrity tournament in Santa Barbara next weekend. Come on, I'll take you out to the courts."

"Thanks."

"So, what did you think of the club special?" Jeremy asked as they walked through the exercise rooms and into the hallway.

"I feel pretty good right now. Tomorrow morning may be a different story. I'm not exactly in shape for the kind of workout Rocco put me through."

"A few more like it, and you would be."

"I'm not staying that long."

"Where will you be going back to?" Jeremy asked as he opened the door and headed toward the pool area.

Maggie blinked at the sudden blast of sunlight. She pulled out her sunglasses and put them on, pleased not just because they darkened the glare of the sun, but also because they protected her eyes from Jeremy's careful scrutiny.

"I live in San Diego," she said lightly, preferring to name the larger city rather than the smaller suburb of Solana Beach.

"I've never been there."

"You should go. It's beautiful. We don't have nearly as much smog as L.A. and not half as many earthquakes."

He grinned. "Is that the city slogan?"

"No, but it's true."

"Is someone waiting for you in San Diego?"

"I have lots of friends there."

"Then why are you here?"

"I told you—Serena."

He eyed her speculatively. "Yes, the lovely Serena. I still don't see you two as friends."

Maggie paused as they neared the tennis courts. She suddenly realized that having professed to be Serena's friend, she could hardly ask Jeremy to point her out.

"Well, what now?" he drawled as they both looked at the group of people in trendy tennis clothes sipping mineral water and chatting about the matches.

Maggie didn't know how to answer him. Was Serena here or not? She bit down on her lip as she studied each woman. Serena had been wearing hot pink as she recalled, and none of these women were wearing anything remotely pink.

"You don't really know Serena, do you?" Jeremy asked, turning her around so she had to look into his inquisitive eyes. "You're not her friend at all. Who are you? And what are you doing here?"

"Mother, what on earth are you doing here?" Lisa demanded as Silvia Alvarez walked through the front door of Maggie's house. Silvia wore a colorful peasant blouse tucked into an even more colorful skirt, adorned with a shiny gold belt. Long gold earrings dangled from her ears, sparkling against jet black hair that was pulled back in a bun, but which Lisa knew would drift down to her hips when released.

"I came to help you," Silvia proclaimed, kissing Lisa on the cheek and gathering her into a warm hug.

Lisa felt some of the coldness seep out of her body, as if Silvia's body heat were enough to warm them both. Silvia had always been fire and sunshine, colors and craziness. Lisa loved her mother very much, but often with a sense of bemusement that they could actually be mother and daughter. They were different in so many ways. And while Lisa appreciated her mother's sincere interest in her life, she was wary of exactly what course that interest would take.

"You're too thin," Silvia declared, taking a step back so she could scrutinize her daughter. "And pale, too. Don't you ever let the sunshine kiss these cheeks?"

Lisa stepped back before her mother could pinch some color into her face. "I'm too busy working to lay in the sun."

"Grandma Silvia," Mary Bea shouted from halfway down the stairs.

Lisa turned, shocked to see Mary Bea, who had barely given her a smile, run into her mother's arms—as if they knew each other, as if they were family. But Silvia wasn't related to Maggie in any way. Silvia was Lisa's mother, and Lisa had cut her ties to the Maddux family eight years ago, long before Mary Bea had come along.

"Did you bring me something?" Mary Bea asked.

"Of course." Silvia opened her large canvas bag and pulled out a small package. "This is for you."

Mary Bea knelt on the floor and opened the wrapping paper. She squealed with delight at the sight of a colorful beaded necklace. "It's beautiful. *Gracias.*"

"De nada," Silvia replied. "Your Spanish is getting better."

"Can I show this to Roxy?"

"Yes, and tell her I have something for her and Dylan, too." Silvia straightened and smiled at Lisa. "She grows like a weed."

"You've seen her?"

"Of course. I only live fifteen minutes from here."

"But why?" Lisa suddenly felt left out. "She's not related to you."

"Maggie was your best friend, your sister-in-law, and one of my favorite girls. I watched you grow up together. I couldn't divorce her simply because you did."

Lisa flinched at the criticism. "I didn't divorce her. I divorced Nick."

"And that's why you've seen Maggie only a handful of times in the past few years. When her husband died, you snuck in and out like a thief in the night."

"I was busy."

"That's right. You have a place to live, a great job, a new man, new friends. I'm surprised you haven't found a new mother yet."

"Sometimes, I'm tempted." Lisa knew it wasn't rational to feel bothered by her mother's continued friendship with Maggie, but somehow she felt betrayed that her mother had chosen Maggie and even Nick over her.

"Did you get the bracelet?" Silvia asked.

"Yes, and that's another thing," Lisa said, feeling once again righteously indignant. "Where did you get it?"

"From Nick, of course."

"He said he hadn't seen it in years."

"But he kept it." Silvia's dark eyes gentled. "For you. He kept everything for you."

Lisa shook her head. "That's not true. I was at the house, and my room is changed and her—her room is empty. My things are gone."

Silvia didn't say anything for a long moment. Then she reached into her bag and pulled out her key ring. She worked the metal ring in her fingers until a single key slid off. She handed it to Lisa.

"What's this?"

"The answer to your question."

"I didn't ask one."

"1427 San Vicente Boulevard, Number 134."

Lisa stared at her mother, not sure if the address was supposed to make sense. It wasn't her mother's address. It wasn't Nick's.

Silvia walked over to the side table and jotted the numbers down on a piece of paper. "In case you forget," she said, covering the key in Lisa's palm with the piece of paper.

Before Lisa could reply, Roxy, Dylan and Mary Bea descended the stairs like a herd of cattle, each begging for their present.

Silvia laughingly complied, pulling out a wooden marionette for Dylan and a pair of hand-painted earrings for Roxy. The children were delighted with their gifts. Their exuberance, their loving hugs with Grandma Silvia, both touched and troubled Lisa. She supposed it was only natural that Silvia would visit with the children. She'd always loved kids. And she didn't have any grandchildren of her own.

Lisa swallowed back that memory and tried to smile as Dylan showed her his puppet.

"Maybe you could put on a show," Lisa suggested.

"Cool." Dylan and Mary Bea ran off to the family room

to plan their show, and Roxy headed for the phone to call her best friend.

"Now that they're settled, I'll get started on dinner," Silvia said as she turned toward the kitchen.

Lisa followed her mother down the hall, knowing it was pointless to argue. When her mother was on a roll, it was impossible to stop her. Lisa watched as Silvia pulled out various food items from her never-ending canvas bag.

"You look like Mary Poppins," Lisa said grumpily. "I'm expecting you to start singing about a spoonful of sugar any minute now."

"Maybe I will. If it would put a smile on your face."

Lisa leaned against the counter. "Did Nick call you?"

"No. Why would he?"

"He doesn't think I can handle taking care of the kids for the weekend."

Silvia sent her a steady look. "Is that what he said?"

"It's what he thought. He spent the night here on the couch."

"I'm not sure you have any idea what's going on in Nick's head."

"That might be true," Lisa agreed. "So, how did you know I was here? Maggie?"

"I just knew, Lisa. I woke up this morning and I opened the curtains to let in the sunlight. Then I made myself a cup of coffee and took it into the garden; it was such a beautiful morning. That's when I saw it."

"Saw what?" Lisa asked as a wave of uneasiness swept through her body.

"The robin," Silvia replied, meeting her eye. "It came back, and so did you."

Lisa stared at her mother for a long moment as a tiny seed of wonder began to grow in her heart. The robin. Could it have special meaning? No. No. It was just a bird, and her mother was once again trying to make her believe in magic.

Lisa finally looked away. "I'm only spending the weekend. Tomorrow I go back to L.A." She walked over to the cupboard and pulled out a glass, then took some ice tea out of the refrigerator. "Would you like some tea, Mother?"

Silvia simply stared at her reprovingly.

"I'll take that as a no." Lisa poured herself some tea, then put the pitcher back in the refrigerator. When she turned around, Silvia hadn't moved.

"I suppose you want to tell me about the robin." Lisa took a sip of tea. "How it's some sign of something magical, mystical. Well, go ahead."

Silvia looked saddened by her sarcasm, and for a moment, Lisa felt guilty. Her mother didn't deserve to be attacked. Lisa didn't understand how she could deal with irate clients with complete calm, but become a sulky, annoyed child when she was with her mother.

"I'm sorry," Lisa said. "It's been a long day."

"I can see that."

Lisa pushed her hair off her face in a gesture of weariness. "I don't know what you want from me. I don't know what Nick wants from me. You both seem to expect me to do something, but I don't know what it is. I can't come back here. I can't make things the way they were."

"All I want is for you to stop running away from everyone who loves you."

"I'm not running, Mom. I've been in L.A. for a long time. And I'm planning to be with the man who loves me on a daily basis in the very near future."

Silvia shook her head. "He's not for you. He's too old. He's too safe. I don't see love in your eyes. I don't hear it in your voice."

"Because you don't want to hear it. You can't accept the fact that I'm getting married again and that that man is not Nick," Lisa retorted. "You adored him. He could do no wrong—even when he was doing plenty wrong." She took a deep breath, trying to calm down. "How can you say Raymond isn't for me? You don't even know him."

"No, I don't, do I?"

Lisa knew she couldn't defend against that accusation. She had deliberately kept Raymond and her mother apart, just as she had kept her past away from her present. Now they were blurring together, and she was losing control just as she had known she would.

She forced a smile to her face. "If you want to come up one day next week, we can go out to lunch or dinner, whatever you like."

"Why can't he come here?"

"Because he's busy."

"And I'm not?"

Lisa sighed. "I know you think I'm looking for a father figure, but you're wrong. Raymond and I have a great deal in common. We talk business. We know the same people. We have a good time together, and, most importantly, Raymond will never hurt me."

"Love is the most important thing."

Lisa instinctively wrapped her arms around her waist. "Love hurts."

"So you don't love this man?"

"I care for him deeply. Yes, I love him," Lisa added, realizing she didn't sound all that confident.

"The way you loved Nick?" Silvia's eyes softened as she looked at Lisa. "The way you couldn't keep your hands off each other, the way you finished each other's sentences, the way you laughed at the same jokes?"

"I'm older now. I'm different. He's different. Our love was a lifetime ago."

"Are you going to have children with this older man?"

"No!" The word rang through the kitchen like a shotgun blast.

"No," Silvia agreed, surprising her. "I don't see a child with you and this man. Only with you and Nick."

"That child is—gone." As Lisa said the words, a lump grew in her throat, and a wave of self-pity filled her heart. She had lost so much. Her life hadn't just swerved in a new direction, it had been shattered into a zillion irretrievable pieces. "I need some air," she muttered.

Lisa opened the back door and stepped out on to the deck that overlooked the backyard. She stared up at the darkening twilight sky, letting the beauty of the night ease her tension.

After a moment, she sat down in one of the deck chairs and took several deep, cleansing breaths of fresh air.

There was a slight evening breeze, which carried with it the scent of the sea and memories of long summer days, warm evenings, love and laughter and dreaming.

Lisa remembered sitting out on the front porch of her house with Nick the night they'd brought Robin home from the hospital. Robin, who had been blessedly quiet when they were surrounded by doctors and nurses, had become a red, squealing tyrant the minute they'd stepped foot in the house. She could still see Robin's tightly scrunched eyes, and feel Robin's ridiculously long fingernails clawing into her arm.

Lisa and Nick had spent most of the afternoon caught between tender love and utter bewilderment over how they could possibly take care of Robin. It wasn't until dusk had fallen, until Nick had brought out his guitar and they'd sat in the swing on the porch that the baby had finally quieted down, lulled to sleep by the music, surrounded by two people who loved her more than anything.

Lisa put a hand over her heart, swept back into the past, into a place where she could almost feel Robin's little head snuggled against her breast, her tiny curls tickling Lisa's chin. She could hear her quiet breathing, smell the baby powder. Lisa remembered the way she'd held her baby, one hand protectively cradling the back of her neck, the other against her tiny bottom.

Oh, God!

It hurt so damn much. There was a hungry ache in her soul that wouldn't go away, that could never be filled. Over the years, she had forced herself to overlook it, but it had never gone away, and tonight it felt as bad as it had felt all those years ago.

A tear crept out of the corner of her eye. Lisa wiped it away, terrified of the pressure that was building behind her eyes, the emotion that threatened to spill out. She would not cry. She couldn't. If she let the tears come, she would simply drown in a sea of emotion.

Nick stood in the doorway for a long moment, watching

Lisa's face. She was fighting something, breathing as hard as if she'd just finished running a marathon. He wanted to yell at her to let it out. He wanted to shake her until her perfect hair fell down around her shoulders the way he remembered, until the hardness left her eyes, the coldness vanished from her voice. He wanted her soft and trembling, the woman he'd fallen in love with, not the hard-hearted warrior she'd become.

"Lisa? Are you all right?" He knew she would say she was fine. There had been a time when she'd told him everything, all of her deepest and darkest fears, and he had told her his. That time was past.

Lisa put a hand over her mouth to stop any words from erupting between her lips. The shakiness of her hand told him how hard she was fighting to stay in control.

Nick walked around her chair and knelt in front of her. He looked into her beautiful blue eyes and saw a wash of unshed tears. "Cry, dammit. You know you want to."

"I won't," she said defiantly.

"Why? Are you afraid you won't be able to stop?" He read the answer in her eyes. "I couldn't cry for a long time either. The only time I could let go was when I was drunk out of my mind. I could pretend it was the booze that was crying, not me."

"Are you suggesting I get drunk?"

"God, no. I'd be the last one to suggest that."

She breathed in and out for several seconds as silence settled between them. He realized how much he'd missed her face, her mannerisms, the tiny freckle at the corner of her eyebrow, all the little things that were her and some that were Robin's as well. Robin had looked like Lisa, with her dark hair and her blue eyes.

"Stop staring at me," Lisa said.

"Do I make you nervous?"

"You know you do."

He smiled as he touched the side of her face, enjoying the feel of her silky skin beneath his roughened fingertips. "What's this? Truth?"

"Maybe." She paused. "It would probably be better if you didn't touch me."

"Better for who?"

"For both of us."

He dropped his hand away from her face and stood up. He walked to the edge of the deck and looked out at the yard. "You're right. It would be better if I didn't touch you, because it only makes me want you again. We both know that can't happen."

"No, it can't. Our life together was a foolish fantasy, Nick. I don't know what we were thinking, getting married when we did. You didn't have a job. I hadn't finished college. And we made love without any protection, never thinking about the future. We didn't make plans. We didn't act responsibly. We let our hormones run wild. Everything we did was stupid, and we paid for it."

His lips twisted in disbelief as he turned to look at her. "It's amazing how you can turn the love affair of the century into a series of reckless sexual encounters. I was in love with you, Lisa, and you were in love with me."

"I was in love with love," she cried as she stood up. "I adored you and Maggie and your American white-bread family. Your mother was June Cleaver, and you and your brother were Wally and the Beaver. I wanted what you had. A mother who stayed home, who didn't work all the time, who wasn't a single parent, who didn't believe in crystal balls and magic. I wanted the house with the white picket fence and the baby carriage on the porch. I wanted a man in my life, one who would stand by me through thick and thin till death do we part."

"And we had that."

"Yeah, until God decided his little practical joke had gone far enough."

"We could have had it again if you hadn't walked out. I was willing to stand by you, Lisa."

"No, you weren't. You'd like to remember it that way, but that's not the way it was."

Nick turned away from her and took a deep breath. He

wanted to argue but couldn't. There was a memory at the back of his mind, one that ran consistently through his nightmares. And it was starting again. He could see the morning fog, the grass, the tiny white casket, the flowers, the people—and Lisa.

"Hey, Lisa. Babe." Nick waved as he stumbled out of his brother's car. He knew he was in trouble when he saw her face, so cold, so unforgiving, and her skin was so pale against the heavy, depressing black of her suit. A sudden burst of shame ran through him, but he quickly shoved it away. So what if she was angry because he was late. She'd blamed him for everything else. She'd even kicked him out of their bedroom the night before. What was the difference?

"Where have you been?" she asked, storming over to him. She grabbed him by the arm, her grip as tight as a vise.

"I've been getting some breakfast."

"My God. You're drunk. It's eleven o'clock in the morning, Nick."

"No kidding. Gee, thanks for pointing that out."

"I don't know you anymore," she said with a shake of her head.

Nick looked into her eyes and saw nothing familiar. *"I don't know you either."*

She stiffened. *"How could you do this today—of all days?"*

"Do what?" He burped, tasting the beer on his lips.

"Don't you have any respect for Robin's memory?"

His stomach turned over at her words, and he felt like throwing up. His beautiful baby was dead, and his wife—his wife hated his guts.

Lisa turned her back on him and started to walk away.

"Where are you going?" he asked.

"I'm going to say good-bye to my daughter."

"Without me?"

"You do what you want. That's your specialty."

"And turning your back on me is your specialty."

She sent him a ferocious look. *"Goddamn you, Nick."*

"He already has, Lisa. He already has."

Nick let out a breath as the memory finally receded. He still felt guilty about his behavior at the funeral. And even though he'd tried to apologize to Lisa the next day, she'd obviously never forgiven him.

"I'm going inside," Lisa said from behind him.

Nick turned around. "I'm sorry."

"What?" She looked taken aback, wary.

"I'm sorry for the way I acted at the funeral. I'm sorry that I got drunk, that I let you down."

"Okay. Thank you."

"That's it?"

"What do you want me to say?"

He ran his fingers through his hair in frustration. "Oh, hell, I don't know. Maybe I'd like to hear some honest emotion in your voice. You know, maybe I didn't stand by you, Lisa, but did it ever occur to you that maybe you could have been the one to stand by me?"

"How could I, Nick? It was a dream to start with—a fantasy. It wasn't real." She turned toward the house, but he moved across the deck and grabbed her arm.

"How dare you pretend what we had wasn't real."

"It wasn't," she insisted.

"You're a liar and a coward."

"And you're a drunk!"

"Used to be," he corrected. "I admit I had a problem, but I didn't turn to booze until you turned away from me."

"So, it was my fault."

"Oh, dammit. Do we always have to assign blame?"

"You just blamed me."

"Okay, I apologize again. Why can't you forgive me, Lisa? Everyone else has."

"I forgive you for being drunk at the funeral."

Nick's eyes narrowed as he saw the mix of emotions run through her eyes. "Then what can't you forgive me for? Robin's death?"

"No." She shook her head.

"Then what?"

The back door flew open, and the flash of light from the

kitchen took them both by surprise. Nick dropped his hand from her arm.

Silvia sent them an inquiring look, her smile fading at the stress on Lisa's face. "You have a phone call, dear. Your fiancé. He said it was important."

"I'll be right there."

"Very well." Silvia returned to the house.

"I have to take that," Lisa said as she walked toward the door.

"Lisa?" Nick asked.

She paused before entering the house. "What?"

"One of these days I'm going to walk out on you, and you're going to know what it feels like to be left behind."

She already knew what it felt like, Lisa thought as she entered the house. She'd been left by two very important people—her father and her daughter.

Chapter 9

*L*isa took a deep breath and picked up the telephone receiver, trying hard to change gears from her past love to her present love. "Raymond?"

"Elisabeth, how are you?"

His sharp, clear voice gave her an anchor to hold on to, and she grabbed it. "I'm fine. How are you?"

"Missing you."

His words took the rest of the tension from her body, reminding her that she had another life now, one that didn't include Nick, one that didn't include reckless, passionate emotions spilling out every other second.

"When are you coming home?" Raymond asked. "We have a million things to do in the next month. By the way, I went to Monty's party today," he continued without waiting for her to comment. "He really wanted to meet you. I had to do some fancy talking to convince him you wouldn't have missed that party if your friend wasn't terribly sick."

"She's not sick, Raymond."

"For Monty, she's on her deathbed. Look, Beverly Wickham is gunning for this account. She was a woman possessed today. Determined, ambitious, ruthless. We'll have to pull out all the stops for this one. We'll have to fight down and dirty, whatever it takes."

Lisa looked up as Nick walked into the kitchen. She barely registered the rest of Raymond's comments. Something about Beverly trying to charm Monty out of a million dollars.

115

Instead she watched Nick kiss her mother on the cheek. Nick muttered something that put a smile on Silvia's face. Then he swiped a carrot off the vegetable tray she was preparing and settled back to listen to Lisa's telephone conversation. In fact, his cocky smile told her that he knew she wanted him to leave and he had no intention of doing so.

"Elisabeth?"

She started at the sound of Raymond's voice. "I'm sorry. What did you say?"

Nick smiled at her obvious lack of attention. She turned her back on him.

"Weren't you listening?" Raymond demanded. "I was telling you about my ideas for the campaign."

"It's so chaotic around here," Lisa said defensively. "Can I call you back later?"

"Why don't you just come home?"

"I—I can't. My friend went away for the weekend. She needed some time to herself, so I'm baby-sitting."

"You're baby-sitting? For that you rushed down to San Diego when we're in the middle of a huge campaign and our wedding?"

Lisa wondered why he never put their wedding first. But she wasn't about to say anything that damning in front of Nick and her mother. "Maggie needed me."

"Loyalty is an admirable quality. I respect that. I just wish your loyalty was to me."

"It is—of course it is."

Silence fell between them, and Lisa realized it was the first time they'd clashed on a personal matter. Their arguments were usually about which font size to use in an advertisement. They rarely disagreed about anything personal—probably because she'd never done anything that wasn't Raymond's idea—until now.

She'd been happy to let him organize their life. He did it so well and so thoroughly, making her feel she was as well put together as he was. If he only knew. She'd have to tell him, at least some of it. She'd known that for awhile, she'd just never been able to find the words.

Lisa turned her head as Nick burst into raucous laughter, accompanied by her mother's guilty giggle. The two of them looked perfectly delighted with each other.

"Sorry," Silvia said, waving her hand in the air in an apologetic gesture. "Nick just told me a funny story."

"Elisabeth. Who else is with you?" Raymond asked. "It sounds like you're in the middle of a party."

"My mother's here with a friend of hers." Lisa frowned at Nick. "She's helping me with dinner."

"I'll let you go then. Elisabeth . . ."

"Yes?"

"Hurry back."

"I will." She hung up the phone, annoyed with both Raymond and Nick, not to mention her mother.

"No love and kisses?" Nick asked. "And you're planning to marry the man in what—three weeks?"

"Four." Lisa faced her mother. "I'm going to check on the children, Mom."

"There you go again, running off just when things get interesting. Does Roland know that about you?" Nick asked.

"His name is Raymond, and he knows all the important things." Lisa paused at the door. "I wouldn't have to run off, if you'd leave. Don't you have something else to do? Some other woman to harass?" As she said the words, it occurred to her that she knew nothing about Nick's personal life. Now she couldn't help but wonder. Surely there had been a woman or two in all the time they'd been apart. "Well?" she demanded, crossing her arms in front of her chest, pleased that Nick suddenly looked uncomfortable. "Do you have a woman in your life?"

"I have lots of women in my life, sweetheart."

"Then why haven't you gotten married?"

"I did that already."

"You can do it again."

"I don't think so."

"You can't stay single for the rest of your life."

"Why can't I?"

She shrugged. "You'll end up alone."

"Being married didn't stop that from happening, did it?"

After that comment, Lisa wanted desperately to turn on her heel and leave, but Nick was waiting for her to do just that, and it irritated the hell out of her. He thought he knew her so well. But he didn't. He might have known the girl, but he didn't begin to know the woman she was today.

Lisa glanced at her mother, who was smiling to herself as she stirred the browning meat on the stove. "I'll set the table for you, Mother," Lisa said. "Is there anything else I can do to help with dinner?"

"I thought you were going to see to the kids," Nick said. "You know, the kids in the other room?"

"Why don't you do that? You seem to have a tremendous need to leave a room first, so go right ahead." She waved him toward the door.

"Fine."

He walked out of the kitchen without a backward glance, and Lisa couldn't believe how much it bothered her that he'd gone. She'd told him to go. She'd wanted him to go. But it did feel odd, being the one to stay behind—not that she'd ever tell him that.

"You still haven't told me who you are and why you're pretending to be a friend of Serena's when it's obvious you don't even know what she looks like." Jeremy Hunt leaned forward in his chair, minimizing the distance between Maggie and himself, his brown eyes intent on her face.

Maggie wanted to look away, but there was something about his eyes that held her gaze, something about him that made her want to linger. She should have left an hour ago.

After the embarrassing moment by the tennis courts when he'd accused her of not knowing who Serena was, she'd considered confessing everything. Then they'd been interrupted by two men eager to talk to Jeremy about a screenplay, and she'd found herself swept along to the bar with the three of them.

Since she thought she'd have just as good a chance of tracking down Serena in the club restaurant, she'd gone along. Unfortunately, she'd now had two glasses of wine and was not a speck closer to finding Serena. Although she was more than a speck closer to Jeremy. Since his friends had left, he'd moved his chair next to hers. If she shifted her leg ever so slightly, it would touch his thigh. She felt downright excited by the thought.

Jeremy looked devastatingly handsome in the candlelight, sexy and somewhat dangerous—at least dangerous to her, to her good sense, to her plan of finding Serena and going home.

"Crystal?"

The name shattered the intimacy between them. Good Lord! What was she doing? She wasn't Crystal. She was Maggie. Or maybe she was Crystal. Maggie certainly wouldn't have gone to a bar with a man she didn't even know. Great. Now, she was thinking of herself in the third person.

"What did I say?" Jeremy asked, his gaze roaming across her face. "You look frightened."

Maggie licked her lips. "I—I should be going."

"Why? Because I know you're not a friend of Serena's?" He paused. "Are you out to hurt her? Because if you are, as her neighbor, I would in good conscience have to stop you. If you're not, why don't you tell me what's going on?"

She was tempted to do just that, but the story sounded so ridiculous even to her own ears that she couldn't imagine telling this man, this stranger, that she didn't trust her own husband. Still, she had to tell him something.

"All right. I'm not her friend. But I don't want to hurt her," Maggie said hastily. "She's a friend of a friend, and I need to ask her something."

Jeremy smiled somewhat sardonically. "That really clears things up for me."

"I'm sorry. It's complicated."

"You're very beautiful."

Maggie's mouth dropped open at his blunt statement, which had completely changed the subject. "Uh—thank you. I've always been partial to candlelight."

"It's not the light. It's you."

The look in his eyes was pure male, pure desire. She hadn't seen that look in a long time, and it made her ache. She wished she knew what to say, how to act.

"You're scared of me, aren't you? I wish you weren't."

"You're a stranger. I don't know you at all. You could be a serial killer for all I know." Good heavens. He could be just that! And she was sitting here alone with him in a town where she knew no one, where sex and drugs and women who ended up dead after a drink with a stranger were commonplace.

"Relax, Crystal. I'm not a serial killer."

"Like you'd tell me if you were."

"That's true."

"And everyone says afterwards, 'But he was such a nice man, we never suspected a thing.' "

"You're right." His brown eyes gleamed with amusement. "So, what are you going to do now?"

She took a sip of wine. "Leave, I guess. That would be the safe thing to do, the smart thing to do."

"Is that what you want to do?"

Maggie ran her finger around the edge of her wine glass as she set it down on the table. "It's what I should do."

"Do you always do the right thing?"

"Always." She smiled at him. "I'm pretty boring that way. What about you?"

"I'm not all that exciting either. I spend most of my days envisioning imaginary conversations with people who don't exist outside of my mind."

"Oh, heck, I do that, too," Maggie said with a laugh. "And I'm not even a writer."

"Don't leave." He covered her hand with his. "Live dangerously."

Oh, my, she was tempted to do just that, especially with his warm fingers creating all sorts of delicious shivers down her spine.

"You're not going to drive back to San Diego tonight, are you?" Jeremy continued. "You haven't seen Serena yet."

"I have a feeling I may never see her." Maggie checked her watch. It was past seven. She needed to call the kids and check on Lisa, then find a hotel room. He was right about one thing; there was no point driving all the way home tonight. Plus, she could try to find Serena in the morning. "I think I'll stay in town, and see if I can catch up with Serena tomorrow."

Jeremy nodded, pleased with her decision. "Good. Then we can have dinner. We'll take two cars. I promise not to lead you down any deserted roads. You can leave whenever you want. What do you say?"

"If I say yes, will you let go of my hand?"

He looked down at their hands, then grinned. "My insecurity is showing, huh?"

She never would have suspected that this man could feel even an ounce of uncertainty. He seemed so confident, so strong, so alive. When she was with him, she felt a bit the same way.

"Yes," she said. "To dinner, not your insecurity. But I have one condition. Tomorrow morning, you make sure Serena doesn't leave her house before I get there."

"I'll do my best, but I can't make any promises." He shrugged. "Serena doesn't always come home at night, if you know what I mean. She has an active social life."

"Is she really beautiful?" Maggie asked.

"Gorgeous."

Maggie's heart sank.

Jeremy frowned. "Serena and I don't have anything going on, Crystal, if that's what you're thinking. We're neighbors, that's it. And even if we weren't neighbors, she'd never give me a second look."

"Why not? You're very attractive."

A gleam came into his eyes. "I am?"

She felt herself turn red. "Yes. But you already know that."

"It's nice to hear it from you. As far as Serena is concerned, I'm too footloose and fancy-free. Serena prefers her men with a few more attachments."

"You mean like wives?"

"Serena has this incredible fascination with wanting what she can't have. Instead of accepting that something is out of reach, she works that much harder to get it." He paused. "You really don't know her at all, do you?"

"No."

His eyes connected with hers. "What is it you need to ask her?"

Maggie wanted to tell him the truth, but she couldn't. She wasn't ready to give up the pretense just yet. It was fun being a single woman for a change, and if she could keep the guilt at leaving her children out of her mind, she just might be able to enjoy a nice dinner in the company of a very nice man. Everything would end if she told him who she really was, a neurotic, anxiety-ridden single mom with three children and a deep suspicion that her husband had been having an affair.

"I didn't think the question was that difficult." Jeremy sat back in his seat, studying her with an intensity she found very appealing. She'd had to fight for Keith's attention. They'd rarely had a conversation without the television on, one of the kids shouting about something, the phone ringing or Keith sneaking peeks at his scientific magazines the minute she got distracted. Now, she was all alone with Jeremy, and he wanted to know her.

Actually, he probably wanted sex, a one-night stand, she told herself. Not that she was going to provide it. She wasn't that crazy—at least not yet. She'd just have dinner with him, flirt a little, then go home.

"I'm still waiting," he said with a smile.

"I need to ask Serena about a friend's husband. My friend found something of Serena's, and well, she's afraid her husband might be having an affair, and she wanted me to check things out for her."

Jeremy's smile faded. "Maybe she'd be better off not knowing."

"It's the not knowing that's driving her crazy."

"And what if he is having an affair—do you think your friend can handle it?"

"I guess she'll have to." Maggie got to her feet, determined to change the subject before he discovered the mysterious friend was her. "If we're going to have dinner, let's go. I'm starved. You know I worked up quite an appetite today, and since I'm sure I burned off at least two-thousand calories, I'm ready to replace them."

"Thank God, a woman who eats." Jeremy stood up, and they walked toward the door. "I may never let you go." His words were light, but his tone was serious.

Maggie took a deep breath, feeling once again out of her league in this situation. She hadn't gone on a date in fourteen years, and she had no idea how to act. She just knew she had to make one thing perfectly clear. She put a hand on his arm, stopping him at the door.

"Jeremy?" She hesitated, then took a deep breath. "I'm not going to sleep with you tonight. I just wanted you to know that."

He smiled at her. "I can live with that. Is that what you think this is about?"

"Isn't it?"

"Sex is pretty easy to come by in this town."

"So, you weren't thinking about—you know."

"Oh, I was definitely thinking about it. I still am." He pulled her to one side of the doorway as another couple pushed past them. "You stated your intentions clearly up front, so I'm going to state mine." He looked deep into her eyes. "Before you leave tomorrow, you and I are going to share one hell of a kiss."

Maggie swallowed hard. "I can live with that."

The phone rang just as the ten o'clock news came on the television. Lisa turned down the sound and reached for the phone, hoping it was Maggie. "Hello."

"Hi, it's me," said Maggie. "How is everyone?"

Lisa felt an enormous sense of relief at the sound of her friend's voice. After the hectic evening she'd spent with her mother, Nick and the kids, she needed to talk to someone who really understood her. "Maggie. Thank goodness. I was beginning to worry when you didn't call back."

"I got a little distracted. How are the kids?"

"They're great. Mary Bea crashed early. The birthday party wiped her out. Dylan's asleep, too, but I think Roxy might be up if you want to talk to her."

"In a minute. Tell me first about you. Are you holding up okay? Should I come home?"

"No, I'm fine." Lisa leaned back against the pillows on Maggie's bed. "Tell me what you've been up to."

"A whole lot of exercise," Maggie said with a laugh.

"That sounds good. Are you still feeling stressed?"

"Not as much as I was. In fact, I feel better than I have in ages."

"I'm so glad."

"Thanks for rescuing me, Lisa."

"It was my pleasure."

"I can see why you like the big city. It's got a pulse, an excitement that I haven't felt in a long time."

Lisa sat up in the bed, disturbed by Maggie's choice of words. "The big city? Where are you, Maggie? I thought you were in San Diego."

Maggie uttered a small laugh. "I was—last night. I'm in Beverly Hills at some incredibly posh hotel that's probably going to set me back a month's mortgage payment."

"Oh, my God, you went looking for that woman."

"Guilty."

"Did you find her?"

"Not yet. I'm hoping to see her tomorrow." Maggie paused for a long moment. "I think she might be a hooker."

"What?"

"You know, a professional call girl."

"What on earth would she have wanted with Keith?" Lisa groaned as the foolish words fled from her mouth. "I'm sorry. I'm sure she had a legitimate reason for contacting Keith."

"I'm not so sure. Everything is different here, Lisa. And

I can't help remembering the fact that Keith took several trips to L.A. in the few months before he died."

"Maggie, come home," Lisa ordered.

"I can't. Not yet. I have to know."

"Why? What good will come of it? Keith's gone. Whatever relationship he had with this woman is over. Why not just let yourself believe it was innocent?"

"Because it's driving me crazy," Maggie said. "I want to know. I want to understand. I want to be free of the stress and the tension. And every step I take seems to bring me closer to that freedom."

Lisa switched the phone to her other ear. "So, what time do you think you'll be home tomorrow?"

"I'm not sure. I'll call you in the morning. And Lisa?"

"What?"

"If for some reason I need to stay until Monday, is there any way you could cover for me?"

Another day with Nick? Impossible. Lisa could hear the strains of music coming from his guitar right now. He'd taken it out to the backyard so as not to wake the kids, but Maggie's bedroom was right over the deck, and Lisa could hear every note of the haunting melody.

How could she stay here with him? How could she listen to his music, hear his voice, watch his smile, feel his warmth? How could she do all that and address her wedding invitations at the same time? She looked down at the box on the bed. She'd brought it with her, knowing that the invitations absolutely had to go out on Monday. She'd already procrastinated far too long for good taste and proper etiquette. Now, she had to do it while her ex-husband played love songs. Life was full of irony.

"Lisa, did you fall asleep on me?" Maggie asked.

Lisa started at the voice in her ear. "Sorry, I was thinking about my schedule."

"I wouldn't ask if it wasn't important. I have to find Serena. I have to end this."

"All right, I'll stay until Monday, if you need me."

"Thanks, you're the best."

"You're the only one who thinks so. Nick's here, too, Maggie."

Maggie drew in a quick breath. "He is? I thought he was out of town. That's why I called you. Are you two . . ."

"I don't know what we are," Lisa said with a sigh. "I look at him and it feels like yesterday. But it was eight years ago when we were together, a lifetime. Everything should be different, but somehow it seems very much the same. He took me to the house today."

"Oh, dear." Maggie's husky murmur said it all. "I'm sorry. I didn't do this to throw you two together."

"I know. Nick wants to stay here until you get back. The kids really love him, and they want him to stay, so I said it was okay."

"Is it okay with you?"

Lisa had a lie ready and willing to be told, but this was Maggie after all, her very best friend. "I'm a little scared." She looked up at the ceiling as Nick's music played through her soul. "I loved him so much. I think I'd forgotten just how much until I saw him again. I try to remember how bad it was at the end, but instead I keep thinking about all the good times."

"Is that so bad?"

"Yes, it is! I'm getting married in a few weeks, Maggie. In fact, I'm sending out the invitations on Monday. Once I do that, I can't turn back."

"Then don't do it, not until you're sure."

"I am sure. At least, I think I am."

"Lisa, hang on a second."

Lisa frowned as she heard Maggie call to someone in the background that she'd be there in a minute. Then Maggie giggled like a schoolgirl.

"Maggie, is someone with you?" Lisa asked.

"Uh, sort of."

"Who is it?"

"You don't know him."

"Him?" Lisa squealed. "It's a him? You have a him in your hotel room?"

"Lisa, I have to go. I'll call you tomorrow."

"You're not hanging up until you tell me what's going on," Lisa said, but the only reply she received from Maggie was a dial tone.

Chapter 10

Sunday morning the kids and Nick slept late, which gave Lisa a chance to finish addressing her wedding invitations and down two cups of strong, caffeinated coffee. She'd slept little the night before, her dreams a mix and match of old and new, Nick and Raymond, Maggie, the kids, her old house, her current apartment and the robin, of course.

As she carried her cup to the sink, she heard the faint sound of a bird, and she couldn't help looking out the window. The robin was sitting on a branch, singing his heart out to no apparent avail. Then the singing stopped as the robin seemed to stare right at her.

"Go away," Lisa muttered. "Shoo now. Find some other yard." The bird stared at her as if she were crazy, which of course she was. "I'm getting married. I've found my mate. He's in L.A. Go visit him."

"Who are you talking to?" Nick asked, stumbling into the kitchen dressed in nothing but a pair of low-riding blue jeans.

Her breath caught at the sight of his tousled hair, sexy eyes, tanned, muscular chest, and the strong arms that had once held her so tight. Mornings had always been their best time together. They'd made love so many times in the early light of dawn, still dreamy with sleep, but awake with desire.

Lisa forced herself to look away from Nick. Unfortunately that only brought her gaze back to the robin, and they both disturbed her peace of mind.

"He's back," Nick said, joining her at the window, his

arm brushing hers in a touch so brief, so impersonal it should have meant nothing.

Instead she felt a jolt of awareness, a shivering parade of goose bumps that fled down her arm. She stepped away quickly as if she'd touched a hot stove.

Nick looked at her, not saying a word, but his eyes said it all. He knew. He'd always known. Damn him.

She walked over to the coffeemaker and refilled her cup.

"That looks good," Nick said.

"Help yourself."

"You never used to drink coffee," he commented as he poured himself a cup.

"I never used to do a lot of things." She sat down at the kitchen table. "Maggie called last night. She said she might not be back until Monday, but she'd call this morning."

"What in the hell is she up to?"

Lisa debated whether or not to tell him that Maggie had a man in her hotel room, then decided not to. Maggie was a grown woman. If she wanted to have a fling, who was Lisa to criticize? "I'm not sure," she prevaricated.

"Not sure? Or won't say?"

"A little of both."

"Fine, have it your way." He took a sip of his coffee. "What are your plans for the day?"

"I thought I might take the kids to the beach."

"They love the beach."

"Nick, you can go home now. The kids will be fine with me today. Unless you still don't trust me to take care of them." She could have kicked herself for revealing her insecurity, because it was clear from Nick's expression he knew exactly what she was thinking.

"You're very good with the kids," he said quietly. "I always thought you were a good mother."

"That's not what you said—" She stopped herself and took a deep breath. "Never mind."

Nick sat down in the chair next to hers. He stared at the box of invitations, then pulled one out. "Raymond Curtis and Elisabeth Alvarez cordially invite you to attend their wedding.'' He looked at Lisa, who wished she'd never brought the invitations downstairs. "Elisabeth?"

"It is my name."

"Is that what he calls you?"

"Yes."

Nick put the invitation back in the box. "I guess you're really doing it."

"I told you I was."

"You did," he agreed. "It will be here before you know it. In fact, aren't you sending these out a little late?"

"I've been busy."

"There sure are a lot of them. Must be over a hundred in that box."

"Raymond has a lot of friends."

"What about your friends? Is Maggie invited?"

"Of course."

"What about me?"

"You didn't make the cut."

"I'm hurt." Nick slid his chair so close to hers that their legs touched. Lisa was about to back away when she saw the challenging glint in his eye. He was waiting for her to get up and run, and she refused to give him the satisfaction.

"What are you doing?" she asked, as he set his cup down on the table and placed his hands on top of her thighs.

"I'm conducting a test."

"Of what?"

"You and me. You said we're over. Until yesterday I would have agreed with you. Now, I'm not so sure."

"Why not?"

"Because I have this incredible urge to kiss you."

Lisa's heart sped up. "Don't do it." She put up a hand to stop him from coming closer, but touching his bare chest only made it worse. Instead of pushing him away, her fingers curled in the dark strands of hair on his chest.

"God, I've missed you doing that," he said huskily, his gaze dropping down to her mouth. "And I've missing doing this."

He covered her mouth with his, pushing, prodding, persuading until she could do nothing more but open her mouth and kiss him back the way he wanted her to. His tongue slid into her mouth and he tasted like coffee and Nick, the taste she'd loved and hungered for. She tilted her head, unconsciously deepening the kiss, as his arms slipped around her waist.

"Wow! Are you guys French kissing?" Roxy asked, her voice tearing them apart.

Lisa put a hand to her flushed cheeks. "Uh, uh . . ." She looked over at Nick for help, but his breathing was as ragged as her own.

"I've never done it. Is it fun or is it sort of gross?" Roxy asked. "Because it sounds a little gross, you know."

Nick smiled at Lisa, that slow, heart-stopping smile that made her mouth water. "It can be really great with the right person," he said. "And when you're a lot older."

"Like how old?"

"Thirty."

Roxy made a face. "I don't think so, Uncle Nick." She skipped over to the breakfast table and sat down. "Hey, what are these?" She picked up an invitation, then looked at Lisa in confusion. "Is this you?"

"Yes," Lisa said. "I'm getting married in a couple of weeks."

Roxy looked from Lisa to Nick, then back at Lisa. "Then how come you're kissing Uncle Nick?"

"That's a good question, Lisa," Nick said.

It was a good question. She just wished she had an answer.

"You came." Jeremy smiled at Maggie with satisfaction when she arrived on his porch just before eleven o'clock on Sunday morning.

Maggie smiled somewhat nervously. Jeremy looked as good as he had the night before. He was wearing jeans and a long-sleeve rugby shirt. His hair was still wet from a recent shower, his face cleanly shaven.

She felt a surge of pleasure at the enthusiasm in his greeting. She'd spent most of the night telling herself that he was just amusing himself with her, that she was different from the women he dated, thus interesting for awhile anyway. Not that he knew who she really was.

They'd talked until two o'clock in the morning, arguing, debating, but never getting personal. At least she hadn't. He'd talked about his family in Nebraska, the life he'd left behind, his dreams of making it big in Hollywood, and she'd listened. It reminded her of all the times she'd listened to Keith talk about his ambitions, how she'd encouraged him and supported him in every way she could.

But there was one difference. Keith had never expected her to be anything but a wife and a mother. They had met in high school, married when she was eighteen and he was twenty-two. They'd conceived a child on their honeymoon and spent the next thirteen years building a life together, growing up together.

Jeremy had asked her lots of questions about who she was, what she did for work, where she lived, what kinds of movies she liked, who she'd voted for in the presidential race. She'd dodged most of his questions while admitting to being a Republican, which seemed almost sacrilegious here in Hollywood.

"Crystal, hello," Jeremy said, waving a hand in front of her face. "Are you still with me?"

She flushed with embarrassment, realizing she'd once again drifted into a daydream in the middle of a conversation. "Sorry."

"Don't be. Especially if you were thinking about last night, because last night was incredible."

She twisted the strap of her purse between nervous fingers. "You make it sound like we did something."

Jeremy laughed. "We did do something. We talked, we ate, we drank. We laughed a lot. I haven't enjoyed myself that much in a long time."

"I meant, well, you know what I meant."

"I told you before that that wasn't what this was about."

"I didn't believe you before, and I don't really believe you now," Maggie confessed. "Men always want sex."

"That's true. But sometimes we want more."

"More sex," she said with a laugh.

He shook a finger at her. "Maybe you need to broaden your experience with men."

"Maybe I do. Are you volunteering?"

"Ready and willing." He took her hand and pulled her inside. "Come on in."

She hesitated, looking through the trees that separated Serena's condo from Jeremy's. "Have you seen Serena this morning?"

"No, I just got up. Do you want to go over there now, or come in and have coffee?"

"I better try her now, before it gets late."

"Do you want me to come with you?"

She thought of all the questions she had to ask Serena. "No, thanks. I'll stop back when we're done."

"Promise?" He put a hand on her shoulder. "Whatever she says, whatever you find out, don't let it drive you away, not without saying good-bye."

"I'm not sure I can promise that," she said slowly.

"This isn't about a friend, is it? It's about you."

Maggie knew he could read the truth in her eyes, but she couldn't bring herself to say the words. "I better go."

"I hope she gives you the right answer."

"Me, too."

Maggie walked quickly down the path and around the corner. She wanted to ring Serena's doorbell before she changed her mind.

She heard the bell ring through the house, but it seemed awfully quiet inside, so she pushed it again. At this point, she didn't much care if Serena was asleep. She just wanted to see her face-to-face and ask Serena why the heck she'd written a letter to her husband.

After a moment, Maggie heard footsteps. Her heart quickened. Serena was home. She was finally going to meet her.

"Did you forget your goddamn keys again—" A male voice grumbled as he flung open the door.

Maggie took a step backward. She'd been expecting Serena, not a tall, well-built man wearing nothing but hot red bikini underwear and a gold chain.

"Who the hell are you?" he demanded, making no move to cover his glorious, almost naked, body.

"Uh . . . uh . . ." Maggie stumbled, trying to find a safe place to look. She settled on his angry, unshaven face. "Is Serena here?"

"Who wants to know?"

"A—a friend."

"You don't look like a friend." The man's eyes narrowed as he checked out her blue jeans, beige knit top and the oversize brown purse that had become her constant companion since she began having children who seemed to need an endless array of supplies to get through every excursion. "What have you got in that purse?"

Her jaw dropped open at his question. "What difference does it make?"

His face tightened. "Shit. You've got a camera in there, don't you? Alma sent you after me, didn't she? Well, it won't work." He grabbed the purse off her arm.

"Hey, wait a second, that's mine." Before she could stop him, he'd opened her purse and dumped half her things out on the side table inside Serena's front door. "What are you doing?" Maggie demanded, stepping through the doorway.

"No camera," he said grimly, staring down at the pile of things that made up her life—crayons, peppermints, lipstick, scissors, a troll doll, three plastic black spiders, a comb and the letter from Serena to Keith.

"Why would I have a camera?"

"What about a tape recorder? Are you wired?"

She saw his gaze move from her face to her chest and had the sudden feeling he was about to rip open her shirt. "Don't even think about it," she warned, grabbing her stuff and piling it back into her purse. "Are you crazy or something?"

"You tell Alma that her little plan won't work. She's got nothing on me."

"Who is Alma?"

"Like you don't know," he scoffed. "I'll admit you're

better disguised than the last dick she sent after me. But I can spot a setup a mile away.''

''A dick?'' Maggie spluttered. ''You think I'm a private eye?'' Good heavens! Had the world gone mad? Jeremy thought she was Crystal, and this man thought she was a private eye spying on him for some woman named Alma.

The man grabbed her arm and shoved her onto the porch.

''Wait. Wait,'' she cried. ''I came to see Serena.''

''Yeah, right.''

''Is she here?

''I don't know anyone named Serena.''

''Then why are you in her condo?''

''I got lost.'' He slammed the door in her face.

Maggie silently fumed, debating whether or not to ring the bell again. It was probably pointless. She wouldn't be able to get that jerk to listen to reason even if he did open the door.

Taking a few deep breaths, Maggie tried to calm the flutters of panic and uncertainty. That obnoxious man had only reminded her that she was completely out of her depth here in L.A. and she would no doubt be better off going home. But she hated to leave now, when she was so close. Maggie turned and walked down the path. She had to admit that it was somewhat amusing to be mistaken for a private investigator. She almost felt like she was in a television movie. By the time she pushed open Jeremy's front door, she was feeling better and determined to come up with another plan.

She knew Jeremy would help her. And he was a writer. Surely he could think of some way for her to meet Serena.

Jeremy wasn't in his living room, but at her questioning call, he told her to come in, so she did. His condo was warm and inviting, the feel of the Pacific Southwest apparent in the Indian rugs on the floor and the series of spectacular photographs lining the hallway, boasting aerial photography of the Grand Canyon, the red cliffs of Sedona, and old town Albuquerque.

There were books and magazines littering every available table. Jeremy had obviously turned his dining room into an office, with papers strewn endlessly about. It was a man's house, endearingly messy, she thought with a smile.

"It's a mess, I know." Jeremy walked out of the kitchen with two mugs of coffee. "I like to spread out when I'm working."

"I can see that."

He handed her a mug. "I thought you'd be back sooner since Serena isn't home."

She sent him a confused look. "Why didn't you tell me she wasn't home before I went over there?"

He tipped his head toward the phone. "Serena just called to ask me to pick up her newspaper for a couple of days. She was at the airport. I thought you'd ring the bell and come right back. What took you so long?"

"A man answered her door. He seemed to think I was spying on him. He kept asking me if Alma sent me."

Jeremy smiled. "Oh."

"Do you know him?"

"Can't say that I do."

"He acted so oddly. I mean, why would he think I was spying on him? He must be paranoid."

"Or married." Jeremy took another sip of his coffee.

She stared at him in dismay. "I bet you're right. He kept saying Alma wasn't going to get anything on him."

"So, what now?"

Maggie thought for a moment. "Go home, I guess."

"Serena went to San Francisco," Jeremy said abruptly, a speculative gleam in his eye.

Maggie felt her pulse quicken at the new lead. "San Francisco?"

"It's only an hour by plane."

"No, I couldn't." Maggie immediately shook her head. Or could she? Lisa had agreed to stay until Monday. She could be back by tomorrow morning.

"I love watching you think," Jeremy said. "Everything goes through your eyes. You're worrying about something." His smile faded. "Someone's waiting for you, a man."

"No, not a man."

His expression lightened. "Good."

"This is foolish. I shouldn't even be considering it."

"Serena told me she was meeting someone in San Francisco, someone she hadn't seen in a long time. In fact, she said it had been so long she thought he was dead. It turned out he wasn't."

Maggie's stomach lurched. Her heart raced. Her palms began to sweat, and the mug fell from her fingers and smashed against the floor, splashing hot coffee in every direction. She barely felt the stinging drops of burning liquid that sprang up to her bare arms.

Serena thought he was dead, but it turned out he wasn't. Oh, God. What did that mean? Was it possible? No, of course not. Still . . .

"Crystal." Jeremy grabbed her arm and gave her a shake until she finally focused on his face. "What's wrong? What did I say?"

"You said he might not be dead."

"Who?" Jeremy asked in bewilderment.

"My—my husband."

Chapter 11

Lisa felt like she was part of a family again as she and Nick loaded the kids into his car, along with a stack of towels, some beach chairs, a Frisbee, a football and a picnic basket loaded with food. The kids squabbled as they squeezed into the backseat, arguing over who would sit in the middle. The tension broke when the dog leapt into the car and settled down in the center of the bench seat, barking with excitement.

"You're not going, Sally," Nick said. "Go on, get outta here." He waved his hand at the dog.

"Sally loves the beach," Dylan protested, throwing his arms around Sally's neck. "And she needs to run. Mom usually walks her every day, and since Mom is gone . . ."

"Yeah, yeah, yeah," Nick grumbled. "Fine. She can come. The rest of you buckle up."

Lisa smiled as she slid into the passenger seat. Nick was a complete pushover where the kids were concerned. He tried to be stern but failed every time, and they knew exactly which buttons to push.

"Did you remember the sunscreen?" Lisa asked as Nick turned the key in the ignition.

He sent her a disgusted look. "Sunscreen? You mean we don't have one bottle of sunscreen in the eighty-six bags you threw into the back?"

"It was just a question."

"I put some in, Aunt Lisa," Roxy piped up. "I don't want to get more freckles."

"Anything else?" Nick asked.

"You know you wanted to come," Lisa pointed out. "Because your car isn't working, and I'd hate for the kids to be stuck in the house all day."

"Then let's go."

"We're going." He backed out of the driveway, then stopped. "Oops, I almost forgot."

"What now?" Lisa asked.

Nick rolled down the windows and punched in a tape. "Music, baby."

He smiled at her, and she couldn't help but smile back as the sound of the Beach Boys came blaring through the car. "I haven't listened to them in ages."

"They used to be your favorite group."

"I remember," she said with a sigh as he drove down the street. The beach music pulsed through her body, and with the warm wind in her hair and Nick by her side, she felt nineteen again—and in love. Her lips curved into another smile. She couldn't help it. She knew she had plenty of reasons to dislike Nick, but at the moment she had a hard time remembering what they were. The good memories were coming back, and she wasn't sure she could stop them even if she tried that is, if she wanted to try.

For the moment, it was easier to simply sit back in her seat and enjoy the day.

Nick smiled to himself as the song ended and another one began. Lisa looked suddenly younger, more carefree, the way she'd been when they had first begun to date.

Although Lisa had grown up under his feet, she'd always been Maggie's friend. Besides that, she was two years younger and had always been too young to fool with, until he ran into her after her high school graduation. By then he was living on his own in an apartment on the beach with two other guys. He had just begun his junior year at San Diego State and hadn't seen Lisa in almost two years.

When he saw her at a party, he couldn't believe she was

all grown up. He'd been drawn to her beauty, of course, but also her quiet. She didn't talk a lot. In fact, she'd often seemed vulnerable to him, with fragile feelings that could easily be hurt. Once he got to know her, he realized she had a quick wit, an easy laugh, a loving smile, a killer competitive instinct, and a good heart.

And she'd listened to him, to all his crazy dreams about playing guitar in a rock and roll band even though they both knew he didn't have nearly enough talent. In those days, their dreams had touched the sky.

Although Lisa had been reluctant to share her own goals at first, she'd finally come to trust him enough to tell him how much she wanted to write a novel. She'd even shown him some of the journals she'd kept throughout her childhood, pages of daydreams that had kept her company in a family where she seemed the odd one out.

Not that he'd ever seen her that way. It had always been obvious to him that Silvia adored her daughter. They were just different. Silvia was hot, fast, impetuous. Lisa was cool, calm and thoughtful. And her great-aunt, Carmela, had only widened the divide between mother and daughter with her weekly spiritual gatherings, as she liked to call them.

Lisa hadn't wanted to introduce him to her family at first. For awhile, he thought she was ashamed of him. Then he realized she was worried about his reaction to them. Finally, he'd managed to convince her that he loved her unconditionally. And finally, she'd trusted him enough to believe that.

It was funny. Lisa had always been an optimist where his dreams were concerned, but she'd always been a pessimist about herself. Not that she didn't try to win. Despite her inherent insecurity, she loved to compete and adored winning, especially card games, where her incredible memory made her remember every hand. They'd had a great time in Vegas one year.

In fact, they'd always had a good time together, whether they were going to the movies or a comedy club or the beach. They'd been surprisingly compatible, or maybe they'd just been willing to share everything. He'd suffered through the tear-jerking movies she'd loved, and she'd gamely stayed out until three in the morning so he could hear a new band play. The most important thing was that they were together. Nothing else had mattered.

Nick snuck a glance in Lisa's direction. She seemed content to look out the window while the kids chattered in the backseat. He'd missed her, he suddenly realized. When she'd left, he hadn't just lost a child and a wife, he'd lost his best friend. He wondered if she'd missed him. Probably not, he decided. He knew one thing about her that hadn't changed. When someone hurt her, she never forgave them.

Lisa turned and looked at him. She raised an eyebrow inquiringly. "Something wrong?"

It was such a simple question to cover just how much was wrong between them. How had they ever gotten to this place, two strangers who had once been everything to each other?

He shook his head. "Everything's fine. Maggie tells me you're in advertising now. Do you like it?"

"Yes. Although I like the writing better than everything else. Not that I don't enjoy meeting clients and all that, but I still get a thrill out of coming up with just the right slogan." She smiled somewhat self-consciously. "I know it's not brain surgery, but it suits me."

"You always did want to write. I'm glad you found a job where you could do just that."

"Me, too." She was quiet for a moment, then smiled at him. "Thanks, Nick."

"For what?"

"Understanding." She turned away as if she were sorry she'd said something so personal.

Nick didn't press her for more. He wasn't sure he'd get it, nor was he sure he wanted it. He and Lisa had closed the door on their relationship a long time ago, and whether or not he'd been in favor of ending it at that time was water under the bridge. It had ended. That was the bottom line. Whoever said you can't go back was probably right.

*   *   *

"I'm old," Nick said a half hour later as he tossed down the football and collapsed on the sand next to Lisa, his breath coming fast, sweat beading along his forehead. "I've just been trounced by an eight-year-old."

Lisa shaded her eyes against the sun as she checked on the kids. Roxy had found a friend, and they were lounging about twenty feet away, pretending to be completely alone on the beach, so that the group of boys a few feet away might come over and start flirting. Dylan and Mary Bea were throwing a stick into the water, watching in delight as Sally jumped into the waves to retrieve it.

It was early spring, and although the day was warm, the ocean water was cold. Dylan and Mary Bea seemed content to let Sally do the wading, which was fine with Lisa, who had no desire to stick even her big toe into the ocean. She'd always loved to sunbathe. Swimming through waves that usually pounded her into the sand had never been her idea of a good time.

Lisa looked at Nick. His eyes were closed, and he wasn't moving. His face was red, and he appeared hot. A devilish thought came into her mind, and, acting on impulse—something she hadn't done in years—she scooped a couple of small melting ice cubes out of the ice chest and let the cold water drip onto Nick's face.

His eyes flew open as he sat up. "What the hell—"

"Just wanted to make sure you weren't asleep," she said with a laugh.

She knew she'd made a huge mistake when Nick reached into the ice chest and came up with a large chunk of ice. She scooted back on the blanket, but she couldn't get away from him fast enough.

Nick grabbed her arm, pulled open the neck of her shirt and dumped the ice down her chest. She gasped and jumped to her feet, shaking the ice cubes out from her shirt. "That wasn't fair."

He laughed. "You started it."

She glared at him. "Fine. You're right. You win."

He didn't look like he believed her. "You're going to let me win that easily?"

"I'm not a child. I can take losing."

"Since when?"

"Since—oh, shoot. Do you think Mary Bea is too close to the water?"

As Nick turned to look at the children, Lisa grabbed another handful of ice, pulled open the back of Nick's shorts and dumped the ice.

"Yow!" Nick started dancing, hopping up and down on one foot as he tried to shake the ice out of his shorts. "That does it. Now you've made me mad."

At the look of murder in Nick's eyes, Lisa took off down the beach. Nick ran after her. She sprinted past Roxy and her girlfriends and headed toward Mary Bea and Dylan.

"Are you playing tag?" Dylan asked.

"Yes," Nick shouted. "Anyone who can push Aunt Lisa into the water gets ten bucks."

"Cool!" Dylan tossed down the stick in his hand as he ran after Lisa.

Lisa ran faster as they gained on her, but it wasn't long before Nick, Dylan and Mary Bea tackled her.

She hit the ground hard, getting a fistful of sand, which she promptly tossed into Nick's face while Dylan and Mary Bea laughed, and Sally barked with delight.

Nick pushed her back on the sand and pinned her hands over her head. She would have yelled at him, but she was completely out of breath.

"Say it," he ordered.

"Uncle," she gasped.

"Uncle who?" Mary Bea asked curiously.

"It means I give up," Lisa said. "Let me go."

Nick laughed. "I don't think so. You haven't said the magic words."

"Which are what?"

"You win, Nick. You're the best."

"You win, Nick. You're the best," she said with a mocking smile.

"I'm always wrong and you're always right," he added.

"You got that right," she said.

He frowned. "That's not what I meant. You say, 'I'm always wrong, and you're always right.' "

"Not in this lifetime."

"Okay." He looked over at Dylan and Mary Bea. "Guess we'll have to tickle her."

"Don't you dare," she warned, but it was too late. Mary Bea and Dylan dived into her, their little hands tickling every sensitive spot until she begged for mercy.

That's when Nick picked her up and headed toward the water. She flung her arms around his neck and hung on for dear life. "Nick, please. It's cold."

He waded in deeper. "What will you give me if I don't drop you?"

"What do you want?" she cried as the ocean spray hit her hot face with shocking coldness.

"I don't know. What are you offering?"

She stared into his teasing eyes. "I'll give you a hug."

"How about a kiss?"

"On the cheek."

"Open mouth, all tongue."

"No way. Think of the children. Think of our—our divorce. Think of Raymond."

"Are you thinking of Raymond, Lisa?"

She should be thinking of Raymond, but Nick's face was too close, his eyes too bright, his lips so damn sexy.

"Raymond is a great guy," she said desperately.

"So am I, and I'm the one who's holding you. So what's it going to be?"

"Nick, think of the children. We'll only confuse them more."

Nick glanced over his shoulder at Mary Bea and Dylan, who had lost interest in them and were tossing a stick to Sally. "The children are fine. They're not paying any attention to us." He began to lower her toward the water.

"Wait. Wait. All right. One kiss on the mouth—no tongues."

Nick laughed. "You seem to be under the misguided impression that you have some say in this."

"You don't really want to kiss me that way."

"Oh, but I do," he said with a gleam in his eyes. "I really do." And he did. He covered her mouth with his, pushing past her lips with a confidence and sureness that felt absolutely right, absolutely perfect. His tongue danced against hers, filling her mouth, her soul, the empty places in her heart.

She was mindless to her surroundings. The noise of the beach, the children, everything else faded away—until she hit the water with a resounding splash.

The cold stopped her heart. "Damn you," she spluttered, coming up for air.

Nick held out his hands in apology. "Sorry, I forgot where we were."

"I'll just bet you did," she said, wading out of the water.

"It's true." The smile faded from his face. "You sure can kiss. I'd almost forgotten." He shook his head. "That was a mistake. I won't let it happen again."

Anger flared at his arrogant statement. "Maybe you won't have a choice next time. Maybe I'll kiss you." Good heavens, what was she saying? She clapped a hand over her mouth to stop any other stupid statements from erupting past her lips.

Nick looked amused again. "That will be the day. You don't want me, remember? Or have things changed?" Without waiting for an answer, he smiled at her. "I'm going to dry off. See ya."

"Wait a second," she called, but he'd already turned his back on her. She kicked some water at him, but it fell woefully short, and she realized that for the second time in two days he'd walked away from her. "Fine, dry off," she yelled. "See if I care."

He stopped about ten feet from her and laughed. "Oh, you care all right. Finally, you care about something. I'd rather see you mad and spitting at me than the way you were when you left all those years ago, so cold and distant like a robot.

Now, you're all . . ." he paused, raking her body with his glance. "Now, you're all woman again. God help me." He turned and strode up the beach.

"God help both of us," she muttered as she slowly followed him back to the blanket.

"Your husband?" Jeremy repeated, as he took Maggie by the shoulders. "What are you talking about?"

"Never mind." Maggie tried to slip away from him, but his hands tightened around her arms.

"Don't you think it's time you told me the truth? You think your husband is having an affair with Serena, don't you?"

"Sort of." She took a breath. "My husband died in a fire almost a year ago."

"He died? I don't understand. You just said—"

"About two weeks ago, I received a letter from Serena. It made me suspicious of everything that had happened. I thought if I could just ask her how she knew him, I could let it all go."

Jeremy pulled her over to the sofa so they could both sit down. "I think you better start at the beginning. If your husband is dead, why did you panic when I told you Serena was meeting a long lost friend in San Francisco?"

Maggie felt foolish for even considering a confession. She would sound like an idiot. "I—forget it. I don't know why I reacted that way."

"Yes, you do. Tell me."

"I can't," she whispered.

His expression turned serious. "You can trust me, Crystal. Don't you know that yet?"

Obviously she didn't, since she hadn't yet told him her name was Maggie. Still, it would be nice to tell someone, especially someone she would never see again. So what if he thought she was crazy? What did it matter?

It mattered because she liked him, because he seemed interested in her. She hated to see all that disappear, and she knew it would when she told him what she really thought.

"Okay," Jeremy said. "Let me guess."

"You couldn't."

"I've got a good imagination. Your husband died, and although you used to think he was faithful, now you think he was having an affair with Serena. And there's something else. Something that happened that's made you doubt other things about him, about your life together." He paused. "Lastly, you suspect that he might still be alive."

"You are good."

"All that plotting experience," he said, settling back on the sofa.

Maggie turned, suddenly eager to discuss her theory with him. Maybe he could make sense of it. "Okay, what would you think if a man increased the terms of his life insurance policy two months before his death, made a large cash withdrawal only twenty-four hours before his death and then received a letter from a strange woman asking him if he was still planning to meet her as he'd promised?"

Jeremy stared at her for a long moment, his eyes speculative, considering. "I'd think something was going on."

"Then you don't think I'm crazy?"

"No."

Maggie couldn't help the sigh of relief. "There's something else, Jeremy. They never found Keith's body. There was an explosion, a chemical fire deep within a lab. They found . . ." She stumbled over the gruesome details, but knew she had to get them out. "They found bits of bones and some teeth, fragments of Keith's shirt. But not a body. The firemen said the force of the explosion, the chemical makeup of the fire was so strong that the body was basically incinerated." She shook her head. "I'm probably just grasping at straws."

"Maybe you are," Jeremy took her hand in his. "Maybe you want him to be alive so much you're imagining everything else. Did you love him?"

"Yes, very much. We were happy. At least I thought we were. After he died, I tried not to think about the money and everything, but then I got that letter from Serena, and I knew

I had to find out the answer to at least one of my questions.''

"Makes sense to me. So, are you going to San Francisco?''

"I shouldn't.''

"That's not what I asked.''

She smiled. ''You already know the answer, don't you?''

"Want some company?''

She looked into his eyes and saw the same look of desire she'd seen the day before. ''Why?''

In reply, he cupped her face with his hands and kissed her. The warmth of his mouth, the persuasion of his lips, the seductive scent of his aftershave drew Maggie in like a moth to a flame. He was a stranger. His face was so different from Keith's, his skin rough and sexy, his lips demanding, his arms pressing her close to him. His body felt right—yet wrong. His jeans pressed against her bare legs—jeans, not a suit.

The sensations hit her in waves as desire raced through her body. She liked the way Jeremy kissed her, the way his hands caressed her back, spreading across her waist until his fingertips glanced lightly against her breasts. She suddenly wanted him in her mouth, in her body, in a completely lustful, sexual way that shocked the hell out of her.

"Oh, God,'' she murmured, breaking away from him. ''What am I doing?'' She jumped to her feet. ''I have to go. I have to . . .'' She didn't know what she had to do. She could barely remember her own name. Was it Crystal or was it Maggie? She put her hands to her face, feeling the heat in her cheeks. ''This is getting complicated.''

Jeremy stood up, desire darkening his eyes. ''It's pretty simple really. I'm attracted to you. You're attracted to me.''

"But I'm married.''

"Are you?''

"I might be,'' she whispered, putting a hand to her mouth.

"Whatever happened, whether he's dead or he left you, he's still gone. You're still alone.''

Maggie took in a deep breath as his sharp words hit home.

"That was pretty blunt. You don't know anything about me, Jeremy."

"Then tell me about you. Tell me on the way to San Francisco."

"I can't go with you."

"I won't hurt you. I won't even touch you again, not unless you ask me to."

"That's the problem. I have a feeling I might ask you to," she said with complete honesty.

He smiled. "You're a lousy flirt."

"I haven't had a lot of practice." She paused. "Jeremy, I haven't been single in a very long time. I don't know how to date, or how to play the games that men and women play these days. I don't mean those kind of games," she quickly amended as he began to grin.

"Too bad."

"I'm serious," she said, with a gentle slap on his arm.

"Far too serious." He drew a line down her cheek with his finger. "Just relax. This isn't a movie. You don't have to remember your lines. You don't have to be someone you're not. Just be you."

She tried one last argument. "Jeremy, if Keith is alive, I don't know what I'll do."

"Why don't we leave that for when it happens, if it happens?" He walked over to the phone. "I'll call the airport and check the flights. I assume you want to leave as soon as possible."

"Yes."

He picked up the phone, then paused. "Shall I make the reservation for Crystal—or someone else?"

Chapter 12

When Lisa and Nick returned to Maggie's house with a carful of weary children and a droopy dog, they found Silvia and Lisa's great-aunt Carmela waiting on the porch. Silvia was dressed like a rainbow, in a long red skirt and a bright white peasant blouse that set off the trio of necklaces she wore around her neck. Carmela, Silvia's aunt, went to the other extreme of dress, a long-sleeve black knit dress that hung loosely on her thin frame and touched the tops of a pair of serviceable black leather shoes. Men's shoes, Lisa thought, both pleased and bothered by the familiar sight.

"Looks like we have company," Nick said with a wry smile.

"Looks like."

Nick turned off the engine. "What do you think they want?"

"Probably a big black cauldron and some rat's toes or something like that."

"Rat's toes?" Dylan echoed in amazement.

"A very important ingredient in magic potions," Nick said solemnly.

"Cool," Dylan replied.

"I am not having anything to do with some diseased, disgusting little rat," Roxy declared.

"I like mice," Mary Bea added. "They're not cooking a mouse, are they?"

"No. No. It was a joke," Lisa explained.

Nick laughed as Lisa tried to work her way out of her impulsive comment.

"I was kidding," she added. "Why don't you three go on up and say hello? Nick and I will be right there."

"Grandma Silvia says your great-aunt Carmela makes magic," Dylan said, as he slid out of the car.

"Can she pull a rabbit out of a hat?" Mary Bea asked.

"She can't pull much of anything out of anything," Lisa replied. "But be nice to her. She's old."

"She's also scary," Nick muttered as Mary Bea joined her brother and sister on the porch. "I'm going to drop you off. I have some work to do. I'll be back later."

"Chicken."

"Hey, she threatened to curse me into eternity when you left. Or turn me into a toad."

"That might have been an improvement."

"Ha. Ha."

Lisa smiled. "You don't really believe she could turn you into a toad, do you? This is a woman who hand-washes her clothes because she can't figure out how to use her washing machine."

"I don't feel like taking any chances. She always looks at me like she knows something I don't."

Lisa looked at the two women sitting on the porch, who were a big part of her family. Her grandparents had died when she was a child. Silvia's brother had returned to Mexico shortly after he married, and Silvia's sister had followed her army husband to Texas, leaving Silvia, Carmela and Lisa pretty much on their own in San Diego. They had shared a town house, and Carmela had often watched Lisa when she was a child, allowing Silvia to work.

Although Lisa knew that both her mother and Carmela loved her, she had always felt out of place with them. Her mother was flamboyant, loud and gregarious, while Carmela was mysterious, dark and moody. Lisa had never known what to expect upon entering her home.

As a child she'd been deeply embarrassed by her family. She'd never brought anyone home, because she'd always felt so different, not just because she didn't have a father, although that was part of it, but because Silvia and Carmela could be so odd.

Of course, Maggie and Nick and the whole Maddux family had found Silvia and even Carmela at times to be delightful. Or at least they'd always pretended to think that way. Maybe it had been for her benefit.

Lisa glanced at Nick, who also seemed lost in thought. Then he turned his head and caught her eye. "What did you do with the bracelet?" he asked abruptly.

"It's in my purse. Why?"

"I never would have believed the bracelet would bring you home." He shook his head. "Yet here you are."

"I came because of Maggie, not because of the bracelet."

"Yeah. But why did Maggie leave so suddenly? Why did she call you? She has other friends in town she could have asked. Hell, she could have asked me."

"I think she tried. You weren't home. The bracelet is just a bracelet, Nick. If it was magic, do you really think our baby would have died?"

Nick didn't have an answer to that.

"I better say hello." Lisa got out of the car but hesitated before shutting the door. "Are you sure you have to go?"

"Yeah, I'll catch up with you later. I need to check out some things at my store."

"It can't wait until tomorrow?" She felt like a complete coward, but she could see from here that Carmela was in one of her intense moods. In fact, she hadn't stopped staring at the car since they'd pulled in the driveway.

Nick raised an eyebrow. "You actually want me to spend more time with you?"

"Not with me, with the kids and my mother and my aunt."

"So you don't need me at all?"

"Me? Of course not."

"Liar." He smiled wickedly. "If you'd told me the truth, I would have stayed." He leaned over, pulled her door shut and backed out of the driveway.

Great. He was leaving again. She was getting damn tired of watching him leave.

"Lisa. Lisa," her mother waved. "Come on up. I have some interesting news to tell you."

Lisa walked slowly up to the house, wishing the children hadn't already disappeared inside. She had a feeling that whatever reason had brought Silvia and her aunt to the house was not going to be to her liking. Still, she dutifully kissed her aunt on the cheek. "Hello, Aunt Carmela. How are you?"

The elderly woman studied her in silence. Lisa tried to stare back without feeling intimidated, but Aunt Carmela, with her black hair, black eyes and long pointed nose, had always reminded her of the wicked witch in the *Wizard of Oz*.

"Carmela," Silvia encouraged. "Tell Lisa your news."

Carmela hesitated. Then she pointed to the tree at the side of the yard. A small bird hopped along one branch as if called forth by some secret call. A robin. Another damn robin.

"I know, the birds are back," Lisa said. "But that has nothing to do with anything." She took a deep breath. "I'm getting married in less than a month, Aunt Carmela. You have to accept that. So do you, Mother," she added pointedly.

Carmela shook her head, her hand shaky as she reached up to stroke the crystal she wore around her neck. "You came home. You should not have done that if you wished to marry someone else."

"I came home because my friend needed a break."

Carmela's eyes appeared even more troubled. "Your friend. Margaret. She—she is confused."

Lisa felt a tingle run down her spine in spite of her disbelief in Carmela's predictions. "What do you mean?"

"She is embarking on a journey—"

"She's coming back this afternoon."

"No. She will not be back for awhile. And she may not come back alone."

"Who? What?" Lisa shook her head. She couldn't believe she was getting sucked into her great-aunt's mystical world. "Never mind. I don't want to know. I'm sure Maggie will come home as soon as she can."

"I'm not sure if she will even make the celebration," Carmela continued.

"What celebration?" Lisa asked suspiciously, trying to catch her mother's gaze, but her mother seemed more interested in plucking a piece of lint off her skirt.

Carmela leaned heavily on the cane that had been her constant companion for more than thirty years. Lisa was never quite sure if she really needed it to walk, or if she used it more as a prop. But it would have been disrespectful to do anything but put a hand out to steady Carmela as she adjusted her weight.

"*La dia de muertos*—the celebration of the dead," Carmela said finally.

"That's in November."

"No, we have a special day for Robin, the anniversary of her death. Next Sunday, it will be eight years."

"No, absolutely not." Lisa was horrified by the thought of celebrating her baby's death. She knew all about *la dia de muertos*. She'd celebrated the holy day many times with her mother and her aunt, but it had never meant anything to her. She had never known the people who had died. This would be different. This would hurt.

"It is necessary to honor those who have gone before us. You have missed the other celebrations, but you are here now. You will stay." Carmela's voice allowed no argument.

Lisa looked at her mother, finding at least compassion in Silvia's eyes. "I can't."

"We just talk about her, Lisa, about who she was—" Silvia began.

"Who she was?" Lisa asked incredulously. "She wasn't anybody. She died before she had a chance to be anything. What on earth is there to talk about?"

"Her smile. The sounds she made. What made her happy.

The little things. Then we talk about our family, about those who have also passed on, who are with her now. It can be very comforting. I know when my grandmother died, I found it to be a lovely tribute.''

All Lisa could think about was the pain the memories would bring. And what was the point? It wouldn't change anything. She simply couldn't do it. ''I won't be here next Sunday. I have to go back to work as soon as Maggie returns.''

''Don't you think it's odd that Maggie called you this weekend, so close to the anniversary of Robin's death?'' Silvia asked.

''It's a coincidence.''

''And the robins have come back to San Diego this weekend,'' Silvia added.

''Another coincidence. It is spring.''

''Open your eyes, *mija*, before it is too late,'' Carmela said.

''It's already too late. It has been for a long time.''

Silvia pursed her lips. ''You are so stubborn. But come, let us go inside. Carmela and I will cook for you and the children and for Nick. He will be back, *si?*''

''I don't know what his plans are.''

Silvia smiled. ''He can be as stubborn as you.''

''We must talk about the celebration,'' Carmela added, ignoring Lisa's previous statement.

''Maybe later. I have to get some—some milk,'' Lisa said. ''Since you're both here, maybe you could watch the kids for awhile.'' She turned to her mother. ''Can I borrow your car? Mine doesn't seem to be working.''

''Because you are not meant to leave,'' Carmela said quietly.

''Because it has a dead battery,'' Lisa corrected. ''I don't believe what you believe. Please, try to understand that.''

Carmela shrugged. ''Because you don't believe does not make it false.''

Silvia pressed her car keys into Lisa's hand. ''Take as long

as you need. We'll watch the children for you.'' She turned
to her aunt. ''Come, Carmela. It's getting chilly out here.''

Lisa hurried to her mother's car and slipped into the
driver's seat. It wasn't until she opened her hand to insert
the key that she saw the piece of paper tucked into her
palm—the address her mother had given her earlier, wrapped
around yet another key.

Raymond drove through the busy streets of Westwood, a
trendy shopping area near the UCLA campus and high-priced
neighborhoods of Bel Air, Beverly Hills and Pacific Pali-
sades. It was a gorgeous Sunday afternoon, with not a trace
of fog or L.A. smog. Unfortunately, he wasn't in the mood
to enjoy the weather.

Beverly was trying to seduce Monty Friedman and his
million dollar account right out from under him. Raymond
could not allow that to happen, which was why he was
spending the afternoon looking for a parking spot instead of
relaxing.

One of his account executives had just called him from
Duke's, a popular sports bar, to inform him that Beverly was
having lunch with Monty Friedman, and they were planning
to watch the basketball play-offs on the big-screen television.

Raymond knew Monty was a sports nut. He just hadn't
acted on it. Trust Beverly to find the man's passion and milk
it for all it was worth, which might be a lot in this case. He
could not lose Monty Friedman's account to Beverly, and it
wasn't just because of the money. His pride and his reputation were also at stake. He'd already lost one smaller account
to Beverly earlier in the year. He couldn't afford another to
go her way, not if he didn't want to make his other clients
nervous.

The industry magazines would be announcing the competition for Nature Brand in Monday's issue. He'd already
been interviewed by one reporter who had somehow dug up
information on every account they had ever lost. The reporter
had speculated that Raymond had lost his touch. Raymond
had tried to be patient and calm, to act unconcerned, but deep

down he felt stressed and edgy, nervous about the ground that seemed to be slipping beneath his feet.

He wished again that Elisabeth had not chosen this particular time to go away. He needed her at his side, and dammit if she shouldn't be there. Her loyalty should be to him, not some friend she hadn't seen since high school.

He sighed as he finally located a parking spot and managed to pull in before anyone else could steal it from him. Then he picked up his cellular phone and punched in the number Elisabeth had given him.

After two rings, a woman answered the phone. *"Hola."*

"Hello. This is Raymond Curtis. Is Elisabeth there?"

"Hello, Raymond. This is Silvia. I'm sorry, but Elisabeth is out. Can I take a message?"

"Actually, I was wondering what time to expect her back in town. I thought she might have left by now."

"I'm afraid not. Maggie isn't home yet. I'll have Lisa call you."

Although Silvia was outwardly pleasant, Raymond didn't sense he had a supporter in Elisabeth's mother. He didn't know why she'd taken such a dislike to him. Maybe the age gap, he decided. "Do you know when her friend will be back?" Raymond asked, determined not to let Silvia off the phone without getting more information.

"I really couldn't say." She paused. "I don't think Maggie will be returning until tomorrow at the earliest."

"Tomorrow?" Raymond's gut tightened, and he felt a surge of anger. "This is ridiculous. Elisabeth and I are working on a big account. I need her here."

Silvia didn't say anything, and Raymond realized he was not helping his case. "And of course, the wedding's coming up in just a few weeks," he added. "I'm sure Elisabeth has told you all about it." Raymond hated the silence that followed his words. Something was wrong; he could feel it. "You will be coming to the wedding, won't you?"

"Of course, I love my daughter."

Now why did that sound like an accusation? "So do I."

"Good. You shouldn't marry someone unless you love them."

"That's true." He cleared his throat. "Uh, by the way, Elisabeth showed me the bracelet you sent her to wear on her wedding day—something old, she said, something you'd always treasured."

Silvia laughed, but it sounded more sad than happy. "Is that what she told you?"

"It's not true?"

"The bracelet never belonged to me, Raymond. It's Lisa's."

His stomach turned over. Why would Elisabeth have a bracelet with a pair of baby shoes on it? But he couldn't ask Silvia. He couldn't let on that he seemed to know less and less about Elisabeth each second that passed. She'd only been gone two days, but it felt like longer.

"I have to go." He decided to save his questions for Elisabeth. "Please have Elisabeth call me as soon as she can. Tell her she can reach me on the cell phone. She has the number."

"I'll tell her."

Raymond hung up the phone, disturbed by their conversation. He told himself it was silly to worry about a bracelet. It was nothing. Lisa hadn't been eager to wear it. In fact, she'd looked at it like she hated it. Silvia was just trying to make trouble. But Raymond didn't have time to worry about her right now. He had another troublemaker to deal with—Beverly.

Duke's was crowded, both the restaurant and the bar area. After ascertaining that Beverly and Monty were not in the restaurant, Raymond walked into the bar. The basketball game was in full swing on the big screen, and the bar was crowded.

"Can I get you a drink?" a waitress asked him.

"I'll take a Corona, thanks."

"No problem."

He scanned the crowded room, hoping that Monty was in

fact there, as his source had led him to believe. The people in the bar suddenly went crazy as a basket was sunk from midcourt, and the Lakers went up by two points. Raymond jostled for position as high fives were exchanged. Finally, he spotted Monty and Beverly seated on the far side. He was in luck—there was an empty chair behind them.

"Monty, hello." Raymond tapped Monty on the shoulder.

Monty didn't look any more surprised to see him than Beverly did.

"I figured you'd be along once you realized I was here with Beverly," Monty said with a laugh as he shook Raymond's hand.

"We saw Paul in the restaurant," Beverly added, referring to the senior account executive who had called Raymond. "Small world, isn't it?"

"It seems to be getting smaller every day. I hope you'll give me as many chances to make my pitch," Raymond said to Monty. "I don't usually disturb my clients on the weekend, but if you have some time later, I'd be happy to sit down with you, and—"

"Sorry, Ray," Monty said with an apologetic but amused smile. "Early bird gets the worm."

"How about tomorrow morning, breakfast, as early as you like?"

"Now that would be fine." Monty checked his watch. "I have to be going. I have a tennis match at four." He extended his hand to Beverly. "Thank you for lunch. I'll look forward to hearing more of those ideas. I certainly do appreciate the personal attention."

"That's what I specialize in," Beverly said. "My firm is small so that we can meet every client's needs, whatever those needs may be."

Raymond rolled his eyes at her blatant sexual invitation. Is that how she was beating him? By sleeping with her clients? He wouldn't put it past her.

"Raymond, I'll meet you at seven-thirty at Alana's restaurant on Wilshire," Monty said. "Do you know it?"

"Yes. I'll be there."

"Bring Elisabeth along. I'd like to meet her."

"Uh—I can't. Elisabeth is still in San Diego."

Monty raised an eyebrow. "Perhaps you should consider bringing in another account executive."

"That won't be necessary. She's already working on the campaign. In fact, she faxed me some ideas earlier today," he ad-libbed. "I'll share them with you tomorrow."

"Good enough." Monty offered Beverly a casual salute, then left.

Raymond sat down in Monty's chair and glared at Beverly. "Do you really think you have the capability to seduce the man out of a million dollars? Do you believe you're that good?"

Beverly smiled, her bright red lipstick emphasizing her generous mouth. "I am that good, Raymond." She paused, letting her words sink in. "But contrary to what you might think, I don't have to sleep with clients to get business. They come for a lot of other reasons, one of which is my brilliant mind."

"You're an egomaniac."

"Thank you, I consider that high praise, coming from you, the man who invented the word."

"What are you talking about?"

"Oh, come on, Raymond. Look in the mirror. Actually, I probably don't have to tell you to do that. You're a man who takes great pride in his appearance. Your clothes cost a fortune. Your body is honed to perfection. Even your hair is the perfect shade of brown with not a hint of gray. And let's examine the rest of your life. Take Elisabeth, for example, a beautiful, much younger woman, who strokes your ego by making people believe that you must be incredible in bed to attract a woman like her."

"I am incredible," Raymond retorted.

"See, I told you. We're a perfect match. And frankly, if we were working together, Monty would have forked over money right now. He likes my fresh ideas, my personal attention, but he loves your reputation as the best, your showmanship. He'd really **like** to have both of us. But of course, he can only have one.''

Raymond knew she was right. He'd had the same feeling himself during his initial pitch with Monty. Every question, every doubt Monty had directed toward his own company had been a strength of Beverly's firm. But he could give Monty what Beverly could. He'd just have to make an effort to do so.

Beverly took a sip of her wine, and they sat for a few moments, watching the game, the revelers, the endless beer commercials. Finally Beverly turned to him. ''Shit. I hate basketball. I can't believe I'm still sitting here.''

Raymond couldn't help but laugh. ''Did you tell Monty that?''

''Of course not. I told him I was a huge fan of Shaq, whoever that is.''

''You have no scruples.''

''Not one,'' Beverly agreed, as she threw back her head and laughed.

Raymond was once again caught by the light in her eyes, the energy in her being, the long, lovely profile of her slender neck, her generous breasts heaving softly against her lace blouse. He felt his body respond in a very familiar way. Unfortunately, there was nothing he could do about it.

Beverly stopped laughing, her expression turning more serious as she saw the look in his eyes. He knew that he was revealing more than just a little of his desire, so he looked away, focusing again on a game that meant nothing to him.

Beverly put her hand on his knee, and he almost jumped out of his pants. They were sitting in a crowded room of strangers, yet there was an intimacy between them, as if they were on an island in a sea of bodies, of voices, of shouts that couldn't touch them.

Her hand moved up his thigh, and he turned hard. Jesus! What the hell was the matter with him? He was acting like an eighteen-year-old boy.

''Maybe we should go somewhere else, somewhere quieter, and have a drink,'' Beverly suggested.

He looked into her beautiful eyes and felt like he was drowning. "I don't think so."

"We could call a truce, a cease-fire, just have a drink like a man and a woman with nothing better to do on a Sunday afternoon."

He smiled at her choice of words, at the deliberate play of innocence in her voice. "Looking for information, Beverly? Or something more personal?"

"Maybe I'm looking for you. The real you. The one you keep hidden."

He knew he should toss out a joke, make a sarcastic comment, hurt her in some verbal punch-out sort of way. But tough-as-nails Beverly suddenly seemed vulnerable. In fact, she stood up and walked away from him before he could think of anything to say.

He got to his feet and followed her out to the street, knowing that if he had any sense he would have stayed put.

Beverly didn't say a word to him as she handed her ticket to the valet and waited for her car.

"So, where are you going?" he asked finally.

"Home, I guess. How about you?"

"Home. Yeah, I might as well go home." He looked around the crowded street. It was a beautiful day, and lots of people were taking advantage of the sunshine. Suddenly, the last place he wanted to be was home, where he'd be alone with his thoughts, with his desires. "I still owe you a dress," he said suddenly.

She nodded. "That's right, you do—a very expensive dress."

"There are some stores around here. Maybe we should," he shrugged, "go buy you one."

"You mean you want to buy it for me, not just pay for it?"

"Same difference."

"I don't think so."

She stared at him, and he stared back. She had such an interesting, complicated face. In fact, there always seemed to be two conflicting emotions running through her eyes, two meanings behind every word. He didn't know what the hell she really wanted. For that matter, he didn't know what he wanted.

"All right. Let's go buy me a dress." She turned to the valet. "I won't need my car after all." She handed him a ten dollar bill. Take care of it for me, won't you?"

The young man gave her a broad smile. "You bet I will."

"God, do you have to flirt with every man you meet?" Raymond asked with annoyance.

"It's a gift, and I feel we should use all of our God-given gifts."

He was already regretting this idea. Still, maybe he could use the time to his advantage, find out what she and Monty had been talking about. That was it, he rationalized. He was simply taking advantage of an opportunity to get the upper hand, to cajole her into thinking he was her friend, not her enemy.

"Where do you want to go?" he asked.

"Let just start walking and see where we end up."

Raymond looked down the street. "There's not much more on this block except a few shops and a motel."

"Like I said, let's see where we end up."

"It won't be in that motel."

"Goodness, Raymond, I wasn't even thinking about the motel. Were you?" She didn't wait for an answer. "Imagine that, and you an engaged man and all."

"That's right, I'm engaged, and don't you forget it."

"Honey, I don't think it's me you have to worry about forgetting."

~❧ *Chapter 13*

L isa stared at the address on the sign. She checked the number. It was the same as the one on the slip of paper her mother had given her. On the other side of the chain-link fence was a series of low buildings, each with a number. The sign over one building read STORAGE.

Storage? Lisa suddenly had a sinking feeling in the pit of her stomach. Did she really want to know what was behind Number 134? Part of her wanted to run, another part of her wanted to know what was behind that door. When a car pulled up behind her and honked impatiently, she knew she had no choice but to pull inside. She drove down the rows until she found her number. Then she stopped the car and sat there for a long moment.

She'd told Nick to get rid of their things. She'd seen nothing at his house. Was it here? Was it all here? The furniture, the memories? Oh God! What if the crib was inside? Had he kept the crib? The stuffed animals?

Her heart began to race. Her palms turned sweaty against the steering wheel. She tried to breathe, to think rationally. Nick wouldn't have kept all those things. Not for all these years. She had to see. She knew she couldn't leave without opening up the door and looking inside.

It took her a few moments of awkward fumbling to get out of the car and insert the key into the padlock. Finally, the door swung open. At first everything was dark. She could only make out shapes and shadows that looked like monsters—big, scary monsters from her past that wanted to suck her into the darkness and slam the door behind her, shadowy monsters that would take her back to a place where she no longer wished to be and hold her prisoner there.

Frantically, Lisa searched for a switch on the wall. Upon finding it, she flooded the room with welcome light. Actually, the light wasn't much, just a dim bulb hanging from a wire, but it was better than the darkness, and with the sunlight coming in from the street, she could see the furniture more clearly.

It took her only a moment to realize it was all there, the crib, the changing table, the high chair, the stroller, the pink and white lacy curtains that she'd painstakingly sewed, feeling she wouldn't be the perfect new mother if she didn't personally make the nest in which her baby would sleep.

Lisa picked up one of the matching pillows, running the lace through her trembling fingers. The white had faded to yellow, and the pillow was covered in dust. It was no good to anyone anymore, she thought with a deep sense of sadness. She traced the heart with her finger. She could almost feel the needle pricking her skin as she stitched the seam in a clumsy, awkward fashion.

Nick had laughed at her. He'd found her bent over the sewing machine at one o'clock in the morning, tired, cranky and nine months pregnant. She'd spent an hour trying to thread the ancient machine only to have the thread snap midway down the material.

When Nick had come into the room and smiled with amusement, she'd picked up the box of threads and thrown it at his head. That had made him laugh even more. A reluctant smile crossed her lips as she thought about that night, the way he'd teased her out of her bad mood with affection and love.

Tears pressed behind her eyes as the memories washed over her. She blinked them back, then set the pillow down in the crib. She walked over to the corner, where she found the jewelry box Nick had made for her their first Christmas together. She opened the lid and smiled at the photo that was taped inside. She couldn't have been more than nineteen when she and Nick had cozied up in the photo booth on the San Diego Pier and paid five dollars to have a silly photograph taken.

She ran her finger over their faces, tracing his long hair, his goofy smile, his beautiful eyes. Life had been so simple then, so full of promises and hope for the future. They'd actually believed they could have it all—love, passion, great careers, a family, a home—everything.

Only it had ended in this, furniture and memories crammed into a square cement box. She glanced around the room one more time, her gaze catching on the musical mobile with Donald and Micky and all the gang. She picked it up and let the wires dangle in the shadowy sunlight.

The pain came sharply and swiftly. Suddenly all the furniture seemed to come to life. The mobile danced in the breeze. The pink lamp in the corner sparkled, refreshed by the burst of sunlight. Lisa could almost see the cradle rocking.

And out of the silence came the sound of a baby, a sweet, sweet baby, suckling at her breast, cooing at the music from her father's guitar. Lisa could see Robin smiling, her eyes so big and blue and filled with wonder. She could feel the baby's hand twisting around her finger, feel the warmth of baby's breath against her cheek.

Then the shadows came back. The sighs of joy turned into crying, angry, relentless crying. The baby would not be comforted. Something was wrong. She didn't like her own mother. She just kept crying and crying and crying until Lisa thought she would go crazy.

"Stop it," Lisa yelled into the darkness. "Stop crying. Please. I love you," she whispered, her heart breaking. "Don't you understand that I love you, that I would do anything for you if only I could make you happy?"

There was nothing but silence, an infinity of silence. The empty cradle said it all.

*   *   *

Nick ran a cloth along the side of the crib he had just finished making, polishing his signature carving with the special oil he used to protect the wood. He felt better in the back room of his store, working with the wood. Everything was simple here, uncomplicated by emotions, by Lisa. He sat back on his heels and stared at the crib.

He couldn't believe how much had changed in two short days. The woman he'd spent the last eight years hating had walked back into his life and changed everything, not that she'd wanted to.

No, Lisa hadn't meant to distract him, to make him shift his focus from his growing business to her. She'd tried everything she could to get him to leave her, to make him remember all the bad times instead of all the good.

It would have been easy to do that if the old Lisa hadn't unexpectedly shown up. The woman he'd seen five years ago had been dressed to the nines in a business suit so cold and sharp that she looked more like a bed of nails than a soft, loving woman. That brief glimpse had reinforced his opinion that the Lisa he'd loved, the woman he'd married and lived with and hoped to die with, had already died, or at least disappeared.

But she was back. Watching her with Maggie's kids, with that scruffy mutt of a dog, with her crazy mother and today with him, at the beach, he'd been taken back in time. He could still see her at the beach, pulling the hair out of her eyes, looking down in horror at the seaweed winding around her ankles.

Nick smiled at the thought. She had been so angry with him, but so alive, the woman he remembered, the woman he'd loved. He'd wanted to kiss her earlier, to strip the wet clothes off her body and make love to her right there on the sand, in front of God and his witnesses.

She'd never have done it. She hated him. No, she didn't, he realized. Maybe she had at one time, but no more. Of course, just because she didn't hate him didn't mean she cared about him either.

"Nick, goddammit, where are you?" Lisa shouted.

Nick's jaw dropped as he glanced at the partly open door that separated the storeroom from the showroom. Lisa was here? He'd never told her where he worked, for good reason. Lisa had no idea what he did for a living, and as he glanced down at the robin, he knew she wasn't going to like it. Maybe that's why she was angry. Because she was definitely angry.

He listened as his store clerk tried to reason with her.

"Excuse me, ma'am, is there a problem?" the clerk asked.

"There sure as hell is. Where is he?"

"Uh, uh," the clerk stumbled. "Can I tell him who you are?"

Nick smiled as his trustworthy employee tried to protect him from what she thought was an irate customer.

"Oh, he knows who I am all right," Lisa said. "Is he in the back?"

"You can't go in there—"

Lisa flung open the door to the back room and stalked inside. Her hair fell wildly about her shoulders, and she looked mad as hell, even more angry than she'd been after he'd tossed her in the water.

"How dare you!" she yelled at him.

"Mr. Maddux. Do you want me to call the police?" his clerk asked, hovering anxiously in the background.

"It's okay. I can handle her," he replied, slowly rising to his feet.

"Handle me?" she retorted, her blue eyes blazing. "Don't even think of handling me. I am so angry with you, I could hit you."

In fact, she did hit him, punching him in the arm, not once, but twice, then again, harder and harder, until Nick had to grab her hands and hold her away from him.

"What is wrong with you?" he demanded, as she tried desperately to free her hands. "Hey, that hurts."

"You deserve pain, lots and lots of pain."

"Okay, okay," he said, trying to placate her. "You want to tell me why?"

"You kept everything. How could you do that to me?

ONE TRUE LOVE

169

How could you let me walk in there without knowing what to expect?''

Nick let go of her hands, suddenly realizing what her anger was all about. The storage unit. Damn.

''It was all there. Everything. Her crib. Her bassinet. The mobile.'' Lisa's voice broke as an unwelcome sob slipped past her defenses. She blinked back angry tears. ''I hate you, Nick. I hate you.'' She brought her fist up to hit him again, but this time Nick stepped aside, and, before she could react, he kissed her.

He could have slapped her, but kissing her seemed a better choice, especially when all that anger and tension turned into passion, when she stopped trying to shove him away and instead wound her arms around his neck, when her mouth began to move beneath his, when her breasts pressed against his chest, when he smelled everything about her that was her—Lisa, his lover, his wife, his friend.

He buried his tongue in her mouth, wanting a piece of her, needing to get past her defenses, to find her, the real her, the woman who'd disappeared so many years ago.

''Lisa,'' he murmured against her mouth when they finally came up for air.

''Nick.'' She lifted her head and stared back at him with tearful, searching eyes. ''Why? Why did you keep her things?''

''I thought you might want them some day.''

''You should have told me. That day, at the house, when her room was empty, you never said . . .''

''I couldn't stand to look at them either. I couldn't have stayed in the house with the room set up for Robin, waiting for her, for you. But I couldn't throw her things away. It didn't seem right.''

''She's gone. She's really gone.'' Lisa took a deep breath. ''I've known that for a long time, but when I saw that empty crib, I really felt it here, in my heart.'' She put her hand to her chest. ''And I missed her,'' she said, swallowing back another sob as her eyes began to water yet again. ''I didn't want to miss her. I didn't want to hear the sound of her little voice cooing, laughing, crying. When I touched her diaper bag in the storage shed, I felt like I was touching her. Remember, how her diaper used to feel beneath her sleeper, all crinkly and soft.'' She sniffed. ''I don't want to do this. Why am I doing this?''

Nick's gut clenched at the wistful longing in her voice, the hunger that he felt reflected in her voice. ''I miss her, too, Lisa. You know what I remember, the way Robin used to squeal when we put her in that little bathtub. She loved the water. She didn't care if it got in her eyes or anything. Did you see her rubber ducky in the shed? I couldn't bring myself to throw it away. She loved it so much.''

''Oh, Nick. Why can't you just learn to throw things away?''

''I believe just about everything can be salvaged, if you try hard enough.'' He paused, knowing his remark had hit home by the way Lisa looked down at her shoes. ''How did you find out about the storage unit?''

''My mother. She gave me the key and the address.''

''Then how come you didn't go home and hit her?''

Lisa reluctantly smiled. ''I don't know. Habit, I guess. You kept some of my things, too, the jewelry box you gave me, the rocker, the birdbath. You should have at least sent me a bill for the storage.''

''If I'd done that, you would have destroyed everything.''

''I could do that now.''

''Do you want to?''

''I don't know.'' She took a step back, and he pushed his hands into his pockets. For the first time since storming into the room, she looked around. He saw her eyes widen again in surprise, and her hand began to tremble as she reached out to touch the crib he'd just finished. ''This—this is what you make?'' she asked, her blue eyes reflecting more shock.

''Yes. I make handcrafted baby furniture, cribs, cradles, rockers, dressers.''

Her eyes darkened with horror just as he had expected. ''Oh, my God. I thought you were normal, that I was the crazy one. But you—you're sick. You're obsessed with her. You're—''

"Stop it," he yelled.

"Stop what? Someone has to say it out loud. Do your customers know that your own baby died in a crib just like that one? Do you think they'd buy this furniture if they knew?"

Nick felt a wave of deep, stunning anger. "How dare you imply there's something wrong with these cribs? This is not a sick obsession; it's a business, and a good one."

"Based on our daughter." She peered down at the robin in the corner, then put a hand to her mouth. "You even use the bird!"

"The name of the business is Robin Wood Designs," he said ruthlessly. "It's all about Robin, our daughter, the one whose name you can't even say out loud."

"I have to sit," Lisa said, weaving slightly.

Nick pushed her down on top of a crate. She rested her head in her hands as if that would stop the dizziness, the madness. After a long moment of silence, Nick knelt in front of her. He put his arms around her and pulled her against his chest. She didn't resist, so he just held her for long, silent minutes, his chin resting on top of her head.

Finally he spoke. "I needed to make something that would last, Lisa, something that would be here when I'm gone. For a long time, after you left, a couple of years I'm ashamed to say, I didn't even know what time it was, what day it was. I got so wasted I lost my job. Then I met an old guy who made furniture, and for the first time in a long time, I actually thought about something besides you, besides Robin."

She lifted her head and looked at him. When she didn't say anything, he continued, knowing that he had to make her understand, that he couldn't let her go back to L.A. thinking he was crazy or worse—abusing their daughter's memory in some twisted way.

"Carving the wood was like therapy, I guess. It felt good to be working with my hands again, to be making something beautiful. It took some of the ugliness out of my life. I stopped drinking, and I started working again. At first I just made rocking chairs. Then one day I made a cradle, then another. It seemed like every time I made a piece of baby furniture, I got a piece of my life back.''

''I don't understand,'' she whispered.

''I know you don't. Because in order to survive, you had to leave, you had to forget. The only way I could survive was to face the memories head-on every day, to think about her, to remember her. Otherwise, I felt like she would have died for nothing. Robin was here on this earth for two months. She was inside you for much longer.'' He stroked her face with his fingers, feeling her soft skin beneath his calluses. ''She was in us always.''

''Oh, Nick.'' Lisa took a shaky breath. ''I don't want to cry.''

''She was beautiful, Lisa. Robin looked just like you. Her blue eyes, her dark hair. Remember her tiny hands, her long fingers?''

''Stop, please.''

''She used to watch you when you left the room. And when she woke up, and she saw you, her smile was so damned bright, it lit up the whole room.''

''Except for once . . .'' Lisa's voice broke as the tears gathered in her eyes and one slid down her cheek. ''She didn't wake up, Nick. She didn't smile at me. And it was my fault. I wasn't good enough. I didn't do the right thing. I—''

''Sh-sh.'' He put a finger against her lips as the tears streamed down her face. ''You did everything right. She just died, Lisa. It wasn't anybody's fault.''

''She was in the crib, and it was too big for her, and she should have been in the cradle, but we wanted her to be in her own room, because we were so tired at night, and it was so difficult to sleep, hearing her breathe and rustle around in the blankets, and that's why we moved her.'' Lisa sobbed the last few words.

Nick tucked her hair behind her ear, feeling his own emotions threatening to spill out. He couldn't stand the look on her face, the pain in her voice, but he knew she had to get it out, that they finally had to face it.

"The crib had nothing to do with it. The doctors all said that."

"But how can anyone die for no reason?" she asked, crying in earnest now. "How can a little innocent baby die without anyone knowing why? *It's not fair*. It's not right. Why did this have to happen?"

"I don't know, honey. All I know is that we loved her as much as any parent could love their child. We didn't kill her with lack of attention, or too many blankets, or put her in the wrong position. We didn't."

"It could have been that. She was on her stomach."

"She loved to sleep that way. She hated being on her back, remember?"

"Now they say that might be bad for babies."

"*Now* they say," he repeated softly. "We didn't know it was the wrong thing to do. We still don't."

His voice was gentle, kind. Lisa felt it cover her like a warm blanket. Looking into his eyes now, she couldn't remember why it had been so difficult to trust him before. "That was always the hardest part, the not knowing," she said. "I wanted a reason, Nick, a logical explanation, and no one could give me one."

"I felt the same way."

"Having Robin was the best thing that ever happened to me. Losing her was the worst."

He looked at her for a long minute. "I think having you was the best thing that ever happened to me and losing you was the worst."

She touched his cheek. "I didn't mean it like that. I didn't mean that you were any less the love of my life than Robin."

"Was I? The love of your life?"

"You know you were."

"I wasn't sure you did." He smiled and grabbed a napkin off his desk so he could dry the tears from her cheeks. "I think these tears were long overdue."

"You always knew how to make me cry," she said, her wry smile taking the sting out of her words.

"Among other things."

As his eyes darkened, Lisa realized she was still attracted to him, so attracted it took her breath away. It seemed like only yesterday when they had been together, when kissing him was as natural as breathing air.

"Lisa?" he murmured. "I want to kiss you again."

Her body tightened in anticipation, and she couldn't deny that she wanted him to do just that. "We seem to be pretty good at this love/hate thing. A minute ago, you were screaming at me, now you want to kiss me."

"A minute ago, you wanted to tear me apart, but now I think you'd like to kiss me back," Nick replied.

"We're both crazy."

"At last, something we can agree on."

Lisa smiled, and Nick lowered his head. His mouth had barely touched her lips when she heard the door opening and the sound of a woman's voice.

"Nick. Are you here?"

Lisa pulled away, surprised and embarrassed by the unexpected appearance of a beautiful redhead in the doorway.

Nick turned his head. "Suzanne."

Suzanne looked shocked as her gaze moved from Nick to Lisa. "I'm sorry. I didn't mean to interrupt. Who—"

"This is Lisa," Nick said. "My ex-wife."

"Your ex-wife? First a sister, now an ex-wife? Next, I suppose you're going to tell me you have a kid?"

Chapter 14

"If you'd told me three days ago, I'd be on a plane to San Francisco with a handsome stranger, I never would have believed you," Maggie said to Jeremy as their plane began its descent into the San Francisco Bay Area.

"The mysteries of life are infinitely frustrating for those of us who try to make sense of them," Jeremy said with a smile.

"You have such a way with words. I can see why you're a writer. What kind of screenplays do you write?"

"Mysteries. Thrillers. Psychological horror."

She nodded, somewhat dismayed by the enthusiasm in his voice. Although they'd talked forever last night and Jeremy had shared a bit of his history, he was still a stranger. And she was still neurotic enough to imagine that he could turn out to be a charming serial killer.

"I've become obsessed with obsession." Jeremy's eyes darkened along with his topic.

Maggie licked her lips. "What—what kind of obsession?"

"Oh, lots of things, like what makes a man become obsessed with a woman so that he can't think of letting her out of his sight, letting her talk to other people, see friends, go out by herself."

Maggie felt her pulse begin to race. "What did you come up with?"

"I think it's about control. A man like that has to control everything and everyone. He can't stand the thought of someone who is supposed to be loyal to him having anyone else in her life.'' He paused. "It's an interesting subject, don't you think?"

"It's kind of frightening, especially for a woman.''

"Would you let a man do that to you? Would you cut your ties with friends and family for him, so that everything you did, said or thought about involved him?"

"No, never. That isn't love.''

"What if he's a great guy otherwise? I'm not talking about someone who abuses his wife, just controls her. What if he buys you pretty things and tells you you're beautiful and says he adores you and can't bear to share you with anyone? What if he's incredible in bed, and you'd do just about anything if it meant another night of great sex?"

Maggie nervously waved a hand in front of her face. "It's hot in here, don't you think?"

Jeremy grinned. "I'm scaring you, aren't I? I'm not talking about me, and that was a hypothetical you.''

"I knew that.''

"You are so gullible, Margaret Mary Scott.''

Maggie sighed at the sound of her real name on his lips. She had had no choice but to tell him who she was. She'd needed ID to check in at the airport, and she certainly didn't have a driver's license with the name Crystal on it. She'd been rather sorry to see Crystal go. Crystal had had a lot more fun than Maggie usually did. Of course, the way Jeremy was looking at her now told her he had some fun still in mind for Margaret Mary Scott. If she dared.

"I'm not all that into control," he added. "In fact, sometimes it's more fun to let a woman take charge.'' He touched her thigh with his hand, causing a shiver to run down her spine. "After all, I'm the one following you at this very moment.''

"And why exactly are you following me?"

Jeremy took her hand and squeezed it. "I'm intrigued.''

"And that's why you're on a plane to San Francisco with a woman who lied to you about her own name? A woman who thinks her dead husband might still be alive?"

"Hell yes. I haven't read a story this good in years, and I haven't written one lately, either."

"You think this is a good story?" Maggie asked, not sure if she should be offended, shocked or pleased. It wasn't a story to her—it was her life.

"I think it's a great story. But I have to admit that I'm here not just because I can't wait to see how this turns out. I like you. I'm attracted to you. I'm hoping that at some point you might return those feelings."

"I already do," she said candidly. "But I've never had a casual affair. I wouldn't know how. And with the possibility of Keith still being alive, I need to focus on finding Serena and figuring out the truth."

"I know that." He smiled again as he patted her leg. "Relax, Maggie. I came along for the ride, because to tell you the truth, I haven't been able to write in a month. I'm stale, burned out, blocked, whatever you want to call it, and when I found you standing outside Serena's condo yesterday, I felt like I'd just been hit by a blast of fresh air. I figure a trip to San Francisco with a mysterious woman is just the ticket to get my creative juices flowing again."

"Well, I hope I can be of help."

Jeremy reached out and touched the corner of her mouth, and the teasing light in his eyes faded into something more serious.

"What—what are you doing?" she asked.

"You had a pretzel crumb," he replied in his deep, mesmerizing voice.

"Oh." She held still while he brushed the corner of her mouth with his finger. "Is it gone?"

"I don't know. Let me check." He kissed her first on the corner of her mouth, then trailed his lips across hers in a sensuous, tantalizing manner that made her want so much more.

He stopped as an announcement came over the P.A.

"Ladies and gentlemen, the captain has asked that you fasten your seat belts," the flight attendant said.

Maggie couldn't help but smile. "Boy, they got that right."

He grinned back at her. "I don't bother you, do I?"

"Not a bit. I'm cool as a cucumber." Maggie fastened her seat belt, then looked out the window, trying to catch her breath, to slow her pulse. Jeremy seemed able to turn her on without even trying. She wasn't used to even thinking about sex. After having been married for so long, she'd pretty much gotten over being attracted to a man every time she sat down next to one.

Today, she felt eighteen again, letting the timbre of Jeremy's voice draw shivers down her spine, letting the touch of his hand on her thigh turn her stomach inside out, letting the scent of his aftershave direct the course of her breathing. This was foolish, crazy.

She'd slept with Keith for years without feeling a rush simply because his body was close to hers. She'd felt comforted, yes, and when they'd made love, she'd felt excited, eager. But when it was over, her mind had moved on to the laundry, and the bills, and the kids' schedules.

Now, she could barely remember her kids' names or why she had gotten on this plane in the first place. She kept thinking about Jeremy, with his long hair, his sexy body, his sensuous voice. She wondered what it would be like to sleep with a stranger, to make love with someone new, to run her hands down a body that was unfamiliar, to have him do things to her she had only imagined.

Good heavens! What was she thinking? She glanced over at him and caught him watching her. "You're staring at me."

"I can't help it. Don't you like looking at me?"

"Yes. No. I think I'm out of my league here. I told you, it's been awhile since I've gone anywhere with a single attractive male and been . . ." she sighed, "single myself. I wonder if I'll ever get used to that idea."

"You will."

"Have you ever been married, Jeremy?"

He shook his head. "I've managed to escape so far."

"You make it sound terrible. What about children?"

"I never saw myself as a white picket fence kind of guy. And I've never had much to do with kids. I was an only child." He shrugged. "I don't know. I guess I never thought much about it. I never met the right woman." He tilted his head as he studied her. "You know, someone who made me want to drop everything and run away with her."

Maggie's heart stopped. "If that's a line, it's a really good one."

He laughed. "You don't have much self-confidence. I wonder why that is." His smile faded. "Tell me about your husband."

"Keith? Why—what do you want to know?"

"Did he love you as much as you loved him?"

"I thought so."

"How long were you together?"

"It seemed like forever."

"Do you really think he would have had an affair with someone like Serena?"

"I'm not sure." She looked into his eyes. "I haven't met Serena yet. From what you told me, from what they said in the gym, she's very beautiful, sexy, fun. I'm sure that must be appealing to a man."

"You're all those things."

"Maybe I wasn't with Keith," Maggie said softly, knowing in her heart of hearts that that was one of the things she needed to find out. Had she driven Keith to an affair because she hadn't been good enough—because she'd let her figure go, her hair, her nails? Had she let him down? Had he been disappointed in her? She had so many questions. She just hoped Serena could answer them.

The plane landed and braked to a stop.

"We're here," Jeremy said. "Are you ready?"

"Yes. Where should we go first?"

"Serena usually stays at the Crestmoor Hotel when she's in San Francisco. She likes all that old rich class."

"Then let's go there."

Jeremy stood up as the passengers began to disembark.

Within a few moments they were standing in the middle of the terminal. As they walked toward the exit, Maggie saw a bank of phones.

"I need to make a call," she said. "Do you mind?"

"Go ahead."

Maggie walked over to one of the phones and used her credit card to call home. As she waited for someone to answer, she glanced over at Jeremy. He was watching her again, a small smile on his lips. She would have turned away, but his look made her feel so desirable, so sexy that she hated to let the feeling go.

"Hello?"

Maggie started at the sound of a voice, feeling suddenly guilty as she touched base with her reality, the one she really lived in, not this fantasy world where she was falling in love with a handsome stranger. Not falling in love, she corrected immediately, feeling a touch of panic at the thought.

"Is anyone there?" a voice asked.

"Silvia? Is something wrong? Why are you there? Where is Lisa?"

"She's with Nick, and everything is fine," Silvia replied. "Roxy and Dylan took Sally for a walk, and Mary Bea is playing in the bath."

"So everyone is okay? Mary Bea isn't missing me terribly?"

"She's having a good time getting to know her Aunt Lisa, and Nick is great with her. They don't seem to mind me either."

"They adore you, Silvia."

"How are you, Maggie?"

"I'm—fine," she said simply. "When do you think Lisa will be back? Goodness, did you say she was with Nick?"

Silvia gave a little laugh. "Yes. Isn't it wonderful? I hope you're getting lots of rest, Maggie, darling. In fact, it might be good if Lisa had a reason to stay a while longer."

"Silvia, are you matchmaking?"

"With my stubborn daughter and your equally stubborn brother? You bet. But they don't listen to me. I'm just glad they have this opportunity to see if there's any love left.''

"It's ironic, really. I could have asked Lisa to come down before, but I never wanted to push her.''

"Everything in its own time, dear. Now, when did you say you'd be back?''

"Tomorrow. I'll call again later.'' Maggie paused as an airport announcement rang through the terminal, making it impossible for her to hear. Finally, it ended.

"Maggie, are you at the airport?'' Silvia asked.

"Yes.''

"Should I ask why?''

"No, please don't. I have to go. Tell the kids I love them, and I miss them, and give each one a big kiss.''

"I will. I hope you find what you're searching for, Maggie.''

Maggie looked over at Jeremy's long, lean body and had a feeling she'd found at least part of what she was looking for.

An hour later, Maggie and Jeremy stood in line to register at the Crestmoor Hotel. In a few minutes, it would be their turn, and they would have to get two rooms—or maybe one. Maggie snuck a peek at Jeremy, wondering what he was thinking, wondering what she should do. Should she insist on her own room or take a chance and have a wild fling with a sexy stranger? She had a feeling Jeremy knew how to treat a woman.

But goodness, she'd only known him for two days. He could be into all kinds of kinky things. He might want to tie her to the bed or use handcuffs or . . . actually, she felt a little excited at the thought, then guilty, then stupid.

This was not some fantasy. This was the real world. Men didn't drive women to ecstasy with their lovemaking. It just didn't happen. That was for movies or books where women wore silk underwear that was constantly being ripped from their bodies and men knew how to titillate every part of a female's body with their hands and their mouth, and . . . oh, dear, her cheeks were turning red. She could feel the heat.

Thankfully, Jeremy was studying the line in front of them, instead of her. He had no idea how unsophisticated she was. She'd been married for almost thirteen years and had made love literally hundreds of times, but always and only with one man. There hadn't been anyone before Keith and no one after.

She had no idea if what they did was what everyone did. She had no clue if she was good, bad or indifferent in bed. She and Keith had certainly never ripped off each other's clothes. But the sex had been nice. She'd enjoyed touching him. He'd enjoyed touching her. Was there more? Was she brave enough to find out?

Maybe Jeremy was the perfect candidate for a one-night stand. They lived in different cities. They wouldn't run into each other again. If it was a total disaster, she'd never have to see him again. If it was the best ever—well, she'd probably still never see him again, because if she knew anything at all, she knew that she was capable of handing him the biggest turnoff in the world—three children.

And that was another thing. How could she hide the stretch marks, the not-so-flat tummy? She wasn't a model or an actress, the kind of woman he usually dated. What if he was disappointed? She didn't think she could take his disappointment. It would be safer not to risk it.

"Maggie."

She turned her head to find him watching her again, and her resolve melted away under the warmth of his eyes. He was so handsome, so appealing. And he kept touching her in little ways, a hand under her arm, against the small of her back. Even now, he brushed a piece of hair away from her eyes. He was so attentive. She could imagine him loving her in just that way.

"Jeremy," she said huskily.

"Don't be scared."

"It's hard not to be."

"You don't have to do anything you don't want to do."

"That's the problem. I'm not exactly sure what I want to do."

Jeremy stiffened, then turned his head, craning his neck to look at someone or something.

"What is it?" she asked.

"That woman who just came off the elevator. Where did she go?"

"Who? Did you see Serena?"

"I don't know. It looked like her."

The clerk motioned for them to move forward. Maggie hesitated. "Should we go after her?"

"It might have been her," Jeremy said. "But she was heading for the exit."

"Let's go then." Maggie dashed toward the front door, with Jeremy following close behind. When they moved through the revolving doors to the pavement, they saw a man and a woman getting into a cab.

Maggie stopped dead in her tracks. There was something about the man, the cut of his suit, his hair color.

"That's her, Maggie, come on. They're leaving."

She put a hand over her mouth, shaking her head in denial.

"What? What is it?" Jeremy asked impatiently.

"I think that man was my husband."

Her ex-husband had a girlfriend, Lisa realized, feeling a twinge of bitterness as she drove back to Maggie's house. Suzanne's shocked face was still imprinted in her mind. Not to mention her glorious red hair and incredible figure. She could have been a model. Heck, maybe she was a model.

Lisa drummed the steering wheel as she stopped at a red light. Damn Nick anyway. He'd made such a big deal about her getting married again, when he was dating someone himself. He'd probably been with dozens of women since she'd left. He'd always enjoyed sex.

Her stomach knotted at the thought of Nick with someone else. She'd been able to keep that picture out of her mind for a long time, but now that she'd met Suzanne it was impossible not to think of Nick with another woman. Especially since he'd kissed her only minutes before Suzanne had walked in the door. He had kissed her with hunger and desire and longing, as if he'd missed her, as if he still cared.

And for a moment she'd cared, too. Far too much. She was getting married, she reminded herself, trying to focus on Raymond's face, his smile, his eyes. It was hopeless, though. All she could see was Nick and Suzanne.

She wondered if they were sleeping together. Of course they were. They were both adults, both single, both free. After all, she'd slept with Raymond. But that was different. Raymond made love like a gentleman. He didn't embarrass her or tease her or make her feel like he was trying to see into her soul, get into her thoughts and her heart as well as her body—the way Nick had always done.

With a sigh, Lisa stopped her mother's car in front of Maggie's house, knowing she had to pull herself together before she went inside. The day had brought so many surprises, the storage room, the baby furniture, kissing Nick and still feeling something, and Suzanne—how could she forget Suzanne? Lisa leaned her head against the steering wheel and closed her eyes.

She saw Nick walking over to Suzanne, putting his arm around her shoulders, explaining who Lisa was. But why didn't Suzanne know? Hadn't Nick told her about his marriage? Obviously he hadn't. He also hadn't mentioned Robin. And at Suzanne's question, he'd simply replied that he didn't have a child.

How could he deny having a child?

She was the one who denied it. He was the one who confronted it every day of his life, by building cribs for babies.

For some reason, the thought that he hadn't told Suzanne anything about his past cheered her. It made her feel that their relationship was still private, still special.

Shaking her head, Lisa opened her eyes and got out of the car. Why on earth did she want to think of their relationship as special? It was over. She was moving on.

Lisa walked into the house, said hello to Dylan and Mary Bea, who were watching television, then ventured into the kitchen knowing she'd find her mother and great-aunt there.

Silvia stood at the stove, stirring something in a pot. Carmela sat at the kitchen table, studying the flame of the candle in front of her. They both looked up when she walked into the room.

"Are you happy now?" Lisa asked, setting the key to the storage unit on the counter.

"I thought you should know," Silvia said.

"Why?"

"Because you're insisting on getting married to a man you don't love."

"You barely know Raymond. You have no idea how I feel about him."

Silvia continued to stir without commenting, which irritated Lisa even more. "You know, I don't see how you are such a judge of men," Lisa said pointedly, feeling like a child when her mother looked at her through disappointed eyes.

"Are we back to your father?"

"No, let's just forget the whole thing."

Silvia shook her head. "You brought it up. Why don't we finish it once and for all?"

Lisa crossed her arms and leaned against the counter. "Okay."

Silvia set down her spoon. "I fell passionately in love with your father on our first date. He was different from the boys I'd grown up with. He wasn't serious or macho or passionate. He was like a summer breeze, warm, teasing, fun, full of blarney." She smiled at Lisa. "He was a boy, though, not a man, and when I told him I was pregnant, he became terrified. Being a husband and a father was not in his plans. And his parents . . ." Her face tightened. "His parents wanted so much more for him than me."

"So he left."

"No, he married me to give you a name."

"Which you didn't allow me to take."

"Because I didn't want him for that," Silvia said proudly.

"Then he left."

"The day after you were born," Silvia admitted.

"He hated me."

"He loved you."

"Oh, right. And you think I'm in denial? You're the one who can't see the truth."

"He couldn't be a father, Lisa, but he wasn't a bad person."

"You always want to see the best in people. Why can't you see the best in Raymond? The man has a successful business, owns a lovely home, and is mature, caring and kind. Why do you think our marriage is a mistake?"

"Because he's so much older than you, and because you don't love him."

"The age difference doesn't matter," Lisa said, grabbing on to the one point she could confidently argue.

"It wouldn't, of course, if you did love him, and if you were honest with him. I don't believe Raymond knows you at all. When you're with him, you're not Lisa, you're Elisabeth, this woman you've created who is nothing," Silvia said, waving her hand in the air. "You've become a shadow of yourself, no opinions, no joy, no tears. You've turned your back on everything that you were and everything that you could become to be this man's wife."

"This isn't getting us anywhere," Lisa said, hating the fact that her mother's words had a ring of truth to them.

"You're so afraid of living, you've simply stopped. You might as well be dead."

Lisa stared at her mother in shock. "How can you say that?"

"I say it because I love you, because I've spent almost eight years waiting for you to wake up. I can't wait anymore. Someone has to shake you out of this stupor you've placed yourself in. I want you to be happy, the way you were with Nick."

"You want me to be with Nick," Lisa argued. "But that isn't possible, and it doesn't have anything to do with me. Nick has a girlfriend. He's involved with someone else."

Silvia looked taken aback. "He never said anything."

"He probably didn't feel he needed your permission. You see, we're divorced. We're finished." Lisa grabbed the bag of trash sitting by the door in a desperate move to end the conversation. "I'm taking this outside."

She opened the kitchen door and walked out onto the back deck. As she turned to go down the stairs to the walkway where Maggie kept the trash cans, she heard a rustle and saw a clash of color. She stopped abruptly, dropping the bag on the ground. "Who's there?"

Lisa stepped forward and took a better look. She saw what looked to be two people embracing, and her jaw dropped open. "Roxy, is that you?"

Roxy and the boy jumped apart. "Aunt Lisa. Hi." She straightened her shirt. "What—what are you doing out here?"

"Obviously not what you're doing out here."

"Uh. Well." Roxy looked at the boy, then at Lisa. "I— we were trying that French kissing thing that you and Uncle Nick were doing. I just wondered what it felt like."

"Roxy, get in the house."

"But Aunt Lisa—"

"Go, now, please." Lisa turned to tell the boy to leave, but he was already hopping over the side fence.

"I thought you were cool," Roxy protested as they reached the back door. "You're acting just like Mom."

"Good heavens. How much makeup did you put on?" Lisa asked, getting her first glimpse of Roxy's face in the light.

"Just a little lipstick and blush."

"You used more blush than I'd use to paint my house."

"I look prettier this way and older."

"Which is exactly why you're going to wash your face," Lisa said pointedly. "You're too young to be wearing that much makeup. In fact, I don't even wear that much makeup. And you should definitely not be sneaking out of the house to kiss boys."

"I'm thirteen," Roxy said defiantly. "Girls my age can get pregnant."

"God help us," Lisa said. "Kissing the way you were kissing is not a game, Roxy. It should only be done between two people who care about each other, who are committed to a relationship.''

''But you kissed Nick that way this morning, and you're marrying someone else.''

Lisa was shocked into silence as she tried to figure out how to answer that statement. The screen door opened, and Silvia stepped out on the porch.

''You kissed Nick?'' Silvia asked, obviously eavesdropping.

''She did,'' Roxy said. ''And it was a long one.''

''It was not,'' Lisa protested, feeling as if she were the guilty one.

''They had their mouths open,'' Roxy added.

Lisa sent her niece a dark look, now feeling like she was the one in trouble.

''I thought you were finished with each other,'' Silvia commented. ''Done, over, divorced. Isn't that what you said?''

''This isn't about me. It's about Roxy. You are not to go out of this house again until your mother comes home, or unless I'm with you,'' Lisa said firmly. ''Understood?''

''Fine. But when is Mom coming home? I thought she was supposed to be back by now.''

''She called,'' Silvia said. ''She said she'd probably see you tomorrow or the next day.''

''The next day?'' Lisa asked. ''I have to go back to work. Did she say where she was? Did she leave a number?''

''No, she was rather vague.'' Silvia turned to Roxy. ''Why don't you wash your hands? We're about ready to eat.''

''Okay.'' Roxy hesitated at the door, her face losing its bravado for one vulnerable moment. ''Do you think Mom's all right, Aunt Lisa?''

''She's fine. She just needs a break. When she comes back, she'll be rested and full of energy and more than capable of keeping you out of trouble.''

Roxy smiled and entered the house, leaving Lisa alone with her mother.

''Don't even start with me about kissing Nick.''

Silvia smiled knowingly. "I wouldn't dream of asking you about such a personal matter. Listen, when Maggie called she was at the airport. I don't think she's coming home any time soon."

"The airport. I can't believe this." Lisa shook her head in bewilderment. "Has the whole world gone mad?"

"Sometimes it seems that way, doesn't it? Oh, and Raymond called. He wants you to phone him as soon as possible."

Lisa sighed, feeling exhausted. "I can't do this, Mom. I just can't do it all."

Silvia put her arms around Lisa and pulled her close, the way she'd done when Lisa was a child. Lisa returned the hug. She loved her mother, even though they rarely agreed on anything else.

"I'm sorry," Lisa murmured. "I know you're trying to help, that you want what's best for me."

"I do," Silvia said as they broke apart. "You're my baby. I know you've always felt a little lost without a father. Sometimes I thought about marrying someone else just so you could have a dad. But I couldn't do it. I believed that marriage was sacred, and I still do."

"Your marriage didn't last a year, Mother. And you were left with a baby. I hardly think anyone would have minded if you'd found someone else."

"I would have minded. I took a vow. I kept it."

"The man didn't love you. Why should you deny yourself the chance to be happy with someone else?"

"I loved him, and regardless of his feelings for me, my love was true. It was sacred. I believe in one man, one woman, Lisa. That's why I believe in you and Nick."

"Mom." Lisa shook her head, feeling Silvia's powerful words stir her emotions, knowing she was nowhere near as strong as her mother. "Even if I don't marry Raymond, I can't be with Nick. You know he would want children. He would believe that somehow we could re-create what we had lost, that we could end up happily ever after. How could I go through that again? I couldn't survive a second time."

''Who's to say you wouldn't end up happily ever after? That you couldn't have another child?''

''Me, I guess.''

Silvia stared at her for a long moment, her eyes kind but sad. ''Do you still love him, Lisa? Just tell me that, one time, the absolute truth.''

''Does she still love who?'' Nick asked, as he walked out of the house.

Chapter 15

"Raymond," Lisa said swiftly. "She wants to know if I love the man I'm going to marry, and of course the answer is yes. By the way, your girlfriend is lovely. How long have you been together?"

Nick's smile didn't reach his eyes. "Long enough. She is pretty, isn't she?" He looked her straight in the eye. "And loyal, too."

Lisa swallowed hard. "She sounds perfect. What does she do for a living, save the world?"

"Not quite. Suzanne owns a retail store that specializes in clothing for infants and toddlers. It's very successful."

Lisa's body tightened with sudden, unreasonable tension. "Babies! That's just great. Is she part of your 'face your fear' strategy? Maybe you should just have another baby and attack it head-on. Maybe two or three, to fill up all those cribs in your storeroom."

"Maybe I should," he said through tight lips. "I haven't ruled it out. I'm not afraid of trying again."

"No, you're just—you're just—" Oh, good grief, she couldn't even think of what he was. She just knew she hated the idea of Nick and another baby—and another woman. It seemed unthinkable.

"I'm just what, Lisa? Living in the real world? Some of us do that, you know."

"So, are you serious about her?"

"Maybe." Nick crossed his arms in front of his chest. "What's it to you?"

Lisa glanced over at her mother, suddenly aware that Silvia had heard their entire conversation.

"What is it to you, Lisa?" Silvia asked.

"It's nothing to me. I was just making conversation."

The screen door opened, and Roxy stuck her head out. "Grandma Silvia, the oven timer went off, and Aunt Carmela is chanting something weird over a candle."

"Oh, dear. I'll be right there." Silvia moved toward the door, then looked at Nick. "Carmela is very worried about the anniversary of Robin's death. Perhaps you can convince Lisa to stay, Nick. It would be nice to have both of you."

Lisa's jaw dropped open once again as Silvia left to tend to dinner. "You—you've done the celebration before?"

"Someone had to."

"You don't believe in those customs."

"Your mother and your great-aunt do, and they both loved Robin. I figured it couldn't hurt. Maggie came last year, and Roxy. We thought Dylan and Mary Bea were a little young to hear your great-aunt's stories, but I've taken them by the cemetery a few times, and we've put flowers on Robin's grave. She is their cousin, after all." Nick leaned against the side of the house. "Have you ever gone to the cemetery, Lisa?"

She hesitated for a long moment. "Yes."

"The violets. You left her the violets." He nodded as he smiled to himself. "I found them by the headstone, the day after Mary Bea was born. Did you talk to her, Lisa? Did you say her name out loud?"

His words came softly on the breeze, accompanied by the sound of the wind chimes hanging over the deck. Here in the shadowy darkness, it seemed easier to answer Nick's questions.

"I don't think she's interested in anything I have to say. I'm the one who let her down."

"I thought that was me."

"Maybe it was both of us."

"Or maybe she just died through no fault of ours. No, somehow you just can't accept that. You have to blame someone."

"This is pointless. I'm going inside to help my mother with dinner." Lisa tried to walk past him into the house, but he grabbed her arm.

"Not so fast. We have some unfinished business."

She looked at him in surprise. "I can't imagine what that is."

"This." Nick leaned over and covered her mouth with his, kissing her this time with a passion she found just as compelling as the tenderness he had exhibited earlier. In a way, it was easier to handle, because this kiss was more like a fight than a loving, and she knew how to fight with Nick. It was the love without the hate that she couldn't come to terms with.

Nick finally set her free, but the expression on his face still held her captive. "How can you kiss me like that—and marry someone else?"

How could she? Lisa felt an immediate wave of shame and guilt. "I never should have come here."

"That's not an answer."

Lisa threw her hands in the air. "I had everything figured out, Nick. I knew what I wanted. I *had* what I wanted. Now it's all messed up."

"My fault, I'm sure."

"Partly, yes." She hesitated. "I saw the way Suzanne looked at you. She wants you. And Raymond wants me. We're both moving on. That's the way it should be."

"What if I can't stop thinking about you? What if I call your name when I'm making love to Suzanne?"

Her stomach clenched as she remembered all the times Nick had cried her name, with passion, with joy, with lust, with tenderness. "Don't do this, Nick."

"Here's an idea. You and me—one night of passion, just to see if there's anything left."

"You can't be serious."

"Are you afraid?"

"Of course not." But she couldn't stop a shiver at the thought. Nor could she bring herself to look into his eyes.

Nick cupped her face with his hands, making her look at him. "One night, Lisa. Remember how you used to scream my name and tangle your hands in my hair when I kissed your breasts?"

She shook her head in denial.

"Remember that night when I started with your toes and worked my way up every gorgeous inch of your body?" Desire gleamed in his eyes. "You were so hot by the time we were through, I thought you'd set the bed on fire."

She shook her head again, not wanting to remember, even though she felt that same fire now, burning its way through her body.

"You were so willing to make love anywhere, on the kitchen table, the porch swing in front of our house at two o'clock in the morning, the living room couch."

"Now, that is not true," Lisa interrupted. "I only went along, because you persuaded me."

He laughed. "And you liked the persuasion. Admit it."

Lisa knew she was in danger of losing herself in his eyes, in his voice, in his arms. It had always been that way with him. From their first date she'd been swept off her feet. She hadn't come back to earth until the day of the funeral.

She pushed him away from her. "I am not interested in one night of anything with you, Nick. I'm engaged to be married to a great guy, and I certainly don't intend to cheat on him with my ex-husband."

Nick shrugged. "Whether you sleep with me now or not makes little difference. I still will have had you first."

"My God. You're arrogant."

"Thank you."

"That wasn't a compliment. And don't forget I had you first, too. At least, I was the first important one," she said defiantly. "That's what you always said."

"And I told the truth. I haven't forgotten anything, Lisa. Unlike you, I remember every detail of our life, but then I don't live in a country called Denial." He paused. "Tell me, are you and Raymond going to have children?''

She hesitated, knowing she was about to give him more ammunition, but she refused to lie or explain. "No."

"Why not?"

"I don't want more children."

"Because you're afraid. You can't take a risk. You're chicken."

"I'm not chicken. I'm a mature, sensible woman who does not need to risk losing her mind again over a baby. I've been there, and I've done that. If you're so hot on kids, why don't you marry Suzanne and have your own brood?"

"Maybe I will," he said loudly.

"I hope you do," she shouted back, storming past him to get into the kitchen.

Nick stopped her, determined to have the last line. "If this Raymond is the perfect guy for you, why haven't you sent out your wedding invitations?"

"I haven't had a chance, but I will."

"Second thoughts?"

"Not one. In fact, I'm going to call him right now and tell him how much I love him."

Beverly's foot moved up Raymond's leg, her toes caressing his calf, then his knee, then his thigh with a sensual purpose. Raymond stared at her across the small table in the dimly lit restaurant. He saw smoky shadows of desire in her eyes. He had a feeling the same emotion was reflected in his eyes.

In desperation, Raymond grabbed his glass of water and tried to dislodge her foot from his leg. Instead, he spilled the water halfway down his shirt and accomplished nothing more than making Beverly laugh.

"You're so nervous," she said. "Why?"

"It might have something to do with your foot on my crotch."

"You don't like it?"

"We're in a restaurant, for God's sake."

"So you do like it, just not the location."

Raymond took his hand and removed her foot from his thigh, forcing her to sit up straighter in her chair. "Thank you. Now, are you done? I think we should go." In fact, he should have left a long time ago. They'd shopped for several hours, until Beverly had selected the most expensive, sexiest dress she could find. Then they'd stopped in a restaurant for drinks and finally decided to have dinner. It was now almost nine o'clock at night, and he had yet to call a halt to things.

Being with Beverly was surprisingly enjoyable. They'd spent most of their time arguing about everything from politics to fashionable ties, but he'd found their conversation stimulating. Beverly had an opinion on everything. She also had a sharp wit and a way of looking at him that made him feel ten feet tall. Not that she didn't humble him on many occasions, like this one, when her sexuality threatened to overwhelm him.

"I guess we should go," Beverly agreed. "I hate driving home alone so late at night. I don't suppose I could convince you to follow me, just to make sure I get home safely."

Raymond hesitated. Beverly wasn't afraid of much. He had a feeling this plan had more to do with getting him to her home than anything else. Still, she was a woman alone, and L.A. could be dangerous at night.

"Sure. No problem. Tell me something, are you flirting with me because you think it will give you some sort of an edge over Monty Friedman, or because you're truly interested?"

Beverly smiled, that slow, knowing, self-satisfied smile that reminded him of a cat with a big bowl of cream. "I get to you, don't I?"

"Not at all. I don't know what your game is, but it won't work."

"Then why are we here together? In fact, why did you come looking for me?"

"I wasn't looking for you; I was looking for Monty."

"You knew we were together. Did you really think Monty would give me personal information? Something I could use to beat the pants off of you?'' Her eyes gleamed with delight. ''No pun intended.''

''Obviously you thought you could get something out of him.''

''I was just showing him a little personal attention. I'm very good at that.''

''I'm sure you think so.''

''I do. None of that explains why you're still here with me.'' She paused. ''I think you want me.''

Raymond laughed, shaking his head as if she'd just said the most outlandish thing in the world, instead of the closest thing to the truth. ''Don't be stupid.''

''Why are you so afraid of me?''

''I'm not.'' Raymond tossed his napkin on the table. ''This conversation is over.''

''Fine. The last thing I'd want to do is make you uncomfortable.''

''Sure.''

Beverly remained blessedly quiet as they paid their bill and left the restaurant. It took a few moments to collect their cars from various locations, but Raymond eventually found himself following Beverly's taillights down the freeway. She drove as fast as she did everything else, and it was a challenge just to keep up with her.

He couldn't remember being with a woman who tested him in so many ways. Not that he wanted to spend his life with that kind of woman. Elisabeth was more his type, with her quiet, calm demeanor, her willingness to adapt to his needs, his schedule. Maybe they didn't have a tremendous amount of passion in their relationship, but who the hell needed all the upset anyway? Beverly would drive a man crazy.

Not that it wouldn't be fun while it lasted. She was so bold, so daring. Raymond wondered if she'd be that way in bed—if her fresh mouth wouldn't take him places he'd never been before.

His body hardened, and he rolled down the window to let in some air. He had to stop thinking about her. He was marrying Elisabeth in four weeks. Elisabeth. Elisabeth. He ran her name through his mind like a mantra, trying to remember her face, her beautiful blue eyes, but then he saw the bracelet, the baby shoes.

What if Elisabeth wanted children? What if she changed her mind and got pregnant without asking him?

Of course, he could always have a vasectomy. He'd thought about it for years, but the procedure had never been palatable to him. He was afraid it would decrease his sex drive, make him less than he was, and he was already losing so much of everything else like hair and muscle tone that he hated to do something unnecessary.

He was probably just imagining things. Still, he remembered the softness in Elisabeth's voice when she'd told him about the children she was baby-sitting. He knew she would be a good mother. She had a nurturing instinct that couldn't be denied. That's why she volunteered for the children's organizations. Because she loved kids. Which left him wondering why she didn't want any. It suddenly seemed a contradiction in her character. Was she hiding something? Why had she told him the bracelet belonged to her mother, when it was hers? And why did she have a bracelet with baby shoes on it? Had it been given to her at birth?

Funny, until today he'd never thought Elisabeth capable of hiding anything. But then he'd never anticipated her taking off for San Diego on a moment's notice.

He straightened as Beverly exited the freeway. In a few minutes, she pulled into her parking space in front of a luxurious town house in the Hollywood Hills. He stopped his own car in the guest space and sat there for a moment, knowing that he should not get out of the car. He should not go inside. Absolutely not.

Beverly walked over to his car and tapped on the window until he rolled it down. "Did I mention that Monty Friedman's sister was featured in *Entertainment* magazine last week?"

"No," Raymond said warily. "Why would I care?"

"Well, she does talk about how she and Monty grew up,

what they believe in, some of their family values. I probably shouldn't even be telling you this, but you were so nice today and that dress is going to cost you a fortune, so if you're interested . . .''

"I'm interested. I'll pick one up at the store."

"Suit yourself. But they're probably gone by now. It was last week's issue. If you want to come inside for a minute, I'll find it for you."

Go inside? No way. He shook his head.

Beverly laughed. "What do you think I'm going to do? Attack you in the hallway? Strip off your clothes before you can say you have a headache? And you're not scared of me? That's a laugh."

"Fine," he said stiffly. "I'll come inside and get the article. Then I'm leaving."

"Of course you are."

Raymond followed her into the town house, standing awkwardly in the front hall, turning down her offer to take a seat or have a drink. Although, as he looked around, he had to admit that Beverly's home felt comfortable. Her living room was filled with overstuffed white chairs and sofas and silk flowers in decorative vases. She had a grand piano in one corner and a crystal collection in another, featuring delicate glass animals.

It was a grown-up living room, sophisticated, personal, yet nice, he thought with some surprise. For some reason he'd expected black leather and leopard prints, maybe even some tacky chandelier.

Raymond stiffened as a door opened. He was almost afraid to look up, terrified and excited by the thought that Beverly might be wearing a sexy black nightgown or nothing at all. What would he do then? He couldn't even let an answer form in his head.

"Here it is," Beverly said, handing him the magazine.

When he finally looked at her, he realized she was still wearing her dress, the one she'd had on all day.

"Is something wrong?" she asked, arching one finely penciled eyebrow.

"No. Thanks for the magazine."

She walked him to the door. "I had a nice time, Ray-mond," she said softly. "If we weren't enemies, I could almost think of you as a friend. But you don't want any more friends, do you?"

"I'm getting married."

"You could still change your mind."

"I don't want to. Elisabeth is—is—so nice," he finished lamely. He slammed the door on Beverly's sudden burst of laughter.

Later that night, Lisa checked on the kids. Roxy was sit-ting in bed, reading a teen magazine, which she quickly tossed on the floor when Lisa entered the room.

"I was just getting ready to turn off the light," Roxy said.

Lisa smiled. With Roxy's face cleanly washed, she looked like a girl again instead of a hooker. Lisa sat down on the bed. "It's pretty tough growing up, isn't it?"

Roxy pushed her hair behind her ear, somewhat self-consciously. "I wish I was prettier, like you."

"Me?" Lisa laughed as she sat down on the bed. "Good heavens, Roxy. When I was your age, I thought I was the ugliest thing alive."

"No way."

"Yes way. I had no confidence. I thought my family was nuts."

Roxy grinned. "Mine is, too."

"Your mother doesn't hold séances on the weekend."

"That's so cool, though."

"It wasn't to me. I was afraid people would find out, that they would think I was strange. I never brought anyone home from school. I never told anyone about my family. Some-times, I'd even lie and say my father was a travelling sales-man or in the marines, just so I wouldn't have to admit that he was gone."

Roxy's expression darkened as she plucked at the bed-spread with her fingers. "I miss my dad." She looked up at Lisa. "Why did he have to die? Why did it have to happen to me? Other kids have two parents. It's not fair."

"It sure isn't. My dad left when I was just a baby. I never even knew him."

"Why did he leave?"

Lisa thought about all the explanations she'd heard, including the most recent one provided by her mother. Deep down she knew there was really only one answer. "I guess he didn't love us enough to stay. But my father had a choice, Roxy. Your dad didn't. It was just his time. I think he's looking down on you from heaven right now. In fact, ever since I found you with that boy, I've heard your father's voice whispering in my ear to protect his beautiful daughter from all those eager boys."

"You're making that up."

"Maybe. Roxy, can we have a truce—until your mother comes back? No more sneaking out on me, okay?"

"Okay."

"Good. And in return, I'll show you how to wear makeup so you don't look like you're wearing it."

"What's the point of that?" Roxy asked.

"The point is making those boys think you're naturally beautiful, not a walking paint canvas."

"Oh."

Lisa kissed Roxy on the cheek in an impulsive, motherly gesture, then tucked the covers around her chin. "I'll tell you one other thing. You have lots and lots of time to do it all, Roxy. If you're in a rush to grow up, you might just miss some of the best things of being a kid."

"Like what?"

"Like everything, honey. You can be whatever you want to be. The sky is the limit. And believe it or not, boys usually prefer girls who have their own interests and goals. Because those girls have more to talk about than makeup and clothes. They're fun and interesting."

Roxy made a face. "I don't think I'll ever be popular. My nose is too big, and my legs are too skinny, and I'll never have boobs."

Lisa laughed. "Your mother has great breasts, Roxy, so I

think you'll do just fine. Besides that, you're funny and smart and a good person. That's really what counts.''

Roxy snuggled under the covers with a contented smile. ''Good night, Aunt Lisa.''

''Good night.'' Lisa got up and walked to the door.

''Aunt Lisa?''

''What, honey?''

''I'm glad you're here.''

Lisa smiled to herself. ''Yeah, me too.'' She turned off the light, closed the door behind her, then went into Dylan's room.

Dylan was already fast asleep, sprawled on top of the covers of a messy bed that was littered with sweatshirts and socks. She gently pushed the laundry to one side, then moved him slightly so she could pull the blanket over his bare legs.

''Mom?'' Dylan muttered sleepily, not even opening his eyes.

''It's okay. Go back to sleep,'' Lisa said, not bothering to tell him who she was.

''Love you, Mom,'' Dylan said as he turned on his side and fell back to sleep.

''I love you, too,'' she murmured, feeling a rush of emotion. How lucky Maggie was to have these beautiful children.

''Lisa?''

She turned and saw Nick standing in the doorway. Things had been tense between them all evening, and ever since Silvia and Carmela had gone home, they'd tried to stay out of each other's way.

She walked into the hall and closed Dylan's door before speaking to him. ''I'm tired, Nick. I don't want to argue with you. I don't want to sleep with you. In fact I don't even want to talk to you.''

''Then talk to Mary Bea,'' he said roughly. ''She has a stomachache.''

She turned, startled by his words. ''She was fine at dinner.''

''She's not now.''

Lisa walked across the hall and into Mary Bea's bedroom.

The little girl was curled into a fetal position. Lisa sat down on the edge of the bed and rubbed Mary Bea's shoulder. "What's wrong, honey?"

"My stomach hurts."

"Do you feel like you're going to throw up?"

"I don't know. Kind of."

Lisa put a hand on Mary Bea's forehead. "She feels a little warm. It was probably just something she ate," she said, trying not to worry. She wasn't sure she could deal with a sick child, not after what had happened to Robin. "A good night's sleep, and she'll be fine."

"I hope you're right. But—" Nick didn't finish. He didn't have to. She could fill in the rest as well as he could.

Chapter 16

Maggie finally crept out of bed just after seven o'clock in the morning. She felt uneasy. In fact, she felt downright spooked. She'd tossed and turned and sweated most of the night. Since seeing Keith with that woman, she hadn't been able to think of anything else.

They'd tried to follow the cab, but they had lost it in traffic. It would have been too easy to simply catch up with them and confront them.

Maggie walked to the window and pulled the curtain back. She could see downtown San Francisco from her vantage point—the Transamerica Pyramid, the Bank of America building, the Bay Bridge in the distance. She'd been to the city only once, just after she and Keith had first married. He'd loved the cable cars, the steep hills, the old Victorian houses.

Had he been planning his mad escape from their life even then?

She thought of all the little moments they'd spent together in the months before his death. While she'd been baking meat loaf, had he been thinking of sliding under the sheets with another woman? When he'd made love to her, had he been thinking of someone else? Of Serena?

Maggie felt like she was losing her mind. Nothing was the same anymore. The world had turned upside down, and she was still trying to find a way to get right side up.

Jeremy had tried to distract her last night by taking her

out to dinner at a lovely Chinese restaurant in Ghirardelli Square. She'd smiled and chatted, but she'd barely been able to concentrate on what he was saying. She was surprised he hadn't dumped her right then and there.

Instead he'd seen her back to the hotel and suggested they get separate rooms. She wondered if that was because he couldn't stomach the thought of making love to a woman whose husband had obviously strayed. After all, the logical correlation was that she hadn't been good enough for him.

No, she wouldn't do that. She wouldn't blame herself for everything. Keith could have said something. He could have told her he was unhappy. He could have asked for a divorce instead of killing himself in a fire, instead of making his wife and his children go through a funeral.

Maggie was suddenly so angry she wanted to kill him. But how could she kill a dead man?

She sat down on the edge of the bed, thinking about the money Keith had taken out of their savings account—money she could have used for the children, for the house, for all their bills. Of course, he had taken out more life insurance— guilt money, she decided, to appease his conscience for faking his death and hurting his children and his wife.

His wife. The title seemed so strange now. She'd thought she'd known everything about her husband, but she'd known nothing, certainly not that he had a body desirous of another woman or a mind devious enough to plot his own death.

And why kill himself? Why not just leave? People did that all the time. Then she thought about Keith's parents, their expectations, their strong family traditions. Scotts didn't get divorced. They stayed together, no matter what. Keith had been raised to believe in the institution of marriage, and he'd always been a good son. He'd done everything exactly as he was supposed to do, except he'd died far too young. That hadn't been in anyone's plan, except his, apparently.

A knock came at her door, and her stomach convulsed. She knew she wouldn't find Keith on the other side of that door; she'd find Jeremy. She wasn't sure what to do about him, either.

How could she think of having a sexual fling when she might be married? Who was she kidding? She wasn't married. Even if Keith wasn't dead, he was still out of her life. He'd made his decision. So who was she protecting? What promises was she supposed to keep?

Maggie got up and opened the door.

Jeremy stood before her, wearing beige slacks and a navy blue polo shirt. He looked clean and fresh, his hair still damp from a shower, his cheeks smoothly shaven. He smelled like heaven, and when he opened his arms to her, she could do nothing more than walk into his embrace.

"You worried all night," he said, brushing her hair with his lips. "I knew you would."

"I couldn't help it." She played with the button on his shirt. "I had a lot to think about." She stepped back so he could enter the room, then shut the door behind him.

"I think you're wrong," Jeremy said abruptly.

"What do you mean?"

"Your husband can't be alive. It doesn't make sense. I analyzed everything you told me. There was absolutely no reason for him to take such drastic steps to carry on an affair or to disappear. Unless there's something you've forgotten. You said he worked in a lab. But you never told me what caused the explosion or if there was foul play involved."

Jeremy sat down in a chair by the window, resting his arms on his knees as he waited for her to give him an explanation.

Maggie stared at him blankly for a moment, trying to follow everything he'd said. Foul play was the only thing that stuck in her head. But that didn't make sense either. "They said it was a chemical fire," she said slowly. "My husband often worked with toxic and flammable substances. They told me it looked like an experiment gone awry. No one ever suggested that someone had set the fire deliberately. Although, to tell you the truth, I didn't pay much attention."

"That's understandable. You were in shock."

Among other things, Maggie thought, remembering how upset the children had been. That's when Roxy had become boy-crazy, Mary Bea had started crying all the time and Dylan had taken to spending his day in front of a video game.

"Didn't anyone at the company give you any more information than that?" Jeremy asked.

"Not really. I don't know. Maybe they did. I can't remember. Keith's boss came up to me at the funeral and muttered something about it being a freakish accident, but I didn't know him well enough to really question him. You see, when Keith started working at that company, he changed. He became less talkative, more stressed. At his old company, I knew everyone, but at this place, I didn't even know the names of his coworkers. Everything was classified."

"Why?" Jeremy asked with interest.

"Because some of their work involved national security, chemical weapons, stuff like that. Although Keith didn't make weapons. He was a very peace-loving guy. He told me that his area of interest was in developing substances to protect our soldiers against the use of chemical weaponry." She sighed and flopped down on the bed. "At least that's what he said."

"Wow. Chemical weapons. The plot thickens."

Maggie shook her head at the enthusiasm in Jeremy's voice. "I wish you could have known him the way I did. You would have a lot more trouble believing the man was anything but a nine-to-five guy who never did anything remotely daring."

"Tell me more about the company. You said you didn't know anyone?"

"No, there were never any parties, not even at Christmas, and Keith travelled a lot. I'm not really sure what he did on the road. He was so vague about it. When I tried to ask, he'd just change the subject." And she hadn't tried that hard, because she'd had three kids to worry about. She'd never suspected anything odd about Keith's job or travel until now.

Jeremy stood up and began to pace around the room. "Okay, let's go over what we have. Keith takes a job at a new company that has something to do with national defense about a year and a half before the explosion.''

"Yes.''

"He doesn't introduce you to anyone. You're not welcome to visit or even hear about his experiments. He travels to other cities. You never call him. He always calls you. One night he goes into the lab after everyone has left. There is a mysterious explosion. Items of clothing and his briefcase are found at the site, but no body.''

"And some teeth," Maggie added.

"Right, the teeth. Cavities matching Keith's dental records.''

"Yes. Don't forget about the money. Eight thousand dollars withdrawn from our checking account the day before he died.''

Jeremy paused and looked at her. "I agree it's strange. But, Maggie, I don't know. Do you really believe the man faked his own death? It's so extreme. So dramatic. So final. He could have just left you.''

"I thought of that, too, but his parents would have hated him if he'd divorced me, especially because of the . . .'' She stopped, suddenly realizing she was about to mention her children. But why tell Jeremy about the kids? He'd probably lose interest in her and leave. Right now, feeling as crazed and anxious as she did, she couldn't stand the thought of him leaving. She needed him.

"Because of what?'' he prodded.

"They believed in marriage,'' she prevaricated. "They were very religious, and they wouldn't have approved if he'd divorced me.''

"They'd rather have him dead?''

"No, of course not,'' she said, twisting her wedding ring around her finger. "But maybe Keith preferred that alternative. They put a lot of pressure on him.''

"To do what?'' His eyes lit up with sudden understanding. "To have kids?''

"Well, uh—yes, as a matter of fact, his parents did pressure him to have children. That whole grandparent thing. They really wanted that.''

"And Keith didn't."

"He loved kids. But he was really devoted to his work." She rushed on before he could ask her any more questions about kids. "Anyway, maybe Keith just wanted to escape from me and his parents and all the other pressures in his life."

"Hell of a way to go."

Maggie stood up and stretched her tired, tense limbs, eager to change the subject. "I tried calling Serena's room earlier this morning. She didn't answer."

He met her gaze. "I know. I tried, too."

"And I asked for Keith, but he wasn't registered. So I guess we just have to wait. Or go home. Or give up."

Jeremy slid his arms around her waist. "Maybe we were meant to spend more time together. It's fate."

"I know you think I'm a nut," she said with a self-conscious smile.

"I think you're the most intriguing woman I've met in a long time."

She wasn't intriguing. She was a single mom with three kids and a dog, but she couldn't tell him that.

"Maggie. I know we've only known each other for two days, but it feels like longer. I want you to make me a promise."

"What kind of a promise?"

"That no matter what happens you won't disappear as soon as we find Serena or Keith."

Maggie hesitated. How could she promise that? They lived in different worlds. At least when she was living in reality, which wasn't in a hotel in San Francisco.

"You just say 'I promise,'" Jeremy prodded, worry creeping into his eyes.

"I know I won't ever forget you," she said. How could she forget the man who had brought her back to life? She placed her hands on his chest and kissed him softly on the lips, taking the initiative for the first time in a very long time.

Jeremy groaned as his mouth parted beneath hers. "I want you," he whispered.

Maggie pulled back, frightened and exhilarated. "Maybe we should—we could . . ." She glanced over at the bed, at the rumpled sheets, the soft pillows. She could see herself lying there, losing herself in Jeremy, forgetting about everything.

A knock came at the door, startling both of them.

"Saved by the knock," Jeremy said softly. "We could ignore it."

"No one knows I'm here," Maggie said, suddenly terrified. "Maybe it's Keith. Maybe it's Serena. Maybe they saw us."

"Relax. I ordered room service. You know, coffee," he added, when she didn't reply.

Jeremy strode over to the door and let the waiter in. By the time the waiter had set up the table and pocketed his tip, the mood was broken. Maggie wasn't sure if she felt grateful or annoyed. She took one last lingering look at the bed and knew deep down in her heart that she wasn't quite ready to take that step, at least not yet.

She busied herself by pouring two cups of coffee. "What do you take in it?"

"Nothing. Just black for me."

"I need a little sugar," she said, adding some sweetener to her cup.

He clicked his cup to hers. "To us."

"I've never made a toast with coffee before."

"I have a feeling you and I are going to do a lot of things you've never done before," Jeremy said, his gaze drifting over to the bed.

Maggie took a deep breath and slowly let it out. "Jeremy, I'm not ready."

"I know," he said swiftly. "But I still want you. And I think you want me, too."

"I'm scared," she said honestly. "I've never gone to bed with a handsome, sexy stranger."

"Maybe you should try it some time."

Maybe I will. Maggie took a sip of coffee and wished she had the courage to say the words out loud.

*   *   *

Lisa felt Nick's arm slide around her shoulders as she took the thermometer out of Mary Bea's mouth and smiled down at the bright-eyed, red-cheeked little girl who didn't seem to have enough energy to smile back. "Let's see how we're doing," she said cheerfully. "It's still one hundred," she muttered to Nick. "Not high enough to worry, according to the pediatrician's office."

"Not that that's going to stop you."

"Or you. Don't think I didn't notice that you spent the night with Mary Bea."

"I was tired of sleeping on the couch," he said gruffly.

"You're a softie. Admit it."

"Never."

"My stomach hurts," Mary Bea said, repeating a now familiar phrase.

Lisa sent Nick a helpless look, which he returned with one of his own. "You wouldn't think a case of indigestion would last this long, would you?"

"I don't know. Maybe the food is stuck somewhere."

"Thank you for your diagnosis, Dr. Maddux."

"I want Mommy," Mary Bea proclaimed.

Lisa frowned as she pushed Mary Bea's damp, sweaty hair off her forehead. "I know you do, honey, and I'll tell her you're not feeling well just as soon as she calls."

"Is anyone going to drive me to school?" Dylan asked from the doorway as he slung his backpack over his shoulder. "Hey, how come Mary Bea gets to stay home?"

"She's sick," Nick said.

"She's probably faking," Dylan replied.

"I am not," Mary Bea said hotly.

"Dylan, get in the car," Nick said. "And tell your other sister to hurry up."

"Like that will do anything."

Lisa grimaced as Dylan screamed for Roxy to get off her butt and get in the car.

"Well, at least she heard him," Nick said.

"Along with the rest of the neighborhood. Nick, you better check Roxy's face before you take her to school. I'd rather she didn't look like a hooker while we're baby-sitting.''

"Ah, kids. Aren't they great? Do you want me to get you anything while I'm out?''

"No, I think we're okay. We still have plenty of Tylenol. Maybe that will help her stomachache.'' Lisa stood up. "I'll be right back, Mary Bea. I'm going to get you some more medicine, all right?''

Mary Bea nodded, then closed her eyes against what looked like another wave of pain. It broke Lisa's heart to see her so uncomfortable, but she didn't know what else to do.

Nick followed her into the hall. "You okay?''

"I am. I'm not so sure about Mary Bea.'' She paused, noting the lines of concern under his tired eyes. "What if I do the wrong thing, Nick?''

"You won't.'' He stroked the side of her cheek. "Mary Bea is a healthy child with a simple case of the flu.''

"You're right. I just wish Maggie was here. Or that she'd at least call.''

"I don't get it,'' Nick said. "She's never gone off and left the kids like this. And why isn't she back by now?'' His eyes narrowed speculatively. "You know something, don't you?''

Lisa pushed him toward the stairs. "I'll tell you when you get back. The kids are waiting.''

"Now you've got me worried.''

"It's nothing, really. Don't worry.'' She smiled reassuringly when he looked unconvinced. "Maggie is just going through—''

"Uncle Nick, come on, we're going to be late,'' Dylan interrupted with a shout.

"I'll be back in ten minutes.''

"Nick, if you have to go to work, it's fine.'' Actually, it wasn't, but she was trying to act confident, hoping her act would turn into reality.

"I'll be back in ten minutes,'' he said, then jogged down the stairs.

Lisa felt relief at his words, but it vanished as Mary Bea stumbled out of her bedroom with panic in her eyes and a hand over her mouth. Lisa swept her into her arms and rushed to the bathroom, but Mary Bea threw up before they got there, all over Lisa's slippers, her bathrobe and the bathroom floor.

"I'm sorry," Mary Bea said, sobbing.

"It's okay." Lisa grabbed a towel and wiped Mary Bea's face, then set her down. "Do you feel better now?"

Mary Bea nodded but couldn't help a shiver as her bare feet touched the cool tiles of the bathroom floor.

Lisa gave her a commiserating smile. "How about a bath, honey? We can put in some bubbles."

"Okay."

Lisa reached over and turned on the tub. She added bubbles to the rushing water, then pulled Mary Bea's nightgown over her head. After getting Mary Bea into the tub, Lisa wiped the floor with a towel and a sponge and tossed her bathrobe and slippers into the growing pile of dirty laundry. "I'm going to throw these things in the washer," she said to Mary Bea as she turned off the water. "Will you be all right for a minute?"

Mary Bea nodded, her attention focused on the red fire engine boat floating in a pile of bubbles.

After convincing herself that Mary Bea couldn't possibly drown in the barely filled tub, at least not in the next two minutes, Lisa dashed down to the laundry room and threw everything in. Then she ran back upstairs, checked on Mary Bea and hurried into her own room to change into some jeans and a sweatshirt. She ran a brush through her hair, and went back into the bathroom.

Thankfully, Mary Bea looked a little better now. Lisa hoped it would last. She finished cleaning the bathroom with disinfectant while Mary Bea played with her boat. Then she knelt down on the floor next to the tub and swirled her hand in the water.

She'd pictured moments like this a thousand times, when she'd been pregnant with Robin, when she'd given Robin baths in the kitchen sink. The familiar ache settled into her heart, but it didn't feel as sharp as it used to feel.

"Do I have to wash my hair?" Mary Bea asked.

Lisa shook her head. "Not if you don't want to."

"I hate it when the soap gets in my eyes."

"So do I." Lisa tickled her under her chin, and Mary Bea giggled.

"What's so funny?" Nick asked, as he came through the doorway and surveyed the scene. He tried to make his voice sound light, but there was a catch in his throat at the sight of Lisa and Mary Bea, looking so much like mother and daughter.

Lisa was great with kids. He couldn't believe she was planning to live the rest of her life without ever having another baby. Not that he didn't understand why. He knew the fear of losing another child, the risk of taking another chance. But someday, he wanted to be a father again. He wanted to have moments like this that were his.

"She's just a giggly girl," Lisa said, tickling Mary Bea again.

"I threw up on Aunt Lisa," Mary Bea said proudly.

Nick smiled at Lisa. "I guess I made the right decision in taking Dylan and Roxy to school."

"I guess you did." Lisa pulled the plunger out of the tub. "Come on, honey, let's get you back into bed before your fingers begin to look like raisins." While the water drained from the tub, Lisa wrapped Mary Bea in a warm, fluffy towel.

"I'll take her to her room," Nick said, picking Mary Bea up. She threw her little arms around his neck and pressed her cheek against his face. He almost couldn't stand the poignancy of her simple touch. He looked up and saw Lisa watching him.

"You look good together," she said.

"It feels good. There's something about a child's hug that's better than anything else."

"Yeah," she said softly.

"I better get this munchkin dressed." He took Mary Bea

into her room before Lisa could say anything else, before she could see the moisture in his eyes. Lisa had always hated emotion, the vulnerability of tears, the nakedness of grief. Maybe that's why they'd never been able to really share the worst moment of their lives.

Nick sighed, then got back to the business at hand. He put Mary Bea in a long T-shirt and tucked her into bed with a pile of books and her favorite stuffed animals. Then he went downstairs, to find Lisa in the kitchen cleaning up the breakfast dishes.

Wearing old jeans and an oversize sweatshirt, Lisa was hardly a glamour girl. He should not have been attracted to her, but he was, which annoyed him. He had to stop wanting her. There was no point. She'd made it clear she was going back to L.A., to Raymond.

"So where is my sister?" Nick demanded.

Lisa looked at him in surprise. "What did I do?"

"Nothing."

"Then why are you snapping at me?"

"I asked a simple question."

"I don't know where Maggie is."

"You have an idea," he persisted. "Is there any coffee left? I could use some caffeine."

"Among other things," Lisa said, as she poured him a cup and handed it to him. "You used to be cheerful in the morning."

"You used to be my wife in the morning."

"What does that mean?" she asked in astonishment.

Hell, he had no idea what it meant or why he'd said it. Although it probably had something to do with the fact that he was dying to kiss her, maybe work his hands up under her sweatshirt and let his fingers curve around her breasts.

Lisa must have read his mind, because she caught her breath and turned around so her back was to him. She began washing the dishes, but her hands were shaky as she rinsed each plate and set it in the dishwasher.

"Sorry." Nick walked over and turned off the faucet. "I don't know where that came from."

Lisa took in a breath. "Just one look, and I forget everything."

"You do?"

"I'll admit that no one has ever gotten to me quite the way you do."

"Good."

She gave him a reluctant smile. "Why don't you go to work, so I can have some peace?"

"That's probably a good idea. But first tell me what you know about Maggie."

Lisa wiped her hands dry on a kitchen towel. "Maggie received a letter from a woman a few weeks ago. Actually, the letter was addressed to Keith. Maggie had never heard of the woman, and the note suggested there was a personal relationship between this woman and Keith."

"So what?"

"So, Maggie thinks Keith might have been having an affair."

"That's ridiculous. Keith wouldn't have cheated on Maggie," he said automatically.

"That's what I told her. But . . ."

"What else?"

"Keith took out extra life insurance two months before he died."

"Because he worried about the future. The guy planned out his life to the last detail. He left nothing to chance." Nick thought about the man who had been his brother-in-law for fourteen years. Never in all that time had Keith ever given Nick a reason to suspect he was anything but what he was—a nice guy.

"He also withdrew eight thousand dollars from their bank account the day before he died," Lisa added. "Maggie has no idea where the cash went."

Nick felt uneasy despite his faith in Keith. "Maybe it was lost in the fire."

"Yes, except why would Keith be walking around with eight thousand dollars in cash?"

Nick began to pace. Something wasn't right. No wonder

Maggie had begun to fall apart. "Why didn't Maggie tell me?"

"I think she deliberately forced herself to forget about the money and the insurance, but when the letter came, it stirred everything up. You should have seen her on Friday, Nick. She was beside herself. The house was a mess. The kids were running wild, and she was stricken with anxiety. I've never seen her like that."

Nick felt guilty that he hadn't noticed, that he'd been so preoccupied with the baby fair that he hadn't checked on Maggie in days.

"It's not your fault," Lisa said gently, reading his mind once again.

His gaze flew to hers. "You don't think so?"

She shook her head. "You love Maggie, and you'd do anything for her. But she's a grown woman now. She has to take care of herself. We all do."

"Family takes care of family," he corrected.

"You're right, but I don't think that Maggie is in trouble. She just needed to get away. I'm sure she'll come back happy and well-rested."

Nick started as the phone rang. "That better be her." He grabbed the receiver. "Hello."

"Nick?" Maggie's tentative voice sent a mix of relief and anger through him.

"Where the hell are you? Why did you just—"

"Is Lisa there?" she interrupted.

"Of course she's here. Where else would she be?"

"I'd like to talk to her," Maggie said with annoyance, which only made him more angry.

"Well, I'd like to talk to you. Where are you and when are you coming home?"

"I'll be home as soon as I can."

Nick ran a hand through his hair in frustration. "What does that mean? You make it sound like you have to do something. What on earth requires you to be away from your kids?"

"I have something to do, Nick," she said briskly, "something that could be very important for my children. How dare you imply that I'm letting them down? Lisa's there. You're there. I even spoke to Silvia yesterday. She told me everything was fine, that the kids were happy. Was she wrong?''

"That's not the point." He lowered his voice, trying to hold on to his temper, but sometimes his little sister drove him crazy. "Maggie, what are you doing?"

There was a long silence from her end. "I think Keith's alive, Nick."

Nick almost dropped the phone. "Excuse me?"

"I think he faked his death," she said with more energy in her voice than he'd heard in a long time. "It makes sense."

"No, it doesn't. Explain."

"It's a long story, Nick, but I have to find him. I can't come home until I do. I'm sorry if watching the kids is an imposition, but dammit, I've never asked anything of you or of Lisa. Surely one of you can help me out. I won't feel guilty about this. I just won't."

Nick couldn't focus on what she was saying. All he could hear were the words *I think Keith is alive*. "Maggie, are you out of your mind?" he asked, finally finding his voice. "Keith is not alive. He died almost a year ago."

"That's what he wanted everyone to think," she shouted.

"Come home, Maggie. We'll get you a shrink. We'll talk all this out."

"I am not crazy, and I am not coming home until I find Keith."

Before Nick could say another word, the dial tone rang in his ear. "She's nuts." He shook his head in bewilderment as he put the phone back on the hook. Keith was not alive.

"Nick, what's going on?" Lisa asked, her eyes worried.

"Maggie thinks her husband is alive, that it was all a big misunderstanding."

"Oh, dear. Did she say where she was? When she's coming home?"

"She said she isn't coming home until she finds Keith." Nick flopped down in a chair at the kitchen table.

Lisa crossed the room and sat next to him. "Nick, why didn't you tell her about Mary Bea?"

His head jerked up at her simple question. "Damn, I forgot. How could I forget? Oh, hell. She rattled me, Lisa. I wasn't thinking. I should have been thinking." He slammed the table with his fist and stood up. "I should have told her Mary Bea was sick. She would have come home then."

"It's okay."

"It's not okay," he yelled at her. He took a deep breath. "Shit. I'm sorry. I shouldn't be yelling at you. I'm the one. I screwed up."

Lisa got up and put a hand on his shoulder. "Nick, I think Mary Bea is better, and I'm sure Maggie will call back. She's called every day so far."

"You're right." He latched on to that thought like a drowning man clinging to the side of a lifeboat. "She'll call back. Then I'll be calm, and I'll tell her that Mary Bea needs her, and she has to come home."

"And you won't tell her she needs a shrink."

"Right." Nick looked into Lisa's eyes, and although he saw understanding, he still wished he hadn't messed up. There had to be a way to fix things. But how? "Wait a second. I can push that star button," he said, snapping his finger. "It will call Maggie back."

Before he could take a step toward the phone, it rang. They both dashed for it, but Nick grabbed it. "Maggie. Maggie, I'm sorry. Don't hang up."

"Uh, this is Raymond Curtis. I'm looking for Elisabeth Alvarez."

Nick felt another rush of anger. Not only was he reminded that Lisa had another man in her life, he'd also lost his only chance of getting Maggie back on the phone.

"For you," he said shortly, handing the phone to Lisa.

"Hello? Raymond. No, it's all right. We just thought you were someone else." Nick stormed out of the room, slamming the door behind him. Lisa was grateful he'd left. She preferred to speak to Raymond in private. "How are you?"

"Not so good. I had a breakfast meeting with Monty this

morning. I had Paul and Jeff work up some ideas for me, but Monty didn't like any of them. I need you on this, Elisabeth. What time will you be back today?''

Lisa took a deep breath, knowing Raymond would not like her answer. ''I don't think I'll be back today. Maybe not tomorrow either. My friend hasn't returned, and I can't leave the kids.''

''Elisabeth,'' Raymond said tensely, obviously trying to hang on to his patience. ''Forgive me if I'm not being sympathetic, but yesterday I spoke to your mother, and this morning a man answers the phone. It sounds like there are plenty of people down there who could take care of those kids.''

Lisa twisted the phone cord between her fingers. ''Maggie left them with me, Raymond. I made a promise.''

''You made a promise to me. By the way, did you mail our wedding invitations?''

Lisa hesitated, then lied. ''Yes, they're on their way.''

''Well, thank goodness for that.''

Lisa felt terribly guilty, but she would mail them, she told herself, as soon as she got off the phone.

''Elisabeth. I can't lose this account. You're going to have to find someone to relieve you.''

''What if I work up some ideas and fax them to you?''

Raymond didn't answer for a moment. ''All right. I did get more information today that might help you. I guess that's all I'm going to get, isn't it?''

''I'm sorry,'' she said, sincerely meaning it. ''I didn't know Maggie would disappear like this. But we have several weeks. We can get it done.''

''This isn't something we can throw together at the last minute. Believe me, Beverly Wickham is hot for this account. I'm not sure she isn't in the lead.''

''You've never been afraid of Beverly.''

''I've gotten to know her a little better.''

''Really?'' Lisa asked, hearing something in his voice that sounded odd. ''Why is that? I would think she would be the last person you'd be socializing with, especially in the middle of this contest.''

"She keeps turning up, like a bad penny," he replied. "Does your friend have a fax there? I want to get you this information before you start coming up with copy.''

"Mm-mm, let me check." Lisa put down the phone and walked to the door. She opened it and saw Nick lounging in front of the television in the adjoining family room. "Nick, do you know where I can find a fax?''

"There's one at my store," he said, without turning his head.

"Would you mind if Raymond sent me something?''

"Why would I mind?''

"What's the number?" Lisa asked, trying to ignore his bad mood.

She reached for a piece of paper on a side table and jotted down the number he gave her, then returned to the kitchen and relayed it to Raymond.

"Elisabeth, if you can do this as soon as possible," Raymond said, "it would really help. I want to make sure you and the art department are in sync.''

"I'll try to get you something by this afternoon.''

"All right.''

Lisa wasn't sure what else to say. Their conversation was so business-oriented, so edgy. She was going to marry this man in under a month, and he seemed like a stranger.

"I'll talk to you later," he said finally. "Good-bye.''

"Bye," she said softly, wondering why she hadn't told him she loved him, wondering why he hadn't said the same to her.

Chapter 17

L isa hid in the kitchen for the next thirty minutes, cleaning and straightening the shelves until she had absolutely nothing left to do. When she went into the family room, she found it empty. She had begun to think Nick had left when she heard the strains of his guitar coming from upstairs.

She followed the music to Mary Bea's room, where she found Nick playing a Spanish love song to his niece. Mary Bea's eyes drooped so low they were almost closed. Lisa leaned against the doorjamb and listened to him, feeling the music play through her soul.

The song was familiar. He'd played it for Robin many, many times. At some point, they'd begun to call it Robin's song. She closed her eyes, waiting for the pain, but instead she felt only a bittersweet sense of longing, which slowly turned into pleasure. She'd missed this song, missed hearing Nick play.

The Spanish guitar was one part of her heritage she had never denied. When Nick had learned how to play the songs that were part of her culture, he'd completely won over Silvia and Carmela—and her.

He'd seduced her with that same music. They'd made love to it, and they'd watched their baby sleep through it. So many memories, she thought, as a montage of images raced through her mind. She remembered sitting with Nick on a bluff overlooking the ocean, content to share a little music, a big sunset and a long bottle of wine. She could see them

222

walking down Pacific Avenue on Sunday, when the artists took over the sidewalks. With Nick holding her hand, kissing her mouth, laughing, always smiling, she'd felt like her life was one beautiful love story. Nick had coaxed her to try so many new things, riding a motorcycle, taking a dune buggy ride in the desert, eating praline pecan ice cream and Ruby's hot, hot chili.

They had shared a lot of good times, she realized, and when she'd turned her back on her life with him, she'd locked away not just the bad memories but the good ones as well.

Nick stopped playing, and she opened her eyes. He looked at her inquiringly, obviously not sure of her response.

"That was nice," she said softly.

"Sh-sh." He tipped his head toward the sleeping child, then slid off the bed and met her in the hallway. They both looked back to see if Mary Bea was still asleep. She was, so Lisa pulled the door halfway closed.

"That was beautiful," Lisa said, as Nick set his guitar down on the floor next to the hall table.

"Thanks."

He stared at her with so many questions in his eyes—questions she couldn't begin to answer. "I'd forgotten how well you play," she said finally.

"I'm a little out of practice."

"Do you—do you play for Suzanne?"

"No."

"Why not?"

His eyes met hers. "You're treading on dangerous ground, Lisa."

She knew she was, but she couldn't stop herself. "I asked a simple question. I didn't think it was that big of a deal. Obviously it is."

"Liar." Nick took a step closer. "You don't just want to know if I play the guitar for Suzanne, do you?" He took another step closer, until his face was just inches from hers. "You want to know what goes on between us, how serious we are, if we've made love, if you were better—"

"Stop it, Nick." She shoved him backward, out of her face, out of her space.

"Why should I stop? You wanted to know. You asked."

"About your music, nothing else. Why do I even try to talk to you?"

"I'll make it easy for you. I'll leave."

"Good." She took a breath, wishing she could just walk away, but she couldn't. "When do you think you'll be back?" she asked grudgingly.

"I don't know. Why?" He sent her a mocking smile. "Will you miss me?"

"I need that fax that should be at your store by now, so I can do some work this afternoon."

"Right." His expression turned grim at the reminder of Raymond. "I'll come back at lunch. Will that be soon enough to hear from your lover?"

"It's business, Nick."

"Excuse me? I thought you were in love with the man."

"The fax is business. You're twisting my words."

"Yeah, well, you wouldn't believe what you're doing to my head." He put his hands on his hips and glared at her.

She glared right back, refusing to walk away or back down. She had done nothing wrong, except ask him to pick up a fax for her. "What's the big deal? If my receiving a fax at your store was such a problem, why did you give me the number?"

"It's not the fax. It's you."

"What am I doing that is irritating you so much?"

"It's what you're *not* doing."

She put a hand to her head, feeling the onset of a headache. "What does that mean?"

"It means, I can't stand it anymore." He grabbed her around the waist and pulled her up against his body so she could feel every long, lean inch of him, hard and male, and hauntingly familiar.

His mouth pressed against her lips and stole her breath away. His lips punished her for loving another man. She tried to push him away but couldn't. Once she touched him, her resistance fled. Her hands refused to pummel his chest and instead slipped around his waist, bringing him that much closer to her.

With her resistance gone, Nick's kisses changed from angry to passionate to needy, and she couldn't help but respond to that longing. With each kiss, he took back a part of her that had once been his.

Eight years of absence disappeared into nothingness as his mouth demanded and she gave, as his body tightened and hers softened, as his hands caressed her shoulders and her hands clung to his waist.

Nick backed her up against the wall so there was no place for her to go. His mouth left her lips to travel across her cheek, to the curve of her neck. His tongue drew a line around the lobe of her ear, and she thought she might just die with the pleasure of it.

When Nick's hands came up under her sweatshirt, she didn't slap them away. She wanted him to touch her breasts. She wanted his hands all over her body, and suddenly that's exactly where they were.

"Nick," she breathed, as he teased one nipple into a sharp point of pleasure.

"I love the way you say my name," he murmured, kissing her mouth again and again and again.

His fingers fumbled with the snap on her jeans. Finally, it was open, and his hand caressed the flat of her stomach, the edge of her panties, teasingly, until she knew she wanted more and more and more.

"You're driving me crazy. I can't sleep at night. I can't think about anything or anyone but you," he said against her mouth. "I thought you were out of my head, but you're right back in it."

He pulled away and looked deep into her eyes, searching them for some sort of truth. She tried to hide from his gaze, but there was nowhere to go, no way to disguise the way she felt—overwhelmed and seduced by his eyes and his hands and his mouth. And it wasn't just her body that was responding—it was her heart and her soul.

He took her hand and pulled her down the hall toward Maggie's bedroom. Lisa didn't think about resisting. Her body wanted more of his touch. Her mind seemed lost to reason.

Try to think, she told herself, as Nick kissed her again. She moaned with the pleasure of it. How could she fight herself and him, too? The task seemed daunting, but as Nick pulled off his shirt, a cool breeze blew in her face, and she suddenly realized she was standing in the middle of Maggie's bedroom. This wasn't her house or her life or her man.

"We can't." She held up a hand as Nick stepped toward her. "Mary Bea—"

"Is asleep."

She eyed his bare, muscular chest and felt her resolve slipping away. He looked so good, so damn good, and it had been a long, long time. The years between had starved her for this moment. She took a deep breath and tried to count to ten. She counted seven twice and eight three times, but she finally made it to ten. "We're divorced, Nick."

He laughed, but the sound was harsh and unforgiving. His mouth tightened, his eyes turned bleak, and the light of desire changed into anger. "We're divorced. So that should stop us from wanting each other? I have a news flash for you. It doesn't change a thing. We promised to love each other forever, till death do us part. If you think a piece of paper will destroy that—"

"It was till death we do part," she reminded him.

"I'm not dead."

"You know what I mean."

"The promise was between us," he said fiercely. "I've never even considered marrying anyone else."

His statement shocked her. "You haven't? What about Suzanne?"

He ran a hand through his hair. "Suzanne is a very nice woman, who thinks we make a good couple. But she doesn't know me. She doesn't even know about Robin. I've tried to tell her, to trust her, but I can't do it. And I can't marry her, knowing I don't love her the way I loved you. It wouldn't be fair to her."

His words made Lisa feel like the biggest cheater in the world. Was she shortchanging Raymond, giving him only a part of herself? Didn't he deserve a woman who absolutely adored him, who would love and cherish him all the days of his life?

But she would be good to Raymond, she told herself. She would treat him with respect. She would make his life easier. She would be his partner, his friend, his mate. Surely, at his age he didn't expect mind-blowing passion.

At his age. What was she thinking? Was that why she was marrying him, because she thought he would have less expectations than a younger man? Was that true? Was it fair? And did Raymond deserve a woman who still wanted to make love to her ex-husband?

Suddenly, she had so many questions and not one answer.

"Lisa." Nick put his hand under her chin, forcing her to look at him. "Just admit one thing. You still want me in your bed."

"I can't admit that."

"Then you're lying to yourself as well as to me, because a minute ago you wanted me inside your body and in your bed. We both know that. Oh, to hell with you. If you want to lie, lie." He grabbed his shirt off the floor and stormed toward the door. "It won't change the truth."

"Which is that we're finished," she called after him, determined to have the last word.

He paused in the doorway. "You'll never be finished with me, no matter who you marry. I'm in your blood. I'm under your skin. I'm in your head. Now that you've kissed me again, do you really think you won't see me when you're kissing him?"

"You're an arrogant, obnoxious jerk."

"Who knows you better than anyone."

As Nick left the room, Lisa had a terrible feeling he might just be right.

* * *

"Great news," Jeremy declared as Maggie opened her hotel room door.

"Really?" she asked hopefully, noting his pleased expression. "You talked to Serena?"

His smile altered slightly as he stepped inside the room. "No. I spoke to the concierge. I told him I was trying to catch up with a friend of mine and wondered if she'd stopped by to ask directions for an activity we were planning."

"That sounds inventive."

He walked across the room and opened the drapes, allowing the sunshine to stream in through the windows. "That's better."

"Go on," Maggie urged, impatient to hear the rest.

Jeremy laughed. "You know, I'm pretty good at this undercover stuff."

"Would you get to the point?"

"Okay. I described Serena to the concierge, and he had seen her. In fact, he'd spoken to her at some length. He remembered because he thought Serena was gorgeous."

Maggie frowned. She hated to think about Serena's good looks. It only made her feel worse. "Did he know what Serena's plans were?"

"Yes. She and a friend went to the wine country to do some wine tasting."

"Was the friend male?"

Jeremy nodded again.

She grabbed his arm and twisted the sleeves of his shirt between her anxious fingers. "Did he say the guy's name? Did he tell you what he looked like? Was it Keith?"

Jeremy slowly peeled her fingers from his shirt. "I don't know for sure, Maggie. The concierge didn't notice the guy. His attention was focused on Serena, because she's so—"

"Gorgeous. I get the picture." Maggie flopped down on the edge of the bed, feeling anxious and panicked and depressed, all at the same time. They were so close, yet so far away.

"Maggie, we know where they went. That's good news," Jeremy reminded her.

"Yeah, they went to the wine country. Great. Do you know how many wineries there are in Napa Valley? That is, if they went to Napa and not to Sonoma. In which case, we'd have to cover another valley."

"Heroines do not get discouraged. They get tough. They fight back," Jeremy said. He pulled her to her feet to get her going, but once he let go of her, she sat back down on the bed. "Hey, come on. Don't give up on me now."

"I'm not a heroine, Jeremy, and this is not a book."

"No, it's better," he said with a broad grin, that enticed her to smile back.

"Why is that?" she asked somewhat reluctantly.

"Because we're living it. We're not reading about some- one else's adventure. We're having our own. I haven't had this much fun in a long time."

"Jeremy, this isn't fun. It's serious. I'm looking for a man I was married to for thirteen years. If he faked his death and lied to me, my whole life will have been one big lie. I won't know who I am any more." She sighed. "Actually, I don't know who I am at the moment, so that probably won't change."

"Maggie, I know this is hard for you," Jeremy said, once again pulling her to her feet. This time he held on to her as he gazed into her eyes. "I'm sorry if I seem to be taking it lightly. But we can do this. We can find Serena. I know we can." He let go of one of her hands to pull something out of his pocket. "And the task isn't as difficult as you might think. The concierge circled the wineries he recommended to Serena." Jeremy held up the brochure in his hand. "And there's more good news. Serena only left a half hour ago. With any luck, we should be able to catch up to her before the end of the day."

"With any luck," Maggie echoed doubtfully. "I haven't had much luck lately." She pulled herself out of his grasp and walked over to the window, gazing down at the city of San Francisco. What was she doing in a place so far from home, with one man she barely knew, chasing after another man she apparently had never known?

Jeremy put his arms around her waist, letting her rest against his chest. "What else happened?" he asked quietly. "You weren't this upset when I left you an hour ago."

Maggie thought back to her phone call with Nick. She shouldn't have told Nick about Keith. She should have known he'd be skeptical. On top of that, she'd lost her temper and never had a chance to ask how Lisa and the kids were doing. Of course, if there was a problem with the kids, Nick would have told her. He would have used that information to get her to come home.

Still, Maggie felt uneasy, probably because she hadn't been away from the kids for this many days in a long time. Which was why she needed this break, she told herself firmly. The kids were fine. They had Nick and Lisa and Silvia. They could do without her for a few more days. She'd call in the afternoon when the kids were home from school and talk to them directly.

"Maggie? Where are you?" Jeremy snapped his fingers in front of her face.

She turned in his arms. "Sorry. I was just thinking about what to do next."

"We'll find Serena. I promise you that. I don't know when or how, but I know it will happen. Have some faith."

She kissed him on the cheek. "You're great, you know that?"

"I don't mind hearing it from you."

She saw the desire flash in his eyes yet again, a physical connection between them that seemed to grow more with each passing minute. "Why?" she asked somewhat helplessly.

"Why what?"

"Why me? I have a mirror, Jeremy, and it does not tell me I'm the fairest in the land. In fact, I don't even come close." She smiled self-consciously, trying to act like she didn't care, when deep down her insecurity ate away at her confidence.

Jeremy sent her a thoughtful look. "I don't think you see what I see." He pulled her over in front of the mirror. His hands cupped her head so she couldn't twist away. "Look, Maggie."

"I know what I look like."

"You have beautiful blond hair that turns gold in the sunlight and silver in the moonlight. I know because I've seen you in both." He paused for a moment as their eyes met in the mirror. "You have a perfect oval face."

"With lines," she whispered.

"Laugh lines. Life lines. They make your face interesting."

"You are a good writer," she said with a reluctant smile.

"And you have the lushest mouth I could ever imagine, just made for all kinds of wicked things."

Maggie licked her lips, watching in the mirror as Jeremy's gaze followed her movement with lustful fascination. A shiver ran down her spine as their eyes met again. Here with him, in the mirror, she did look somewhat different, sexier, sultrier. She almost didn't recognize herself, but then she'd seen herself for so long through Keith's eyes and her children's eyes that she'd forgotten she was a woman.

"Beautiful Maggie," Jeremy said.

"Thank you."

"For what."

"Everything." She turned to face him. "I lived with Keith for a long time. I became comfortable in our love, and I didn't bother much with makeup or hair. When he died, the little vanity I had completely disappeared, and I didn't care. But when I saw Keith last night getting into that car with Serena, I felt abandoned and used and really, really ugly." She took a breath and offered him a shaky smile. "Thanks for making me take another look. I don't think the supermodels need to be worried about me honing in on their territory, but it wasn't as bad as I feared."

"You don't need makeup, Maggie. You're real. Believe me, it's a lot more appealing. I went to bed with an actress one night, and the next morning half her face was on the pillow. It scared the hell out of me."

Maggie grinned. "You're making that up."

"It was that bad. And did I tell you about the time I thought I was getting my hands on two of the biggest hooters I had ever seen in my life, only to find out she was wearing one of those miracle bras?"

Maggie laughed at his disgruntled expression. "Poor baby. Unfortunately, with me, what you see is pretty much what you get."

"So when do I get it?"

She punched him on the arm. "We're supposed to be tracking down Serena. Remember?"

"We could always wait here until they come back. I'm sure we could find a way to make use of our time."

She was sure they could find more than one way. But how could she concentrate on Jeremy when her mind was on Keith?

Jeremy cleared his throat. "I sense a rejection coming."

"Not a rejection, exactly."

"You want to go wine tasting, don't you?"

"I want to find Serena and Keith."

"All right. I must admit, I have a sudden thirst for a full-bodied Bordeaux."

Maggie couldn't help the giggle that escaped her lips. "You make it sound X-rated."

He sent her a sexy grin. "If you want X-rated, I can do better than that."

"Right now, I just want a glass of wine, and a long rope to throw around Serena's neck." She walked over to the dresser and checked her purse to make sure she had her wallet and lipstick and the note from Serena. She intended to confront her with it in case she tried to deny writing to Keith.

"When we find Serena, maybe you better let me do the talking," Jeremy suggested. He eyed her large bag with distrust. "You don't have a weapon in there, do you?"

"Only enough crayons to color her to death."

"Crayons?" he asked in surprise. "Why would you have crayons?"

"Uh—uh." She searched desperately for an answer. "Sometimes I volunteer—at a—at a school, a preschool, where they color a lot, with crayons, lots and lots of crayons.'' She pulled open the door. ''Shouldn't we go?''

He sent her an odd look. ''Sure. But . . .'' He walked over to her. ''After we solve the mystery of Keith and Serena, we'll solve the mystery of Maggie.''

''There is no mystery.''

''You know, every time you lie, you push your hair behind your ear.''

Maggie caught herself doing just that. ''It's a habit.''

''That's what I intend to find out, Maggie, all of your habits, especially the bad ones.''

Maggie dug her hands into the pockets of her blue jeans. ''I don't have any bad habits,'' she lied.

''Your left eye also twitches when you lie.''

''Oh, it does not.'' But Maggie couldn't help glancing in the mirror just to make sure.

Chapter 18

*L*isa put a stamp on the last wedding invitation and set it in the box with a sense of finality. She could not procrastinate any longer. She had to mail the invitations before she changed her mind. Not that she planned on changing her mind, she told herself firmly.

She stood up and glanced out the kitchen window at the empty driveway. It was past one o'clock and Nick hadn't returned. He probably loved the idea of making her wait for the fax, just because it was from Raymond.

A small impulsive smile curved her lips. Nick was jealous. She saw the green fire in his eyes every time she said Raymond's name. Maybe she ought to say it more often just to torture him. Of course, then he'd probably start saying, Suzanne, Suzanne. Her smile turned into a frown.

Lisa opened her soft leather briefcase and pulled out a notepad, determined to concentrate on work. Roxy would be dropped off after band practice, which ended around four-thirty, and Nick would pick up Dylan from baseball practice around five. As long as Mary Bea slept, Lisa could work. She could forget about Nick and his taunts and his kisses.

Lisa sighed, unconsciously touching her fingers to her lips. It shocked her to think she still wanted Nick. Eight years ago, she'd hated him. The night of the funeral he'd come to bed with alcohol on his breath, and she'd loathed his touch, not just because he was drunk, but because making love was what had started everything in the first place. Their love had

234

given birth to Robin, and when Robin had died, the love had died, too.

When she'd left San Diego and started her new life, she'd managed to shove Nick completely out of her mind, with a ruthlessness that was probably the one thing that had kept her going.

Not that she'd ever forgotten. And even though she'd consciously locked Nick away in her past, he'd invaded her dreams, night after night. Sometimes, she'd wake up in a sweat, his touch so fresh on her mind that she could almost believe she'd just made love to him. But she always woke up alone.

Think about cereal, Lisa told herself with a sigh. With newfound resolve, she pulled out the advertisement that Monty Friedman had run with his previous agency, and she studied it for color and content, font size and graphics. She listed three good points and three negative points. Then she stared at her pad of paper and tried to think of a catchy slogan.

Nothing came to mind. She began brainstorming evocative, powerful words that would create an image in the reader's mind. Mother Nature. Healthy. Satisfying. Great taste. No fat. Your kids will love it. Nobody believed that one anymore, she decided, and crossed it off her list.

Nick was healthy, Lisa thought idly, remembering the strength in his arms and his hands when he'd held her. She'd always loved his body, and although he'd filled out with age, he still had a vitality that made everyone else seem insubstantial. Not that Raymond wasn't in shape. He worked out religiously. But Nick had that nice tan to go along with the muscles.

Cereal. Think about cereal. Lisa chewed on the end of her pencil, then practically jumped out of her skin when she heard a car door slam outside. Nick was back. Her pulse sped ahead in a crazy, reckless fashion that made a mockery of her pretended disinterest in the man.

It's just old-fashioned lust, she told herself firmly, a physical reaction that had more to do with chemistry than with love. She and Nick had always been combustible together. Knowing that, she could avoid the danger. She could stop kissing him for one thing and touching him for another. Even looking at him tended to create heat. So, she'd have to stop looking at him, too.

When Nick finally entered the kitchen, Lisa continued scribbling on her notepad, although her words made no sense. She hoped he wouldn't notice.

Nick tossed a bunch of papers onto the table, careless of where they landed. "There you go. Love notes from lover boy."

"Gee, thanks," she said, as she straightened the papers into a pile. "You're a real peach."

"And you're a real pain in the ass."

"I see your mood hasn't improved. Why don't you go back to work?"

Nick sprawled into the chair across from her. "I'm hungry. Did you eat?"

"I made vegetable soup." She tipped her head to the pot on the stove.

His expression lightened. "Can I have some?"

"You want soup made by a pain in the—"

He reluctantly smiled. "I take it back. Please, may I have some soup, oh, darling, wonderful Lisa?"

"Help yourself," she said airily, unexpectedly touched by his deliberately, meant-to-be charming words. No one had called her darling in a very long time. Not that he meant it. He was just making time to get food, and she was not that easy.

Nick stood up and got a bowl out of the cabinet. He filled it to the brim, then returned to the table, eating quietly while Lisa read through the faxes.

They made little sense to her. She was acutely aware of Nick. Every nerve ending in her body felt like it was on fire. Nick sat so close, barely a foot away. She could touch him if she wanted to. She could probably kiss him if she wanted to.

Think about cereal, she told herself again.

"So what's all that about?" Nick asked, waving his hand toward the work spread out in front of her.

"Cereal," she said. "Also breakfast bars and whole-grain breads. It's very healthy."

"If it's not, I'm sure you'll convince me." He pushed his empty bowl to one side. "Aren't you the queen of words?"

"As a matter of fact, I am."

"What's the worst thing you've ever had to advertise?" he asked with a curious smile.

"The worst thing?" She thought for a moment. "Bug killers."

"Bug killers?"

"Yes. We did a Cinderella campaign about the roach coach. Send your roaches off to the ball in this coach and they won't come back at midnight."

Nick burst out laughing. "No way. That was you? I remember those commercials."

"That wasn't the exact wording, and it was better with the music and the visuals."

"You sold me. I actually bought one of those roach coaches, and it worked." He sat back in his chair, his eyes still smiling. "Wow. I'm impressed."

"You're impressed by my roach coach slogan? Next time you're yelling at me, remind me to feed you," Lisa said. "I forgot how much it improves your mood."

"I'm a simple man, Lisa, a little food, a little—"

"Don't even think about it."

"I was going to say—"

But he didn't say anything, because they were interrupted by a piercing scream. Nick's smile shattered. Lisa jumped from her seat, colliding with Nick in the doorway. She finally struggled free, then ran up the stairs, Nick following behind her.

Mary Bea wasn't just moaning now, she was crying full force, clutching her stomach and moving her legs in a desperate manner, as if she were trying to crawl out of her own skin.

Nick took one look at Mary Bea and paled. "I'm calling the doctor. This can't be normal."

"It hurts," Mary Bea screamed.

Lisa gathered her into her arms. "It's okay, honey. We're calling the doctor. Where—where does it hurt?"

"My stomach. Make it stop. Please make it stop."

Lisa stared at the little girl, feeling completely overwhelmed and panicked. She couldn't make the pain stop. She didn't know what to do, what to say. And Mary Bea was looking at her for answers, for help, for relief.

"Oh, God. I can't do this," Lisa said as Mary Bea's cries intensified. "I can't." She looked over at Nick, her breathing coming in ragged gasps as anxiety took over her mind and her body. She felt nauseated herself.

"You can do it. You can," Nick repeated forcefully.

"What if I screw up again? This isn't even my kid. Maggie should never have left her with me. I'm jinxed or cursed. I can't do this. I'll only make it worse." The words tumbled out of her mouth before she could stop them.

"Get a grip, Lisa. We've got more important things to deal with than your insecurity," Nick said sharply. "You're scaring Mary Bea."

Lisa bristled with anger, directed both at herself and at him. Nick was right. She had to get a hold of herself. She glanced down at the wide-eyed child, whose eyes were bright with fever and pain. "I'm sorry, honey. It's going to be okay. Call the doctor, Nick. His number is on the dresser in Maggie's room."

Nick disappeared, and Mary Bea threw her arms around Lisa's neck, burying her face in Lisa's chest. Lisa could feel the child's faith, her blind trust. She desperately hoped it wasn't misplaced.

"The nurse wants to know if the pain is in the stomach or the abdomen," Nick said, returning to the room with the portable phone.

"She's five years old. Her stomach is about as big as my hand."

"Lisa, she wants to know."

Lisa adjusted Mary Bea so she could gently touch the girl's stomach. "Does it hurt here?" she asked Mary Bea, pressing slightly on the upper stomach.

Mary Bea whimpered slightly. Lisa ran her hand down lower on the right side. "How about here?"

Mary Bea screamed as if Lisa had cut her with a knife.

"Her abdomen," Nick said into the phone, retreating to the doorway so he could hear the nurse's advice over Mary Bea's screams. "Right side or left?" he asked Lisa.

"Right. Although I'm afraid to even try the left side."

"Right side seems to be worse," Nick said. He listened for a moment than looked at Lisa. "Does she have a temp?"

"An hour ago it was still one hundred. It's been one hundred since last night."

Nick relayed that information to the nurse. "Has she thrown up?"

"Only the one time, a few hours ago. But tell her the pain has been going on for hours."

Once again, Nick repeated her comments. He waited, then put a hand over the phone. "She's checking with the doctor."

Lisa felt like every second they waited was an eternity, when in reality it was probably just a few moments.

"Don't go. Don't leave me," Mary Bea moaned as Lisa tried to settle her more comfortably on the pillows.

"I'm not going anywhere. I will not leave you, not for one second."

"Do you promise?" Mary Bea asked, her eyes filled with fear.

Lisa couldn't find the words. Could she promise to stay? What if Mary Bea got worse? What if it turned out to be like the last time? Wasn't this exactly why she didn't want to have children, so she wouldn't have to face these situations, wouldn't have to make a terrifying dash to the hospital, wouldn't have to be afraid that someone she loved, someone who counted on her to protect them, was going to die?

But Mary Bea was not going to die. She was a healthy little girl with a stomachache. Lisa tried to convince herself that's all it was, but deep down she knew it was more, and Mary Bea knew it, too. That's why she wanted Lisa to promise not to leave. Mary Bea was scared. Lisa was beyond scared.

"Lisa, did Maggie leave any sort of consent form?" Nick asked, interrupting them once again. "The nurse says we need the mother's consent to get treatment."

"Yes. Yes, she did," Lisa said, thankful that at least the old Maggie had been thinking before she left home.

"We have a consent form," Nick said. "Okay, we'll be right there."

"Does the doctor want to see her?" Lisa asked, noting the worry in Nick's eyes.

"Yes, but he wants us to take her to the Emergency Room at Children's Hospital."

"He thinks this is an emergency?"

Nick looked at Mary Bea, who was writhing in pain. "He thinks she might have appendicitis."

"Oh, no," Lisa said as panic slammed into her like an onrushing wave. "Nick, we can't do this without Maggie," she whispered. "This is her baby."

"Maggie's not here. We're all she's got, Lisa. Now are you going to fall apart, or are you going to help? Because I can't take care of both of you."

"I'm going to help." His sharp words cut through her panic. She touched Mary Bea's face with her hand. "I promise I'll stay with you honey. We're just going to take you to the doctor so he can make you better. Okay?"

Mary Bea nodded. "You're coming with me?"

"You bet I am." She turned to Nick, digging down deep for a strength and a calm she didn't know she possessed. "Take Mary Bea down to the car. I'll get my purse and the permission slip Maggie left for us."

He nodded, offering her a tight smile, which she did not return, still offended by his notion that she wasn't capable of holding herself together in a situation like this, although she had to admit she'd given him good reason to think that way.

*   *   *

Nick drove as quickly as possible to the hospital in San Diego. Fortunately, it was the middle of the afternoon and they didn't hit much traffic. Mary Bea cried uncontrollably, gasping for breath at times, her face turning red and wet and sticky from tears and sweat. She cried all over Lisa's knit shirt, soaking the material, until Lisa shivered from the wetness. But she held on tightly to the little girl, saying everything she could think of to reassure her.

All the while, terrifying images of the past ran through Lisa's mind. She once again heard her baby's cry. Then the silence. Nick had convinced her that Robin had gone to sleep—at last. He'd asked her to come to bed.

She could see him, sitting there in bed, his bare chest, his hand reaching out to her, desire in his eyes. They'd made love with a hunger that came from not getting enough of each other since the birth of their child. When she'd checked on Robin an hour later, the baby had looked so still, so peaceful.

Too peaceful, too still.

Robin lay on her stomach, her face turned to the side, one cheek pressed against the mattress. Her dark hair lay sweaty and matted against her small head. One of her little fists was pressed to her mouth as if she had shoved it against her lips to stop her own cries.

Lisa remembered bending over, trying to catch the sound of Robin's breath, watching her back to see if it was moving, convincing herself that it would be okay. But she couldn't see or hear anything, so she'd poked the baby with her finger, a nasty little poke, she still thought, cruel to wake a child up just to see if she was breathing.

Robin hadn't woken up. She hadn't opened her eyes or cried.

That's when Lisa had screamed, a piercing, anguished scream. Nick had run into the room in a panic, asking her what the hell was wrong. Lisa closed her eyes against the memories, the pain.

She could still hear the siren on the ambulance, still see

those two hulking men pounding on her tiny baby's chest. She could feel Nick's arm restraining her from running forward in a desperate attempt to blow her own breath into Robin's body.

"Oh, God!" she said out loud, her eyes flying open. "It feels like the last time."

"It's not the same, Lisa," Nick said tightly, his fingers gripping the steering wheel like a lifeline. "Mary Bea will make it. She's strong and she's tough, and I will not let anything happen to her."

Lisa didn't say a word. They both knew they'd had no choice the last time, and it was quite possible they would have no choice this time.

She hadn't prayed in eight years. Today, she inwardly cried out for help. *Please God, don't take Mary Bea, too.*

Nick pulled into the parking lot outside the Emergency Room. Lisa waited for him to open her door. Nick tried to take Mary Bea, but the little girl wouldn't let go of Lisa.

"It's okay. I can carry her," Lisa said.

Nick held the door open as she struggled to get out of the car without causing Mary Bea more pain. They walked up to the double doors together.

"Oh, shit," Nick said.

Lisa looked at him in alarm. "What's wrong?"

He tipped his head toward one of the tree branches that graced the side of the building. A small bird let out a familiar call.

"The robin," Lisa whispered, meeting Nick's eyes. "Do you think it's a good sign or a bad one?"

"How the hell would I know?"

Lisa took one last look at the robin before walking into the Emergency Room.

The receptionist asked for insurance information. Nick handed her the paper Maggie had left with them. The receptionist tried to ask a few questions, but Mary Bea began to cry again, the motion of their trip having caused her more pain.

Five minutes later, a nurse came out and escorted them into an examining room. Lisa tried to lay Mary Bea down on the table, but the little girl refused to let go.

"It's okay," the nurse said. "It might be easier if you just hold her for the moment. I understand her mother is away."

"Yes. I'm her aunt, and this is her uncle."

Nick couldn't believe how calmly Lisa said the words, tying them together the way they used to be—aunt and uncle, husband and wife. He knew Mary Bea's illness was taking its toll on Lisa. Her face was pale, her blue eyes bright with worry. Somehow she held herself together. Whatever insecurity she had seemed to be under control.

He, on the other hand, felt like he was losing control. A little girl he loved desperately was in tremendous pain, and he couldn't do a damn thing about it. Not only that, if it weren't for him, Maggie would be here right now, holding her daughter. If only he hadn't lost his temper, hadn't screwed things up.

"Nick, could you hold my purse?" Lisa asked, sliding it off her shoulder.

"Sure."

He held on to her purse like a life jacket. It made him feel better. He didn't know why. Maybe it was the connection with Lisa. Then he began to get a strange sensation of warmth in his hands. He felt a tingle in the tip of each finger, and he had the sudden need to open her purse.

For a moment, he fought the urge, watching as the nurse took Mary Bea's temperature and pulse. But he couldn't get rid of the sensation that it was important for him to open Lisa's purse.

Finally, he gave in, feeling like a fool. He was a man, and there was something about a woman's purse that seemed intimate, personal. There didn't seem to be anything unusual in her purse, just her wallet and checkbook, a hairbrush, lipstick and a small white box. The bracelet.

He took out the box and opened it. The bracelet glittered more than he remembered, taking on a shine, an energy that felt like an electric shock when he picked it up and held it between his fingers.

"What are you doing?" Lisa muttered, while the nurse jotted down notes in Mary Bea's chart.

"I think Mary Bea should wear this."

"No." Lisa shook her head.

"It feels—" Nick didn't know how to describe it without sounding like an idiot. Before he could explain, the nurse began to speak.

"Your pediatrician ordered a blood test, to check for infection," the nurse said. "I'd like to do that now, then the Emergency Room physician will be in to examine your niece."

"What about Mary Bea's pediatrician? Shouldn't he be here?" Nick asked, still hanging on to the bracelet.

"We'll be in touch with him after we know more," the nurse replied, as she prepared to take Mary Bea's blood. She smiled at Lisa. "If you can turn her face against your chest, so she isn't looking directly at me, that would be helpful."

Lisa did as requested, trying to distract Mary Bea from the needle the nurse was preparing to inject into her skin. "Maybe you should tell her what's going to happen," Nick suggested.

"You tell her," Lisa said.

Nick smiled at Mary Bea. "The nurse is going to give you a little pinch in your arm. That will help the doctor know what's wrong so he can make it better."

Mary Bea looked at him with wide, frightened eyes.

"I brought the magic bracelet with me," he said, holding it in front of her. "Isn't it pretty?"

"Is it really magic?" Mary Bea asked as the nurse wrapped a piece of tubing around her arm.

"Aunt Carmela says it is."

"If I touch it, will it make my stomach stop hurting?"

Nick looked into Lisa's eyes, not sure how far he should go with this. Lisa didn't seem to want any part of this conversation. "It might help," he said, watching Mary Bea's eyes fill with moisture as the nurse inserted the needle into her arm. She tried to jerk her arm away, but Lisa and the nurse managed to hold her still.

"Hurts," she whimpered.

"All done," the nurse said. "You can relax for a few minutes. The doctor will be in shortly."

As the nurse left, Nick touched Mary Bea's cheek with the bracelet, hoping she could feel the warmth, the energy that he was feeling. It seemed to help. She closed her eyes for a moment.

"Take it away," Lisa said in a rush, her eyes panicked. "She's going to sleep, Nick. Just like before. I was wearing the bracelet that night, don't you remember?"

Nick remembered everything about that night. It was indelibly printed on his brain. "You weren't wearing it, Lisa." He looked into her eyes and saw confusion.

"Of course I was. I wore it every night. I never took it off."

"The clasp broke when you accidently caught it on the edge of the diaper table. Don't you remember? You were heartbroken."

She stared at him blankly.

"I found a jeweler who could fix it, so we left it with him. That was the day before Robin died."

She put a hand to her mouth. "You're right." She looked absolutely stunned by the revelation.

"The bracelet didn't come back from the jeweler until after the funeral. Of course, you didn't want any part of it by then."

"I'd forgotten."

Nick slipped the bracelet over Mary Bea's wrist, letting it dangle loosely over her arm. "You forgot a lot of things, Lisa."

"I guess I did. But if the bracelet was supposed to be magic, it sure didn't work."

"Maybe because we didn't have it when we needed it."

"Like that explains what happened?"

Nick offered her a sad smile. "Nothing will ever explain what happened. Nothing. That's a fact we both have to accept."

Lisa adjusted her arms around Mary Bea as the girl seemed to doze in her arms, the waves of pain having receded for the moment.

"I never really believed in the bracelet. It's pretty, but magic?"

"Your Aunt Carmela said she made the bracelet out of gold that was passed down from the ancient Aztecs. They were renowned for their mystical powers."

Lisa rolled her eyes. "That's the difference between you and me—you don't need much of a reason to believe in the impossible. I want a written, money-back guarantee before committing to any big dreams."

"I know. I wish I could have given you one."

Lisa stared at the shiny gold bracelet. "I'm sure you would have if you could. I never believed in anything until I met you. You made me believe, Nick. I guess that's why I had to blame you when everything fell apart. But it wasn't your fault, it was mine."

"Maybe we just didn't give the magic a chance to work," Nick said. "Maybe if you'd put the bracelet back on . . ."

"How could a bracelet be magic?"

"How could a robin be following us all over town?" he asked as he shoved his hands into his pockets. "How could two people who promised to love each other for all time get a divorce?"

Lisa looked away, but not before he saw a glimmer of pain in her eyes.

She gently stroked Mary Bea's hair. "I don't understand much of what's happened in my life."

Mary Bea opened her eyes and squirmed on Lisa's lap, once again tormented by pain. She was trying so hard to be brave that it almost broke Nick's heart.

"I can't believe the damn doctor isn't in here by now," Nick said. "What's he doing?"

"I'm sure he's busy with other patients."

"She's hurting, Lisa. She needs to see the doctor now. I'm going to find him."

"You're staying right here, Nick. Get a hold of yourself. As you said before, we have to stay calm."

"You're right." Nick sat down on a stool, irritated by her sudden cool. She was supposed to be the one falling apart, not him. He'd always taken care of her; it had never been the other way around. He had to admit she'd impressed him with the way she'd taken charge since entering the hospital, dealing with Mary Bea, the receptionist and the nurse.

Mary Bea cried again, and Lisa kissed her forehead. "It's okay, honey. Hang on. It will be better soon."

Nick got to his feet again, unable to stay still while Mary Bea was in so much pain. He had heard Mary Bea cry many times in his life, but not with this type of intensity. He was afraid something was terribly wrong.

"I could kill Maggie," he said abruptly. "She should be here."

"It's not her fault. She doesn't know."

"She should have left a phone number." He ran a hand through his hair. "I know it's my fault. If I hadn't yelled at her, you could have talked to her and told her about Mary Bea. Then she would have come home."

"Nick?"

"What?"

"Shut up."

"I feel so damn helpless."

"I know. Me, too."

He looked into her eyes and saw the worry behind the calm. It made him feel better to know she was scared, too. Maybe he still needed her to need him. It was a pitiful thought for a grown man to have, but he couldn't deny it wasn't there.

The door finally opened, and a man walked in carrying Mary Bea's chart. The doctor appeared to be in his early thirties and wore an outrageous red tie with puppies all over it. He smiled at Mary Bea.

"You've got a bad tummyache, I hear," he said kindly.

Mary Bea blinked away some tears and stared at the doctor. "Hurts."

"I bet it does." He squatted so he could look into Mary Bea's eyes. "I need you to do me a big favor. I have to ask you to lie down on the table over here so I can see where it hurts."

"No. Want Aunt Lisa." Mary Bea hugged Lisa more tightly.

"Well, Aunt Lisa will stand right next to you and squeeze your hand really, really tight. Say, what do you think of my puppies?" He flicked his tie in front of her.

"Silly tie," Mary Bea said.

"Really? I have one with hamburgers on it, too. And one with Garfield. Oh, and I have one with the Little Mermaid. I bet you like the Little Mermaid."

Mary Bea's arms loosened as the doctor talked, and Nick could hardly believe his eyes when the doctor lifted Mary Bea out of Lisa's arms and laid her down on the table. As promised, Lisa took Mary Bea's hand and squeezed it reassuringly.

The doctor continued to talk about cartoons and movies and dolls. He seemed to know quite a bit about little girls. First, he checked Mary Bea's throat, ears and glands, then worked his way down to her chest and stomach and, finally, the abdomen. He carefully avoided the right side, starting with the left, pressing gently here and there, and asking if it hurt.

He slowly worked his way over to the right side, and as soon as he did so, Mary Bea shrieked, her eyes suddenly wild with pain. The doctor eased up, but continued the examination for another very long minute.

Nick had to force himself not to drag the man away from Mary Bea. He knew the examination had to be done, but he couldn't stand to see his niece in so much pain.

Finally, the doctor finished. "Her appendix appears inflamed," he said. "We should have her blood test in a few minutes. I'll have one of our surgeons check her, but I think she has appendicitis."

"Surgeon. Why do you need a surgeon?" Nick asked. "Can't you get rid of it with antibiotics?"

"No. She'll need to have her appendix removed. How long has she been complaining of pain?"

"Since last night, around ten or so."

"That would be about sixteen, seventeen hours?"

"Yes, I guess."

"I have to tell you, there's a danger of rupture within twenty-four hours."

"Rupture?" Lisa swayed slightly, and Nick moved over to stand behind her, supporting her and Mary Bea. They faced the doctor like a united family.

"Is the surgery dangerous?" Nick asked.

"We have an excellent pediatric surgeon on staff. She's done this particular surgery thousands of times, but I'll let her explain everything to you." The doctor stepped out of the room, and they were once again left to wait.

"Surgery," Nick muttered. "I can't believe it."

"It's a simple procedure, I think," Lisa said, but she looked as worried as he felt.

Five minutes later the doctor returned with a woman.

"I'm Dr. Connelly," she said with a warm smile. "I understand someone in here has a stomachache."

Mary Bea turned her head into Lisa's chest, obviously wary of another doctor.

"I'm sorry," the woman said, "but I'll need to examine Mary Bea as well."

"It hurts her so much," Lisa protested.

"I'll do it as quickly as possible, but we want to make sure we have the right diagnosis before we go into surgery."

Lisa tried to get Mary Bea back down on the table, but the little girl fought her all the way. Finally Lisa managed to get her flat on her back, although she couldn't remove Mary Bea's arms from around her neck.

The surgeon had obviously had a great deal of experience with reluctant children and managed to examine her quickly and surely. She had just finished when the nurse entered the room with the results of the blood test. The surgeon studied them for a moment, then turned to Lisa with a solemn smile.

"It's my opinion that your daughter has an inflamed appendix that needs to come out as soon as possible," the surgeon said.

Daughter! Nick's heart almost stopped at the word. Mary Bea wasn't his daughter. His daughter had died in a hospital just like this.

"She's our niece," Lisa corrected when Nick couldn't find the words with which to speak.

"Is her mother available?"

"No, but we have permission to seek treatment."

"Good."

Nick drew in a long breath as the surgeon explained the procedure to them. She reviewed the risks of the surgery, which seemed to include a myriad of horrible possibilities, including death. Nick had second, third and fourth doubts about letting them operate. What if something happened to Mary Bea? Once again, he found himself fighting an urge to sweep Mary Bea up in his arms and take her as far away from the hospital as possible.

. He knew he couldn't do that. Mary Bea was very sick, and she needed treatment. He just couldn't stand the thought of losing her, too.

"I don't want to wait," the surgeon said. "There is always a danger of rupture, which can cause a lot of other problems."

"Then let's do it," Nick said.

"Can I stay with her?" Lisa asked.

"Yes. I'll have the nurse give her a mild sedative now, so we can ease some of her distress. Then we'll take her up to surgery. As soon as it's over, I'll let you know how it went."

"Will she be okay?" Lisa asked, sounding as desperate as Nick felt.

The surgeon smiled at them both. "There's always a risk, but I think she'll be fine. I really do."

Nick let out a breath. "Thank you."

"I'll be back with the medication," the nurse said, as all three of them left the room.

"Do you think we're making the right decision?" Lisa asked.

"Yes."

Lisa nodded. She put her hand around Mary Bea's wrist, touching the bracelet with her fingers. "Goodness, this feels so hot. I guess Mary Bea's body heated it up."

"It felt that way when I took it out of your purse."

"I don't remember it ever being so warm."

"Maybe it's the magic. I pray it is. I'll believe anything if it will help Mary Bea," he said defiantly, daring her to contradict him, but for once Lisa didn't argue.

"I guess I will, too," she said simply.

The nurse came back a few moments later with a hospital gown that was way too big, and a needle that looked just as bad. Mary Bea seemed resigned to being stuck again, and within a few minutes, she became drowsy.

"I'm sorry, I'll have to remove the bracelet as well," the nurse said.

Lisa took it off of Mary Bea and slipped it onto her own wrist. Then she kissed Mary Bea on the cheek and whispered in her ear. "I'll be here when you wake up, honey. Just take a nice nap, and you'll feel better."

Nick kissed Mary Bea, then put his arm around Lisa as an orderly took their niece up to surgery.

He turned Lisa into his arms as soon as they were alone, and she slipped her hands around his waist, resting her head on his chest. Nick hadn't held her in such a loving, tender way in a very long time, and he'd missed it. He felt his emotions threatening to spill out, all the love and anger and fear coursing through his body like an onrushing wave. She'd been his wife, his lover, his best friend. How had he lost her? Why?

Lisa slowly lifted her head and looked at him. Her own eyes were wet with moisture, her face pale and tense.

"I can't believe we're here again. I didn't think I'd ever be in this position again."

"You were great."

"After a few anxious moments," she admitted. "You kept me on course."

"You did the same for me."

She sighed. "Now we wait."

"Yeah, we wait."

"Are you going back to work?" Lisa asked as they walked out of the Emergency Room and down the hall toward the main bank of elevators.

"No, I'm staying here with you."

"It will be nice to have company."

"Even mine?"

"Especially yours. I couldn't have done this without you."

"Me either."

"I guess I'll call my mother and see if she can pick up Dylan from school and wait at the house for Roxy to come home. We should have asked the doctor how long it will take."

"I'm sure we can find a nurse or someone to tell us that."

The elevator doors opened, and Nick stepped inside. He was surprised to see Lisa still standing in the corridor. "What's wrong?" he asked.

"I—I just remembered. I was supposed to fax something to Raymond this afternoon."

"He'll have to wait," Nick said, feeling a surge of satisfaction.

Lisa slowly walked into the elevator. "I'm sure he'll understand. He's really a great guy."

Chapter 19

"I do not understand why Elisabeth hasn't sent me some copy," Raymond said, checking his watch. It was almost four. He had faxed her the information just after ten. Surely, she had something by now.

Raymond stood up and looked out the large window behind his desk, while Paul Evans, one of his senior account executives, sat quietly in a chair, obviously not sure how to reply. Elisabeth was, after all, not just an employee but Raymond's fiancée. Raymond knew the other staffers had grown wary around her, seeing her as an extension of him.

He also knew Paul would love a shot at the Nature Brand account, which created his current dilemma. Did he wait for Elisabeth to come home? Or did he bring Paul in on the account? He felt torn between loyalty to his fiancée and loyalty to his company.

"I'm sure Elisabeth will fax you something soon," Paul said casually. "She's very reliable."

"Yes, she is," Raymond admitted, without turning around. His mind focused for a moment on the sight before him—downtown Los Angeles, tall skyscrapers, narrow streets, traffic, smog, excitement, even a little danger, everything he loved. He'd grown up in the nearby San Fernando valley, in the backyard of Hollywood and Beverly Hills. His father had worked in special effects for MGM studios, and he'd spent hours watching his father create magic with his

camera. It was probably one of the reasons he'd gone into
advertising, another way of creating magic.

There was no doubt that L.A. was where he wanted to
spend the rest of his life. He loved the flash of this southern
California city, the weather, the movies, the fantasy women
haunting the streets for their chance at a part in a movie, the
clothes, the jewelry, and the money. Most of all he loved
being a success, dining with powerful people, being invited
to premieres, living the good life. And he wanted that good
life to continue. He wanted the Nature Brand account, yet
he'd lost an entire day because of Elisabeth.

He couldn't stop the surge of anger that filled his body. It
occurred to him that Elisabeth hadn't called him once since
she'd left. He'd called her—every damn day.

He turned around and found Paul watching him with a
speculative glint in his eye.

"I want you to work up some more ideas for me, Paul,
and they have to be better than the last ones. Monty thought
they sucked. And I'll need them by tomorrow night, because
I have a lunch meeting on Wednesday with the Marketing
V.P. at Nature Brand."

Paul straightened in his chair, trying to look unconcerned,
but Raymond knew the younger man had been longing for
this opportunity. He was a young hotshot eager to make his
mark, and Paul wouldn't care if he left muddy shoe prints
all over Elisabeth's back in the process.

Elisabeth would hate him for bringing Paul in on the account. She'd already had a couple of run-ins with Paul and
found him to be arrogant and unprincipled. At the moment,
Raymond was more concerned with whether or not the
younger man could come up with some dynamite copy.

"I'm not taking this account away from Elisabeth," Raymond added. "But she's in a difficult situation right now,
and I think we should support her."

"Whatever you say, boss." Paul leaned forward in his
chair. "By the way, I have a friend who just got a job at the
Wickham agency. She's only working in the mailroom, but

sometimes interesting information comes in the mail, if you know what I mean.''

Raymond understood exactly what Paul was trying to say. He'd never stolen from a competitor before—at least not blatantly. Still . . . no, he forced the thought out of his head. He didn't need to cheat to beat Beverly.

"I think we can win this one on our own without any help from a clerk in the mailroom," Raymond said.

"Sometimes it's good to know your enemy."

"That's true. Ask Connie for my file on Nature Brand on your way out," he added.

Paul stood up and sauntered out of the office, standing a lot taller than he had when he'd walked in. Raymond stared down at the papers on his desk, knowing there were other matters that needed his attention.

The phone rang, and he smiled. Elisabeth. He eagerly reached for it, without waiting for his secretary to pick up. "Raymond Curtis."

"Hello, this is Rachel Carstairs."

Raymond sighed at the sound of his wedding consultant's voice. "Hello."

"Elisabeth was supposed to come in at lunch today for her final fitting," Rachel said. "I hope she's not ill."

"No, she had to go out of town unexpectedly."

"Oh, dear. We really need to take care of this as soon as possible."

"I'll have her call you."

"Please do. And what about the invitations? I know Elisabeth wanted to handle that herself, but she did promise to give me the list so I could double-check the numbers."

"I'll have her call you," Raymond repeated somewhat helplessly.

Mrs. Carstairs didn't say anything for a moment. "Very well. I won't take up any more of your time, Mr. Curtis. Have a nice evening."

"You too," he muttered as he hung up the phone. He might as well go home and have that nice evening, since he wasn't accomplishing anything here. Or maybe—maybe he should drive down to San Diego and surprise Elisabeth.

He pushed the button on his intercom. "Connie? I need to track down the address of Maggie Scott," he said, pulling out the note Elisabeth had left for him with the phone number. "She lives in Solana Beach, and I know if anyone can find her, you can." He sat back in his chair with a satisfied smile. He'd never liked to wait. Taking action was much more his style, and that's exactly what he was going to do.

Maggie heard the sound of her own voice coming over the answering machine, requesting her to leave a message. She checked her watch. It was almost four. Lisa and Nick were probably picking the kids up from their various activities.

"Hi, it's Mom," she said cheerfully. "I just wanted to see how everyone is doing. I love you guys. I'm blowing you a kiss. Here's one for Roxy, my smart teenager, who I hope isn't giving Aunt Lisa any gray hair. Here's one for Dylan, my big boy—don't watch too many video games. And here's one for Mary Bea, my sweet baby. Love and hugs to all of you . . ." Her voice caught in her throat as she thought about the kids and how much she missed them, but she wasn't just doing this for herself—she was doing it for them, too. If Keith was still alive . . . "Anyway," she said, knowing she was running out of time. "Lisa, I hope it's okay that you stay with the kids. If it's not, make Nick stay. I hope you guys understand. I have to do this. I'll call again when I know more. Bye."

Maggie hung up the phone, took a deep breath, and headed toward the winery entrance where Jeremy was waiting.

He sat on a bench outside a train station. This particular winery was built on top of a hill, and a small open air train took visitors up and down to the winery. Since it was a Monday, the visitors were sparse, and aside from the ticket taker, Jeremy was the only one in sight.

He smiled when he saw her, that slow, knowing smile that made her heart catch, her stomach clench and a thrill run down her spine. She was becoming addicted to his smile, to the look of desire in his eyes.

With him she was simply a woman and not somebody's mother. It had been a long time since she'd felt that way. Not that she didn't love her kids, she told herself again. But somehow in the hoopla of marriage and kids, she'd lost a bit of herself, and she was just now getting it back—with Jeremy, a handsome stranger. Who would have thought she could have attracted a man like him?

Jeremy stood up as she approached. "Ready for more wine?"

"You might have to carry me before we're through."

"Promise?"

She laughed at his devilish smile. "I weigh more than you think."

"I'm stronger than you think." He playfully flexed a muscle as he winked at her.

"You are so great. Why hasn't some woman snatched you up before now? There must be something you're not telling me, some deep, dark secret of why you're still available at the age of what—thirty-three?"

Jeremy shook his head. "Hey, I'm only thirty. Don't age me like that."

Thirty? He was younger than her by a year. Younger. She suddenly felt the gap was about twenty years instead of one. She'd been married. She'd had children. A lifetime of experience separated them.

Jeremy's eyes turned serious. "What's the problem? You don't like thirty-year-olds?"

"I'm thirty-one."

"Ooh, an older woman."

Maggie tried to smile but couldn't. She took her ticket out of his hand and walked over to the train entrance. "We better go. It's getting late, and I want to check this place before it closes."

Jeremy stepped into the waiting train and sat down across from her. They were both silent as the train lurched out of the station, then up the hill to the winery.

"Do you really think a year makes that much difference?" Jeremy asked.

"No, of course not." It wasn't the year, it was everything else he didn't know.

"Something is bothering you."

"It's not. I'm just moody. See, you're starting to get to know me, and the bloom is already off the rose," she said, drumming her fingers on the seat beside her.

Jeremy got up and sat down next to her. Before she could say another word he leaned over and kissed her. It was a hot, lush kiss, more potent than the wine they'd tasted earlier.

Jeremy's hand worked its way inside her collar, his fingers warm against her skin. She moaned as his tongue slid into her mouth, tasting him as he was tasting her.

"You're driving me mad," Jeremy whispered, as he bit down gently on the tip of her earlobe.

Maggie closed her eyes against a bolt of sensation that hit every erogenous point in her body, leaving her tingling, wanting.

When she opened her eyes, Jeremy was staring at her. "I want to make love to you."

"There are things—"

He cut her off with a finger against her lips. "That I don't know about you. There are things you don't know about me. For instance, I really enjoy making love."

Maggie swallowed hard. "That's—that's good."

"It can be really good. Especially with a woman who is willing to explore."

"Explore what?" she asked, feeling both excited and dismayed by his titillating words.

"Explore the ways a man and a woman can find pleasure."

"Would these ways be painful?"

He smiled. "Am I scaring you?"

"You're turning me on," she admitted. "But I'm not— I'm not all that experienced."

"You don't have to be experienced, just attracted, interested, willing. You know I want you," he said bluntly. "You know I came with you because I want you."

"Yes." Maggie licked her lips, then gasped as Jeremy's tongue followed the same motion as hers.

He trailed his lips down the side of her face, her neck, her collarbone. He undid the top button of her dress so his tongue could drawl a swirl of pleasure along the curve of her breast, until she wanted to rip her shirt open so he could have better access to the parts of her that wanted his greedy, hungry mouth.

The train jerked to a stop.

"What—what happened?" Maggie gasped.

"I don't know, but I'm sure we'll get going in a moment."

Maggie looked around. They were halfway up the hill, not a soul in sight. "How long do you think it will take before we start moving?"

"A few minutes probably."

"I feel so vulnerable."

"Don't think about it. Think about this." He kissed her again, his hand moving against her chest, unbuttoning two more buttons on her dress. His hand slipped inside, cupping her breast. After a heart-stopping moment, his fingers pulled aside the lacy cups of her bra and caressed her bare skin.

Maggie would have gasped with pleasure, but Jeremy's mouth made a mockery of every other kiss she'd ever received. His fingers worked magic against her breast. She completely forgot about where they were and put both arms around his neck and pulled him closer.

His mouth left hers, and she almost begged him to come back, until she felt his fingers unhooking the front clasp of her bra. His mouth replaced his fingers in the valley of breasts, the curve of one, then the other, finally settling in on the center of her being, feeling, tugging, tasting, sending electric shocks throughout every part of her body.

And she wanted more. Maggie shamelessly pressed his head against her breast, and when his hands slid up under her breast, she welcomed them, yearning for his touch.

Maggie ran her hands through his hair, loving the feel of

his mouth on her breast, his hand on her thigh, slipping inside her panties. She did gasp then as his fingers found her hot spot, as he caressed, first slow, then fast, until she felt herself losing control.

"Don't stop," she whispered.

And he didn't, not for several mind-blowing minutes of pleasure that left her shaky and breathless. He lifted his head and smiled at her. She felt a little embarrassed that it had all been for her.

"I had a good time, too," he said with a smile, reading her mind.

"Not as good as me." She suddenly sat up, hooking her bra, fumbling with her buttons, as she realized where they were. "I can't believe you just did that, and I let you. Anyone could have seen us."

"No one did."

"I know, but—but I've never done anything like that before. I feel wild."

"Oh, man, I wish you hadn't said that. It makes me wish . . ." He took a deep breath and let it out.

"Maybe I could help you." She put her hand on his thigh, and he jumped.

She smiled, feeling a delicious sense of power now that the tables were turned. "I want to be fair."

"Hey, it's broad daylight."

"That didn't stop you."

"Well, it's going to stop you," he said, removing her hand from his thigh. "Unless you want to end up completely naked on this bench."

"Mm-mm, I have a feeling you could make me forget just about anything."

His eyes darkened, and his breathing grew ragged. "Damn. Damn. Damn. I wish to hell we were in a nice private bedroom right now."

"No one can see," she teased, repeating his own words.

"Okay, let's do it."

His hand moved to his belt buckle and Maggie felt a rush of excitement, followed by fear.

"I—uh."

His eyes twinkled. "Second thoughts, Maggie?"

Maggie didn't get a chance to reply as the train jerked into motion. "Well, too late," she said, feeling both relieved and grateful.

"Saved again," Jeremy said, settling back on his seat. "I guess I'll have to hope the third time's the charm."

Maggie simply smiled as the train continued its slow ascent up the hill. She still couldn't believe her behavior or Jeremy's. Keith wouldn't have dreamed of kissing her like that where anyone could see. Or maybe he had dreamed of such a thing—just not with her.

"You think too much," Jeremy said.

She found him watching her again. "It's a bad habit, I know."

"Come here." He put his arm around her, and she rested her head on his chest. She could hear his heartbeat next to her ear, and she felt comforted by it. She had only known him a short time, but it seemed like she'd known him forever. Kissing him, wanting him, loving him seemed so natural, so right. Loving him? No! She couldn't be falling in love! That would be stupid and foolish and impossible. She might even still be legally married.

"Your shoulders are suddenly tense," Jeremy said, rubbing his hand against her tight neck muscles. "What happened? Don't tell me, you were thinking again."

She sat up and looked at him. "Jeremy, am I leading you on?"

"I sure hope so."

"Are you leading me on?"

His smile faded as his eyes turned serious. "What are you asking me, Maggie?"

"I don't know. I just—you make me feel things."

"Good things?"

"Very good."

"Then why don't we just go with that—for the moment."

Maggie slowly nodded. He was right. She didn't have to commit to any feelings right now, and neither did he. And if she was falling in love with him, well, she'd just have to stop.

The train finally pulled into the station at the top of the hill and came to a grinding halt.

"Sorry about the delay, folks," the operator said as he opened the door.

"No problem. We enjoyed ourselves," Jeremy replied.

The man smiled. "It's a great view, isn't it? One of the best in the valley."

"The best I've ever had," Jeremy said.

Maggie nudged him in the ribs, but Jeremy was obviously enjoying himself. "The valley is so lush, so sweet. You can almost taste the wine in the air."

The operator sent him a strange look, then nodded. "Some people say you can get drunk up here just by breathing deep."

"I'll bet. I know I felt—"

"Jeremy, let's go." Maggie steered him away before he could say anything risqué. "You're terrible," she said as they walked into a nearby courtyard.

"I was having a little fun."

"Too much."

"Life is fun, Maggie." He tipped her chin and gave her a quick kiss. "You have to stop worrying so much about everyone and everything."

"Another bad habit. See, you're perfect, and I am terribly flawed."

"Looks that way," Jeremy agreed.

She socked him in the arm.

"Ow."

She laughed. "You're right, life is fun. Come on, let's see if we can get you a little more drunk."

"I think that was my line," he said, following her down the path that led to the winery.

They entered the main building and strolled into the tasting room. It was quiet inside, just one other couple sipping wine, and it wasn't Serena and Keith. They tasted several different wines, then decided to call it quits.

'Do you want to take the tour?" Jeremy asked.

"No, I'm tired, and I've seen enough vats today to write a book about wineries."

"I was thinking the same thing. Only I was plotting out how a body might wind up in one of those big barrels."

"You have a dark side, Jeremy."

He winked at her. "Baby, you don't know the half of it. Wait till I get you alone."

She knew he was teasing, but she couldn't help the nervous shiver that raised goose bumps along her arms. Every time she thought she knew who he was, he said something to unsettle her.

"I'm going to get some water," Jeremy said, heading toward a drinking fountain down the hall. "I'll meet you out front."

"Okay." Maggie wandered into the courtyard. It was quiet, the late afternoon sun casting shadows through the trees. She rested her elbows on top of the brick wall that wound its way around the grounds. She imagined there would be a spectacular sunset in a few hours. She suddenly felt as if she were a million miles from home, from her life, from herself. She felt guilty, because it felt good to be away.

She had always loved sunsets, the time of night when dusk settled over the city and the stars came out one by one. It was the time when she felt invincible, as if there was a huge world out there waiting for her to conquer. Not that she'd ever tried to do such a thing. She'd always wanted to be a wife and a mother. That had been her goal since she got her first doll and played her first game of house.

But what now? She was still a mother but no longer a wife. How could she play only part of the game? Everyone knew you needed a mother and a father to play house.

Jeremy wouldn't fit into the game. His life was Hollywood. Lights, camera, action. Soon he'd go back to his world, and she'd go back to hers.

They had now, a little voice inside her said. She could have him tonight. She could make every fantasy about sex come true with him. Instinctively, she knew that. She'd never before met a man who could drive every logical thought out of her head with one kiss.

"Maggie! Maggie!"

She turned to see Jeremy waving impatiently at her from the other side of the courtyard. She hurried over to him. "What's wrong?"

"I just saw Serena. Come on."

He ran down the path toward the train station. Maggie hoped they wouldn't be too late.

By the time they got to the station, the train was just pulling away.

"Sorry, folks," the operator said. "The next one will be up in a few minutes."

Maggie caught her breath at the sight of the two people on the train. A woman turned around and looked back at the winery.

"Serena," Jeremy said.

He waved, but the woman didn't wave back. Instead she laughed and swayed as the man next to her nuzzled her neck.

The man's face was buried behind Serena's long blond hair, so Maggie couldn't get a good look at him. The next thing she knew, Serena had turned around and kissed the man on the mouth. Then the train disappeared from sight.

"They're as bad as we were," Jeremy muttered.

Maggie couldn't speak. The sight of Serena kissing that man had caused her blood to run cold. Keith had never kissed her like that, especially not in public.

"Damn it all," she said in frustration, stamping her foot like an annoyed child. "I can't believe we missed them again. We were so close."

"Was it him?"

"I think so. The hair color is exactly the same color, but I need to see his face. I want to look into his eyes and see the truth."

"You will. We're close."

"We've been close for the past three days."

"It hasn't been all bad," Jeremy reminded her.

"I know, but . . ." She walked over and sat down on the bench.

"But what?"

"I'm running out of time."

"When do you have to be back in San Diego?"

"I should have been back yesterday." She got to her feet, restless again. "And I'm sure you have better things to do than chase after Serena."

"Not really." Jeremy tipped his head toward the station, where another train had arrived. "Let's go down the hill and see if we can catch them in the parking lot."

The ride down was a lot shorter than the ride up, with no unexpected stops, and Maggie was too tense to even think about fooling around again. When they exited the train, the parking lot was empty.

Maggie felt her heart sink once again, even though she hadn't really expected them to be there. She'd been one step behind Serena for three days now, and she still was.

"I'm sorry," Jeremy said. "I know you're disappointed."

"It's not your fault. I guess we just aren't meant to catch them."

"If it's them. You still haven't really seen his face. Are you sure it's your husband Serena is with?"

"About ninety-nine percent sure. He was kissing her, Jeremy."

"I saw. I bet that hurt."

"Only about as much as cutting off my arm." She walked toward their rental car, which was now the only one left in the parking lot. "We might as well go back to the hotel."

"Might as well." Jeremy unlocked the passenger door but paused before opening it. "If your husband truly left you for Serena, he's a fool. You are a beautiful, smart, and exceptionally wonderful woman."

"You don't have to say that." She smiled. "But if you want to, go ahead."

"It's true, Maggie. You're special. I knew that right away."

"You're really good for my ego."

"You're really good for me."

"But we're so different."

"Are we?"

She gazed into his eyes, all thoughts of Keith forgotten as she got caught in the gleam of desire . . .

"Even if we don't find Serena tonight, we can still have a great night," Jeremy continued. "We can make love. We can dance. We can tell each other all of our fantasies. We can even act some out if you want. So, my little worrier, if you're determined to think about something, why don't you think about that?"

As if she would be able to think of anything else.

Chapter 20

"Five card stud, jacks are wild," Lisa said.

Nick watched as she dealt five cards for each of them. They were the only ones in the hospital waiting room, which boasted a couple of lime green chairs, a beige couch and a small television set. After a half hour of tense silence, Nick had gone down to the gift shop and bought a deck of cards. Two hours later, they were still playing.

Nick picked up his cards and groaned when he saw his hand. "Great. You're almost unbeatable, you know. Are these cards marked?"

Lisa smiled. "No. But just so you know, you do owe me two hundred dollars."

Nick stared at the packages of Sweet'n Low he'd swiped from the hospital cafeteria. There were at least ten on her side and only two on his. "That's two hundred dollars?"

"They're each worth ten dollars," she said, checking her hand.

"Says who?"

"Me. How many cards do you want?"

Nick took a look at his hand and sighed again. "I'll just stick with these. I'll be broke soon anyway."

"You're so easy. I'll bet ten." She tossed one packet onto the table.

"I'll see your ten and raise you ten."

"Feeling cocky, I see." Lisa tossed two more packages onto the table. "I'll call, since you have nothing left to bet."

"Oh, rub it in, why don't you?" He showed his hand. "Three aces."

Her jaw dropped open. "No way. You looked like you had two threes at best."

He grinned. "That is called bluffing, sweetheart."

She threw down her cards in disgust. "You must have cheated."

"You dealt."

"You cut the cards."

He laughed out loud. "You're a sore loser."

"I am not," she said, sitting back in a huff, her arms crossed in front of her chest.

"You still have more packets than me," he pointed out.

She straightened in her chair. "Okay, double or nothing."

"Forget it, I'm done." He stretched out his arms and legs, tired from sitting for so long.

"You can't quit on a winning hand, Nick."

"Why not?"

"I deserve a chance to get my money back."

Nick leaned forward until their heads were almost touching. "I hate to break it to you, Lisa, but we're not playing for money, we're playing for artificial sweetener."

She made a face at him. "It's the principle."

He shook his head. "Does Raymond know how competitive you can be?"

"Yes, and he likes it. Because he's a shark in business, far worse than me." She shuffled the cards, her fingers flying with practiced speed.

"And you like that?" Nick asked, watching her, wishing she'd look at him instead of the cards.

"Of course. I admire him a great deal."

Funny how she never said the word love. "Do you think it will be easy to work together and live together at the same time?" he asked. "Or maybe you are already?" For some reason, that thought left a bitter taste in his mouth.

"No, we aren't," Lisa said, still shuffling the cards with restless fingers. "I have a nice one-bedroom condo in Studio

City. I've enjoyed having my own place to decorate. I even wallpapered the bedroom myself.''

"I remember the first time you put up wallpaper."

She grinned as she looked at him, her blue eyes sparkling. "The glue didn't stick, and in the middle of the night all the paper in our bedroom started falling down."

"And you ran around the room naked, trying to push it back up."

"I couldn't believe how much time I'd spent to have it fall apart. But this time I got it right."

His smile disappeared. *This time she'd gotten it right.* Her life was so much better now, without him.

"I still kill plants, though," she said, watching him closely. "If it's any consolation."

"It is."

"That's what I figured." She threw the cards down, stood up and walked across the waiting room, then back again. She checked her watch. "It's been over three hours. How long could it take?"

"I don't know." He hated the look of worry that crossed her face. For awhile, they'd managed to keep the fear at bay, but it was back.

"Maybe I should call Silvia again."

"She has everything under control, Lisa."

"I know, but it would give me something to do." She paused. "I should be working on my cereal slogan."

Nick stroked his chin. "How about this? If you've got a brain, try our grain. Not bad, huh?"

She laughed. "That was beyond terrible."

"Like you've got anything better. At least you know your boss won't fire you."

"I still want to do a good job. I don't use our relationship to take advantage at work," she said, her voice tightening. "I wouldn't do that."

"Hey, hey, hey. I didn't say you did. It sure as hell doesn't take much to piss you off these days."

"That's because you're so good at it." She paused, putting a hand on his arm. "I'm sorry, Nick. I'm a little tense."

"Me, too. Are you going to slug me if I put my arm around you?"

"No." He sat down, and she sat next to him, resting her cheek on his shoulder. They stayed that way until the surgeon came into the waiting room about fifteen minutes later.

As soon as they saw her, they stumbled to their feet. Nick wasn't sure if the surgeon's neutral expression was good news or bad. Lisa's hand slipped into his, and he held it tightly, needing her support.

"She's fine," the surgeon said, offering a bright smile.

"Oh, thank heavens." Lisa let out a long, relieved sigh.

"I want to keep her overnight, but if everything looks good in the morning, we'll send her home."

"That soon?" Lisa asked in surprise.

"As long as she does well tonight, there's really no need to keep her here."

"I'm staying with her," Lisa said. "I can't leave her alone all night in a hospital."

"That's fine. She's in recovery right now. One of the nurses will be in shortly to take you to see her. She'll sleep for awhile, though."

"Thank you, doctor," Nick said.

The surgeon nodded, then left.

Lisa turned in Nick's arms and hugged him. "She's okay. She's really okay."

He squeezed her tightly, having the sudden urge to never let her go. "We made it."

Lisa smiled up at him. "Yeah, we made it."

"Not everything has to turn out bad. You were great with Mary Bea." Nick paused as he looked into her eyes. "You shouldn't deny yourself the chance to have another child, Lisa. You would be a good mother."

Her smile disappeared, and her eyes darkened with a yearning he hadn't seen in a very long time. "It would be a risk. It's not like Rob—like she died of something specific. What if the same thing happened? What if there's something genetically wrong with me?"

"It could have been my genes."

"I don't see you rushing to have another child."

"I would do it again—with you."

Her eyes widened in shock. "That—that could never happen. I couldn't. I wouldn't."

"Then I guess I won't have children, either."

"You and me, us, together," Lisa said, waving her hand in the air. "That was the problem, Nick. If you had a baby with someone else, it probably wouldn't happen again."

"Then why not you and Raymond?" He paused, giving her a chance to reply, but she didn't say a word. "You don't have to answer that, Lisa. I know why, because you're afraid. I'm afraid, too. That's why I could only do it again with you, because we both know what it feels like to lose a child. We would go into the situation knowing exactly the same things."

"This conversation is pointless because we're not together any more, Nick. Remember?"

His arms locked around her waist, mocking her statement.

"Let me go," she said.

"No." He leaned over and kissed her. Lisa was so surprised she didn't have time to close her mouth, and he took immediate advantage of that fact, letting his tongue dance along her lips and inside the warm cavern of her mouth.

Her hands tightened on his arms, but she didn't push him away. In fact, she seemed to pull him closer, and when he deepened the kiss, he heard a soft sigh of delight. It undid him completely. He had only meant to kiss her briefly, but now he couldn't stop.

"Excuse me?" a voice said.

He let Lisa go, feeling somewhat shell-shocked to realize they were still standing in the middle of the hospital waiting room. Another minute, and he'd have ripped open her shirt and let his hands go where his mind had already wandered.

"Would you like to see your niece now?" a nurse asked, with a wry smile on her face.

"Of course." Lisa stepped away from Nick, patting her hair self-consciously. "We were so happy and relieved that our niece will be all right, I guess we got carried away"

"You two make a great couple."

"Oh, we're not a couple. We're divorced," Lisa explained.

"Really? If my ex-husband had kissed me like that, I sure as heck wouldn't have divorced him." The nurse turned her back and walked to the door.

"Where was she eight years ago?" Nick muttered. Lisa shot him a dark look, and they seemed to be right back where they'd started.

Lisa spent the night at the hospital, with Mary Bea sleeping alongside her in the bed. She'd worried that her presence might cause Mary Bea pain, but the little girl had insisted that they snuggle together.

Lisa hadn't slept much, but she had enjoyed holding Mary Bea in her arms. It brought back the maternal feelings she'd thought were dead and buried. Along with those feelings came thoughts of Nick. Things had changed between them in the few days they'd been together. Somehow they'd climbed the mountain of guilt and anger together and come down the other side. She didn't know how it had happened exactly. But she did know that she didn't hate him anymore. She didn't blame him for Robin's death. She didn't even hold him responsible for his behavior at the funeral. Drinking had been Nick's answer to the pain. Flight had been hers. How could she blame him for wanting to escape when she had done exactly the same thing?

Lisa glanced over at Mary Bea's sweet face, peaceful in sleep. Maggie was so lucky to have her children. She might have lost her husband, but at least she had them. When Robin had died, Lisa had had nothing. Actually, that wasn't true. She'd had Nick. She just hadn't wanted him then.

Trying not to wake Mary Bea, Lisa checked her watch. It was past seven. The night before she'd been so busy with Mary Bea, trying to keep her entertained and unafraid of the hospital, that she hadn't had a chance to call Raymond, and she needed to do that.

In fact, she should have made time to call him yesterday

when Nick was telling Mary Bea a good-night story. Instead, she'd stayed and listened to the story. Nick had always had a way of telling a tale that was completely captivating. But it wasn't just the story that had held her there, it was Nick. He was working his way back into her heart, under her skin, into her blood, just as he'd predicted. She couldn't let it happen. She couldn't take another chance with him. It was far too risky.

And Raymond was a great guy, she told herself firmly. He was kind and caring and ambitious. He liked the theater. He let her play classical music in the car. He even let her sleep without touching her—not like Nick, who hadn't been able to make it through the night without resting his hand on her breast or her waist or her thigh. She felt a tingle just at the thought of Nick in bed, naked and hot, cozying under the covers with her on a cold morning.

Then she felt guilty at the traitorous thought. So what if Raymond wasn't one for snuggling? That didn't make him any less desirable. And it gave her more space. She liked space.

With Nick, there was no space. When Lisa was with him, he took over her life, her thoughts, her body, her bed, everything, until they were practically the same person.

Still, it was kind of nice the way he'd been unable to sleep without touching her, she thought with a wistfulness that surprised her. Of course, Nick had obviously learned how to sleep alone in the past eight years, or how to sleep with Suzanne.

Lisa made a face at the ceiling, realizing she was stalling. She needed to call Raymond and explain. Surely he would understand once he knew about Mary Bea. It wasn't like they didn't have time to work up some ideas, although she had no idea when Maggie would return.

Maggie had left a message the day before, according to Silvia, but Maggie still didn't know Mary Bea was sick, and she still hadn't left a phone number where she could be reached.

It was so unlike Maggie to take off mysteriously, and to

think that Keith was alive; that was preposterous. Lisa just hoped Maggie wasn't having some type of breakdown all alone somewhere without family or friends to help her. At least she continued to call regularly. That was a good sign.

Call Raymond, Lisa told herself firmly. She slid off the bed slowly, taking care not to jostle Mary Bea. Once away from the bed, she stretched her arms overhead and yawned. She was exhausted but happy. Mary Bea was okay. That was enough to feel good about.

There was a phone next to the bed, so she picked it up, and after obtaining an outside line, dialed Raymond's home number. He was an early riser, so she didn't worry about waking him up. The phone rang several times, but no one answered. Finally, the machine answered in Raymond's no-nonsense voice.

Lisa waited for the beep, then left a message. "Hi, it's me. Are you there? I can't believe I missed you. I've been tied up down here. One of the kids had to go to the hospital. I'm really sorry that I didn't send you anything for Nature Brand, but I hope to do some work today, and I'll talk to you later. Bye." She hung up the phone feeling unsettled. Where would Raymond be at seven-thirty on a Tuesday morning?"

The hospital room door opened, and Silvia peeked inside. Lisa waved her in. "Hi, Mom."

Silvia tipped her head toward Mary Bea. "Is she all right?"

"She slept like a rock all night."

"How about you?"

Lisa tucked her hair behind her ear. "Not nearly as good as Mary Bea."

"But you survived."

"Yes," Lisa replied, looking down at Mary Bea and realizing how close they'd been to an even worse situation. The nurse had told them Mary Bea's appendix was severely inflamed. They were lucky to get it out before it ruptured.

"Now you know you can do it," Silvia said, putting her arm around Lisa's waist.

Lisa hugged her, then stepped away. "I don't know what you mean."

"Of course you do."

"Mom, please." She held up her hand. "I'm exhausted."

"Okay. At the moment I'm more concerned with Maggie."

"Maggie? Did she call again?"

"No, just the one message, but she sounded so odd, Lisa, and your Aunt Carmela thinks she's in trouble."

Lisa pulled her mother over to the far side of the room so they wouldn't be overheard by Mary Bea. "Maggie thinks Keith might still be alive. That's what she told Nick yesterday."

"Oh, dear." Silvia's eyes filled with worry. "Perhaps I should have asked her to come home instead of . . ."

"Instead of what?" Lisa asked, suddenly suspicious.

"Oh, nothing."

"You told her not to come back, didn't you?"

"I wouldn't do that."

"But you told her Nick and I were spending time together."

"It's the truth," Silvia said, looking as innocent as she possibly could. "Okay, I told her I thought it was good that you and Nick had a chance to talk about your lives. But that's it. I certainly didn't know Mary Bea would get sick. I feel terrible about that."

"It's not your fault, Mom. I doubt whatever you said had any effect on Maggie anyway. She seems determined to find out the truth—whatever that is."

"Lisa, why don't you go back to Maggie's house, take a shower, change your clothes, and catch up on some sleep? I'll stay with Mary Bea."

Lisa immediately shook her head. "No, I can't leave her. Besides, the doctor said she can go home later this morning. I'll just wait. Nick's with Roxy and Dylan. He said he'd get them off to school, then come down here."

Silvia smiled somewhat sadly. "You and Nick sound like a family when you talk like that."

They did sound like a family, and it was beginning to feel comfortable, cozy, loving, warm. But the kids didn't belong to her, and eventually their mother would come home and Lisa would go back to her own life, a life without children. She suddenly wondered if she was making a mistake.

"I think it was a mistake to let you sleep alone last night," Jeremy said when Maggie answered her hotel room door.

She pulled her robe around her shoulders and wished Jeremy wasn't such an early bird. She was still half asleep and could feel her hair sticking up from her head.

"I didn't sleep a wink," Jeremy added. "I couldn't stop thinking about you." He slid into her room before she could think of asking him to wait while she changed. He kissed her before she could think of brushing her teeth. Not that he seemed to care, and once his mouth touched hers, she didn't much care either.

"I like you like this," Jeremy whispered against her mouth. "Beautiful and dazed and ready to go to bed with me."

"Uh—I'm still asleep."

"Good, then you won't resist." He picked her up and tossed her on the bed.

She squealed in protest, but he climbed on to the bed and pinned her arms over her head with one hand. Then he let his glance drift down the length of her body, pausing just long enough on her breasts to cause them to tingle. Finally, his gaze came back to rest on her face. He suddenly looked serious. "Call him," he said.

"What?" Maggie was having a little trouble following the conversation, considering Jeremy's crotch was resting against her upper thighs, and if they didn't have clothes on, if he slid forward just an inch or so, they could do all the things she'd dreamed about the night before—only this time he'd really be in the room.

"Maggie. Maggie." Jeremy let go of her hands and snapped his fingers in front of her face.

"What?"

"Call him." Jeremy got off of her and sat on the edge of the bed. He tipped his head toward the phone.

"Call who?" she asked as she sat up.

"Keith. I want to know if you're still married, and I want to know now."

She looked into his eyes and saw desire and impatience. "He's—he's not registered, Jeremy."

"I know that. Call Serena. I'm sure they're together."

"Ouch," she said softly.

"Sorry." He touched her hand. "I just need to know if you're free, Maggie. We're good together. I think we could be great together if you'd give us the chance to find out."

She was so tempted to say yes, to have the ultimate adventure, the fantasy of her life. Who would blame her? No one. Everyone wanted her to be happy. But how could she be happy with Jeremy, when he knew nothing about her? At least none of the important things, like Roxy, Dylan and Mary Bea.

Maggie reached for the phone. Jeremy was right about one thing. They needed to end the mystery. They'd tried calling Serena the night before, but she'd never answered.

Taking a deep breath, Maggie called the operator and asked for Serena's room. She wished they would give her the room number. She would have liked to knock on the door and stare Keith right in the face.

The phone rang once, then twice, then three times. A man answered. "Hello," he grumbled.

Maggie's heart skipped a beat. "Keith? Oh, my God, is that you?"

"What? What?" He sounded confused, then alarmed. "Who is this?"

"It's your wife."

"I—I don't have a wife. You must have the wrong number."

"But—" Maggie stared in disbelief as the dial tone rang in her ear. She turned to Jeremy. "Keith answered the phone."

"What did he say?"

"He said he didn't have a wife."

Jeremy stared at her for a long moment. "Are you sure it was him?"

"It sounded like him." She looked at the receiver still clenched in her hand. "He said I had the wrong number."

"That's it. Give me the phone."

Maggie handed him the receiver, and he dialed the operator once again. She watched him with worry and anticipation and fear. After a moment, he hung up.

"No answer."

They'd spooked Keith. Now he knew someone was on to him. "He's going to leave," Maggie said.

Jeremy nodded. "Get dressed, then meet me downstairs. I'll keep an eye out in the lobby. If they try to leave, I'll stop them." He stood up, then bent back down to kiss her. "Don't worry, Maggie. We'll find out the truth."

"He hates me," she whispered. "What did I do to make him hate me?"

"Maybe you should hate him. He's the one who left, who treated you abominably. Help me out here, Maggie. Get mad. Fight. That's the only way you'll get through this."

"You're right." She thrust her chin up in the air. "I'm not some wimp he can just walk out on without an explanation. I want him to answer to me, to tell me to my face why he faked his own death."

"What are you going to do then?"

"I'll probably kill him."

"That works for me."

Lisa tucked Mary Bea into her own bed just after one o'clock Tuesday afternoon. The little girl was exhausted, and Lisa hoped she would sleep for a few hours and give her body a chance to rest. Lisa had worried that Mary Bea was going home too soon, but the doctor had assured her that Mary Bea would recuperate just as fast, if not faster, at home. Lisa had a feeling that's what they told everyone these days, insurance being the way it was. But she forced herself to take the comments at face value.

"Everything okay?" Nick asked from the doorway.

She turned her head and sighed at the sight of him. He looked so damn good in his faded blue jeans and navy blue knit T shirt, rugged and handsome and fresh from a shower. She, on the other hand, felt like a rumpled bed. "Everything's fine," she said, scolding herself for even noticing her ex-husband's looks. She didn't need to stare at him. She knew what his body looked like. She'd traced it with her mouth a hundred times. Goodness, where had that thought come from?

"Lisa? What are you thinking about?" Nick asked curiously.

She knew she couldn't tell him the truth. "I was thinking about taking a shower, then a nap. I'm tired." She walked into the hall and pulled Mary Bea's door closed so they wouldn't disturb her.

"I'll bet you are. Mary Bea told me she loved you," Nick said softly. "She said she was glad you were her aunt."

Lisa felt a rush of warmth steal across her body. "She really loves me?"

"Yeah, and she wants to know if we're getting married again."

Lisa cleared her throat. "What—what did you tell her?"

"I didn't say anything."

"Why not? Why didn't you tell her that you don't want to marry me?"

Nick sent her a steady look. "I'm not sure that's the truth."

She stared at him in amazement, then shook her head. "I can't have this conversation with you right now. I'm so tired, I can't think."

"You're right, I'm sorry. Listen, I know you probably want a shower and a nap more than anything else in the world right now, but I made you a surprise."

"You did? What?"

"Homemade chocolate chip cookies. Your number one comfort food, as I recall."

"Oh, man, I thought I smelled cookies when we walked

in the door.'' Lisa immediately turned toward the stairs and, despite Nick's laugh, hurried to the kitchen.

The cookies were on a plate on the counter and were still warm.

"They're only the slice and bake kind,'' Nick warned.

"I don't care.'' She broke one in half and popped a bite into her mouth, then closed her eyes as the delicious warmth of chocolate and sugar melted in her mouth.

"You look like you're having an orgasm,'' Nick commented.

Lisa opened one eye and scowled at him. "Yeah, and you're interrupting.''

"It would be a lot more fun if I could share it with you.''

"Get your own cookie.''

He walked over and slid his arms around her waist, then pressed his mouth against hers, tasting the chocolate on her lips. "Mm-mm, I like this cookie the best.''

She pushed him away with a laugh. "You think you can sweet-talk me with a cookie?''

"I know I can,'' he said confidently. "Just let me—''

He stopped when the doorbell rang.

"Probably my mother,'' Lisa said.

"Maybe it's Maggie.''

"She wouldn't ring her own bell,'' Lisa replied, as they walked to the front of the house to answer it.

Lisa opened the door and almost fell over. The man in the expensive, three-piece gray suit and red silk tie was definitely not Maggie. "Raymond,'' she gasped. "What are you doing here?''

He sent her a satisfied smile. "I was worried about you, so I thought I'd drive down and see if I could help speed your return home.'' His smile faded as he saw Nick standing behind her.

Lisa followed his gaze, realizing that Nick's mouth was spotted with chocolate, the same chocolate that was on her lips, because she'd been kissing him when she was engaged to Raymond. She suddenly felt as if they'd been caught in bed together.

"I'm Raymond Curtis, Elisabeth's fiancé," he said to Nick, extending his hand.

Nick ignored the gesture. "I'm Nick Maddux, Lisa's ex-husband."

"Ex-husband?" Raymond's arm fell to his side. His eyes widened in shock as he looked from Elisabeth to Nick, then back to Elisabeth. "You never told me you were married."

"You never told him you were married?" Nick asked with a mocking smile. "Gee, I wonder what else he doesn't know."

Chapter 21

"Raymond, let me explain." Lisa took Raymond's arm and pulled him inside the house. "Come in and sit down. Would you like some coffee or a cookie?" She self-consciously wiped her mouth with the back of her hand, catching Nick's sardonic grin out of the corner of her eye.

"Some coffee would be good," Raymond said tensely, obviously taken aback by Nick's unexpected revelation.

"I'm pretty thirsty myself," Nick said, following them down the hall to the kitchen.

"I'd like to speak to Raymond alone." Lisa paused at the door to the kitchen.

"I've been wanting to meet your fiancé, Lisa, I mean Elisabeth. I understand you're quite the businessman, Raymond."

"Well, yes," Raymond said with little false modesty. "I run a very successful advertising firm, Curtis and Associates."

"Lisa told me. She said you're a shark."

Raymond darted a curious glance at Lisa. "I hope that was a compliment."

"It was, of course it was," she said, feeling like a spectator at a tennis match. But she wasn't a spectator. This was her life, not Nick's. "Excuse us," she said firmly, pulling Raymond into the kitchen and shutting the door behind her.

Raymond stared at her like she was a stranger, and as his gaze ran down her rumpled slacks and blouse, his expression grew more incredulous. "You look like you slept in those clothes."

"She did," Nick said, stepping into the kitchen.

"My God, did you sleep with him?" Raymond demanded.

"No," Lisa snapped, trying to ignore Nick's amused smile. "I slept with my five-year-old niece in the hospital. Didn't you get my message?"

"No." Raymond didn't look as if he believed her.

"I called you early this morning, around seven-thirty. Where were you?"

"You know I always work out on Tuesday mornings."

Lisa sighed, then nodded. Of course she knew that. Raymond's habits were quite predictable, especially when they involved his obsession with exercise. "I forgot."

"After that, I had a meeting with Paul to discuss his handling of the Nature Brand account."

"Paul?" She couldn't believe what she was hearing. "You gave Paul my account? How could you do that?"

"I waited for your ideas," Raymond replied, his voice sharp, his expression tense. "They didn't arrive as promised. I have to have something to present tomorrow at my lunch meeting. I can't go in empty-handed."

"You can't reschedule?"

"No, dammit, I can't," Raymond said, practically shouting. He seemed to become aware of Nick's curious presence and lowered his voice. "I have a business to run, and you're showing an amazing lack of reliability."

"My friend is in trouble."

"Your ex-husband?" Raymond tipped his head toward Nick, who was lounging against the counter.

"No, my ex-husband's sister, Maggie. That's why Nick is here, Raymond. He's helping me take care of the kids."

"So you're living here together?"

"Not exactly together."

"I wouldn't say that," Nick said.

"You won't say anything, because you're leaving." Lisa walked around the kitchen island, grabbed Nick's wrist and dragged him out of the room. "Stay out, this is my business." She slammed the door in his face.

Raymond looked at her in bewilderment. He shook his head, opened his mouth, then shook his head again. "I can't believe you were married to that man. You never said a word. Why?"

"I was very young when we were married. It was over almost eight years ago."

"I told you about my ex-wife. What's the big mystery?"

Now that he asked, Lisa didn't know why she hadn't told him, except that she hadn't wanted to think about Nick, much less talk about him. "There is no mystery. I just don't think about him anymore."

"What else haven't you told me?"

Lisa hesitated, realizing that part of why she hadn't told Raymond any of it was because it put her in a bad light. That age old fear of rejection reared its ugly head once again. She didn't want to lose Raymond to the truth, but she knew that she couldn't marry him without telling him all of it.

"Sit down." She pulled out a chair for him at the kitchen table.

Raymond sat down, waiting for her to begin.

She took a deep breath, wondering if she could really get out the words. She hadn't told anyone about Robin, hadn't spoken about her from the day after the funeral until she'd arrived at Maggie's on Friday night.

"Elisabeth, what is it?" Raymond prodded. "Surely, it can't be that bad."

"It is bad, Raymond." She sat down and folded her hands together on the table. "Nick and I had a baby, and she died when she was two months old of sudden infant death syndrome, which means they don't really know what killed her." Her words came out in a terrifying rush, and she wasn't sure any of them made sense.

Raymond didn't reply for a long moment. Then he put his hand over hers. "I'm sorry, Elisabeth. I had no idea."

"I know." She looked into his eyes, uncertain as to what she would find—rejection, disgust, wariness. Instead, she saw compassion and a bit of confusion. "Nick and I separated a few days after the funeral," she added. "It was a very painful episode in my life, and I never told you, because I didn't want to relive it. I suppose I was afraid of what you would think."

"Is there more?" Raymond asked.

"No, that's pretty much it. The bracelet you saw was mine, not my mother's. She sent it to me because she wanted me to have it."

"And that's why you don't want children, because of this baby that you lost?"

"Exactly."

Raymond sat back in his chair. "I have to admit I'm surprised. I never imagined you'd been through such a terrible experience. You've always seemed so young and pretty, untouched by life."

Because that's the way she wanted to look, and the way she suspected he wanted her to look. "I should have told you. In the beginning, it didn't seem important and after you asked me to marry you, I feared it might make a difference."

"Why would it?" he asked, but he didn't look as compassionate as he had a moment earlier.

She licked her lips, trying to find the right words, the diplomatic answer. "Because I thought you liked the fact that I didn't have any baggage, no ex-husband, no relatives to speak of, no friends of my own, except the ones we have together."

"Elisabeth, I have plenty of my own baggage. I wouldn't have held a previous marriage against you."

"But I failed, Raymond. I know how you hate failure."

He looked at her in astonishment. "Elisabeth, I failed too, and I left behind not just a spouse but a kid."

She knew all that. But she had always believed he expected more from her than he did from himself. "I'm glad this is all out in the open. And I'm sorry that I didn't call you yesterday when I took Mary Bea to the hospital. I got caught up in what was happening and didn't think about work. I hope you'll accept my apology."

"Of course." Raymond hesitated, his eyes searching hers. "Elisabeth, do you think I'm too old for you?"

"No, absolutely not."

"You're sure? When I saw you with that guy, your ex-husband, I couldn't help but notice that you were the same age."

"That didn't keep us together."

"No, I guess it didn't."

"And you and your first wife were the same age, and it didn't help you."

"All right. You've convinced me."

Lisa offered him a somewhat shaky smile. Good, she'd convinced him. Now she just had to convince herself. Deep down she knew it wasn't the age difference that was the problem.

"Come back with me now, Elisabeth."

She tensed. "I can't leave Mary Bea. We just brought her home from the hospital, and her mother hasn't returned yet."

"Why can't you leave her with her uncle?"

"Because I promised Maggie I would stay."

"You promised me you'd help me win this account," Raymond reminded her, suddenly all business again. "This is very important to the agency, to our future together. You should have a sense of responsibility, a loyalty to me, to the company, to your job."

"I thought you'd given the account to Paul," she replied, still irritated that he'd moved ahead without her and now was questioning her loyalty.

"Not officially. But he wants it."

"Of course he does. He'd like your entire agency, in fact. He's a cold-blooded, ruthless little shit."

"Elisabeth!" Raymond looked shocked by her language.

"I'm sorry, but it's true. I have held my tongue where he's concerned, but you have to know who he really is."

"I'm more interested right now in finding out who you really are, because I have to tell you, you don't look like the woman I proposed to a few months ago or the woman I'm used to seeing in the office. That woman is cool and calm and professional, and she knows what her priorities are. She doesn't act without thinking first. She doesn't take off at a moment's notice, and she certainly doesn't wear clothes she spent the night sleeping in.'' His mouth curled with distaste.

"I'm a little wrinkled,'' Lisa said, suddenly losing patience with his questions, with his needs. What about her needs? What about the sleepless night she'd just spent worrying about her niece? "Give me a break, Raymond. I spent the night at the hospital. I'm exhausted. I'm sorry I don't look as crisp and clean as a new hundred dollar bill.''

He held up a hand. "I'm sorry. That was uncalled for. I just don't understand you anymore.''

"I've only been gone a few days, Raymond. I haven't changed all that much.''

"I think you have.'' He stood up. "This was a mistake. You need to take care of your business, and I need to take care of mine. I'll see you when you return.'' His glance drifted to the box sitting on the counter. "Maybe I should say if you return. You never sent out the wedding invitations. You lied to me.''

"I addressed them. I meant to send them,'' she defended. "It's just been so crazy around here.''

"Do you want me to mail them, Elisabeth?''

"No, I'll take care of it. I will.''

"Elisabeth, are you sure you want to marry me?''

She stared at him, stunned by the question. "Of course, I do. I—I love you. I thought you loved me.''

"I do.'' He shook his head. "We'll talk when you get back, when things are normal again.''

As he turned to leave, Lisa put a hand on his arm, knowing she had to cross the breach that had developed between them. "I appreciate your driving all the way down here to see me. It means a lot to know that you care that much about me. I'm sure Maggie will be home today or tomorrow, and I promise I will come home as soon as she walks in the door.''

"Where did she go?''

"That's a long story.''

"Forget it, I don't want to know.''

Lisa followed him to the front door. She hoped he would stop and kiss her good-bye, especially since Nick was sitting in the living room, but Raymond simply walked out the door.

As his car pulled away from the curb, Nick came to stand behind her.

"He's gone already? What did you have—a quickie in the kitchen?"

"No, we didn't have a quickie in the kitchen. Raymond is far too sophisticated for that."

"And far too old. The man has to be at least fifty."

"Fifty-two," she said tightly. "Not that it matters. We have a great deal in common."

"And he takes care of you," Nick taunted. "You finally found that father you were always looking for."

"That isn't it at all. Raymond understands me. He doesn't try to change me, to take over my thoughts, to rule every aspect of my life."

Nick stared at her for a long moment. He could not for the life of him understand what he saw in the guy. "Do you really have fun with him, Lisa? He has enough starch in his shirt to dry up Niagara Falls."

"We have a great time together. He's very, very kind."

"Nice, kind, ambitious—when are you going to tell me you're madly in love with the guy?"

"I'm madly in love with the guy," Lisa repeated, slamming the front door, because it released some of her tension. "It's your fault that he left, announcing I was your ex-wife that way."

"I didn't know you hadn't told him. You're the one who yelled at me for not telling Suzanne, and I'm not even engaged to her."

"She probably wouldn't have you."

The doorbell rang again.

"Maybe that's Raymond," she said hopefully.

Lisa threw open the door. "Ray—" The word died on her lips, for standing on the porch were Bill and Kathy Maddux, Nick's parents. Bill was an older version of Nick, long, lean legs, a strong build and gray hair. Kathy, on the other hand, was a short, rather plump blond with the biggest smile Lisa had ever seen.

"Lisa," Kathy said with genuine delight. "Good heavens, I haven't seen you in ages." She opened her arms, and Lisa couldn't help but give her a big hug. It felt nice to hug Kathy again. In many ways, she was the kind of mother Lisa had always wanted. Although she felt like a traitor to her own mother for even thinking that.

"Mom, Dad, what are you doing here?" Nick asked. "Your trip doesn't end until Friday."

"Tell him, Bill," Kathy said to her husband.

"You tell him."

Kathy rolled her eyes. "Your father got seasick."

"The boat was just too damn big. Couldn't find my way half the time."

"They were on a cruise of the Greek islands," Nick said to Lisa.

"That's right," Kathy said. "We went halfway across the world, and all your father wanted to do was read his golf magazines."

"Now if they'd had a golf course on board, I'd have been happy," Bill said. "Where's Maggie?"

"Anyway, we decided to come home early. We missed everyone. Where's Maggie?" she asked, repeating Bill's question.

Nick shot Lisa a questioning look.

"Why don't you both come in and sit down?" Lisa suggested. "Nick made cookies. Would you like one?"

"Nick made cookies?" Kathy asked, putting a hand to her heart. "Good heavens! What exactly did he want from you, Lisa?"

Lisa blushed a thousand shades of red.

Bill laughed and punched Nick in the arm. "Like we don't know the answer to that question, huh, son? I must say I never thought I'd see the two of you together again."

Nick looked somewhat embarrassed. "I made the cookies for Mary Bea. She just had her appendix out."

Kathy's expression turned to worry. "Not my baby. Is she okay?"

"She's fine," Lisa said. "She's sleeping."

"Oh, I have to go see her. I promise I won't wake her up. Come on, Bill. Let's go check on our sweet thing."

As they left the room, Lisa turned to Nick. "What are we going to tell them about Maggie?"

"I don't know. I'm thinking."

"What are you thinking?" she demanded. "They'll be back any second."

"I'm thinking I should leave you here to explain."

"No way. They're your parents. Besides, I don't think they like me much anymore."

Nick looked at her in amazement. "Are you kidding? They love you."

"Not after I left you the way I did."

"They told me it was my fault."

"They wouldn't have said that." Lisa paused, lowering her voice so she wouldn't be overheard. "Sometimes I think your dad blamed me for what happened. I know he never said anything, but he just couldn't look me straight in the eye after that night."

Nick put his hands on her arms and shook her. "You could find rejection in an ant who decides not to make his home in your kitchen. My father doesn't look anyone in the eye when it comes to personal, emotional matters. He can't let his feelings show, whether they be good, bad or indifferent. You used to tell me that."

"Yes, I guess I did," she said slowly. Something else she'd forgotten. Why was her view of the past so distorted?

"She's still asleep," Kathy said, as she walked down the stairs with Bill at her heels. "Now, tell me what's going on."

"How about a cookie?" Lisa asked again, heading toward the kitchen. "I can make some coffee."

Kathy followed them into the kitchen while Bill muttered something about catching the news on television.

"All right. What's going on?" Kathy demanded, giving

Nick a motherly glare that told him he'd better answer or else.

"Cookie, Mom?" Nick asked with a smile, offering her the plate.

"Chocolate chip, huh? Lisa's favorite." Kathy sent them each a speculative look. Then she took a cookie and sat down. "Okay, talk."

Nick sat down across from her while Lisa leaned against the counter by the sink. She suddenly realized how quickly they'd swapped positions. With Raymond, she'd been at the table with Nick at the sink. Now it was reversed, yet they were both still involved. In fact, everything seemed to involve Nick. It was as if he were living in every molecule of the air she breathed.

"Maggie needed to get away for a few days to get her head straight," Nick said. He glanced over at Lisa, drawing her attention back to their conversation.

"Straight about what?" Kathy asked.

"Oh, jeez, I don't know." Nick rubbed the back of his neck with his hand. "She's a little nuts at the moment."

"What does that mean?" Alarm rang through Kathy's voice, and she leaned forward. "Is she having some sort of a breakdown?"

"Nick, you're scaring your mother." Lisa softened her voice deliberately, hoping to ease some of the anxiety she could see on Kathy's face. "Maggie had some questions about Keith's death that she needed to resolve. That's all."

"She thinks Keith might still be alive," Nick said bluntly.

"Well, don't sugarcoat it, Nick," Lisa said in disgust.

"She's a mother, she can take it."

Kathy put a hand to her heart and took several deep breaths. "Why would my usually sensible daughter think that her husband is alive, when we all know that he died in a fire almost a year ago?"

"She thinks she saw him," Nick replied.

Kathy gasped. "What?"

"It's a long story. There are all sorts of other things, insurance money, missing cash." He shook his head. "I'll admit, I'm getting worried. Maggie was supposed to be back on Sunday. She doesn't even know Mary Bea had her appendix out, because she didn't leave us a number where she could be reached.''

"That doesn't sound like Maggie."

"None of it sounds like Maggie. I'm not sure she's even in San Diego."

"She's not," Lisa said. "When my mom spoke to Maggie, she heard an announcement in the background. She thinks Maggie went to San Francisco."

"What's in San Francisco?" Kathy asked, confusion drawing her brows into tiny sharp points. She tossed her half-eaten cookie down on the plate as if she had suddenly lost her appetite.

Lisa hated the look of worry that crossed Kathy's face. She and her husband had just come back from a long overdue second honeymoon. They were rested, relaxed. At least they had been.

"I don't know what's in San Francisco, Mom, or maybe the better question is who," Nick replied.

"Maybe she went to see Joey," Kathy said, her face lighting up with hope. "She always looked up to her big brother."

"Joey's in Santa Cruz."

"It's not that far from San Francisco. Maybe she just flew into the San Francisco airport, then drove down the coast . . ." Her voice trailed away. "But she would have told you if she went to Joey's house."

"If Maggie was in trouble, the last person she'd ask for help is Joey," Nick said with a shake of his head. "He criticizes first and thinks second."

"You're right. How long has she been gone?"

"Since Friday," Nick replied.

"Five days? So long?"

"But she called us just yesterday," Lisa interjected. "I'm sure she'll call again today and everything will be fine. We'll find out where she is and when she's coming home."

Kathy nodded, looking more relieved as she turned to Lisa.

"I'm glad you're here, Lisa. It's good to see you again, and it's especially nice to see you and Nick together."

"Forget it, Mom. She's marrying someone else in a month." Nick shoved back his chair and stood up.

"Oh." Kathy looked taken aback, but she quickly recovered. "Congratulations. I hope you'll be happy."

"Thank you. I think I'll check on Mary Bea. If you'll excuse me . . ."

As Lisa left the kitchen, Nick walked over to the window and looked out at the backyard. He knew what was coming, and it didn't take more than a minute.

"You still love her, don't you?" Kathy asked.

He shook his head.

"Oh, Nick. I'm sorry."

His mother obviously did not believe him. He felt a wave of anger mixed with self-pity. "I don't love her," he denied, because it was what he was supposed to say. You weren't supposed to love a woman who'd walked out on you at the darkest moment of your life. He was just as afraid of Lisa as she was afraid of him. Having suffered the worst together and fallen apart, how could he think of taking that chance again, of letting himself love her, then having to say goodbye when things got tough?

But Lisa hadn't left yesterday, not even when he'd given her the chance to go. She'd honored her promise to Maggie. She'd stuck by Mary Bea and by him. Maybe she'd changed. He knew he had. Was he a fool to think the impossible could happen after all these years?

Kathy walked over to him, put an arm around his waist and leaned her head on his shoulder. "You two were so in love. I used to envy you."

"Why would you envy us?"

"Because you reminded me of the way I used to feel when your father and I first met."

"Yeah, but you lasted, we didn't," he said, his voice suddenly so tight he could barely say the words.

"We didn't go through what you did. You and Lisa were both very young when Robin died. Heavens, Lisa was still breast-feeding. Her hormones were going crazy. I never held her responsbible for the way she acted then. She didn't know what she was doing.''

"Yeah, well my hormones were just fine, so what's my excuse?'' He shook his head in self-recrimination. "I had no excuse.''

"You were hurting, Nick. Drinking was not the answer, but you were so overwhelmed with pain that you couldn't handle the real world.'' She paused. "You have a great depth of love. When you commit yourself to someone, you go all the way, no holding back. You give everything you have to give. When you lost Robin, you lost a big part of yourself. When Lisa ran away, she took the rest.''

"Well, I won't make that mistake again.''

"That's what I'm afraid of. You haven't been serious with anyone since Lisa. I don't want you to end up alone, Nick, without a wife, without children.''

"Maybe I'm better off without children. I certainly couldn't protect the one I had.''

"That's the hardest part about being a parent, accepting that you can't protect your children from getting hurt. You can take all the precautions in the world and worry yourself like crazy, but each individual comes to this world with a life to live, no matter how long or how good or how scary it might be. We give our children life, but sometimes we forget that they're the ones who actually have to live that life.''

Nick put his arms around Kathy and hugged her. "Thanks, Mom. Sometimes I need a kick in the butt.''

"Here's another kick,'' she said pointedly. "Lisa's not married yet.''

"Do I have a sign on my back that says sucker?''

"No, it says stubborn fool. You still love her. And she's here.''

"Because of Maggie, not because of me.''

"So what?'' She waved her hand in the air. "You've got a second chance. Take it. If you don't, I think you'll regret it more than anything else that's happened.''

"I'll think about it."

"Good. Now what are we going to do about Maggie?"

"I thought you just said children have to live their own lives. How come you're giving me advice and worrying about Maggie?"

"Oh, shut up and give me another cookie. On second thought, give me the whole plate. I need something to do while we wait for Maggie to call."

Nick handed his mother the plate of cookies, then looked over at the phone and willed it to ring. It remained ominously silent.

Chapter 22

L isa wasn't baby-sitting, she was hosting a family reunion, she thought wearily as she brewed another pot of coffee. Kathy and Bill refused to go home until Maggie called. Silvia and Carmela had arrived just before five to check on Mary Bea, and they'd all ordered out for pizza before Lisa could think of suggesting that anyone go home.

Now it was after eight and there was still no call from Maggie. Lisa stared at the coffee slowly filling the pot and had to admit she was worried, too. Maggie had been gone a long time, and this business about Keith was unsettling. There was no way he could be alive. No one could have survived the fire.

"My father wants to know if there are any cookies left," Nick said as he entered the kitchen. "Your Aunt Carmela wants to know if we have any mint tea and your mother—"

Lisa held up a hand. "Do they think this is a restaurant?"

"Yes. And we're the waiters."

"They're treating us like children. Have you noticed that? I swear my mother gives Roxy more respect than she gives me. 'Lisa, dear, are you sure you told the pizza man how to get to the house?'" she mimicked.

Nick laughed. "And my father suggested I didn't know how to work the remote control because I couldn't find golf on any one of sixty-seven channels. Can you imagine?"

"You not know how to work a remote control? Is the man nuts? You are the master. The grand master."

"Okay, that's enough."

She smiled. "So when are they leaving?"

"They're not."

"What do you mean, they're not?"

"My mother says she's not going anywhere until Maggie calls. Roxy graciously offered my mother her bed, and Dylan suggested my father take the bed in his room and he'd sleep on the floor. You'll notice that Dylan never offered to do that for me."

"I guess you don't rate. I should just give them Maggie's bed. Then they could sleep together. After all, they're still on their honeymoon."

"I know. My father actually kissed my mother when she handed him some pizza." Nick shook his head in bemusement. "It's disgusting, really."

Lisa couldn't stop the smile that spread across her face. "I think it's nice. They're still in love after all these years."

"It is nice, kind of sappy, but nice." Nick sighed as his father shouted for his coffee. "That's it. We're out of here."

Lisa looked at him in surprise. "We can't just leave. The children . . ."

"There are more baby-sitters here than there are children."

"Mary Bea is still weak," Lisa protested, although it was halfhearted. Getting out of the house was the best idea she'd heard all day.

"Mary Bea is propped up like a princess in the living room with six people seeing to her every whim. Her fever is gone. She has no more stomachache, and my mother and your mother know more about taking care of kids than we do." Nick sent her a wheedling smile. "Come on, let's go. We'll sneak out the back."

"My purse is in the other room."

"I'll pay."

"We should at least leave a note."

"Fine." Nick grabbed a piece of paper off Maggie's To Do list and scribbled the words "Back later, Nick." Then he took Lisa by the hand and pulled her out the door before she could think of another reason to say no.

They snuck down the side yard like thieves in the night, or at least like two runaway teenagers. Unfortunately, they had to pass very close to the living room window, and Nick paused as they heard his mother ask his father to close the window. They were literally trapped, because to move on the crunchy leaves would only draw attention to themselves. To stay might mean discovery if Nick's father happened to look out the window.

Suddenly the situation struck Lisa as funny, and she couldn't help the giggle that snuck past her lips. Nick put his hand over her mouth.

"Sh-sh," he said. "They'll hear you."

Lisa bit down on her lip to prevent another laugh. Heavens, she hadn't had this much fun in years.

Bill pulled the window down halfway, but he didn't bother to look outside. "Is that better, dear?"

"Yes, sweet 'ems," Kathy said in a cooing voice. "You're a darling. Come here and give me a kiss."

"Oh, God, I might just be sick," Nick muttered. "I don't know who those people are in that house, but they are not my parents."

"They're honeymooners."

"Who have been married for forty years. Come on, let's go, before they start looking for us."

They dashed across the lawn to the driveway and slipped into Nick's car. He put the car in neutral and rolled down to the edge of the driveway, not turning the ignition or hitting the lights until they were as far away from the house as possible.

As they turned the corner and headed toward the highway, Lisa let out a sigh of relief. "We've escaped."

"And not a moment too soon." He flung her a quick glance. "So, where do you want to go? And don't you dare say L.A."

"Anywhere, Nick. Surprise me."

"All right. I will."

Los Angeles was actually the last place she wanted to go right now. Lisa still felt disturbed by her conversation with Raymond, not just the fact that he'd given her account away so quickly, but he'd seemed different after learning about Nick and Robin. He had said all the right things—that it didn't matter, that he had made more mistakes than she had—but she had still sensed disappointment.

Maybe Nick was right. Maybe she anticipated rejection so much that she made it happen, or believed it had happened even when it hadn't.

Still, even if Raymond hadn't rejected her, she knew that he was not happy with her decision to remain in Solana Beach until Maggie returned home. He didn't like that she was putting family before work. He also didn't care for the fact that she had friends outside of their world. It hadn't bothered her before, because she hadn't wanted these friends. Now, she did. She'd learned that in the past few days.

She'd missed Maggie, and now that she'd gotten to know the kids, she knew she would miss them, too. Even Silvia and Carmela had brought a sense of fond nostalgia to her heart. And there was Nick.

She was acutely aware of his presence, fine-tuned to his body, the way he moved, the way he smelled, the way he breathed. Years had passed. But she still felt him within her as if it had only been yesterday when they made love.

How could she marry Raymond, knowing she still had feelings for Nick? How could she act on those feelings when she knew she and Nick could have no future together? She wouldn't go down that road again. She couldn't. It was too frightening.

But how could she marry a man without loving him the way she'd loved Nick? Was that fair to Raymond? Did he deserve more?

She knew she could be a good wife. But could she be a great wife? Could she give Raymond everything he needed and still protect herself from getting hurt?

Lisa looked out the window at the dark night, the lights of the passing cars, and she knew she'd been worrying about this marriage for far longer than the past few days. That's why she'd resisted hiring the wedding consultant and had insisted on doing the invitations herself, because she had wanted to control what was happening—maybe even stop it if she had to.

The wedding invitations were still sitting on Maggie's counter, untouched, unmailed. Who was she kidding? She couldn't send them out now. Not with so much unsettled in her mind.

Do you love me, Elisabeth? She could still hear Raymond's voice, his sharp, tense question. *Are you sure you want to marry me?* She was terribly afraid that she couldn't answer yes to either of those questions.

Lisa looked down at the ring on her finger and twisted it with her hand. It felt heavy and pretentious and wrong. She slipped it off and stuck it in the pocket of her jeans, even though it seemed sacrilegious to stick a two-carat diamond in a denim pocket. But without the ring on her finger, Lisa felt lighter, better, less anxious.

She glanced at Nick and caught him watching her. She waited for him to say something, but he didn't say a word. He just gripped the steering wheel and stared straight ahead. Ten minutes later, he turned off the main highway and drove down the street that lined one of the harbors at Mission Bay.

She thought they were going to a restaurant. But when she stepped out of the car, Nick led her toward the boats.

"Where are we going?" she asked, suddenly nervous.

Nick took her hand. "It's not far."

She followed him down the pier, until they stopped in front of a sailboat. "Whose boat is this?"

"It's mine." He pointed to the bow, where something was written.

She took a step closer so she could read the words. "*Blue Eyes*," she said out loud. Her heart thudded against her chest. "You named your boat after Frank Sinatra?"

Nick laughed. "No, I named it after you, Blue Eyes."

"Oh, Nick. Why?"

"Because I missed you." He closed the gap between

them, drawing her into his arms, threading his hands through her hair so she had to tilt her head and look at him. "I missed the way you made me laugh, the way you made me want to play the most seductive music I could find because you always made love to me afterwards. I missed the way we could read each other's thoughts without even trying, finish each other's sentences, eat half our dinners, then swap plates." His voice turned husky. "I missed my best friend."

Lisa's eyes filled with moisture. "I missed you, too—the music, the laughs, all the secrets we told each other. I've never been as open with anyone as I was with you."

He kissed her on the mouth with tenderness that immediately rose to passion. Her best friend became her lover with one long, tingling kiss.

"Would you like to see the rest of the boat?" Nick asked. "I think you'll like it."

"Yes." She answered one question aloud, the other with her eyes. "Just don't—don't let me think too much," she whispered.

"Honey, the last thing I want you to do is think."

He helped her on board, but didn't bother to point out anything but the stairs that led to the galley, and her brief view of that was cut off by the sudden descent of Nick's head, blocking out everything in her vision but him, his green eyes, his curly hair, his strong, wonderful face.

She cupped his face with her hands and smiled at him. He smiled back, but didn't move. He seemed strangely hesitant to proceed, now that they were alone together. Lisa knew it was her turn to step forward. Nick had brought her this far. She had to take them the rest of the way. If she dared.

The boat rocked lazily in the water, the slippery motion making her only that much more dizzy with desire and need. Nick turned her world upside down. He overwhelmed her senses. He made her feel things that scared the hell out of her, because they were so deep, so personal, so private.

If she made love to him now, Nick would take everything she had to give. He wouldn't let her hide behind the walls she'd built, and she would risk losing everything she'd worked so hard to attain—her independence, her resolve to move forward.

"You're thinking," Nick muttered. "We can't have that."

He kissed her on the cheek, trailing his lips across her face to her ear, tugging on the lobe with his teeth, until she shuddered. He pulled her shirt out of her jeans and slid his hands up the bare skin of her stomach, raising goose bumps in his wake.

Lisa tensed as his hands grazed her breasts, as his fingers teased the skin above her bra and all the while his mouth was moving slowly down her neck until she closed her eyes and let the sensations wash over her.

The want was too powerful, the need too strong to be denied. His mouth left her skin and she felt a rush of unwelcome cold, the silence of a chilling question. She opened her eyes and saw Nick watching her, desire firing his eyes, but control steadying his hands as they slipped to her waist.

She answered him the only way she could. She started with the top button on her blouse and slipped it through the hole, then moved down to the next one and the next. Nick followed each move with his eyes, his hungry, starving eyes.

Lisa suddenly felt in control, powerful, and wanted. When she finished with the buttons, she slipped the blouse off her shoulders and stood before him in a lacy black bra. She moved to undo the front hook.

Nick stopped her with his hand. "Let me." He undid the hook and slowly opened the bra.

"Oh, God," she whispered. "I feel like I'm about to fall off of a cliff."

"Don't fall." He looked into her eyes. "Jump."

She drew in a breath, then let her bra fall to the floor.

Nick's hands covered her breasts, followed by his mouth, moving greedily from one breast to the other, arousing her senses, until she wanted to sink to the floor and pull him on top of her, inside of her.

Suddenly impatient, she reached for him, for the edges of his T-shirt.

He lifted his head long enough to pull the shirt off, then

pressed his chest against hers as he kissed her with a powerful longing that was both familiar and new, raising the old feelings of desire along with new feelings of passion that had come of age.

Lisa mirrored every move he made, delighting in the feel of his rough chest against her soft breasts. When he drew circles around her nipples, she drew circles around his. When his hand dropped to the snap on her jeans, she did the same to his, until they were moving in a beautiful, perfect duet.

Her jeans hit the floor just a second before his. Her panties fell on top of his boxers, and finally they were totally naked, skin to skin in every wicked curve and secret corner of their bodies.

She was hot and ready. He was hard and ready.

He slipped his hands between her thighs. She cupped his buttocks, then slid her hands around to the front, to stroke the long, silky length of him, until Nick impatiently pushed her down on the bed.

"Too much," he muttered.

"Not enough," she said. "More." And she wrapped her arms around his neck and pulled him back for another kiss.

Nick sank his tongue into her mouth, while his fingers slid down her body once again, delving into the curls at her thigh, touching and caressing until she moved her hips restlessly on the bed.

Nick raised his head. "You want me."

It wasn't a question, but she answered him anyway. "I want you."

He parted her legs and entered her in one powerful thrust that took her breath away. It was the past and the present. It was nothing and everything blending together. They were young, they were old. Their bodies and their souls recognized each other and welcomed the reunion. And when Nick went over the edge, she went right along with him, falling, falling, falling.

He caught her the way he always had. His arms tightened around her, his mouth comforted her with a kiss, as her heart slowed down and her mind came back to earth.

Nick rolled onto his back, taking her with him, until her head rested on his chest and her arm fell across his waist. His hand stroked her back. His breath blew through her hair, and she felt loved.

The boat rocked gently on the water as silence covered the cabin like a warm blanket.

Lisa didn't know if Nick was as afraid of conversation as she was, but they both remained silent, and Nick held her as tightly as she held him. There was love in the small cabin. There was also fear. Because Lisa didn't know what came next, and she had a feeling Nick didn't either.

Chapter 23

Raymond smiled hello to various people as he walked through the banquet room at the Beverly Wilshire Hotel. The room was filled with advertising and public relations people gathered together for their regular monthly meeting. Raymond had always enjoyed the dinners; it was a good place to make contacts and catch up on what was happening with the other agencies.

Tonight he felt restless, frustrated with Elisabeth for staying in San Diego and irritated with himself for not being able to convince her to come home. He'd barely been able to concentrate on the evening speaker, and he had no idea what his dinner companions had had to say.

He kept seeing Elisabeth's face and that man's face—her ex-husband. They had looked so good together. The thought had run through his mind like a maddening refrain all day long. And Elisabeth was connected to that man emotionally. They'd lost a child together. He couldn't imagine the horror of that. Which brought him to the next question. Why hadn't she told him about her marriage, her child?

He'd always thought of her as an open book, only to discover now that she had once had a completely different life. He also couldn't shake the image of the box of wedding invitations sitting on the kitchen counter. She hadn't mailed them. In fact, even before she'd gone to San Diego, she'd been stalling. He could see that now—her missed appointments with Mrs. Carstairs, her unwillingness to turn over the

305

entire wedding to a professional consultant, her desire for a small, private wedding rather than the splashy one he preferred.

He'd wanted to show her off. He thought of them as a public couple, one who would be invited to movie premieres and grand openings. They would attend cocktail parties at fancy homes—the successful rich advertising executive and his beautiful young bride.

Elisabeth had had a different idea. She'd always talked about a small wedding, quiet evenings at home where they could work on new campaigns over wine and bread. He'd thought she was being shy, and that with a little encouragement from him she would open up and blossom as young women often did.

But she'd already blossomed with that other guy, he thought in disgust. She wasn't just shy, but secretive. What else hadn't she told him?

He felt like he didn't know her anymore. He'd never seen her so crumpled looking, tired, wrung out. With him, she was always put together, always beautiful, always young. That's the way he wanted her to be. And she would be that way if she married him, because he would make sure that she had household help and money for hair styling and clothes and jewelry. He would make her life incredibly easy. They would have no children to worry about, no responsibilities except work and each other. It was the perfect match.

Yet he'd felt old standing next to Elisabeth in her friend's kitchen. He'd felt out of place and unwelcome. Their conversation had been stilted. He'd tried to act mature, understanding, kind, and compassionate in the face of her obvious distress. But to hell with all that. Elisabeth wasn't supposed to make him feel old; she was supposed to make him feel young. That's why he'd deliberately sought out a younger woman.

He stopped at the bar in the corner of the banquet room and ordered a gin and tonic. While he waited for the bartender to fix his drink, he glanced around the room and saw Beverly standing at the far side of the room, deep in conversation with the head of another advertising agency.

Of course, Beverly had come to the meeting. She thought exactly the same way he did. Too bad she wasn't fifteen years younger.

Beverly looked up and caught him staring. She waved and smiled, apparently glad to see him. He didn't know why, really. They drove each other mad most of the time. He grinned, thinking about the time he'd dropped shrimp cocktail down the front of her fancy suit. Now, that had been fun.

Beverly finished her conversation and walked over to join him.

"Hello, Raymond. We meet again. Are you following me?"

It was a teasing question, but deep down Raymond wondered if he hadn't come to the meeting just to see her. No, that was impossible. Although her flirting did make him feel good, and after the day he'd had, feeling good wasn't such a bad thing.

"It's a public meeting," he said. "Actually, I'm surprised you're here. I thought you might take this opportunity to break into my office and steal all my ideas."

"You don't have any worth stealing. And, I don't need to cheat to win. Although you apparently don't feel the same way. I saw your young hotshot taking my new mail room girl out to lunch. Coincidence?" She tilted her head to one side. "I think not."

"Paul is friends with your employee, nothing more. And do you really think I'd depend on someone in the mail room to give me good information?"

"No. You're too smart for that. Besides, I'd just plant the wrong information with her and send you off on a wild-goose chase."

He smiled. "I know you would."

"Where's Elisabeth?"

He took a sip of his drink. "She's not back yet."

Beverly's eyes widened in surprise. "Not yet? But she's been gone for days."

"It hasn't been that long."

"Are you going to ask Monty for an extension?"

"I won't need one."

Beverly sent him a sharp, piercing look that he tried to avoid. "Is she working from San Diego then?"

"I don't think it's any of your business."

"It's not, but I'm curious."

"Curiosity killed the cat."

"I'm not a cat."

"You sure do have cat's eyes," he said softly.

Her eyes gleamed with that comment, and suddenly the air between them became intensely personal. "Maybe you should find out if I have claws."

"I already know the answer to that question."

"You might be surprised."

"Beverly, we're competing against each other for a big account." He looked around to make sure no one was listening to him. "I'm not going to sleep with you."

"What I have in mind does not involve sleeping," she replied with a wicked smile. "However, I must admit I'm surprised by your choice of excuses. Shouldn't you have reminded me that you're engaged? Shouldn't that be the reason why you don't sleep with me?"

"It is. Of course, it is."

"You're not very convincing. Did something happen between you two?"

"Nothing much." He finished his drink. "Although I did find out she was married before." Now, why had he told her that?

"No kidding." Beverly whistled under her breath. "I never would have guessed. Who was he? Somebody in advertising?"

"I have no idea what he does for a living. It was years ago. Look, forget I said anything. It's not any of your business."

"Elisabeth is not that old. It couldn't have been that many years ago that she was married."

"I don't want to talk about it." He set his glass down on an empty table. "I have to go."

"I'll walk out with you. Don't worry, I won't try to seduce you again."

"I wasn't worried," Raymond said, but inside he felt a little disgruntled at her lack of effort. Not that he would say yes. He had too much on the line to show any weakness in front of a competitor, and Beverly was definitely that. Making love with her would make him vulnerable. He couldn't afford that risk.

They walked out of the hotel together and into the parking lot. Raymond accompanied Beverly to her car and waited until she'd unlocked it. Instead of getting in, she paused, her hand on the door.

"If we weren't competitors . . ."

"Maybe," he said, reading the question in her eyes.

"But I'm old."

Raymond suddenly smiled. "So am I." He laughed. The realization took a huge weight off his shoulders. "I think I just realized that."

"It's about time." She stepped forward, playing with the edge of his collar. "You know, with me you wouldn't have to pretend to be dignified and mature and all-knowing. You could just be sexy and wild. Think about it." She kissed him quickly on the mouth, then got into her car and shut the door.

Raymond put a hand to his mouth, still tasting her lips long after she'd driven away. Think about it, she'd said. Like he could think about anything else. Maybe it was good Elisabeth hadn't sent out the wedding invitations.

"I don't know what to do," Maggie declared. She got up from her seat on the couch in the lobby of the Crestmoor Hotel. "We have just spent twelve hours watching a door. Do you realize that?"

"Actually, I've been writing. You've been watching the door," Jeremy replied.

"Yeah, and a lot of good it's done me. I don't think I'm cut out for stakeouts." Maggie frowned as she glanced at the notebook he'd been scribbling in off and on all day. "What are you writing about, anyway?"

He smiled mysteriously. "I have a new idea for a book."

"Is it about a woman looking for her supposedly dead husband?"

"Maybe."

"You can't write about me."

"It's fiction, Maggie. Relax, it's not about you. I was kidding. I love it when you get mad. Your eyes take on this great fiery glow."

Maggie sent him a disgusted look and stood up. "I'm hungry, I'm tired and I'm cranky. I've spent the entire day glued to this chair with only three trips to the bathroom to break up the monotony of watching people walk in and out of this hotel. The only two people who haven't gone through this lobby are Serena and Keith. They're probably in their room having an orgy of sex. I would give anything to find out their room number."

"You already flirted with three bellboys, the concierge, and a desk clerk. Then you tried bribery, which also didn't work. I don't think you have anything left to give." Jeremy scribbled another sentence in his notebook, then closed it.

"Well, obviously seducing information out of men is not my forte. It's Serena's."

"She's not so bad."

"Jeremy!"

"Sorry." He stood up and walked over to her, turning her around so he could massage her shoulders with his hands.

The tension eased as he worked his fingers against her tight muscles. "Let's call it a night. There's a great restaurant here. We can have dinner, drinks, maybe dance a little in the lounge. What do you say?"

"I'm sure Serena and Keith will walk into this lobby as soon as I leave."

"That's entirely possible."

"Then I'm staying here." She turned in his arms. "But you don't have to stay, Jeremy. In fact, if you want to go back to L.A., I will understand."

"And not see how this ends? Are you kidding?" He

paused. "I'll go to the coffee shop and see what I can drum up for our dinner."

"Could you wait just one second?" Maggie asked. "I need to make a phone call."

"Actually, I do, too. I want to check my messages." Jeremy followed her to the bank of phones at one end of the lobby.

"You go ahead," Maggie said, urging Jeremy to finish his call and head down to the coffee shop so she could call home without him standing next to her. While Jeremy made his call, she kept her eyes focused on the lobby. After investing so much time in this stakeout, she didn't want to miss them at this late date.

"Oh, damn," Jeremy said. "I can't believe this."

She looked at him in surprise, but he held up a hand while he jotted something down in his notebook.

"Maggie, you have to hear this," he said, motioning for her to join him.

"But Serena—" Maggie hated to leave the lobby unwatched for even a second.

"Serena is on my message machine," he said, punching in a code to retrieve the messages once again. "Listen."

Maggie took the receiver out of his hand somewhat reluctantly. She didn't like the look on his face, the grim tone in his voice. After hearing one message from a producer asking Nick to call him about a script, Serena's voice came on the line.

"Jeremy. I've had a change of plans. My friend, Wanda, is going to come over to pick up some of my things tonight, but I need you to let her in, since you have an extra key to my condo. It should be around nine. I hope you're back by then. You won't believe what's happened."

Maggie caught her breath as Serena's voice softened.

"I'm with someone special. He finally left his wife for me. I know you always tell me that married men are a bad idea, but I just couldn't resist him, and now he's finally mine. But his wife is trying to get him back, and she keeps calling my room, and it's a mess. Anyway, we're leaving now to drive down the coast to Santa Barbara. I'll call you when we get to the Miramar. Thanks. 'Bye.''

Maggie hung up the phone and strode toward the lobby, determined to confront Serena and Keith as soon as they came downstairs. Jeremy caught her by the arm.

"Maggie, the time on the message was three o'clock."

She looked at him in confusion, hearing his words but not really understanding them.

"She's gone," he said.

"That's impossible. We would have seen them leave." Maggie walked back to the telephone. She dialled the operator and asked for Serena's room.

"She's checked out," the operator said.

"She has to be there," Maggie insisted.

"I'm sorry, but she's no longer registered, ma'am."

Jeremy took the phone out of her hand and hung it up. "They must have gone directly down to the garage level and rented a car," Jeremy said. "That's the only thing I can think of. Or else they saw us sitting here and found another way out of the hotel."

"It was all for nothing. All day, we waited, for nothing. I can't do this." Maggie felt light-headed and swayed on her feet, trying to focus on Jeremy's face, on his shirt, on the floor, anything to stop the dizziness.

"Hey, Maggie." He pulled her against his chest. "Easy now. We're not done."

"Yes, we are."

"No, we're not."

"I'm going home, Jeremy. I should have gone home a long time ago."

He looked into her eyes, and she saw a stubborness she was beginning to find as exasperating as it was endearing. "You can't go home," he said. "You can't leave in the middle of an adventure."

"It's not an adventure. It's a nightmare, and—"

Jeremy's mouth cut off the rest of her sentence. She pushed against his chest, trying to end the kiss, but he was too strong, and far too good a kisser. He drew her resistance out along with her breath.

Who the heck was she fighting anyway? Keith didn't want her. Jeremy did.

But you have children and a dog and no job, a little voice whispered.

"Sh-sh," she said.

Jeremy raised his head and smiled at her. "I didn't say anything."

"Don't say anything, not one word. Just take me upstairs and make love to me."

His eyes darkened. "For revenge? Or because you want me? On second thought, I don't want to know."

"I don't think you can have a great adventure without a love scene. Write me one, Jeremy. Tell me what to say. How to act. Where to touch you."

"Maybe we should start with the elevator." He pulled her over to the bank of elevators and pushed the button.

"I've never made love in an elevator before," Maggie said as they stepped inside.

"Neither have I, and I wasn't planning on doing it here." Maggie smiled. "Why not? The train was fun."

"That was for you."

"Well, this could be for you." Maggie reached for the top button on his jeans.

Jeremy grabbed her before she could undo it. "I don't think so." He breathed a sigh of relief as the elevator doors opened on their floor.

Maggie didn't feel scared anymore, but excited and eager. Tomorrow she would face reality. Tonight she was going to let herself have one hell of a fantasy.

Jeremy unlocked his door while she unzipped his pants. They stumbled into the room together.

"I think I created a monster," Jeremy said. "What happened to the woman who wanted me to write the love scene?"

"She decided it's about time she wrote her own love scene."

"So how does it start?" Jeremy asked.

"You take off your clothes."

"Me? What about you?"

"You can take off my clothes after you take off yours."

Jeremy pulled his shirt over his head, revealing a solid, muscular chest. Maggie caught her breath at the sight of him. He was beautifully made. No flab. Just enough light brown hair to tangle her fingers in.

His pants fell to the floor, and he stood before her in a sexy black bikini with a very large bulge in the front. He put his thumbs on either side of the bikini and slowly peeled it down.

"Oh, my God!" Maggie said in wonder and delight. "You're incredible." She looked into his eyes. "Can I touch you?"

"You'd better."

She started with his shoulders, then let her fingers drift down his chest past his navel, around his hip bones, the flat of his abdomen and down into the heart of him, which was as hard as everything else.

Jeremy groaned. "Your turn," he said. "I want to watch you."

"Me?" Maggie asked somewhat nervously. She knew what she had—lots of generous curves, a few stretch marks, a thirty-one-year-old body that had only seen the light of day in front of one man to this point.

"You. Take it off."

Maggie stepped back against the wall. She pulled off her knit shirt, embarrassed by her white linen bra. But Jeremy seemed more interested in the luscious cleavage now showing. She'd always had big breasts. In fact, she'd been self-conscious about them for most of her life, but in front of Jeremy's interested gaze, she couldn't help feeling proud.

She slipped off her jeans.

"I never thought white underwear was sexy," Jeremy said. "Until now."

Maggie licked her lips, not sure she had the nerve to pull off the rest of her clothes. It would be so much easier if he would do it. No! She was writing this love scene. She opened her bra before she could find a reason not to and flung it on the floor. Then she pushed her panties down, hoping Jeremy would like what he saw.

"My God!" he said, echoing her words with a smile. "Is that all for me?"

"Yes." She slid her arms around his waist, pressing her white breasts against his tan chest, the delicious friction sending a tingle from one end of her body to the other. His hands cupped her buttocks, pulling her into the curve of his thigh until she could feel him pressing against her. She'd never felt so ready so fast.

"Maybe we should try out the bed," Jeremy said.

"No, here, standing up. I want to wrap my legs around your waist and—"

Jeremy's mouth sought hers, hot and wet and greedy. He lifted her up, and she wrapped her legs around his waist as he brought her back down, penetrating her body, filling her with himself, taking away her sense of emptiness until she felt complete.

Chapter 24

*L*isa slipped out of bed with the sun. As she pulled on her clothes, Nick sat up. He rubbed the sleep out of his eyes—not that they'd gotten much sleep after making love all night long.

"Where are you going?" he asked, suddenly realizing she was once again making the decision to leave without bothering to consult him.

"I think we should go back to Maggie's." Lisa zipped up her jeans and refastened her bra.

He could hear the distance in her voice, and he didn't like it. "What's your rush? Maggie isn't there. My parents are probably still asleep."

"Exactly. I'd rather not see them until I've had a chance to change and shower." She carefully avoided his gaze. "Where's my shirt?"

"You're that eager to wash me off? Last night you couldn't get enough of me. More, more, more, you begged."

She did look at him then, fire bursting out of her blue eyes. "Stop it! Last night was a mistake."

Nick jumped out of bed, uncaring of the fact that he was buck naked. He grabbed her with both hands. "Don't you dare call last night a mistake!"

"It was just sex, Nick."

"We made love, Lisa. You can't deny that no matter how much you want to."

"I'm engaged," she cried, the anger in her eyes turning

316

into hopelessness. "Don't you understand? I feel like a cheater. I *am* a cheater. How can I go to Raymond now?"

"You don't have to go to Raymond. You can stay here with me."

"And do what? My business, my home, my—my life is in L.A. I had everything planned out. And it was working so well. I never should have come here."

"But you did." He couldn't help but give her a little shake, if only to make her stop lying to herself. "Things changed, Lisa. The past few days proved that we are just as good together as we always were."

"In bed maybe."

"And everywhere else. At the hospital, with the kids, at the beach—you're a fool if you can't see that. We were meant to be together. I was supposed to be your destiny— not Raymond."

Lisa took a deep breath. "I'd like to go back to Maggie's house now. Will you take me? Otherwise, I'll walk along the pier until I find a pay phone and call myself a cab."

"You don't have any money."

"I'll borrow some from your parents when I get there." She slipped out of his grasp and tossed him his pants, then reached for her shirt.

Nick slipped on his jeans. "Then what? You pack your bags and head back to L.A.—to Raymond? What about Maggie? What about the kids?" *What about me?*

Lisa pulled her hair up in a ponytail and fastened it with a rubber band she found on the desk. He'd seen her do the simple movement a thousand times, but now it seemed sad, bittersweet. He'd thought he'd found her again last night. But once again, she was leaving, choosing a life without him in it.

Lisa finally turned and looked at him, and for a brief second he felt a glimmer of hope. She was fighting herself, he realized, as much as she was fighting him.

"I'm not running away this time, Nick. I'll do whatever it takes to find Maggie and bring her home. But I can't . . ." her voice faltered. "I can't be with you."

"Why not? Just answer the damn question honestly for a change, and don't give me this bull about loving Raymond, because you and I both know it isn't true."

Lisa didn't say anything for a long moment. Finally, she spoke. "I love you, Nick."

His heart pounded against his chest so loudly that he wasn't sure he'd heard her correctly. "You what?"

She sighed. "You're going to make me say it again? Fine. I love you. I admit it." She took a breath and let it out. "I probably never stopped loving you."

"Then why leave?"

"Because you scare me. You ask so much of me. You want to take over my life—a life that took me a long time to build after I left you. I can't go back to where we were. I can't be the woman I was."

"I don't want that woman."

"Yes, you do."

"No, I don't," he said more strongly, realizing the truth for the first time. "That woman was young and insecure and needed constant reassurance. She didn't know what she wanted and had no clue how to go about finding her dream. Worst of all, she ran away when things got tough."

Lisa looked down at the floor, not bothering to deny anything he said.

"And I know you don't want that man, either, the one who drank all the time, the one who dreamed big dreams but never did anything to achieve them, the one who failed you when you needed him the most."

Her gaze flew to his. "Nick—"

"We're not those people anymore, Lisa. We grew up. We matured, thank God." He looked her in the eye. "I don't want to go back, either. I want to go forward. But you're right. I do want everything with you, a marriage—and children."

Her quick intake of breath was followed by an immediate shake of her head. "No, never. I couldn't."

"It would be the ultimate gamble for both of us," he said fiercely, trying to make her understand. "But at least we'd be living. Aren't you tired of pretending to be happy? Because I know I am. I want another baby, Lisa. I want to feel that small head tucked under my chin, the fine baby hair tickling my lips. I want to smell that baby smell. I want to feel those little arms around my neck. I want to hear the little burp and the giggle. I want to—''

"Stop! You're breaking my heart." She wiped the back of her hand against the corner of her eye. "Don't you think I've thought about all that? It always ends up the same way, with us alone, with our arms empty." She held out her hands as if to demonstrate the point, then positioned them the way she would have held Robin.

Nick sucked in a gasp of air, because his chest suddenly felt so tight he could hardly breathe. Watching Lisa hold nothing in her arms but air and painful memories was almost too much to bear.

"Sometimes I find myself doing this," she whispered as a tear streaked down her cheek. "And I can almost see Robin, her bright blue eyes, the little dimple in her chin, her mouth just starting to pout." Lisa looked down at her arms. "I can almost see her now. But she's not there, Nick. She'll never be there. And now you want me to have another child to put in these arms?"

"Yes," he said firmly. "I do want to put another child in your arms. And then another and another, until our lives and our hearts are full."

"And forget . . ."

"No, we could never forget Robin." He took her hands and put them on his waist. "Hold *me*, Lisa. Let's start there. We've been given another chance. We have to take it."

"You ask too much, Nick. Maybe if it was just you—but a baby. If my choice is all or nothing, I have to pick nothing."

He let out a frustrated breath. "Damn, you're stubborn."

"So are you. It has to be your way or no way."

"No, I think that's your line." He pushed her away. "Fine."

He grabbed his shirt and finished dressing while she did

the same. He knew she wanted to leave without any further conversation, but he had one last thing to say before she left him.

"Lisa?"

"What?" she asked wearily, pausing at the bottom of the steps. "Haven't you said everything there is to say?"

"No, I haven't." He looked her straight in the eye. "You're still a coward. We could have it all, but you're so damn afraid of losing that you won't even get into the game."

"We lost before, Nick. What makes you so sure we'd win this time?"

"Because this time, I wouldn't quit, and you wouldn't either. You've made a success of your life. I've made a success of mine. We'd be equal partners this time around, and we wouldn't let life play us like a couple of suckers. We'd fight back, and we'd win."

"I wish I had your confidence, your courage."

"I wish you did, too." He picked up his keys. "Come on, I'll drive you back to Maggie's so you can start forgetting this night ever happened." He stomped up the stairs to the deck, then stopped so fast Lisa ran into his back. She put a hand on his body to steady herself, then followed his shocked gaze.

The robin stood on the rail. At the sight of them, he began to chirp and sing—a song that sounded remarkably like the one Nick had played on his guitar for her and for Robin. Lisa felt her heart skip a beat. Another robin here? Where were they all coming from? And why was it only one bird that seemed to be following them around?

"Where are the other robins?" she asked in bewilderment.

"There are no other birds. He's looking for his mate." Nick looked down at Lisa. "He's singing as loud as he can, but she doesn't hear him. So, he's alone."

"Maybe she's too far away to hear."

"Or maybe she doesn't want to listen." His eyes met hers in one long, poignant glance. Then he turned his back on the robin and on her. "I thought you were in a hurry to leave."

"I am," she muttered, but she lingered behind when Nick stepped off the boat. "What do you want from me?" she whispered to the robin.

The bird chirped in response, but she had no idea what it meant. Then the bird flew across the boat, landing on the ground. The robin skipped along the sidewalk at Nick's heels, then flew on top of the fence at the end of the pier, as if he were trying to get their attention.

Nick saw it and swore. "Go away," he said, waving his hand at the bird. "She doesn't want you. Isn't that obvious? Give it up."

"Maybe he'll find another bird," Lisa said quietly.

"Maybe he doesn't want one." He shook his head in disgust. "That bird is as stupid as I am."

The robin finally flew away, and Lisa followed Nick to the car.

They drove home in deafening silence. When they arrived at the house, they found deafening chaos.

Bill, Kathy, Silvia and Carmela were standing in the living room, all four talking at once. In fact, they seemed to be arguing.

"What's going on?" Lisa asked.

The four stopped talking, looking from one to the other. Lisa glanced at Nick. Suddenly they were back on the same side. He stepped up next to her.

"Okay, you look guilty as hell," he said. "Somebody talk. Mother?"

"I spoke to Maggie," Kathy said.

"That's great," Lisa said. "Where is she?"

"She's on her way to Santa Barbara," Silvia interjected. "To find Keith, she says."

"Keith is dead," Nick said forcefully, as if he could make it true simply by sheer will.

"There is a man. He looks like Keith," Carmela offered in her dark tones. "And another man, a stranger. You must go to her, Lisa. She will need you."

Lisa hated to believe anything Carmela said, but how

could she doubt the possibility that something was terribly wrong? Maggie had obviously gone off the deep end, and she needed help regardless of whether or not Keith was alive.

"You have to find her," Kathy said to Nick. "Both of you. I'm worried. She didn't sound like herself, and when I asked her to come home, she said no." Her eyes crinkled with worry.

"There, there now, honey," Bill said, slipping an arm around his wife's shoulders. "Maggie is a grown woman."

"She's confused and scared."

"Did she sound scared?" Lisa asked.

Kathy hesitated. "Well, maybe not scared. Actually, she sounded determined, angry. She practically bit my head off when I asked her a question. I didn't even get a chance to tell her about Mary Bea before she hung up on me." Kathy turned to Bill. "My own daughter hung up on me."

He gave her a quick hug. "She wasn't herself, Kat. You know that."

"I can drive up to Santa Barbara," Nick said slowly. "Do you know where she is specifically?"

"The Miramar Beach Inn," Kathy replied. "She didn't want to tell me, but I told her I simply had to have a number for her."

"I'm on my way," Nick said.

Lisa smiled to herself. Nick, the hero, the dragonslayer. He'd risk anything for his family. And she knew that family included her. He'd said he loved her. Why couldn't she let herself love him back? She thought she was being realistic, but maybe she really was just a coward.

"Lisa," Silvia said, drawing her attention back to the situation at hand. "Will you go with Nick?"

"What about the children?"

"Bill and I will stay here, of course," Kathy said.

Lisa looked at Nick. "Do you want me to go with you?" After this morning's scene, she wasn't sure he wanted to spend another minute with her, much less a four-hour drive in the car.

"It's up to you. If you'd rather return to L.A., to your job and everything else you have waiting, I certainly won't try to stop you. Not that I could.''

She sent him a wry smile. "My car isn't working, remember?"

"Why haven't you gotten it fixed, if you're in such a hurry to go home?"

Why hadn't she gotten it fixed? Why hadn't she mailed her wedding invitations? Why the hell had she slept with Nick? And why was she even considering going to Santa Barbara when she had an advertising campaign on the line and her relationship with Raymond needed mending?

"I don't know," she said, answering all of her questions. Maybe she was stalling for time. Maybe she just couldn't stand the thought of leaving Nick, and this gave her a reason to postpone their good-bye. Whatever the excuse, she knew she wanted to go with him. Maggie was her friend, her very best friend. And Lisa had let Maggie down far too many times already.

"What's it going to be?" Nick asked.

She lifted her head and gazed into his eyes. "I'll come with you to Santa Barbara. If Maggie is in trouble, I want to help."

He nodded, looking more pleased with her than he had previously.

"By the way, where have you two been all night?" Kathy asked with a gleam in her eyes. "And why did you sneak out without telling us where you were going?"

"Mom, I'm a grown man, I don't have to tell you where I spend my nights anymore," Nick replied.

"And I'm a grown woman," Lisa said, cutting off her mother before Silvia could say a word. "So don't even think of asking me the same question. By the way, what are you and Carmela doing here so early? Did you spend the night here?"

"No, we arrived a few minutes before you. And I didn't ask where you were," Silvia retorted.

"Because we already knew," Carmela said with one of

her rare smiles. "Go now, quickly," she urged. "And wear your bracelet."

Lisa glanced down at her wrist, realizing she hadn't taken off the bracelet since she had put it on in the hospital room. "Why?"

"Because you will then know where to go and what to do." Carmela waved them toward the door with her cane. "The robin will help you, too."

"Great." Lisa retrieved her purse from the coffee table. "Follow the little bird and rub the magic bracelet. Now we just need to find the yellow brick road."

"Don't piss off the magic, Lisa," Nick said with a smile as he followed her to the door. "We may need all the help we can get."

Maggie stretched out her legs in the cramped front seat of their compact rental car. They'd been driving most of the morning and were only a few minutes north of Santa Barbara. With any luck, she'd have her hand around Keith's neck within the hour.

Jeremy glanced at her and smiled, a warm, knowing smile, the kind a man gives a woman he's made love to. They'd had an incredible night together. She'd done things that made her blush now. Things she'd never known were possible. Jeremy was an inventive lover. But then he was a fantasy. In a few hours, he'd be history.

Unless, of course, their wild-goose chase went in another direction and they were forced to hop a plane for Barbados or something crazy like that. Not that she could. She'd left her children for far too long. And as her mother had reminded her a few hours earlier, she was not a kid. She couldn't just run away from her life.

But she had done just that, and as Jeremy said, they'd had a great adventure. It was almost over. A wave of depression swept through her. Maggie couldn't imagine never seeing him again, never touching him or tasting his lips. It was more than just physical attraction; she felt a strong connection to him both mentally and emotionally. In other words, she'd

gone and fallen head over heels in love with a man she'd
probably never see again after today.

"What's wrong?" Jeremy asked.

He read her mind so easily. "Nothing."

"Thinking about saying good-bye, aren't you?"

"You have to get back to work. I have to get back to
reality."

He didn't say anything for a long minute. "What if I asked
you to stay in Los Angeles? What would you say?"

She gave him a sad smile. "I'd say no."

"That's it?"

"Yes. I mean, no. I mean that's it," she said, rambling
on nervously. "I have other commitments."

"I see." His clipped answer left them sitting in awkward
silence.

Tell him, a little voice inside ordered her. Tell him about
the kids and the dog and the carpools and the baseball games
and the hormone-driven teenagers hanging around your
house. No, she couldn't. Not yet. Maybe never. She wanted
to leave with the fantasy intact. She didn't want to see the
desire in his eyes replaced by disappointment, by rejection.

Jeremy pulled off the freeway as they entered the city of
Santa Barbara. He seemed to know the streets and headed
toward the beach without asking for directions or checking
the map the rental car agency had given them.

"Have you been here before?" she asked tentatively, not
sure if he was angry with her or not.

"Yes. Many times."

"You've been to the Miramar?"

He nodded.

Silence fell between them again.

"It's him," Jeremy said finally. "You still want him."

"Keith?"

"Of course, Keith, the man we've been chasing all over
hell and back."

Did she want Keith back? He was her husband. He was
the father of her children. They could use two parents. But
Keith had gone to such elaborate lengths to disappear; she

doubted he even wanted to come back. How could she compete with Serena?

It was a question she had asked herself dozens of times in
the past few days, so utterly convinced that Serena beat her
in every category—looks, body, brains, sex. That's why
Keith had wanted out of his marriage to her, because Serena
was his ultimate woman—*his* fantasy.

But last night had taught Maggie some new things about
herself. Maybe it wasn't her fault that Keith had wanted out.
Maybe it was his fault. Maybe he was the problem, not her.
She sat a little straighter in the car.

"You haven't answered my question, Maggie," Jeremy
said tightly.

She knew she hadn't. Because while she didn't know if
she could ever forgive Keith and take him back into her heart
and into her body, he was still the father of her children. If
he wanted to come back for them, would she still have the
courage to say no? Could she deny them the chance to have
their father back?

"It's complicated," she said.

"I don't think so. You either want him back or you
don't."

"All I want right now are answers," Maggie replied. "I'm
sorry, but I can't answer your question until I know what
really happened to my marriage."

Jeremy turned a corner and pulled to an abrupt stop in
front of the Miramar Beach Inn. "Looks like we're about to
find out."

Maggie took a deep breath and stepped out of the car.
Jeremy came around to her side, and they entered the lobby
together. Jeremy walked directly to the courtesy phone in the
lobby and dialled Serena's room. Maggie held her breath,
hoping the story they'd plotted on the way down the coast
would work.

"Serena, it's Jeremy." His eyes lit up with excitement as
he looked at Maggie and mouthed the words "It's her." "I
brought your things because Wanda had something to do,
and frankly, I needed a long drive to clear my head. What

room are you in?'' He listened for a moment, then nodded. ''406. I'll see you in a few minutes.''

He hung up the phone and turned to Maggie. ''Got it.''

''I can't do this,'' Maggie said in sudden panic.

''Yes, you can. Whatever happens, I'll be right behind you.''

Maggie sucked in a breath, then let it out. ''Okay. I'm ready. Let's find my husband.''

~⚬ Chapter 25

Nick pulled up in front of the Miramar Beach Inn and turned off the ignition. Lisa let out a sigh of relief that they'd actually made it to Santa Barbara in one piece. She didn't know if Nick was trying to avoid conversation or if he was simply in a hurry to find Maggie. He hadn't said. In fact, he hadn't spoken more than a few words during the four-hour trip.

She'd tried to sleep but couldn't. Although she was tired, every time she closed her eyes she saw Nick's face and his body and remembered every excruciatingly wonderful detail of their lovemaking the night before. The first time had been passionate and stormy and rushed, years of pent-up desire driving them on in a fast fury. The second time had been tender and loving, between two longtime friends who'd found each other again, and the third time had been an adventure, a discovery, a way of making love they'd never shared before.

Three times. She'd made love with him three times. If the night had been any longer, it probably would have been four. How could she go back to L.A. and marry Raymond? How could she stay in San Diego with Nick? Two impossible choices.

"Are you getting out?" Nick demanded impatiently, his door already open. "We're here, in case you hadn't noticed."

"I'm waiting for my stomach to catch up with us," Lisa

328

said sharply. "I think it's back on that last curve you took at a hundred miles an hour."

Nick shrugged off her sarcasm. "You never used to be such a wimp in the car."

"You never used to drive like you were on the last lap at the Indy 500."

"I just want to find Maggie. Are you coming or not?"

"I'm coming." Lisa stepped out of the car and took a moment to stretch. Across the street was a long expanse of beach, the waves breaking just a few hundred yards away. It was a beautiful spring day, blue sky, blue ocean, children laughing, birds singing. Birds! She looked around somewhat warily, but there was no sign of a robin.

"Lisa, let's go," Nick said impatiently.

"I was just admiring the view. It's nice here, isn't it?"

"Yeah." He paused. "We talked about moving once, remember, starting out fresh, just the two of us, no family, no friends."

"Then I got pregnant, and the rest is history."

"You could always move here, Lisa."

"I don't know anyone here."

"Neither do I."

Lisa saw the speculation dawning in his eyes. "That would be crazy. You have a very good business in San Diego, and I have a wonderful job in L.A."

Nick shook his head, a fond but frustrated smile crossing his lips. "You can read my mind, but you still can't give me the answer I want. Damn you."

Lisa turned toward the hotel. "Let's find Maggie. That's why we're here."

Nick followed her across the parking lot and through the double doors that led into the lobby of the hotel. Of Spanish-style design, the floors were tiled, the walls covered with stucco. There were plants everywhere in the atrium-like lobby, and a fountain in the middle of the building sent up a spume of mist with its bubbling stream of water.

"Nice place," Nick commented as they looked around. "I don't see Maggie."

"I doubt she would be hanging around in the lobby. Why don't you check and see if she's registered?"

Nick walked over to the registration desk and had a brief conversation with the clerk. When he returned, his face was grim. "She's not registered," he said in disgust, planting his hands on his hips.

"She has to be here," Lisa said somewhat desperately. They couldn't have driven all this way for nothing. Then she heard a familiar chirp, and both she and Nick turned around at the same time.

Lisa smiled as a robin flew into the lobby and lit on the edge of the fountain, chirping impatiently at them. She glanced at Nick. "I think Maggie is here."

Nick stared in wonder at the bird. "How did he get here?"

"Magic!"

"You don't believe in magic."

"I didn't used to," she said with a hopeless sigh. She held out her right arm. "There's something else. My wrist is getting hot."

Nick followed her gaze to the bracelet. "It's almost glowing."

Lisa moved her arm out to the side, then back in front of her. The warm sensation increased and decreased with her motion. When she moved it back toward the right, she felt as if her arm were on fire. That's when she realized she was pointing to the elevators.

"I think we have to go that way," she said, somewhat bemused by the energy flowing through her arm. She almost felt disconnected from herself, a mere appendage to the bracelet.

"Go which way?" Nick asked. "Did you suddenly see the beginning of the yellow brick road?"

"We don't need a yellow brick road. We're simply going to follow the bracelet. You're the one who said not to piss off the magic, so shut up."

Nick rolled his eyes. "Fine. After you." He glanced over at the bird. "You stay here."

Lisa laughed. "You're talking to a bird."

"For some reason, I think he understands me."

"For some reason, I think you're right."

The elevator doors opened before they even punched the button. "Wow, that bracelet is good," Nick commented as they stepped inside. He stared at the rows of buttons. "What now?"

"I don't know." Lisa pointed her fingers at each button, trying to tell if the bracelet grew warmer or colder. "Four," she decided. "Definitely four."

"You know we'll probably wind up knocking on some stranger's door and have to explain that your bracelet sent us there."

"No, we're going to find Maggie," Lisa said confidently. "Magic bracelet or not, I have the definite feeling she's not too far away."

"You're stalling," Jeremy said, watching Maggie with his dark, piercing eyes. "Serena is on the other side of this door. All you have to do is knock."

"I know it sounds simple." Maggie swallowed a lump of anxiety. She had nothing to fear. She was in the right. They were in the wrong. A little self-righteous indignation would be good, she told herself firmly. *Get mad. He cheated on you He lied. He betrayed you.*

Maggie thrust back her shoulders and rapped sharply on the door. She heard a woman's voice call out that she would get it, a patter of footsteps, the clicking of the double locks. Then the door slowly opened.

A woman stood on the threshold, slender and curvy in hot pink shorts and a white midriff top. Her long blond hair drifted down her back. She was a man's fantasy, long legs, big breasts, great hair.

Maggie put a hand to her stomach, feeling suddenly sick. How could she compete with this?

Jeremy's hand touched her back, a subtle reminder that she couldn't run away. She had to go forward.

"Jeremy?" Serena asked curiously, looking from Jeremy

to Maggie. ''You didn't tell me you were bringing someone with you.''

''This is Maggie Scott,'' Jeremy said.

Serena looked at Maggie, the name obviously meaning nothing to her. Keith hadn't told Serena her name. The anger rolled through Maggie like a runaway truck.

''Your lover's wife,'' Maggie said forcefully.

Serena looked taken aback. ''Oh, shit! You're that woman who was calling our room in San Francisco.'' She tried to shut the door, but Maggie stuck her foot out.

''Not so fast—'' Maggie stopped, struck by the sound of a man's voice coming from behind Serena. It called to her like a ghost from the past. Keith was here, in this room, with this woman.

''You have to leave,'' Serena said. ''Jeremy, how could you do this to me?''

''She needs to talk to her husband, Serena. Let her in.''

''No. I won't. He left you. He's mine now.''

''Let me in,'' Maggie yelled. ''I want to see my lying, cheating, son-of-a-bitch husband right now, and you're not going to stop me.'' Before she could move, she heard some-one call her name.

''Maggie,'' Lisa shouted as she and Nick dashed down the corridor.

Maggie sent them a blank look. What on earth were they doing here?

''What's going on?'' Nick asked. ''Maggie, please, what-ever you're thinking of doing—''

''Go away,'' Maggie said. ''You can't stop me.''

''Who are these people?'' Serena asked, as she folded her arms across her chest.

''I'm her brother,'' Nick said.

''And I'm her best friend,'' Lisa added.

''Great. Then you can all have coffee. I'm closing the door now.''

''No, you're not,'' Maggie said, putting her hand on the door. She turned to Nick. ''If you want to watch, you can watch. My husband is in this room—with his lover—and

I'm not leaving until I see him. Now, all of you get out of my way.''

Maggie practically knocked Serena over as she stormed into the room. The bedroom was empty, but she heard whistling coming from the bathroom. She caught her breath at the familiar sound. The whistling stopped. The doorknob slowly turned.

Maggie felt like she was about to explode. ''Open the damn door, you bastard.''

''Maggie—''

She shook off Nick's attempt to calm her with an angry shake of her head. She would not be stopped, not now, not when she was so close.

The door finally opened, and a man stepped out wearing khaki shorts and a navy blue polo shirt. Her heart stopped.

He was the same height, the same build. His hair was the same color; his face the same shape. Maggie forced herself to look into his eyes, to find the truth.

His eyes were blue, not brown. Blue! That was wrong. And his nose was short and broad, not long and pointed. That was wrong, too. She began to shake.

''Who are you?'' the man asked.

Maggie shook her head back and forth in utter confusion. ''You're not Keith. You're not Keith.'' She put a hand to her mouth, feeling suddenly nauseated. He wasn't Keith. This man was not her husband. She'd been following a stranger. A stranger!

Maggie felt Jeremy move behind her. His hands came around her waist, and she leaned against him, grateful for the support. ''It's not him,'' she whispered.

Jeremy bent his head. ''Are you all right?''

''No.''

''What the fuck is going on?'' the man demanded as Serena walked over to him.

''She said she was your wife, Mitch,'' Serena said.

''That woman is not my wife.''

Serena looked at Maggie. ''Who are you, then?'' she asked in complete bewilderment.

"I'm Maggie Scott." Maggie said the words slowly, finding comfort in the security of her name. At the moment, it was the only thing that seemed real.

"Am I supposed to know you?" Serena asked again. "Jeremy, could you explain, please?"

"Maggie." Jeremy squeezed her waist. "Do you want to tell her?"

"Yes." Maggie took a deep breath. "You wrote a letter to my husband, Keith Scott, about a month ago."

"I don't remember the name . . ."

"You said you missed seeing him on his weekends in L.A. You wanted to know if he'd ever found the courage to tell his wife or if he'd simply changed his mind about the whole thing. You signed it with love, Serena."

Serena's confusion slowly turned into understanding. "Oh, that letter. Keith. Yes, I remember him."

"I should hope so. You were having an affair with him," Maggie said, still trying to put the pieces together, only they didn't seem to fit anymore.

"I wasn't having an affair with Keith Scott," Serena said, rolling her eyes as if she found the idea utterly ridiculous. "Is that what he told you?"

"He didn't tell me anything." Maggie put a hand to her mouth as the bile of reality rose in her throat. "Oh, my God, he's dead. He's really dead." Her eyes blurred with tears. "He's not here. He's not alive. It wasn't a game. It was real. The fire was real." She turned to Jeremy in desperation. "My husband is really dead."

Jeremy stared at her with compassion. "I'm sorry."

"He's dead?" Serena asked, once again looking bewildered. "I don't understand."

"Do you want to finish it, Maggie?" Jeremy asked quietly.

"Who the hell are you?" Nick demanded.

"Someone who cares about your sister," Jeremy replied.

Maggie ignored both of them, her attention focused solely on Serena. "You didn't know he was dead, did you?"

Serena shook her head. "I wouldn't have written him if I

did, although I guess that explains why he never got back to me. I was surprised, because he was so taken with the ring.'' She paused. "Did he tell you about the ring?"

"What ring?"

"The ring he wanted to buy."

"He never said anything about you or a ring," Maggie replied. "When I got your letter, I couldn't help wondering who you were. There was perfume on your stationery. Your words sounded so personal, intimate. You mentioned weekends in L.A. with Keith, weekends when he was supposed to be on business, weekends when I couldn't call him; he could only call me."

"I didn't mean to imply—"

"The day before he died, he withdrew eight thousand dollars in cash," Maggie said, cutting her off. She needed to tell Serena everything, to get rid of every last doubt. "The withdrawal and your letter seemed tied together. I decided to find you, so I could ask you if he'd given you the money. But when I heard you'd gone to San Francisco with a man you'd once thought was dead, and then we saw you getting into the cab . . ." Her voice drifted away as she once again looked at the man standing next to Serena. "You look like my husband. When I saw you, I started thinking maybe he hadn't died. Maybe he'd taken out extra life insurance as an attempt to ease his guilt on running off with Serena."

"I think I can answer one of your questions," Serena said. "The eight thousand dollars was the price of a diamond ring I showed your husband. I sell jewelry, Mrs. Scott. Your husband came in to the Beverly Hills store where I work several times last year. He fell in love with a ring that he wanted to give you for your anniversary. He told me that you'd married young and didn't have a proper ring."

Maggie stared down at her empty finger. She'd taken off the ring to sleep with Jeremy. Now, she felt like a traitor to Keith.

"Your husband was a nice guy," Serena continued. "Although he never could quite get the courage to buy you that ring. He said he'd been brought up to be sensible, and you'd probably rather have a new car than a new ring.'' Serena smiled. ''I told him he was crazy. Any woman would want a ring over a car.''

Maggie nodded, her eyes filling with tears. It sounded just like Keith, practical to the end.

''He told me how much he loved you,'' Serena added. ''He said you'd been together forever, but the marriage just got better and better. It sounded like a fairy tale to me. I guess that's why I wanted him to buy you that ring. It seemed like a good way to have happily ever after.''

Happily ever after. Her husband had loved her. The tears fell down Maggie's cheeks unchecked. Keith had been faithful to her and the children. And she'd doubted him. How could she have doubted him? He had never given her any reason to doubt him, but somehow she'd let it happen. ''I'm sorry,'' she whispered. ''I'm sorry I didn't believe in you.'' She hoped that somewhere he could hear her, he could understand that it was only loneliness and grief and fear that had led her to such a ridiculous conclusion.

Maggie's gaze swept the group. Nick stared furiously at Jeremy as if Jeremy were responsible for her crazy behavior. Lisa looked worried and had a firm hand on Nick's arm. Serena and her lover seemed a bit bemused by the entire scene. Maggie knew it was time to end it.

''I'm sorry for barging in on you, Serena. We'll go now.'' She headed toward the door, breaking free from Jeremy, brushing by Nick's outstretched hand and Lisa's concerned face.

Once in the hall, Maggie leaned against the wall and took several deep breaths. It was over. It was really over. Keith was dead. And this time he would stay dead.

Lisa walked over to Maggie and hugged her. ''Are you all right?''

''I will be.''

Nick frowned. He tipped his head toward Jeremy. ''What are you doing with this guy?''

''He's a friend.''

''Really? Since when?''

"Since I went to L.A. looking for Serena."

"I'm Serena's neighbor," Jeremy offered. He extended a hand to Nick, who ignored it. Jeremy smiled and dropped his hand to his side.

"Nick, don't be such a jerk," Lisa said. "He's just worried about his sister," she told Jeremy.

"I'm worried about your sister, too." Jeremy's glance moved from Maggie to Nick. "I wish I could say I'd heard a lot about you, but I can't."

"Likewise," Nick replied tersely. "And if you've been messing with Maggie—"

"Don't yell at him, Nick." Maggie straightened up. "He only tried to help me."

"By doing what, taking you on a wild-goose chase?"

"No, by listening to me and being there and not telling me I was crazy."

"You should have called your family."

"I did. You told me I needed to see a shrink." She sighed. "Although you were right." Maggie turned to Lisa. "I wanted Keith to be alive so much that I tried to make it come true. But he's really dead."

"I know, honey."

"There was no mystery at all. The money was for my ring. He was leaving for L.A that weekend. And our anniversary would have been a week later."

Lisa hugged her again, and Maggie couldn't help but cling for just a moment. She felt like the rug had been pulled out from under her for the second time in less than a year.

"It will be okay," Lisa murmured. She pulled back and gazed into Maggie's eyes. "You won't have to go through anything else alone, Maggie. I'll be there for you, whatever you need, whenever you need it."

"And so will I," Nick said.

Maggie smiled at their somber faces. "I didn't go nuts because you two weren't around, although I am happy to hear you'll be around a little more often in the future. It was me, all me. I created this in my mind. But I'm okay now. It's over."

"Are you ready to go home?" Lisa asked. "The children have missed you."

"Children!" Jeremy's sharp word drew Maggie's attention to him. "You have children?"

Maggie looked into his dark eyes and saw not anger but hurt. "Yes, I have three children. Roxy is thirteen. Dylan is eight, and Mary Bea is five. I have a dog, too. Her name is Sally. She likes to bring dead animals into the house." Jeremy stared at Maggie without blinking. "And I don't work at a school. I carry crayons in my purse for when the kids and I go out to eat, and they want something to do. I'm a mom, Jeremy. A single mom with a house in the suburbs, a station wagon, and a lot of baggage."

"Why didn't you tell me?"

"I didn't want to ruin the fantasy," Maggie said in a whisper. She leaned over and kissed him on the lips. "I'll never forget you."

"This is it? The end?"

"Do you think you could write a better one?"

"Hell, yes." He grabbed her by the shoulders. "You can't just walk out on me."

"Then walk out on me, Jeremy."

"No! Maggie . . ." He twisted a strand of hair through his fingers. "Last night . . ."

His husky words tore apart what little was left of her heart. She felt as if she had betrayed not only Keith but also Jeremy.

"Last night was incredible," she said, cupping his face with her hands. "But I have to go back to reality, to my kids. They need me. And I need them. It will be okay now, because I know the truth. I don't have any more questions. I'll find a way to live without Keith, and . . ." She stroked the side of Jeremy's face, feeling the tears well up behind her eyes once again. "And somehow I'll find a way to live without you, too."

"You don't have to."

"I do. I really do."

She pulled away from him, struggling to maintain the little

control she had left. She turned to Nick. "Can I have a ride home?"

He nodded. "Of course you can. I'm sorry I wasn't there for you."

"You were there. You just weren't the one I wanted." Maggie turned one last time to Jeremy. "Good-bye. Take care of yourself."

"You, too."

"Let's go home," Maggie said. "Let's all go home."

Chapter 26

"*T*here's no place like home," Lisa whispered as she unlocked the door to her condo and walked inside. It was late Thursday afternoon, and she'd been gone almost a week. Six days away should not have changed her life, but they had, and her oasis of comfort and security suddenly seemed strange and unsettled.

The wallpaper she'd lovingly put up, the couch she'd paid bundles of money for, the pictures she'd chosen so carefully—it was all an illusion, a pretense of a normal life. But her life here in L.A. had never been normal or honest. She'd denied her past, her husband, her child, her mother and her friends. Now her condo didn't seem calm and cool and unfettered by emotion—it just felt lonely and empty.

Lisa dropped her overnight case on the floor and sat down on the couch, closing her eyes for one long, restful minute. As soon as she did, she was once again swept back to the day before, when they'd talked and talked about Maggie's adventures, and, finally, when Nick had come to say good-bye.

He'd picked up her box of wedding invitations and asked her if she was still planning to marry Raymond. She hadn't been able to say no. So, Nick had kissed her good-bye and taken her wedding invitations to the mailbox. His action had dared her to say "stop," to deny that she would marry Raymond, but the words refused to come out of her mouth. So, it was done. The invitations were finally in the mail. She was home. And her reunion with Nick was over.

Oh, damn. Her eyes filled with tears, and her stomach clenched into a familiar knot. She didn't want to miss Nick. Not now, not so soon. With time she'd forget him, the way she'd done before.

Liar. Her own conscience mocked her, and she tried not to listen, but the word ran around and around in her head.

"Stop it," she said out loud.

Great, now she was talking to herself. Lisa got up and walked over to her answering machine. It was time to get back to reality. There were three messages from Raymond on the machine, each one asking her to come to the office as soon as she got back, each one more impatient than the last. How could she blame him? She'd let him down. She'd let Nick down. She'd let everybody down. Why? Because she was a coward. Nick was right about that.

Lisa sighed and twirled the bracelet on her arm, but felt only a cool breeze, not the exciting, tingling heat of magic. She suddenly wanted it back, that feeling of being alive, of being on fire, of excitement and joy and all the colorful emotions she'd painted white the last eight years. Impulsively, she ran to the window and searched the nearby trees for a robin. The branches were empty.

"Fool," she whispered to herself. "There is no magic in life. Go to work. Forget him. You did it once. You can do it again."

Lisa reported to work at eight o'clock on Friday morning, and after a brief, unsatisfying conversation with Raymond, she closeted herself in her office until past six that evening writing copy for the Nature Brand account.

Raymond asked her to have dinner, but she declined pleading tiredness and a need to study the box of material he'd collected from the Nature Brand people. Raymond hadn't persisted. Perhaps he sensed that she just wasn't ready to talk yet, at least about anything personal.

Saturday morning she went into the office early and continued to create new ideas for Nature Brand. Raymond arrived just after noon, but aside from a few casual words, he once again retreated to his own office to work.

By late afternoon, Lisa had put together an initial proposal that she knew was good. Now Raymond just had to sell it to Nature Brand.

She stood up and stretched, then walked to her office window, knowing she was still looking for the robin. But there were no more robins in her life. The emptiness in her heart didn't just hurt, it mocked her. Nick had offered her a second chance, and she'd turned him down. Because she was afraid of losing. She'd always been afraid of losing.

Raymond shared the same fear. He didn't want to lose the Nature Brand account, and he didn't want to lose her. But why? Because he loved her or because he was afraid of ending up alone?

Their wedding invitations were being opened in a hundred homes probably this very minute. And Mrs. Carstairs was determined to get them down the aisle. She'd already called five times about final payments on contracts that were coming due.

Lisa started as she saw Raymond walk out of the Coffee Hut down below. She'd thought he was in the office down the hall. Raymond stopped as a woman came up to him. The woman wore a peach-colored linen suit with a short skirt and a box jacket. She put her hand on Raymond's arm and whispered something into his ear, then laughed and pulled away. Raymond laughed, too.

Lisa strained to get a better look. Suddenly the woman's face came into view. It was Beverly Wickham, Raymond's main competitor. But they didn't look like enemies—they looked like friends.

Beverly continued to talk, with Raymond hanging onto every word. She waved her hands a few times, then grabbed his hands, and, to Lisa's complete amazement, twirled around. Then she kissed him on the cheek, waved and took off down the street in the opposite direction while Raymond headed back toward the office.

Lisa sat down in her chair, unsettled by their exchange. She'd never seen Raymond look so young and carefree, she realized, laughing, smiling, twirling Beverly like a dancer when they were standing on a sidewalk in downtown L.A. He'd certainly never acted so spontaneously with her.

Did she know him? Did she really know him? And more importantly, did he know her? No. No. And no. She and Raymond barely scratched the surface of each other. She knew what kind of topping he took on his ice cream, but not what dreams were in his heart. She'd never asked. She'd never wanted that incredible closeness with another man. And Raymond had never pressed her for any confidences. Even now, he'd barely mentioned her trip to San Diego, her ex-husband, her lost child. Was he waiting for the right time, or just hoping it would all blow over?

Somehow she knew it was the latter. How could she marry a man who was still in so many ways a stranger? Yet, how could she marry Nick, a man who would take over her life until she couldn't find herself any more—only him?

Maybe he wouldn't be able to do that now. Maybe Nick was right. Maybe they were different, better able to be partners, to stand next to each other, to share their lives but not live in each other's pockets.

"Elisabeth?" She looked up as Raymond called her name. Actually, the name felt strange. Since returning to San Diego, she felt more like Lisa than she did Elisabeth.

"Hello, Raymond." She stood up so he could kiss her.

His lips hit the corner of her mouth, and he made no attempt to straighten the kiss or to lengthen it. "Ready for dinner?"

"Sure." She paused. "I was looking out the window a minute ago, and I saw you talking to Beverly."

Was it her imagination, or did Raymond's face turn pale? And why couldn't he look her in the eye?

"Right. She was just coming back from a meeting. She said to say hello."

"Really? Was that after you twirled her or before?"

"Oh, that was just a silly . . ." He shook his head. "Beverly had the crazy idea that we could join forces on the Nature Brand account. She said something about making a pretty good dance team, and the next thing I knew she was twirling."

"Actually, you were twirling her," Lisa corrected. "Are you considering joining forces with her agency?"

Raymond hesitated. "I have to admit, the idea has crossed my mind."

"Why? You hate her. You've always called her a sharp, conniving bitch. And I think those were your exact words."

Raymond picked some lint off the edge of his sleeve. "She's not that bad. She's ambitious, forthright, has a fresh mouth." He cleared his throat. "Monty likes Beverly. He likes her innovative ideas, but he likes my stability, my strength and reputation."

"We have innovative ideas," Lisa argued. In fact, they were her innovative ideas, and she was damn proud of them. "You said you loved my copy."

"I like it. You're very good, Elisabeth. You know I have the utmost respect for you."

"But . . ." she prodded. "There's more, isn't there?"

"You don't always take the big risks," Raymond admitted. "You play it safe. Hey, I'm not saying that's bad. We probably get more small accounts by playing it safe, but—"

"Not the big ones," she finished.

"I'm starving," Raymond said, obviously uncomfortable with the tension developing between them. "Are you ready to go to dinner?"

"No." Lisa leaned against the front of her desk and crossed her arms. "Raymond, do you want to marry someone safe or someone who takes risks?"

He didn't answer for a long time, then he looked into her face, his eyes deadly serious. "I thought I wanted to marry you. Why? What do you want? Or should I ask, who?"

"I thought I wanted you," she said, repeating his own words with a helpless smile.

"We can make it work, Elisabeth."
"Can we, Raymond? Can we, really?"

Sunday morning Maggie carried a load of laundry out of the laundry room and headed toward the stairs. It was her second load that morning, and she was tired. Since returning from Santa Barbara, she'd fallen back into motherhood with a vengeance. Her adventure already seemed like a memory, a distant but beautiful memory.

She still couldn't believe Mary Bea had gone through surgery while she'd been away. That guilt would stay with her for a very long time, although Mary Bea didn't seem to hold it against her. In fact, the children had thrived with Lisa and Nick. They'd talked endlessly about their aunt and uncle, as well as their grandparents and Silvia and Carmela. It seemed everyone had rallied to take care of the children in her absence.

Maggie was lucky. She might not have a husband, but she did have a lot of people in her life who loved her. And now that she had no more questions about Keith, she'd finally packed away his things. After convincing her parents and Nick that she was not about to go off the deep end again, she'd spent most of Friday going through Keith's clothes and other personal belongings, a task she had never been able to face.

Now it was done. They still had pictures of him in the family room. The children each had something of his to keep in their rooms, and Maggie had her wedding ring—tucked away in her jewelry box. She would keep it always, but she wouldn't wear it again.

She set the laundry basket down on the dining room table and bent over to pick up a trail of socks that had somehow escaped from the basket. She tried to concentrate on the mundane task, but her mind drifted to Jeremy. She wondered what he would think if he could see her now, a mother, a housekeeper, a cook, a gardener and everything else that came with the job titled Mom.

He'd probably be disappointed, she thought, as she stuffed

the socks into the basket. This was the real Maggie, not that woman who'd made love to him with wild abandon in a hotel room. She smiled to herself. She'd surprised herself as much as him, and she would never regret that night of passion. Jeremy had brought out another side of her. He'd made her feel beautiful and sexy and adored. And he'd reminded her that she was a woman who had a lot of life left to live.

Although part of her felt guilty about being with a man other than Keith, Maggie knew Keith would have wanted her to be happy. He would have wanted her to love again. And she did. She loved Jeremy.

Logically, she knew it was too soon, too fast, too much of a fantasy, but deep down in her heart, she knew that she had fallen in love with Jeremy, and it would be a long, long time before she got over him.

But she would get over him, she told herself firmly. She had no other choice.

The doorbell rang. Maggie groaned. Carmela and Silvia were early, and she was late, as usual. She was supposed to go with them to the cemetery to celebrate the anniversary of Robin's death. This year she would take all the children, including Mary Bea, who already felt well enough to walk slowly around the house, so that her daughter could begin to understand that while people die, they are celebrated forever in the heart.

Maggie opened the door. "Silvia, I'm sorry, we're not quite ready—" She stopped as she realized the person on the porch was not Silvia. "Jeremy."

"Hello, Maggie."

Maggie shifted the laundry basket to one hip, painfully conscious of how much she looked like a mom. Her hair was a frazzled mess, and she hadn't changed out of her blue jeans or put on any makeup. And Jeremy—Jeremy looked great in his beige slacks and white polo shirt. His dark hair was neatly combed, his skin tan, his eyes filled with energy, his lips curved into a warm, sexy smile that made her want to melt. "What are you doing here?" she asked, finally able to get some words out.

"Seeing you. And boy, have I missed seeing you."

Her body tingled under his intense gaze. Maggie cleared her throat. "It's only been a few days."

"It feels like a lifetime. Aren't you going to invite me in?"

"Uh—we're leaving soon."

"You're not gone yet." He took the basket out of her hands. "Let me help you with that."

Once her hands were free, Maggie had no choice but to step back and invite him in.

"Where do you want it?"

"You can set it down there," she said, pointing to the bottom stair.

Jeremy looked around her house, nodding approvingly. "Exactly as I pictured it."

"When did you picture my house?" Maggie asked.

"The first day I met you."

"The first day you met me you thought I was Crystal," she reminded him. "A swinging, single friend of Serena's."

He laughed. "I never thought of you that way. I'll admit the three kids took me by surprise. Where are they? I'd like to meet them."

"Jeremy, you have to leave," Maggie said abruptly.

"Why? Are you ashamed of me?"

"No, but you and I—it's over. I'm a single mother."

"So what? I like kids."

"You do not. You told me you never wanted kids."

"I told you I'd never met the right woman. I think I have, now." He looked at her with sexy, loving eyes that brimmed with tenderness and compassion. "In case you haven't figured it out yet, I love you, Maggie."

"You can't," she whispered. "You're a fantasy."

He pinched her and laughed when she said, "Ow." "Does that feel like a fantasy?"

She rubbed her arm. "No."

"Does this?" He covered her mouth with his, persuading her with his lips what he could not do with words.

"Wow!" she breathed against his mouth.

"I've still got it?"

"Yes. It's better than I remembered."

"So you have been thinking about me."

"How could I not?" Maggie asked as she pulled away from him. "You were so great, Jeremy. It was the best adventure I ever had."

"I know you think you wrote the end of our story, but I'm convinced there should be a sequel," Jeremy said.

"Really?" she asked, unable to stop the surge of impossible hope from spreading through her body. "What would it be about?"

"You and me and your kids, learning how to be a family." He touched her face. "I'm not letting you go, Maggie."

She didn't want him to let her go. She wanted him to hold on to her forever, make love to her, make her laugh, make her be silly, make her feel wanted. But what could she give him but a complicated mess of a life?

"Mom," Dylan cried, as he and Sally ran down the hall. "Sally found a dead lizard. Look."

Sally dropped her offering at Maggie's feet and barked excitedly.

Maggie made a face at the mangled bit of lizard lying on her hall floor. She couldn't stand to look at it. "Dylan, how many times have I told you not to let her in the house with those things. Make her take it out of here."

"She wanted to give it to you, Mom," Dylan said earnestly. "She missed you."

"I missed her, too. Make her take the lizard away."

When Dylan tried to pick up the lizard, Sally grabbed it with her teeth and headed back toward the yard with Dylan following at her heels.

"That was my son, Dylan. My middle child. Still want to stay?" she asked Jeremy.

Before he could reply, Roxy skipped down the stairs in a very short skirt and enough makeup to cover half of San Diego. She stopped when she saw Jeremy.

"Who's he?" she asked suspiciously.

"He's a friend, and you're not leaving this house with all that makeup."

"I'm only wearing blush," Roxy protested.

"And eyeliner and shadow and lipstick. Go and wash."

"You know, Aunt Lisa is more cool than you," Roxy said, as she stamped her way up the stairs.

"I know. Everyone is more cool than me." Maggie looked to see if Jeremy had left yet, but he was still standing in the hall, smiling.

"Is that it?" he asked.

"Mommy, can I take my dolls to the cemetery?" Mary Bea asked from the upstairs landing, her arms filled with four big dolls.

"Just one, honey."

"But they'll be lonely."

"Why don't you put them down for a nap while we're gone?" Maggie suggested.

"Okay." Mary Bea toddled off to do as requested.

"Are you still here?" Maggie asked, throwing up her hands with a helpless laugh.

"I told you I'm not leaving—not unless you tell me that you don't love me."

She met his gaze in one long, heart-stopping look. "I do love you, Jeremy, but that's a long way from turning you and me into some sort of family. I'm still trying to convince myself you're not a fantasy."

"Let me stay. Let me prove to you I'm real." He put his hands on her shoulders. "I wrote more on the road with you than I have in months. And since I've been home, I haven't written a thing. You're my inspiration, Maggie."

"I've never been anyone's inspiration."

"I've never been anyone's fantasy," he said with a smile. "I'll try it if you will."

"Jeremy, you have no idea what my life is really like."

"Show me. Don't shut me out. Give me a chance."

How could she say no when her heart was screaming yes? "Are you sure? I'm just an average, run-of-the-mill mom with stretch marks and a real weakness for chocolate."

Jeremy laughed. "As long as you're willing to share that chocolate, I have no problem with it. But you're not just anything, Maggie. I've seen you in action. I know you have a wild imagination, but you're also a fighter, and you're loyal. You don't quit, Maggie. I like that about you—among other things."

"Really?" Maggie smiled at him for a long moment, just enjoying the connection that had begun that first day. "I guess I should tell you then that I am totally in love with you."

"Thank God," he breathed.

Maggie suddenly realized that Jeremy had not been sure of her answer. "Are you that surprised?"

"Yes. I know you loved Keith very much. I saw how much it hurt you to know that he was really gone."

"It did hurt, and I will miss him, Jeremy. But this isn't about Keith anymore. It's about me and my life and whether or not it could ever mesh with yours. You once said you weren't sure if you wanted children," she reminded him. "I have children."

"I know what I said, Maggie, and you're right, I'd never really thought much about kids. But that's because those kids didn't have names or faces, and they didn't belong to a woman I love." He paused. "I don't know if I'd be a good father, Maggie. I'm sure I'd make a lot of mistakes, but I'd like to try to make you happy. I'd like to try to make all of us happy, if you'll let me. I don't want to lose you. Give me a chance?"

"Yes. Oh, yes, I'll give you a chance." She kissed him on the mouth with a renewed sense of joy and hope and love. "You might as well come with us, then. We have to go to the cemetery."

Jeremy looked a bit disturbed at that comment. "To visit your husband's grave? Maggie, I don't want to intrude."

"No, not Keith. My brother lost a child, years ago. His mother-in-law believes in a special celebration for the dead. It's a long story. I'll tell you on the way. Just be prepared for anything."

"Who else is going to be there?" he asked.

"Everyone." Her smile faded. "Except Lisa."

From the cemetery Nick could see the blue of the ocean in the distance, glistening in the sunshine. The blue reminded him of Lisa's eyes. A heavy, familiar weight settled around his heart. He tried to shake off the feeling of loneliness, but it covered him like a heavy winter coat.

He shouldn't have made love to her again. Now his memories were vivid, sharp and painful, not old and faded the way they'd been before.

A soft chirping drew his gaze to the nearby tree. He smiled at his old friend, the robin. "She's gone, buddy. Flown away."

The bird chirped in response and hopped up to another branch, flapping his wings, sending his mating call out over the hillside, but there was no reply.

"Maybe you should get used to being alone," Nick said. "If I can do it, you can."

He sat down on the grass and pulled out his guitar. The others would be arriving shortly, but he always came early to spend his own time with Robin. He played a few notes, strumming the guitar softly with his fingers. He remembered when he'd first played the melody for Lisa. It had been her song then. Later it had become Robin's song.

He played it now for both of them, for the two girls he had loved more than anyone else in his life. When he finished, he set the guitar down and looked up, wondering if the bird had flown away. He didn't see the robin. He saw Lisa.

"Hello, Nick."

"Lisa."

His sharp intake of breath nearly undid her. "I heard your song, and I—I came."

"I'd almost given up."

"It took me a while to really hear you. I guess I didn't want to." Lisa turned her head toward the small headstone where her daughter's name was written—*Robin Nicole Mad-dux, child of our love.*

Her eyes filled with moisture at the sight. She hadn't been to the cemetery in a long time, because this vivid reminder of Robin's death was almost too painful to bear. But she was here now, because she could no longer run away from her heart—or from Nick.

Nick stood up and set his guitar down on the ground. "Why did you come back, Lisa?"

Lisa turned to face him. She took a deep breath, knowing she was about to open herself up for the biggest rejection of her life. But she had to do it. "I love you, Nick."

He didn't say anything for a moment, and her heart almost stopped. What if he'd changed his mind? What if she'd waited too long?

"Say something," she begged.

"Are you still marrying Raymond?" he asked, with a curt note in his voice.

"No. I just told you I love you."

He shook his head, his eyes still guarded. "It isn't enough."

"What more do you want?" she cried.

"Everything. I want you to marry me again. I want us to have children. I can't settle for anything less."

"You're asking for the sun and the moon and the stars."

"And you," he said softly. "I can't promise that nothing bad will ever happen to us again, but I can promise that I'll never let you down the way I did before. And I'll never let you go. No more leaving me behind, Lisa. If you've come back to stay, then you're staying forever. It's your choice, but you have to decide now."

You never take a risk. You always play it safe.

Raymond's words echoed through Lisa's head. It was the most honest thing he'd ever said to her. And she knew he was right. But she was about to take the biggest risk of her life.

"Then I choose you," she said. "I've come back to stay, and I'll give you everything I have. I'll even give you another baby, because—because I want one, too.''

Nick suddenly let out a long breath, and she realized that he was as scared as she was. She flung herself into his arms and kissed him over and over and over again, until they broke apart with a breathless, loving laugh.

Nick smiled at her. "It took you long enough. I'd almost given up. I've been sitting on my porch, playing that damn song every night, hoping you'd come back to me." He paused. "I love you, you know. I never stopped."

"Me, either." She glanced toward the headstone, then back at Nick. "There's one thing, though."

"What?"

"Robin . . ." She smiled as the name finally crossed her lips. "There, I finally said it."

"Say it again."

"Robin." She grinned. "It suddenly seems so easy. Robin, Robin, Robin." Lisa took a breath. "She'll always be a part of us. You can talk about her, and I'll listen. You can put her picture on the dresser, and I won't turn it over. And I'll even help you think of some good advertising campaigns for your business using her name. But—" She licked her lips. "I can't live in that house again, Nick. I can't go back. I will go forward with you, but somewhere else."

He nodded. "That's fine with me. If you want me to move to L.A., I'll do it."

"You will?"

"Yes."

She kissed him again. "Thank you, but I've missed the beach. There are advertising agencies in San Diego. And I happen to have a great reference from my former boss."

"I take it you didn't break his heart."

"We weren't getting married for the right reasons. We both realized that. In fact, I think Raymond is interested in another woman. He said he needed someone older, someone who made him feel like a kid. I guess I wouldn't have made a very good trophy wife."

"You're too smart to be any man's trophy."

"I still have to call everyone on our list, though. You had to mail those damn invitations, didn't you?"

Nick threw back his head and laughed. "Hell, no. I didn't mail 'em. I threw them in the trash."

"You didn't?"

"Sure did."

"You're terrible."

"I wasn't about to let you marry anyone but me."

Lisa turned her head at the sudden chirping. "I see our friend is back."

"And lonely as hell. Too bad, buddy. I found my mate." Nick put his arm around Lisa's shoulder and held her close.

"Nick, look." Lisa pointed to another bird that seemed to have come out of nowhere. It lit on the branch next to the male robin. "She heard his song, and she came."

They turned as three cars pulled up and parked along the street. The kids hopped out of the first car, followed by Maggie and Jeremy.

"Looks like someone else heard the mating call," Nick said dryly.

Carmela and Silvia got out of the second car, and Bill and Kathy stepped out of the third. Lisa felt a rush of joy and pleasure as their families walked toward them. Today they would celebrate their daughter and their love.

Her arm started to tingle, and she looked down at the bracelet, which had grown warm against her wrist.

"Oh, Nick, look," she whispered, her voice laced with the same wonder that filled her heart.

Nick took her hand and held it up in the sunlight. Next to the pair of gold baby shoes was a tiny gold robin.

Epilogue

"How long are you going to watch him sleep?" Nick asked as he came up behind Lisa in the shadowy bedroom.

"Just a few more minutes." Lisa leaned her head against Nick's shoulder and smiled down at the child before her. Samuel Robert Maddux uttered a brief snore and turned over, his little thumb sneaking into his mouth as he once again fell back to sleep. "I can't believe he's a year old today."

"Maybe you better wake him up so he doesn't miss his party."

"Let him sleep for a few more minutes. He looks so peaceful." Lisa turned into Nick's arms and smiled up at him. "Thank you."

"For what—last night or this morning?"

Lisa laughed. "For giving me another baby to love. And another," she added, patting her rounded stomach.

"You're not scared anymore, are you?"

"Oh, yes, I am. Every day and every night, but the joy Sam brings into our lives is worth every worry line on my face. I love being a mother, and I love being your wife."

"As much as you love advertising?"

"More, but it is nice that I can work at home three days a week. You fixed everything, Nick. I'm so glad we took another chance. Sometimes, I wonder what would have hap-

355

pened to us if I'd never come back. I'd be married to Raymond, and you'd be married to Suzanne.''

"I don't think so. It probably just would have taken a little longer for us to find each other again.''

Lisa walked to the doorway, then sent him a teasing smile. "Can I go change my clothes—or do you still need to leave the room first?''

"You have a very smart mouth, Mrs. Maddux,'' Nick said, as he walked over and kissed her on the lips. "I've begun to enjoy watching you leave. You have a great—''

"Nick!''

"Well, you do. But it doesn't bother me to see you leave anymore, because I know you're coming back.''

"Always. You're stuck with me forever.''

"I'm not sure that will be long enough.''

The doorbell rang, and Lisa groaned. "You know, ever since Maggie married Jeremy, she's become incredibly punctual. Although, how she does it with four kids, I can't imagine.''

"Maggie has changed,'' Nick said as they walked toward the front door.

"For the better,'' Lisa agreed. "She's still funny and scattered and can never find her car keys, but she's so happy.''

"Maggie said she had an announcement to make. I wonder if she's pregnant again.''

"Kristin is only four months old.''

"So?'' Nick said with a grin. "In case you haven't noticed, my sister seems to have turned into a sex maniac.''

"It must run in the family,'' Lisa replied, as she opened the door to greet Maggie and Jeremy. "Hello. Hello.''

"Hello, yourself,'' Maggie said, as she gave Lisa a hug. "Where's the birthday boy?''

"Still asleep.''

Maggie raised an eyebrow. "And you're not sitting in his room watching over him?''

Lisa gave her a sheepish smile. "I was. But I've gotten better. Come on in. How are you, Jeremy?''

"Just great,'' he replied, as Lisa kissed him on the cheek,

then bent down to kiss her niece, who was asleep in Jeremy's arms.

"Where are the other kids?" Lisa asked.

"They took Sally around the back," Maggie replied, as they walked into the house and put their things in the living room.

"So, what's the news?" Nick demanded.

"Goodness, Nick, give Maggie a chance to catch her breath," Lisa said.

"I don't think that will happen even if you give me the next year to catch my breath," Maggie replied.

"Why? What is it?" Lisa searched Maggie's face for some hint of trouble, but all she saw was glowing happiness.

Maggie looked over at Jeremy. "Can I tell her?"

"Can I stop you?" Jeremy asked with a laugh.

"We sold our story to Paramount Pictures," Maggie said in a rush.

"What do you mean, your story?"

"The story of how we met, my search for Keith, my brother's reunion with his first love—everything," Maggie said with delight. "Jeremy and I wrote it together, and my name is going to be in the credits. Can you believe it? I'm a screenwriter."

"Wow. That's incredible. I had no idea you were writing something together," Lisa said, glancing over at Nick. He hadn't said a word, and she wondered how he felt about the idea of their personal love story making it to the big screen.

"Maggie wrote this on her own," Jeremy said. "I was just the backup."

"No, you were my partner, my equal partner," Maggie said. "So, what do you think, Nick?"

"Who's going to play me?"

Lisa laughed. "More importantly, who's going to play me?"

"I have no idea," Maggie said. "But the story is fictionalized, so it's not really you two, exactly."

"It sounds great," Nick said. "I think your going crazy two years ago was the best thing that happened to all of us."

"Well, thanks, I think."

Before Maggie could say anything more, the back door opened and the kids ran into the room.

"Come see, come see," Dylan cried.

"See what?" Lisa asked.

"The robins," Mary Bea said. "The babies are starting to fly."

Lisa rushed through the door, followed by Maggie and Jeremy and Nick. She stopped on the deck and looked at the nest the robins had built earlier that spring. Sure enough, the baby robins were flapping their wings, getting ready to fly. The first one moved to the edge of the nest. Lisa held her breath.

Nick took her hand and looked into her eyes. "She'll make it, Lisa. We all will. Happily ever after."

"I know. I just wish Robin were here to see all of this."

"She is—right here." He placed his hand on her heart. Lisa put her hand over his, and together they watched as the baby robin took off on wobbly wings, only to soar high above their heads, into a world that held so many promises.

THE WORLD OF
AVON ROMANCE SUPERLEADERS

*Cross-promotion and rebate offer in the
back of every book!*

MEET THE MEN OF AVON ROMANCE . . .
They're fascinating, they're sexy—they're irresistible! They're the kind of men you definitely
want to bring home— but not to meet the family.
And they live in such romantic places, from Regency England to the Wild West. These men are
guaranteed to provide you with hours of reading
pleasure. So introduce yourself to these unforgettable heroes, and meet a different man every
month.

AND THE WRITERS WHO CREATE THEM
At Avon we bring you books by the brightest stars
of romantic fiction. Christina Dodd, Catherine Anderson and Pamela Morsi. Kathleen Eagle, Lisa
Kleypas and Barbara Freethy. These are the bestselling writers who create books you'll never forget—each and every story is a "keeper."
Following is a sneak preview of their newest
books . . .

Enter the world of New York Times *best-selling author* **Catherine Anderson.** *This award-winning writer creates a place where dreams really do come true and love always triumphs. In April, Catherine creates her most memorable characters of all in* **Forever After.**

County Sheriff Heath Masters has a hard enough time managing small town crime, and he doesn't need any complications—especially ones in the very attractive form of his new neighbor, Meredith Kenyon, and her adorable daughter, Sammy. But when Heath's giant of a dog causes trouble for Merry, he finds himself in trouble, too . . . of the romantic kind.

FOREVER AFTER
by Catherine Anderson

*H*eath vaulted over the tumble-down fence that divided his neighbor's patchy lawn from the adjoining cow pasture, then poured on speed to circle the house. He skidded to a halt about fifteen feet shy of a dilapidated woodshed. A child, dressed in pink pants and a smudged white T-shirt, stood splayed against the outbuilding. Her eyes were so wide with fright they resembled china-blue supper plates.

Fangs bared and frothing at the jowls, Goliath lunged back and forth between the child and a young woman Heath guessed to be her mother.

"Stay back!" he ordered.

At the sound of his voice the woman turned around, her

pinched face so pale that her dark brown eyes looked almost as large as her daughter's. "Oh, thank God! Help us! Do something, please, before he hurts us!"

Heath jerked his gaze back to his dog. If ever there had been an animal he would trust with a child, Goliath was it. Yet now the rottweiler seemed to have gone berserk.

Heath snapped his fingers. "Goliath, heel!"

At the command, the rottweiler whirled toward Heath, his usually friendly brown eyes glinting a demonic red. For an awful instant Heath was afraid the dog might not obey him. *What in the hell was wrong with him*? Heath's gaze shot to the terrified child.

"Goliath, *heel*!" He slapped his thigh for emphasis.

The rottweiler finally acquiesced with another frenzied bark followed by a pathetic whine, massive head lowered, legs stiff, his movements reluctant and abject. The second the dog got within reach, Heath grabbed his collar.

"Sammy!"

The woman bolted forward to gather her child into her arms with a strangled cry. Then she whirled to confront Heath, her pale, delicately molded face twisting with anger, her body quaking.

"You get that *vicious*, out-of-control dog *off* my property!"

The blaze in her eyes told Heath she was infused by the rush of adrenaline that often followed a bad scare.

"Ma'am, I'm really sorry about—"

"I don't want to hear it! Just get that monster out of here!"

Damn. Talk about starting off on the wrong foot with someone. And wasn't that a shame? Heath would have happily fixed this gal's plumbing late at night—or anything else that went haywire in the ramshackle old house she was renting.

Fragile build. Pixieish features. Creamy skin. Large caramel brown eyes. A full, vulnerable mouth the delicate pink of barely ripened strawberries. Her hair fell in a thick, silken tangle around her shoulders, the sable tendrils curling over her white shirt like glistening ribbons of chocolate on vanilla ice cream.

Definitely not what he'd been picturing. Old Zeke usually rented this place to losers—people content to work the welfare system rather than seek gainful employment. Even in baggy jeans and a man's shirt this lady had "class" written all over her.

Nationally best-selling author **Pamela Morsi** *is known for the trademark wit and down-home humor that enliven her enchanting, memorable romances that have garnered rave reviews from critics and won national awards. This May experience the charm of Pamela Morsi in* **Sealed With a Kiss.**

When Gidry Chavis jilted Pru Belmont and left Chavistown, the nearly wed bride was devastated, the townsfolk scandulized . . . and Chavis was strongly discouraged from showing his face again. But now he's back, a bit older, a whole lot wiser . . . and rarin' to patch things up with Pru.

SEALED WITH A KISS
by Pamela Morsi

*T*he cowboy allowed his gaze to roam among the customers. There was a table full of poker players intent upon their game. One tired, sort of half-pretty woman looked up hopefully and pulled her feet out of the chair next to her. He didn't even bother to meet her glance. A couple of rowdy farmhands seemed to be starting early on a weekend drunken spree. A few other men drinking quietly. No one that he recognized for certain.

At the near end of the bar a dandied-up gentleman in a plaid coat and summer derby sat alone, his traveling bag at his feet.

The cowboy almost smiled. If there was anyone more certain not to be a local, it was a drummer in a plaid coat. Without any appearance of haste or purposeful intent, he casually took the seat right next to the traveling bag.

"Afternoon."

The little man looked up eagerly.

"Good afternoon to you, sir," he answered and in true salesman fashion, offered his hand across the bar. "Arthur D. Sattlemore, Big Texas Electric Company."

The cowboy's only answer was an indecipherable grunt as he signaled the barkeep to bring him a beer.

"Hot weather we've been having."

The cowboy nodded. "A miserable summer," he agreed. "Good for cotton."

"You are a farmer, sir?" Clearly the drummer was surprised.

"No," the cowboy answered. "But when you're in Chavistown, it's hard to talk about anything here without mentioning cotton."

The drummer chuckled and nodded understanding. He leaned closer. "You have the right of it there, sir," he admitted. "I was asked to come present my company to the Commercial Club. I've been here a week and haven't been able to get a word in edgewise. The whole town is talking cotton and what will happen without old man Chavis."

The cowboy blanched. "He's dead?"

The drummer shook his head. "Not as of this morning, but without him to run the gin and the cooperative, the farmers are worried that their cotton will sit in wagonloads by the side of the road."

"Ginning time has just begun," the cowboy said. "Surely the old man will be up and around before it's over."

The drummer shook his head. "Not the way they're telling it. Seems the old man is bad off. Weak as a kitten they say, and the quacks warn that if he gets out of bed, he won't live to see winter."

"Doctors have been wrong before," the cowboy said.

The drummer nodded. "The whole town hopes you're right. The old man ain't got no one to take over for him. The gin's closed down and the cotton's just waiting."

The cowboy nodded.

"They had a meeting early in the week and voted to send for young Chavis, the old man's son."

"Is that so?"

"Young Chavis created some bit of scandal in this town eight years ago," the drummer explained. "Nobody's seen so much as his shadow since."

The cowboy listened quietly, intently.

"So they sent for their son and they're hoping that he'll come and save their biscuits," the little man said. "But for myself, I just wouldn't trust him."

"No?"

The traveling man tutted and shook his head. "They say he was all but married to a local gal and just left her high and dry."

"Is that what they say?"

The drummer nodded. "And I ask you, what kind of man blessed with plenty of money, an influential name, a fine place in the community and an innocent young sweetheart who expects to marry him, runs off with some round-heeled, painted-up saloon gal?"

The cowboy slowly picked up his beer and drank it down in one long swallow. He banged the glass on the bar with enough force to catch the attention of every man in the room.

"What kind of man, indeed," he said to the drummer.

Best-selling author **Kathleen Eagle's** *marriage to a Lakota Sioux has given her inspiration to write uniquely compelling love stories featuring Native American characters. She's won numerous awards, but her most gratifying reward was a note from a reader saying, "You kept me up all night reading." This June, stay up all night with* **The Night Remembers.**

Jesse Brown Wolf is a man living in the shadows who comes to the rescue of kids like Tommy T, a street-smart boy, and Angela, a fragile newcomer to the big city. Jesse rescues Angela from a brutal robbery and helps nurse her back to health. In return, Angela helps Jesse heal his wounded soul.

THE NIGHT REMEMBERS
by Kathleen Eagle

*H*e hadn't been this close to anyone in a long time, and his visceral quaking was merely the proof. He sat on a straw cushion and leaned back against the woven willow backrest and drank what was left of the tea. He didn't need any of this. Not the kid, not the woman, not the intrusion into his life.

A peppering of loose pebbles echoed in the air shaft, warning him that something was stirring overhead. He climbed to the entrance and waited until the boy announced himself.

"I had a hard time gettin' the old grandpa to come to the

366

door,'' Tommy T reported as he handed the canvas bag down blindly, as though he made regular deliveries to a hole in the ground. "Some of this is just, like, bandages and food, right?''

"Right.''

The boy went on. "I said I was just a runner and didn't know nothin' about what was in the message, and nobody asked no questions, nothin' about you. You know what? I know that old guy from school.''

"A lot of people know him. He practices traditional medicine.''

"Cool.'' Then, diverting to a little skepticism, "So what I brought is just roots and herbs and stuff.''

"It's medicine.''

"She might be worried about her dog,'' the boy said, hovering in the worlds above. "If she says anything, tell her I'm on the case.''

"You don't know where she lives.''

"I'll know by morning. I'll check in later, man.'' The voice was withdrawing. "Not when it's daytime, though. I won't hang around when it's light out.''

On the note of promise, the boy left.

The night was nearly over. The air smelled like daybreak, laden with dew, and the river sounded more cheerful as it rushed toward morning. Normally, he would ascend to greet the break of day. The one good thing about the pain was the relief he felt when it lifted. Relief and weariness. He returned to the deepest chamber of his refuge, where his guest lay in his bed, her fragile face bathed in soft candlelight.

He made an infusion from the mixture of herbs the old man had prepared and applied it to the tattered angel's broken skin. He made a paste from ground roots and applied it to her swollen bumps and bruises, singing softly as he did so. The angel moaned, as though she would add her keening to his lullaby, but another tea soon tranquilized her fitful sleep.

Finally he doused the light, lay down beside her, closed his eyes, and drifted on the dewy-sweet morning air.

When you open a book by New York Times *bestselling author* **Lisa Kleypas,** *you're invited to enter a world where you can attend a glittering ball one night . . . and have a secret rendezvous the next. Her sensuous, historical page-turners are delicious treats for readers. In July, don't miss her latest gem,* **Stranger in My Arms.**

All of England believed that Hunter, the Earl of Hawksworth, had disappeared in a shipwreck, leaving a large estate and a grieving widow. But now, a man claiming to be Hunter had arrived at Hawksworth Hall—handsome, virile . . . and very much alive. And Lara, Hunter's wife, must decide if he is truly her husband—or a very clever impostor.

STRANGER IN MY ARMS
by Lisa Kleypas

*H*e was so much thinner, his body lean, almost rawboned, his heavy muscles thrown into stark prominence. His skin was so much darker, a rich bronze hue that was far too exotic and striking for an Englishman. But it *was* Hunter . . . older, toughened, as sinewy and alert as a panther.

"I didn't believe . . ." Lara started to say, but the words died away. It was too much of an effort to speak. She backed away from him and somehow made her way to the cabinet where she kept a few dishes and a small teapot. She took refuge in an everyday ritual, fumbling for a parcel of tea leaves, pulling the little porcelain pot from its place on the shelf. "I—I'll make some tea. We can talk about . . . everything . . ."

But her hands were shaking too badly, and the cups and saucers clattered together as she reached for them. He came to her in an instant, his feet swift and startlingly light on the floor. Hunter had always had a heavy footstep—but the thought was driven away as he took her cold hands in his huge warm ones. She felt his touch all through her body, in small, penetrating ripples of sensation.

A pair of teasing dark eyes stared into hers. "You're not going to faint, are you?"

Her face was frozen, making it impossible to smile, to produce any expression. She looked at him dumbly, her limbs stiff with fright and her knees locked and trembling.

The flicker of amusement vanished from his gaze, and he spoke softly. "It's all right, Lara." He pushed her to a nearby chair and sank to his haunches, their faces only inches from each other.

"H-Hunter?" Lara whispered in bewilderment. *Was* he her husband? He bore an impossibly close resemblance, but there were subtle differences that struck sparks of doubt within her.

He reached inside his worn black broadcloth coat and extracted a small object. Holding it in his palm, he showed it to her. Eyes wide, Lara regarded the small, flat enameled box. He pressed the tiny catch on the side and revealed a miniature portrait of her, the one she had given him before his departure to India three years earlier.

"I've stared at this every day for months," he murmured. "Even when I didn't remember you in the days right after the shipwreck, I knew somehow that you belonged to me." He closed the box in his hand and tucked it back into his coat pocket.

Lara lifted her incredulous gaze to his. She felt as if she were in a dream. "You've changed," she managed to say.

Hunter smiled slightly. "So have you. You're more beautiful than ever."

Barbara Freethy's *poignant, tender love stories have garnered her many new fans. Her first Avon romance,* Daniel's Gift, *was called "exhilarating" by* Affaire de Coeur, *and* Romantic Times *said it was ". . . sure to tug on the heartstrings." This August, don't miss Barbara's best yet,* **One True Love.**

Nick Maddux believed he'd never see his ex-wife, Lisa, again. Then he knocked on the door to his sister's house and Lisa answered—looking as beautiful, as vulnerable as ever. Nick soon discovered that, despite the tragedy that lay between them, his love for Lisa was as tender—and as passionate—as ever.

ONE TRUE LOVE
by Barbara Freethy

Nick Maddux was surrounded by pregnant women. Every time he turned around, he bumped into someone's stomach. Muttering yet another apology, he backed into the corner of his eight-by-twelve-foot booth at the San Diego Baby and Parenting Fair and took a deep breath. He was hot, tired and proud.

His handcrafted baby furniture was the hit of the show. In some cases, it would be a challenge to have his furniture arrive before the stork, but Nick thrived on challenges, and Robin Wood Designs was finally on its way to becoming the profitable business he had envisioned.

Nick couldn't believe how far he'd come, how much he'd changed.

Eight years ago, he'd been twenty-five years old, working toward getting his contractor's license and trying to provide for a wife and a child on the way. He'd kept at it long after they'd gone, hammering out his anger and frustration on helpless nails and boards.

Two years had gone by before he ran out of work, out of booze and out of money. Finally, stone-cold sober, he'd realized his life was a mess.

That's when he'd met Walter Mackey, a master craftsman well into his seventies but still finding joy in carving wood. Walter made rocking chairs in his garage and sold them at craft fairs. Nick had bought one of those chairs for his mother's birthday. She'd told Nick he'd given her something that would last forever.

It was then Nick realized he could make something that would last forever. His life didn't have to be a series of arrivals and departures.

Nick had decided to focus on baby furniture, because something for one's child always brought out the checkbook faster than something for oneself. Besides that mercenary reason, Nick had become obsessed with building furniture for babies that would nurture them, keep them safe, protect them.

He knew where the obsession came from, just not how to stop it. Maybe Robin would be proud of all that he'd accomplished in her name.

Nick felt himself drawn into the past. In his mind he saw Lisa with her round stomach, her glowing smile, her blue eyes lit up for the world to see. She'd been so happy then, so proud of herself. When she'd become pregnant, they both thought they'd won the lottery.

He closed his eyes for a moment as the pain threatened to overwhelm him, and he saw her again.

"I can't believe I'm having a baby," Lisa said. *She took his hand and placed it on her abdomen. "Feel that? She's kicking me."*

Nick's gut tightened at the fluttering kick against his fin-

gers. It was the most incredible feeling. He couldn't begin to express the depth of his love for this unborn child, but he could show Lisa. In the middle of the baby store, he kissed her on the lips, uncaring of the salespeople or the other customers. "I love you," he whispered against her mouth.

She looked into his eyes. "I love you, too. More than anything. I'm so happy, it scares me. What if something goes wrong?"

"Nothing will go wrong."

"Oh, Nick, things always go wrong around me. Remember our first date—we hit a parked car."

He smiled. "That wasn't your fault. I'm the one who wasn't paying attention."

"I'm the one who distracted you," she said with a worried look in her eyes.

"Okay, it was your fault."

"Nick!"

"I'm teasing. Don't be afraid of being happy. It's not fatal, you know. This is just the beginning for us."

It had been the beginning of the end.

Award-winning author **Christina Dodd** is known for captivating characters and sizzling sensuality. She is the author of twelve best-selling romances, including **A Well Pleasured Lady** and **A Well Favored Gentleman.** Watch for her latest this September, **That Scandalous Evening.**

Years earlier, Jane Higgenbothem had caused a scandal when she'd sculpted Lord Ransom Quincey of Blackburn in the classical manner. Apparently everything was accurate save one very important part of Lord Blackburn's body. Jane retired to the country in *disgrace, but now she has come back to London to face her adversary.*

THAT SCANDALOUS EVENING
by Christina Dodd

London, 1809

"Can you see the newest belle?" Fitz demanded.

"No."

"You're not even looking!"

"There's nothing worth seeing." Ransom had better things to do than watch out for a silly girl.

"Not true. You'll find a diamond worth having, if you'd just take a look. A diamond, Ransom! Let us through. There you go lads, you can't keep her for yourselves." The constriction eased as the men turned and Fitz slipped through the crowd. Ransom followed close on Fitz's heels, protecting his friend's back and wondering why.

"Your servant, ma'am!" Fitz snapped to attention, then bowed, leaving Ransom a clear view of, not the diamond, but the profile of a dab of a lady. Her gown of rich green glacé silk was *au courant*, and nicely chosen to bring out the spark of emerald in her fine eyes. A lacy shawl covered her slight bosom, and she held her gloved hands clasped at her waist like a singer waiting for a cue that never came. A mop cap covered her unfashionable coil of heavy dark hair and her prim mouth must have never greeted a man invitingly.

Ransom began to turn away.

Then she smiled at the blonde with an exultant bosom beside her. It was a smile filled with pride and quiet pleasure.

It lit the plain features and made them glow—and he'd seen that glow before. He jerked to a stop.

He stared. It couldn't be her. She had to be a figment of his wary, suspicious mind.

He blinked and looked again.

Damn, it *was* her.

Miss Jane Higgenbothem had returned.

How to get your special rebate on seven Avon romances

Avon Books would like to offer you a rebate on any or all of the following seven paperback romance titles:

A WELL FAVORED GENTLEMAN by Christina Dodd;
FOREVER AFTER by Catherine Anderson;
SEALED WITH A KISS by Pamela Morsi;
THE NIGHT REMEMBERS by Kathleen Eagle;
STRANGER IN MY ARMS by Lisa Kleypas;
ONE TRUE LOVE by Barbara Freethy; and
THAT SCANDALOUS EVENING by Christina Dodd.

We will send you a rebate of $1.00 per book, or $10.00 for all seven titles, when you purchase them by December 31, 1998. To claim your rebate, simply mail your proof(s) of purchase (cash register receipt(s)) with the coupon below, completely filled out, to Avon Books, Dept. ROM, Box 767, Rte. 2, Dresden, TN 38225.

Yes, I have purchased
_____**A WELL FAVORED GENTLEMAN**;
_____**FOREVER AFTER**;
_____**SEALED WITH A KISS**;
_____**THE NIGHT REMEMBERS**;
_____**STRANGER IN MY ARMS**;
_____**ONE TRUE LOVE**;
_____**THAT SCANDALOUS EVENING**, or
_____**ALL SEVEN TITLES**.

My total rebate (at $1.00 per title OR $10.00 if all seven are purchased) is $ _____
Please send it to:

Name_____

Address_____

City_____ State_____ Zip_____

Offer expires December 31, 1998. Void where prohibited by law.

We've got love on our minds at
http://www.AvonBooks.com

Vote for your favorite hero in
"HE'S THE ONE."

Take a romance trivia quiz, or just
"GET A LITTLE LOVE."

Look up today's date in
romantic history in "DATEBOOK."

Subscribe to our monthly e-mail
newsletter for all the buzz on
upcoming romances.

Browse through our list of new
and upcoming titles and read
chapter excerpts.